走跳國外 一定要會的 生活便利句

溝通力 100%

張翔 / 編著

Going abroad and talking like a native

這樣說，英語會話不間斷！

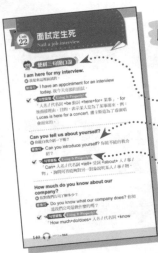

嚴選便利三句

每單元特別選出走跳國外最好用的「**便利三句**」，並提供相同意思的「**替換句**」，讓您隨時都能靈活應用句型；最後的「**句型提點**」分析便利三句的文法重點、增加您對便利句的理解度。

必備回應

有問就有答，「**必備回應**」教您怎麼回答便利三句，雙向溝通不卡關！

小知識補給站

補充一些出國在外一定要知道的小知識以及趣聞，學習語言的同時，也要學習文化、擴充新知。

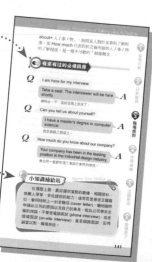

User's Guide

學道地的老外說法

精選各種老外常用的口語說法，熟悉便利三句後，就來加強學習廣度吧！

專業錄製 MP3

特別邀請專業外籍老師錄音，不但知道句子怎麼說、還能學習標準美式口音。

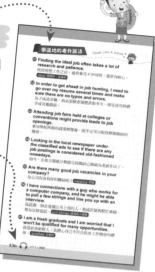

雙人實境對話

模擬實際對話情景，教您怎麼把學到的句子用出來！

篇章索引好查找

標上每個單元所在章節，隨翻隨找超方便、穩穩掌握六大情境。

去國外旅遊、生活時,誰都希望自己能夠順順利利,這時候,如果聽得懂、說得出英文,一定能讓你親近當地、加深你的旅行深度。能用英文溝通,更是邁向國際化的第一步,不但可以與各國旅人交流,說不定還能交到知心好友。本書內容經過嚴選,不佔據你過多的腦容量,還能減輕你背包的重量、心頭的負擔!只要用對句子,就能玩得更順利、旅途也會更有收穫。

想想看,在旅遊途中若是遇到任何問題,但聽不懂、又無法用英文溝通的話,必定會常常會造成誤解,甚至釀成大錯,像是在美國曾發生過的其中一樁槍擊事件之中,一位學生因為沒聽懂 Freeze! (不准動),而慘遭槍殺;或是平常去買個東西,店員忘了找零,你卻不知道怎麼表達,因而錯失自己的權利等等。

至於,怎麼樣做才能加強口說?常常看到許多學生為了練口說,死記硬背大量句子,嘗試複製句型的規則、套用到生活對話當中,遇到外國人時,講出來的英文生硬、不符合情境,甚至會不知道如何應對教科書中沒有出現過的狀況;大部分學生也因為單字不多、沒有完美的文法概念就不敢開口。其實生活會話沒有想像中的那麼困

難，只要多聽、多練習、敢講，不論是誰，都可以成為英語溝通高手。

本書包含了以下特色，希望能幫助讀者說出一口道地英語：(1) 便利三句—只教最精髓的用語，詳細分析句子文法、來幫助理解句型，還有針對便利三句補充的替換句，可以靈活應用；(2) 學道地的老外說法—大量補充老外常用的說法，熟讀便利三句之後，還可以進一步加強自己對話的豐富性；(3) 雙人實境對話—教你怎麼在真實對話情境、把所學用出來；(4) 每個單元補充有趣的小知識，不出國也可以是萬事通；(5) 隨書附贈的MP3，讓你雖然無法身在國外耳濡目染，但可從模仿口音、音調、發音等，來開啟英文對話的第一步。

不管你對「英語會話」有什麼恐懼，想要輕鬆應對，只需要基本的文法以及生活單字，就足以跟老外溝通，只是要知道怎麼把學到的用出來、怎麼在適當的情境下說出合宜的話！所以本書不解釋一連串複雜的文法、也不收錄用不到的困難字彙，希望讀者們能藉由本書，順利突破英語會話的瓶頸！

張翔

Contents

目錄

Part 3 職場應對
許你一個順風順水

Part 4 休閒娛樂
朝 A 咖級玩家邁進

Contents

目錄

Part 5 出國旅遊
愈玩愈樂的必備句

Part 6 愛情來了
情場得意 & 失意

Part 1

自我介紹
社交紅人都這樣說

從建立良好的第一印象開始，
一步一步往好人緣邁進！

How are you?

★ 短短招呼，也能禮貌滿點！

名 名詞	動 動詞	形 形容詞
副 副詞	介 介係詞	助 助詞
連 連接詞	限 限定詞	縮 縮寫

第一印象決勝負
A perfect first impression

便利三句開口說

How do you do?

▶ 初次見面，請多指教。

替換句 ▶ Nice to meet you. 很高興認識你。

✓ **句型提點** Using It Properly!

為初次見面的招呼語，在較正式的場合常常會用到，像是工作場合，態度比較禮貌、客氣。雖然是問句，卻只是單純表達「您好！」的招呼用語。

It's a pleasure to meet you.

▶ 很高興認識你。

替換句 ▶ Pleased to meet you. 很高興認識你。

✓ **句型提點** Using It Properly!

初次認識新朋友時，可以用這句當作禮貌性的開頭招呼語。「It's a pleasure to+ 原形動詞」的句型表示「很開心做（某事）」。本句的 meet 為及物動詞，有見面、認識的意思。

How are you (doing)?

▶ 你好嗎？（過得如何？）

替換句 ▶ How's life? 最近過得如何？

✓ **句型提點** Using It Properly!

和前面帶有禮儀性的問候不同，How are you (doing)? 是親友見面最常使用的實用問候語。除了基本的禮貌問好之外，也同時帶有詢問近況的意思。

有來有往的必備回應

Q How do you do?

A How do you do?

初次見面,請多指教。

Q It's a pleasure to meet you.

A It's a pleasure to meet you, too. / Likewise.

我也很高興認識你。/ 我也是。

Q How are you (doing)?

A I am doing great. / Not too bad.

我過得很好。/ 我過得還不錯。

小知識補給站　Some Fun Facts

最基本的招呼用語除了 Hi、Hello、How are you? 之外,常用的招呼用語,就算同為英語系國家,大家的說法也會不一樣,甚至連同一國的不同區域,也有可能聽到不同的用法。像是美國人與親朋好友打招呼時,常常會說 Hey there!、What's up?、How's everything? 跟麻吉也可以很輕鬆隨意地說 Yo!,還常把 What's up? 省略成 Sup?;美國西南部的人更是常把 How do you do? 簡稱為 Howdy;如果在英國,則可以聽見 Wotcha! (What cheer? 的簡略)、Hiya!、Alright?、How do?;而在澳洲,最道地的莫過於 G'Dday (Good day)!。

Part 1 自我介紹
Part 2 日常雜務
Part 3 職場應對
Part 4 休閒娛樂
Part 5 出國旅遊
Part 6 愛情來了

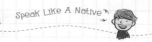
① **Nice to meet you.**
很高興認識你。

② **I'd say the same./Same here.**
我也是。

③ **Let me introduce myself first.**
我先做個自我介紹。 introduce 介紹；引薦

④ **My name is Abby. What's yours?**
我叫艾比，你呢？

⑤ **Could you repeat your first name/last name, please?**
可不可以再說一次你的名字／姓氏？ repeat 重複；重說

⑥ **How do you spell your name?**
請問你的名字怎麼拼？ spell 用字母拼；拼寫

⑦ **I am Sarah, with an h in the end.**
我叫做莎拉，字尾以 h 作結。

⑧ **I can't believe we have finally met! I've heard so much about you!**
不敢相信終於見到你了！久仰大名！ hear about 知道；得知

⑨ **Nice meeting you. I hope we'll see each other soon.**
很高興見到你，後會有期囉。

⑩ **If only we could have met each other earlier! We have so much in common!**
如果我們早點認識彼此就好了！我們的共通點還真多！

⑪ **Have we met? You look very familiar.**
我們有見過面嗎？你看起來好面熟。 familiar 熟悉的

⑫ **Have you met Ted? He is an old friend of mine from college.**
你認識泰德嗎？他是我大學時代的老友。

⑬ I just have one of those faces.
我只是有張大眾臉。 `one of those faces 大眾臉`

⑭ How's it/ everything going?
最近還好嗎？

⑮ How's life treating you?
日子過得如何？

⑯ How's work/ school?
工作／學校生活如何啊？

⑰ What have you been up to?
你最近在忙什麼？ `up to 忙於`

⑱ Not much./Same old, same old.
沒什麼。／老樣子。

⑲ Could be worse.
還過得去。 `worse 更壞的；更差的`

⑳ Couldn't be better!
再好不過啦！

㉑ I've been swamped!
我最近忙翻了！ `swamp 使忙得不可開交`

㉒ I don't want to talk about it.
別提了。

㉓ Everything is going well. Thank you.
一切都很順利，謝謝。

㉔ It's been such a while since the last time we met.
從上次見面到現在已經過了好久。

㉕ It's my honor to meet you here.
遇見你是我的榮幸。

㉖ Dad, this is my friend Jack. Jack, my father.
爸，這是我的朋友—傑克。傑克，這是我爸。

雙人實境對話 oh!

對話情境 1 正式場合初見面

A : How do you do?
B : How do you do?
A : Allow me to introduce myself. My name is Ted Smith, a **senior** engineer in XYZ **Company**.
B : I am Jane Wilson from ABC **agency**. I happen to know someone from your company!
A : What a small world!

A：您好。
B：您好。
A：容我自我介紹一下。我叫泰德‧史密斯，XYZ 公司的資深工程師。
B：我是 ABC 公司的珍‧威爾森，我正好認識你公司的一個人呢！
A：世界真小！

senior [`sinjɚ] 形
年長的；資深的
company
[`kʌmpənɪ] 名 公司
agency [`edʒənsɪ]
名 代辦處

對話情境 2 結交新朋友

A : It's a pleasure to meet you here.
B : Same here. We have so much to talk about.
A : Let me introduce you to my **BFFs** next time.
B : I'd love that. That's very sweet of you.
A : We should all **hang out** together!

A：真的很高興認識你。
B：我也覺得，我們有好多事可以聊。
A：下次讓我把你介紹給我的姊妹淘吧。
B：太好了，你人真好。
A：我們以後應該一起玩樂！

BFF (Best Friend Forever) 縮 死黨；好友
hang out 片
與…相處

對話情境 3 開個小玩笑

Ⓐ：Hi, there. How's it going?
Ⓑ：I'm getting by. How about you?
Ⓐ：I just fell off a cliff and got hit by a bike.
Ⓑ：What? Are you OK? Let me take you to the hospital.
Ⓐ：Just kidding!

A：哈囉，最近怎麼樣？
B：還過得去，你呢？
A：我剛從山崖摔下來，然後被腳踏車撞到。
B：什麼？你還好嗎？我帶你去醫院吧。
A：開玩笑的啦！

get by 🔸 勉強應付過去
fall off 🔸 落下
cliff [klɪf] 🔹 懸崖
kid [kɪd] 🔺 開玩笑

對話情境 4 三人閒聊

Ⓐ：This is my sister, Wendy. Wendy, this is my best friend, James.
Ⓑ：Hi, nice to meet you. My sister has said a lot of nice things about you.
Ⓒ：No way!
Ⓐ：Yes way! You are one of the most talented people I've ever met.
Ⓒ：Wow, I am so flattered.

A：這是我妹妹，溫蒂。溫蒂，這是我的好友，詹姆士。
B：嗨，很高興認識你，我哥對你讚譽有加呢！
C：怎麼可能！
A：有可能！你是我遇過最有才華的人之一。
C：哇，我真是受寵若驚。

no way 🔸 不可能
yes way 🔸 是真的（常用來反駁 no way）
talented [`tæləntɪd] 🔹 有天分的
flatter [`flætə] 🔺 奉承；阿諛

個資情報蒐集
Collecting personal information

便利三句開口說

How old are you?
▶ 你幾歲？

替換句▶ What is your age? 你幾歲？

✓ ➔**句型提點** Using It Properly!

「How+old+be 動詞 + 人名 / 代名詞」用來詢問別人的年齡。疑問詞「How」後面不能直接加名詞，而是接形容詞，用來詢問該形容詞的程度，像是此句接形容詞 old (⋯歲的)。

When is your birthday?
▶ 你哪天生日？

替換句▶ What date is your birthday? 你的生日是幾月幾號？

✓ ➔**句型提點** Using It Properly!

「When+be 動詞 + 人名所有格 / 人稱代名詞所有格+birthday」用以詢問生日是哪一天。When 是用來詢問「時間」的疑問詞。就本句而言，when 用來詢問別人的生日是什麼時候。

What is your sign?
▶ 你是什麼星座？

替換句▶ What's your horoscope? 你是什麼星座的？

✓ ➔**句型提點** Using It Properly!

「What+be 動詞 + 人名所有格 / 人稱代名詞所有格 +sign」，sign 在此句指星座，其他英文說法如

horoscope、Zodiac signs、constellation 也是指星座。

有來有往的必備回應

Q How old are you?

A I am twenty years old.
我今年二十歲。

Q When is your birthday?

A My birthday is on September the 7th.
我的生日是 9 月 7 日。

Q What is your sign?

A I am a Libra.
我是天秤座的。

Some Fun Facts
小知識補給站

　　星座也是一項不分國界的話題，讓人從出生日期就能大致知道一個人的性格。分為四象 (four elements)：(1) 火象 (Fire)：包含牡羊座 (Aries)，獅子座 (Leo)，射手座 (Sagittarius)；(2) 土象 (Earth)：包括摩羯座 (Capricorn)，金牛座 (Taurus)，處女座 (Virgo)；(3) 風象 (Wind/Air)：包括水瓶座 (Aquarius Carrier)，雙子座 (Gemini)，天秤座 (Libra)；(4) 水象 (Water)：包括雙魚座 (Pisces)，巨蟹座 (Cancer)，天蠍座 (Scorpio)。知道這些星座的說法後，試著開口跟外國朋友聊聊你的星座吧！

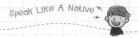
01 **In which year were you born?**
你幾年出生的？

02 **I was born in the 80s.**
我是八〇年代出生的。

03 **I was born on March 2, 1975.**
我的出生日期是一九七五年三月二日。

04 **Do you mind telling me your age?**
你介意告訴我你幾歲嗎？ mind 介意

05 **I am seventeen going on eighteen.**
我現在十七歲，即將邁入十八歲。

06 **I am turning thirty next month.**
我下個月就要滿三十歲了。

07 **Her daughter is in her twenties.**
她的女兒大概二十幾歲。

08 **His student is an eight-year-old kid.**
他的學生是個八歲大的孩子。

09 **She looks much older than her age.**
她看起來比實際年齡老許多。

10 **Those twenty-something boys love to party.**
那些二十幾歲的男孩喜歡狂歡。
-something 年齡大約…；…左右

11 **Are you an adult? Show me your identity card.**
你成年了嗎？給我看看你的身分證。 identity card 身分證

12 **You are not allowed to come in. You are only a minor.**
你不能入場，你未成年。 minor 未成年人

13 **You can only obtain your driver's license when you turn eighteen.**

你滿十八歲才可以考駕照。 driver's license 駕駛執照

⑭ I am five years younger/older than you.
我小 / 大你五歲。

⑮ He was born in July. So, he is either a Cancer or a Leo.
他七月出生，不是巨蟹座就是獅子座。

⑯ Do you believe in astrology?
你相信星座嗎？ astrology 占星術

⑰ I am a Gemini. How about you?
我是雙子座的，你呢？

⑱ I don't think my personality traits match my sign.
我覺得我的個性跟星座不相符。 trait 特徵；特點

⑲ My mom is a Libran and my dad is an Aquarian. No wonder they get along very well.
我媽是天秤座，我爸是水瓶座，難怪他們兩個很合得來。

⑳ I believe in neither horoscopes nor animal signs.
我不相信什麼星座或生肖。 animal sign 生肖

㉑ What is your animal sign?
你的生肖是什麼？

㉒ I was born in the Year of the Dragon.
我是龍年出生的。

㉓ The older generation are more familiar with Chinese animal signs.
老一輩的人比較熟悉中國生肖。

㉔ There are twelve animal signs in the Chinese zodiac.
中國生肖當中有十二種動物。 zodiac 黃道帶

㉕ Many parents want their children to be born in the Year of the Dragon.
很多父母都希望他們的小孩在龍年出生。

自我介紹 日常雜務 職場應對 休閒娛樂 出國旅遊 愛情來了

雙人實境對話

對話情境 ① 時光飛逝

A: My son is **celebrating** his birthday this weekend.

B: How old is he?

A: He is eighteen going on nineteen.

B: Oh my! **Time flies!**

A: Tell me about it!

A：我兒子這個週末要慶生。
B：他幾歲啦？
A：他現在十八，要十九歲了。
B：天啊！時間過得真快！
A：就是說啊！

celebrate
[`sɛlə,bret] 動 慶祝；
慶賀

time flies 片
時光飛逝

對話情境 ② 最棒的讚美

A: Would you **mind** telling me how old you are?

B: **Not at all**. I am thirty years old.

A: We are the same age! You don't **look** your age!

B: What do you mean?

A: You **look** so much younger!

A：你介意告訴我你幾歲嗎？
B：不介意，我三十歲。
A：我們同年耶！你看起來不像這個年紀的人！
B：什麼意思？
A：你看起來好年輕！

mind [maɪnd] 動
介意；注意

not at all 片
完全不會

look [luk] 動
看起來相稱

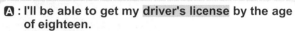

對話情境 3 考駕照

Part 1 自我介紹

A : I'll be able to get my **driver's license** by the age of eighteen.

B : That'll be three years **away**.

A : That sounds like forever.

B : What about me? I am two years younger than you.

A : Well, patience is a **virtue**.

Part 2 日常雜務

A：我十八歲就可以考駕照了。
B：那還要三年耶。
A：聽起來好久喔。
B：拜託，那我呢？我還小你兩歲耶。
A：嗯，耐心是種美德。

driver's license 片
駕照

away [ə`we] 副
尚有 …時間

virtue [`vɝtʃu] 名
美德；優點

Part 3 職場應對

對話情境 4 星座達人

Part 4 休閒娛樂

A : I guess you are a Leo.

B : How do you know that?

A : You are very confident about yourself, and are **straightforward** with your opinions.

B : Well, I guess I **fit** the personality traits of Leos.

A : **Exactly**!

A：我猜你是獅子座的。
B：你怎麼知道？
A：你對自己很有自信，而且勇於表達個人意見。
B：嗯，我想我很符合獅子座的特色。
A：沒有錯！

straightforward
[ˌstret`fɔrwəd] 形
直率的

fit [fɪt] 動 適合；符合

exactly [ɪg`zæktlɪ]
副 確切地；恰好

Part 5 出國旅遊

Part 6 愛情來了

小小外交官
A little bit about your background

便利三句開口說

Where are you from?
▶ 你是哪裡人？

替換句 ▶ Where is your hometown? 你的家鄉在哪？

✓ 句型提點 ‹ Using It Properly!

「Where+be 動詞 + 人名 / 代名詞 +from」主要是詢問對方的國籍或是出生地，口語上經常使用，但要注意別與同樣意思的「Where do you come from?」弄混了。

Where do you live?
▶ 你住哪裡？

替換句 ▶ Do you live in the neighborhood? 你住在這附近嗎？

✓ 句型提點 ‹ Using It Properly!

「Where+do/does+ 人名 / 代名詞 +live」主要在詢問對方居住的地點。例句：Where does John live? 約翰住在哪裡？

Do you live in a house or an apartment?
▶ 你住在獨棟房子還是公寓？

替換句 ▶ What kind of place do you live in? 你住在什麼樣的地方？

✓ 句型提點 ‹ Using It Properly!

「Do/does+ 人名 / 代名詞 +live in+ 地點 A+or+ 地點 B」。主要用來詢問對方是住在哪種房子，替換掉

地點的話，也可以問對方是住在城市還是鄉下、住在 A 城市還是 B 城市等。

有來有往的必備回應

Q Where are you from?

A I am from Taiwan.
我來自台灣。

Q Where do you live?

A I live in this neighborhood.
我住在這附近。

Q Do you live in a house or an apartment?

A I live in an apartment.
我住公寓。

小知識補給站 *Some Fun Facts*

　　詢問國籍或是出生地，也可以用「Where do you come from?」，但別跟「Where are you from?」弄混了，最常見的錯誤是將 are 跟 come 放在同一句裡面，如果要用 come 的話，就必須搭配助動詞 do，而非 be 動詞！根據不同的情境，Where are you from? 也可以詢問你在哪個城市出生、長大；例如在國外旅行時，被問到 Where are you from?，當然是回答 I'm from Taiwan.；但若在台灣被外國友人這樣問，就是回答家鄉在哪個城市。

Part **1** 自我介紹

Part **2** 日常雜務

Part **3** 職場應對

Part **4** 休閒娛樂

Part **5** 出國旅遊

Part **6** 愛情來了

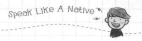
01 What is your nationality?
請問你的國籍是？ nationality 國籍

02 Which city do you live in?
你住在哪個城市？

03 Do you prefer living in a city or the countryside?
你比較喜歡住在市區還是鄉下？ countryside 鄉間；農村

04 What is the capital of your country?
你國家的首都是哪裡？ capital 首都

05 I come from Taiwan, a small island situated next to China.
我來自台灣，在中國大陸旁邊的一個小島。
situated 位於…的

06 I was born in Canada, but grew up in New York.
我在加拿大出生，但在紐約長大。

07 Have you ever been to Taiwan?
你有來過台灣嗎？

08 I live in a suburb close to Taipei.
我住在台北近郊。 suburb 郊區

09 Is there a bus stop close to the place you live?
你住的地方附近有公車站嗎？

10 There's a shuttle bus connecting the MRT station and the place I live.
我住的地方有接駁車可以到捷運站。 shuttle bus 接駁車

11 I commute to work by subway every day.
我每天搭地鐵去上班。 commute 通勤

12 I prefer living in Taipei City because of its nightlife and shopping malls.
我喜歡住在台北市區是因為台北的夜生活跟購物中心。

⓭ I prefer living in the countryside, even if I have to spend an hour commuting.
即使我需要花一個小時通勤，我還是喜歡住在鄉下。

⓮ I am from out of town.
我是外地人。 out of town 外地的

⓯ I live in downtown Taipei.
我住在台北市中心。 downtown 市中心；商業區

⓰ Do you live with your family or alone?
你跟家人住還是一個人住？

⓱ Do you own or rent the house?
房子是你自己的還是用租的？

⓲ I live in a house with a garage.
我住在有車庫的房子。

⓳ I live in an apartment without any elevators.
我住的公寓裡沒有電梯。 elevator 電梯

⓴ I just had my house renovated.
我的房子剛裝修好。 renovate 更新；修理

㉑ I live on the third floor.
我住在三樓。

㉒ I have been living here for ten years.
我在這裡住了十年。

㉓ She lives in a downtown apartment with concierge service.
她住在鬧區裡面一間有管理員的公寓。 concierge 門房

㉔ It is obligatory to mow the lawn in your front yard in the United States.
在美國，修剪前院的草坪是義務。 obligatory 有義務的

㉕ I need to pay a visit to some of my neighbors for I just moved here.
我需要去拜訪一下鄰居，因為我才剛搬過來。
pay a visit to 參觀；訪問

Part 1 自我介紹

Part 2 日常雜務

Part 3 職場應對

Part 4 休閒娛樂

Part 5 出國旅遊

Part 6 愛情來了

雙人實境對話 〈oh!

對話情境① 我來自台灣

Ⓐ : Nice to meet you. Where are you from?
Ⓑ : I am from Germany, and you?
Ⓐ : I am from Taiwan. Have you **ever** heard of it?
Ⓑ : No, I've never heard of it. Where is it?
Ⓐ : It's an **island** in the Asia-Pacific.

A：很高興認識你，你哪裡人？
B：我來自德國，你呢？
A：我來自台灣，你聽過嗎？
B：沒有耶，那在哪裡？
A：台灣是位於亞太地區的一座島嶼。

ever [ˋɛvə] 副 從來；曾經
island [ˋaɪlənd] 名 島嶼；小島

對話情境② 文化交流

Ⓐ : What is your nationality?
Ⓑ : My nationality is French.
Ⓐ : I have been to Paris once.
Ⓑ : How did you like the **city**?
Ⓐ : It is **astonishingly** beautiful, but the people are not really **friendly**.

A：你的國籍是？
B：我來自法國。
A：我去過一次巴黎。
B：你覺得這城市如何？
A：城市美得令人驚豔，不過人們不太友善。

city [ˋsɪtɪ] 名 城市
astonishingly [əˋstanɪʃɪŋlɪ] 副 令人驚訝地
friendly [ˋfrɛndlɪ] 形 友善的；親切的

對話情境 3 該獨立囉

A : Do you still live with your parents?

B : Yes, I do. What about it?

A : Has it ever **occurred** to you that it's about time to live on your own?

B : Well, you're right. Are there any **vacant** rooms in your apartment building currently?

A : I **have no idea**, but I'll keep my eyes open for you.

A：你還跟父母親住嗎？
B：是啊，怎麼了嗎？
A：你從來都沒想過，該是搬出來自立的時候了嗎？
B：也是啦，那你那棟公寓現在有空房可以租？
A：不知道，不過我會幫你留意。

occur [ə`kɜ] 動
發生；想到

vacant [`vekənt] 形
空的

have no idea 片
不知道

對話情境 4 城市還是鄉下好

A : Do you **prefer** living in a city or the countryside?

B : I prefer the **latter**. I've always dreamt of living in a **cottage** by a lake.

A : What about nightlife and convenience stores?

B : I'd rather drive an hour to do the shopping than **put up with** the noise.

A : I couldn't agree with you more.

A：你喜歡住在城市還是鄉下？
B：我喜歡後者，我一直幻想能夠住在河邊的小屋。
A：那夜生活跟便利商店呢？
B：我寧願開一個鐘頭的車去採買，也不想忍受噪音。
A：我也深有同感。

prefer [prɪ`fɜ] 動
偏好；寧可

latter [`lætə] 形
後面的

cottage [`katɪdʒ] 名
小屋

put up with 片 忍受

Unit 04 身家背景深入了解
Running a background check

便利三句開口說

How many people are there in your family?
▶ 你家一共有幾個人?

替換句▶ Do you come from a small or a big family?
你來自小家庭還是大家庭?

✓ **句型提點** Using It Properly!

「How+many+ 名詞 +are there」用來詢問某種情況 / 事物有多少數量。因為 many 修飾可數名詞,故接在 How many 後面的,必須是複數的可數名詞,句尾的 be 動詞則按名詞變化(are)。

Are you single or married?
▶ 你單身還是已婚?

替換句▶ What is your relationship status? 你的感情狀態如何?

✓ **句型提點** Using It Properly!

「be 動詞 + 名詞 / 代名詞 +single or married」用來詢問別人的感情狀態是單身還是已婚。single 意指「單身的」,而 married 則是指「已婚的」。

Do you have any kids?
▶ 你有小孩嗎?

替換句▶ Are you planning to have kids after getting married? 婚後你有計劃要生小孩嗎?

✓ **句型提點** Using It Properly!

「any」用在否定以及疑問句中,表示「任何」之意,

後面可接不可數名詞和複數名詞，例如：Do you have any pets? 你有養寵物嗎？（pet 為可數名詞，用複數表達非指定）；Do you have any cash? 你有現金嗎？（cash 為不可數名詞）。

 有來有往的必備回應

Q How many people are there in your family?

> There are five people in my family. **A**
> 我家一共有五個人。

Q Are you single or married?

> I am single. **A**
> 我目前單身。

Q Do you have any kids?

> Yes, I have one daughter. **A**
> 有啊，我有一個女兒。

小知識補給站 Some Fun Facts

　　美國因為幅員廣大，每個家庭可能都會有住在別州的親戚，每當去拜訪時，都得開上好幾個小時的車，雖然距離遙遠，但與親戚之間卻仍然常常互相拜訪；美國家庭也有較強的家族觀念，像是許多家庭有自己獨特的家庭傳統，例如飯前互相握住手進行禱告、每年夏天去其他州的阿姨、叔叔家玩……等等。而感情狀態方面，除了 single（單身）、married（已婚）之外，還有 in a relationship（有交往對象）、engaged（已訂婚）、separated（分居中）、divorced（離婚）等。

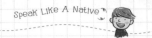

01 There are four people in my family: my parents, my younger sister and I.
我們一家四口，包含我雙親、我妹妹跟我。

02 I was born in a big family in Taipei.
我出生在台北的一個大家庭裡。

03 How many brothers and sisters do you have?
你有幾個兄弟姐妹？

04 I am the oldest/youngest in my family.
我是家裡最年長 / 年輕的。

05 I am the second child of three.
我在家裡三個小孩中排行老二。

06 I am the only child.
我是獨子 / 獨生女。

07 I come from a small family, so I have few relatives.
我來自小家庭，所以我的親戚很少。 relative 親戚；親屬

08 I come from a single-parent family and was brought up by my mother.
我生於單親家庭，是我媽媽把我帶大的。
single-parent family 單親家庭

09 His parents were strict and paid a lot of attention to his academic performance.
他的雙親很嚴厲，而且很重視他的學業表現。

10 My father is stern while my mother is easygoing.
我爸很嚴格，而我媽很隨和。 stern 嚴格的

11 Like father, like son.
虎父無犬子。

12 What do your parents do?

你父母是做什麼的？

⑬ My father is a well-known pediatrician and my mom is a dedicated nurse.
我爸是知名的小兒科醫生，而我媽是個敬業的護士。
pediatrician 小兒科醫生　dedicated 專注的；獻身的

⑭ Unlike in the traditional marriage, it is my mom who brings home the bacon.
不同於傳統家庭，我們家是我媽負責賺錢養家。
bring home the bacon 養家糊口

⑮ I get along pretty well with my family.
我跟家人相處融洽。

⑯ I resemble my father because of my round face and big eyes.
我像我爸，因為我有圓臉跟大眼睛。　resemble 像；類似

⑰ All my siblings are good at music. It runs in the family.
我的兄弟姐妹對音樂都很在行，那是家族遺傳。

⑱ We usually have our family reunion on Christmas Day.
我們家族通常在聖誕節聚會。　family reunion 家庭聚會

⑲ Ever since my grandparents passed away, our family members seldom see one another.
自從我祖父母過世，我們家族成員就很少見到彼此了。

⑳ Sean's brother was a juvenile delinquent, who set a bad example for him.
西恩的哥哥是個問題少年，給他樹立了壞榜樣。

㉑ I am a single mother.
我是個單親媽媽。

㉒ Who looks after your kids while you go to work?
你去工作的時候，誰照顧你的小孩？　look after 照顧；照看

㉓ Rosy thinks that family should come first.
蘿西認為家庭應該排在第一順位。　come first 首先要考慮到的

Part 1 自我介紹

Part 2 日常雜務

Part 3 職場應對

Part 4 休閒娛樂

Part 5 出國旅遊

Part 6 愛情來了

031

雙人實境對話

對話情境 ① 人妻預備之路

A : Are you single?

B : Yes, for now. I am going to get married at the end of this year.

A : Congratulations! You must be busy planning the wedding.

B : Yeah. I am lucky to have my sister as an adviser!

A：你現在單身嗎？
B：目前是，但我年底就要結婚了。
A：恭喜！你一定正忙著籌備婚禮。
B：對啊，我很幸運有我姊提供建議。

for now 片 目前；現在

congratulation [kənˌgrætʃəˋleʃən] 名 恭喜（常為複數）

wedding [ˋwɛdɪŋ] 名 婚禮

對話情境 ② 八卦閒聊

A : Mandy comes from a single-parent family. She hasn't seen her mom since she was born.

B : It must be tough for both her and her father.

A : Not quite. Rumor has it that her father is a famous politician.

B : So you're implying that she might be a love child?

A : You are putting words into my mouth!

A：曼蒂是單親家庭的孩子，她出生後從來都沒看過她媽。
B：對她跟她爸來說，生活一定很辛苦。
A：也不盡然，聽說她爸是個有名的政治家。
B：所以你的意思是…她有可能是私生女囉？
A：這可是你說的，我沒這個意思喔！

single-parent [ˌsɪŋglˋpɛrənt] 形 單親的

rumor has it that… 片 聽說；謠傳

imply [ɪmˋplaɪ] 動 暗示；暗指

對話情境 ③ 團圓聚餐有苦有樂

A : How are you going to spend your Chinese New Year holidays?

B : I have to spend two days in Tainan for my family reunion.

A : I am so jealous! Family reunions sound warm and fun.

B : I wish we could switch places. I don't get along with my relatives!

A : You are such a big child!

A：你過年打算怎麼過？

B：我必須待在台南兩天，參加家庭聚會。

A：真羨慕你！家庭團聚聽起來既溫暖又開心。

B：我真希望能跟你交換，我跟我的親戚們處不來。

A：你真是長不大的孩子耶！

jealous [`dʒɛləs] 形
忌妒的；羨慕的

switch [swɪtʃ] 動
轉換；開；關

get along 片 和睦相處；進展

對話情境 ④ 優秀家人壓力大

A : What does your sister do?

B : She is a surgeon in an overseas hospital, and her reputation is widespread.

A : Wow, it must be stressful living in her shadow.

B : And I always feel that I cannot live up to my parents' expectations.

A : Or maybe you just think too much.

A：你姊從事什麼行業？

B：她是海外一間醫院的外科醫生，她聲名遠播呢！

A：哇，生活在她的光環下，壓力應該滿大的。

B：而且我總是覺得自己沒辦法達到我爸媽對我的期望。

A：或許只是你自己想太多了。

surgeon [`sɝdʒən] 名 外科醫生

widespread
[`waɪd.sprɛd] 形 普遍的；廣泛的

live up to 片 遵守；符合

Part 1 自我介紹
Part 2 日常雜務
Part 3 職場應對
Part 4 休閒娛樂
Part 5 出國旅遊
Part 6 愛情來了

知人知面也知心
Seeing a man's face and his heart

便利三句開口說

Are you an introvert or an extrovert?
▶ 你個性內向還是外向呢？

替換句 Are you an outgoing person or a quiet one?
你是活潑外向還是安靜的人？

✓ **句型提點** Using It Properly!

introvert 為名詞，指「內向的人」，形容詞形式為
introverted；extrovert 則為「外向的人」，為名詞，
但同時也可以當形容詞使用。

······

How tall are you?
▶ 你身高多高？

替換句 What is your height? 請問你的身高多少？

✓ **句型提點** Using It Properly!

「How tall+ be 動詞 + 主詞」。如果主詞是第三人
稱單數或是人名、單數名詞，則 be 動詞要用 is，例如：
How tall is Andrea? 安德莉亞多高？

······

Could you describe your brother's appearance?
▶ 可否描述一下你哥哥的長相？

替換句 What does your brother look like? 你哥哥長得
怎樣？

✓ **句型提點** Using It Properly!

用助動詞 could 開頭，比用 can 更有禮貌。若是與
談話者很熟悉，可以使用 can；若是面對長輩或不熟

的對象，建議使用 could，聽起來才會比較有禮貌。
例：Could you pass me the salad, please? 可否
請你將沙拉遞給我？

 有來有往的必備回應

Q Are you an introvert or an extrovert?

       I am more of an extrovert. A

       我是比較外向的人。

Q How tall are you?

       I am six feet tall. A

       我六呎高。

Q Could you describe your boyfriend's appearance?

       Sure! He has a long face and thick eyebrows. A

       當然可以！他的臉型偏長、眉毛很濃。

 **小知識補給站**   *Some Fun Facts*

美國不用公制單位 (metric units)，而是用英制單位 (imperial units) 如公分 (centimeter)、公尺 (meter)，美國以英尺 (foot)、英寸 (inch) 來度量；表示重量的公克 (gram)、公斤 (kilogram)，美國用磅 (pound)、盎司 (ounce)；台灣用公里 (kilometer)、公尺 (meter) 來計算距離，美國則是英里 (mile)、碼 (yard)；公升 (liter) 為台灣常用的容量單位，美國則用加侖 (gallon)。出國前先有個基本概念，才不會買東西的時候，被不熟悉的單位弄得頭昏眼花！

Part 1 自我介紹

Part 2 日常雜務

Part 3 職場應對

Part 4 休閒娛樂

Part 5 出國旅遊

Part 6 愛情來了

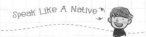
01 **John is an introvert. He keeps everything to himself.**
約翰的個性內向，很多事情他都不會講出口。
introvert 內向的人

02 **My cousin is so outgoing to the point that my aunt is starting to worry about his school work.**
我表哥外向到我阿姨都開始擔心這會不會影響到他的課業。
to the point that/of 達到…的程度

03 **Duke is a man with a short temper.**
杜克是個急性子。 a short temper 急性子；脾氣暴躁

04 **People with Type A blood are considered to be slow and stubborn, but at the same time careful.**
A 型的人被認為是動作慢且頑固的，但同時也很細心。

05 **I don't like to be around with people who are self-centered and think of nothing but themselves.**
我不喜歡跟自我中心、凡事只想著自己的人在一起。

06 **I always use the horoscope and blood types as references to determine people's personality.**
我總是以星座和血型作為判定他人性格的參考。

07 **Debby is not a straightforward person because she always beats about the bush.**
黛比不是個直來直往的人，她總是拐彎抹角。
beats about the bush 拐彎抹角

08 **I think I am a bit impulsive because I sometimes don't think before I speak.**
我覺得自己的個性有點衝動，因為我有時候沒經過思考就脫口而出。

09 **He is a man of his word.**
他是個守信用的男人。 a man of his word 說話算話的人

⑩ She is a persistent woman, meaning she seldom gives up on things.

她是個堅持不懈的女人，也就是說，她不輕言放棄。

persistent 堅持不懈的 give up on 放棄…

⑪ She is five-feet-five-inches tall and weighs 130 pounds.

她身高五呎五吋，體重 130 磅。

⑫ My father has a square face, thin eyebrows and a pair of big eyes.

我爸有一個方臉、淡眉及一雙大眼。

⑬ He has a stout build and wears a Mohawk.

他身材粗壯且留著龐克頭。 stout 結實的

⑭ Jessica is tough on the outside but vulnerable on the inside.

潔西卡外表堅強，但內心脆弱。 vulnerable 易受傷的

⑮ My sister is not satisfied with her single eyelids and decided to have a bit of plastic surgery.

我妹不滿意她的單眼皮，決定要去動整形手術。

single eyelid 單眼皮 plastic surgery 整形手術

⑯ My boss is bald, so he wears a toupee every day.

我老闆禿頭，所以他每天都戴髮片。 toupee 男士的假髮

⑰ She has a pair of long legs that attract everyone's attention every time she walks by.

她有一雙長腿，走到哪都會吸引路人的目光。

⑱ His girlfriend is a blue-eyed brunette with skinny limbs and big feet.

他女友有一雙藍眼及一頭褐髮，四肢乾瘦、有雙大腳。

brunette 深褐髮色的女子

⑲ My son is starting to have zits as he enters into his adolescence.

我兒子進入青春期後開始長痘痘。 zit 青春痘；面皰

⑳ Is that a mole on your right arm?

你右手臂上的是一顆痣嗎？

Part 1 自我介紹

Part 2 日常雜務

Part 3 職場應對

Part 4 休閒娛樂

Part 5 出國旅遊

Part 6 愛情來了

雙人實境對話 〈oh!〉

對話情境 ① 辦公室閒聊

A : What do you think of Andrew, the new guy in the office?

B : He is so my type! I like his smile.

A : **In case** you didn't notice, he smiles at every female colleague **passing by**.

B : So what? He is just being **polite**!

A : You are hopeless...

A：你覺得辦公室新來的那個男生，安德魯怎樣？

B：他是我的菜！我喜歡他的笑容。

A：也許你沒注意到，他對每個經過的女同事都會微笑。

B：那又怎樣？他只是很有禮貌而已嘛！

A：你沒救了…

in case 片 假如；以防萬一

pass by 片 經過；忽視

polite [pə`laɪt] 形 有禮貌的

對話情境 ② 談論老師們

A : What is the word that best describes your teacher?

B : I'd say "patient". She repeats the same **subjects** over and over again simply because a few students don't follow.

A : Mine is "**stubborn**".

B : Do explain!

A : She always **insists** that we turn in our homework on time!

A：用哪個詞來形容你的老師最貼切？

B：我覺得是「耐心」，她會為了一些沒跟上的同學反覆講解同樣主題。

A：我的則是「頑固」。

B：快說為何！

A：她老是堅持我們要準時交作業！

subject [`sʌbdʒɪkt] 名 主題；科目

stubborn [`stʌbən] 形 固執的

insist [ɪn`sɪst] 名 堅持

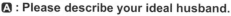

對話情境 ③ 理想類型

Ⓐ : Please describe your ideal husband.

Ⓑ : He should be six-feet tall with average **build** and a handsome face.

Ⓐ : What about personality?

Ⓑ : He should be **considerate**, caring, loving and remember all our **anniversaries**!

Ⓐ : Good luck with you finding him in reality!

A：請描述一下你理想的丈夫類型。
B：他要有六呎高、中等身材及一張俊俏的臉蛋。
A：那個性呢？
B：他應該要貼心、關心他人、有愛心，並且記得我們所有的週年紀念日！
A：祝你在現實生活中找到這樣的人！

build [bɪld]
名 體型 動 建築

considerate
[kənˋsɪdərət] 形
體貼的

anniversary
[ˌænəˋvɝsərɪ] 名
周年紀念日

對話情境 ④ 捉拿要犯

Ⓐ : Can you give the police a basic description of this fugitive?

Ⓑ : Yes, I'll try. He is **approximately** six feet tall and in his late thirties.

Ⓐ : Are there any unique **features** on his face?

Ⓑ : Yes. He has a scar on his left cheek.

Ⓐ : Thank you for your information. We hope we can put this guy **behind bars** in no time.

A：你是否能提供逃犯的基本特徵給警方？
B：好，我盡量。他大約 180 公分、年近 40 歲。
A：他臉上有什麼特徵嗎？
B：有，他左臉頰上有一條疤。
Ａ：謝謝你提供的訊息，希望我們可以盡早將逃犯逮捕歸案。

approximately
[əˋprɑksəmɪtlɪ] 副
大概

feature [ˋfitʃɚ] 名
特徵

behind bars 片
坐牢

039

Unit 06 宗教信仰淺談
Religious beliefs

便利三句開口說

Do you belong to/practice/follow a religion?
▶ 你有信仰嗎？

替換句▶ What is your religion? 你的宗教信仰是什麼？

☑ **句型提點 Using It Properly!**

「Do/Does+ 人名 / 代名詞 + 上述動詞 +religion」。belong to 表示屬於、隸屬；practice 表示實踐；follow 在此處表示追隨信奉。

Do you believe in God?
▶ 你相信上帝嗎？

替換句▶ What is your opinion about God? 你對上帝有什麼看法？

☑ **句型提點 Using It Properly!**

believe in 後面接名詞，表示對「某種信念或存在」表達相信的態度。believe 則指相信一些「表面上的東西或是別人的話」。例如：Do you believe in him? 你相信他（這個人）嗎？/ Do you believe him? 你相信他（說的話）嗎？

Are you superstitious?
▶ 你迷信嗎？

替換句▶ Are you a zealous person when it comes to religion? 在宗教信仰方面，你會很狂熱嗎？

☑ **句型提點 Using It Properly!**

「Is/Are+ 人名 / 代名詞 +superstitious」用來詢問某人是否迷信。superstitious 為形容詞，意指迷信

的。

有來有往的必備回應

Q Do you belong to/practice/follow a religion?

A Yes, I am a Christian.

有，我是基督徒。

Q Do you believe in God?

A No. I am an atheist.

不相信，我是無神論者。

Q Are you superstitious?

A Yes, I think so.

是的，我很迷信。

小知識補給站　Some Fun Facts

　　在國際禮儀上，大都不會開門見山地討論宗教議題，但若具備有關宗教的基本知識，可以加深對別人的了解、也能增加談話的深度。世界上的五大宗教是印度教 (Hinduism)，猶太教 (Judaism)、佛教 (Buddhism)、基督教 (Christianity)、以及伊斯蘭教 (Islam)，現今也有愈來愈多人提倡無神論 (Atheism)。談到宗教，當然也可以把話題延伸到迷信方面，像是西方認為 13 號星期五容易發生不好的事、在屋內打開雨傘會招來惡運、7 代表幸運數字…等等，而日本人認為灑米或豆子可以驅邪、去除霉運；黑貓雖然一般來說，被認為是不祥的代表，在英國卻是帶來好運的象徵，在古埃及甚至被視為神靈的化身。

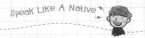
01 Local people worship in temples on a regular basis.

當地人固定在廟宇祭祀。 worship 崇拜;信奉

02 Buddhists and Taoists are two major religious populations in Taiwan.

佛教徒跟道教徒為台灣兩大宗教人口。

03 Have you ever seen any religious ceremonies?

你有看過任何宗教儀式嗎?

04 Using incense while praying for a blessing is part of the rituals in Buddhism.

祭拜時焚香是佛教的儀式之一。 incense 香;焚香時的煙

05 Do you believe in reincarnation?

你相信輪迴轉世嗎? reincarnation 輪迴說

06 Superstition can be seen in various cultures.

迷信在不同文化中都能見到。

07 We call July of the lunar calendar "ghost month".

我們稱農曆七月為鬼月。 lunar 陰曆的

08 People in Taiwan don't play in water during the ghost month of the lunar calendar.

台灣人在農曆鬼月的時候不會去玩水。

09 Fortune telling is considered superstitious.

算命被視為迷信。

10 Jason's parents brought him to have his face and palm read.

傑森的雙親帶他去看面相及手相。

11 Chinese people believe that face-reading can tell a lot about a person's life.

中國人認為面相術可以看出一個人的未來。

⑫ **A prophet is someone who can foresee the future.**

預言家就是可以預見未來的人。 `prophet 先知；預言者`

⑬ **Feng shui is an important part of traditional Chinese culture.**

風水在中國傳統文化中是很重要的一項。

⑭ **Chinese see the number 4 as bad luck, which is the same as how Americans think about the number 13.**

中國人認為數字 4 不吉祥，就像美國人認為數字 13 不吉祥一樣。

⑮ **It is thought to be bad luck not to clean debts with others before Chinese New Year.**

不趕在農曆過年前償還積欠的債務 (欠債欠過年) 被認為會帶來壞運氣。

⑯ **There are a lot of dos and don'ts when it comes to superstition.**

提到迷信，總是有很多該做及不該做的注意事項。
`dos and don'ts 規則；準則`

⑰ **He is very pious because he never misses any church service.**

他很虔誠，因為他從來不缺席教堂的禮拜。 `pious 虔誠的`

⑱ **My friend says prayers before meals.**

我的朋友在用餐前都會禱告。

⑲ **My family goes to church and sings gospel every Sunday morning.**

我家人每週日上午都會去教堂唱福音。 `go to church 上教堂`

⑳ **I'm going to be baptized next month.**

我下個月要受洗。 `baptize 行浸禮`

㉑ **It seems that there are several taboos in the Islamic world.**

在回教世界中，似乎有一些禁忌不能犯。 `taboo 禁忌`

Part 1 自我介紹

Part 2 日常雜務

Part 3 職場應對

Part 4 休閒娛樂

Part 5 出國旅遊

Part 6 愛情來了

雙人實境對話 <oh!>

對話情境 ① 教會禮拜

A: The best part of Sunday service is singing the gospel.

B: What about the sermons?

A: It depends. Sometimes the preachers are eloquent, sometimes not.

B: That only shows one thing-you are not pious enough.

A: True. I still have a long way to go.

A：禮拜天的教會禮拜最棒的部分就是唱福音。

B：那布道呢？

A：看情況，有時候傳教士口若懸河，有時候則不。

B：這證明一件事，你不夠虔誠。

A：是啦，我的學習之路還很長。

gospel [ˋgɑspl] 名 福音

sermon [ˋsɝmən] 名 布道

eloquent [ˋɛləkwənt] 形 雄辯的

對話情境 ② 望彌撒

A: Do you believe in God?

B: Yes. As a matter of fact, I am Catholic.

A: Do you attend Mass or any other religious activities?

B: I live in a remote area, so I attend Mass only once in a while.

A: Maybe you are not that religious.

A：你相信上帝嗎？

B：我信，事實上，我是天主教徒。

A：你有參加彌撒或其他宗教活動嗎？

B：我住的地方比較偏遠，所以我偶爾才參加一次彌撒。

A：或許你比較沒那麼虔誠。

as a matter of fact 片 事實上

remote [rɪˋmot] 形 遙遠的

once in a while 片 偶爾

對話情境 3 拜拜

A : It is the fifteenth day of the lunar calendar.
B : No wonder I saw my boss preparing fruit, snacks and flowers early this morning.
A : My colleagues always buy abundant offerings before worshiping.
B : I am sorry, but I can't join you.
A : Right! You are a Christian.

A：今天是農曆十五號。
B：難怪我今天早上看到我老闆準備了水果、零食及花卉。
A：我同事總是買很多拜拜的供品。
B：很抱歉，不過我無法參與。
A：對喔！你是基督徒。

no wonder 片 難怪
abundant
[ə`bʌndənt] 形 豐富的
offering [`ɔfərɪŋ]
名 供品

對話情境 4 第一次讀手相

A : Your palm tells me you will live a long life.
B : That's not difficult to tell because my life line is long and deep.
A : I can't see your heart line! You will never be in a relationship.
B : As a matter of fact, I am seeing someone now.
A : OK, I'll give you a refund.

A：你的手相告訴我你會長壽。
B：這不難知道，因為我的生命線又長又深。
A：我看不到你的感情線耶！你永遠不會有戀情。
B：事實上，我正在跟某人穩定交往。
A：好吧，我退錢給你。

tell [tɛl] 動 分辨；告訴
refund [`ri.fʌnd] 名 退款

自我介紹

日常雜務

職場應對

休閒娛樂

出國旅遊

愛情來了

045

興趣專長多方了解
Habits and specialized skills

 便利三句開口說

What's your hobby?
◉ 你的興趣是什麼？

替換句▶ What's your interest? 你的興趣是什麼？

✓ **句型提點** Using It Properly!

「What+is + 人名／代名詞（所有格）+hobby」。
hobby 表示嗜好、業餘從事的興趣。例句：What is
your brother's hobby? 你哥哥的興趣是什麼？

What do you specialize in?
◉ 你的專長是什麼？

替換句▶ What's your specialty? 你的專長是什麼？

✓ **句型提點** Using It Properly!

「What+do/does+ 人名／代名詞 + specialize
+in」。specialize in 為片語，指專精在某個領域上，
in 後面接名詞，表示專精的領域、項目。

What's your favorite pastime?
◉ 你最喜歡的休閒活動是什麼？

替換句▶ What do you do in your free time? 平常閒暇
時，你都做些什麼？

✓ **句型提點** Using It Properly!

「What+is+ 人名／代名詞（所有格）+favorite
pastime」，詢問別人最喜歡做的休閒活動是什麼。
pastime 意指消遣、娛樂，特別指用來消磨閒暇時間
的活動。

Part 1 自我介紹

Part 2 日常雜務

Part 3 職場應對

Part 4 休閒娛樂

Part 5 出國旅遊

Part 6 愛情來了

有來有往的必備回應

Q What's your hobby?

A One of my hobbies is playing piano.

我其中一個興趣是彈鋼琴。

Q What do you specialize in?

A I specialize in on-line games.

我的專長是玩線上遊戲。

Q What's your favorite pastime?

A My favorite pastime is writing my blog.

我最喜歡的休閒活動是寫網誌。

小知識補給站

Some Fun Facts

通過聊嗜好，常常可以交到許多興趣相投的好友們，但可別把相關字搞混了！interest 指個人的興趣；pastime 是消遣、閒暇時間進行的活動；hobby 指工作之餘會積極進行、投入的愛好；而 habit 則指習慣、癖好；custom 雖然譯為習俗，有時候也可指個人的習慣，意同 habit。世界上還有形形色色的特殊消遣，例如帶布偶環遊世界的 toy voyaging、英國的極限熨衣 (extreme ironing)、美國威斯康辛州的牛叫比賽 (mooing)、日本的鬥蟲 (bug fighting)、泰國的皂雕 (soap carving)、也有人收集各式各樣的東西 (例如：牛奶瓶、搖頭丸、甚至是機上嘔吐袋等等)。

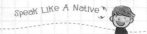
01 **My best friend and I share the same hobbies.**
我好友跟我的嗜好相同。 hobby 業餘愛好；嗜好

02 **My hobbies include oil painting, sketching and pottery.**
我的嗜好包括油畫、素描及陶藝。

03 **Who do you spend your free time with?**
你閒暇時間都跟誰過？ free time 空閒時間

04 **How long have you had your hobby?**
你有這個嗜好多久了？

05 **Do people's leisure time activities change as they get older?**
人喜愛的休閒活動會因年紀漸長而改變嗎？ leisure 閒暇

06 **Judy has had the hobby of knitting ever since her daughter left home for college five years ago.**
自從女兒五年前為了上大學而離家後，茱蒂開始有編織這個嗜好。

07 **Are there any activities that you used to do but don't do anymore?**
有沒有哪些活動是你以前會做，但現在再也不做的？

08 **I spend most of my free time working out at the gym.**
我閒暇時都在健身房健身。

09 **Biking around the island has become one of the major pastimes for Taiwanese lately.**
單車環島近來已經成為台灣人主要的休閒活動之一。
pastime 消遣；娛樂

10 **Do you like gossiping in your free time?**
你空閒時喜歡聊八卦嗎？ gossip 傳播流言蜚語

11 **Which hobbies cost nothing at all to do?**

哪些嗜好完全不用花錢？

12 I think running is one of the cheapest hobbies.
我覺得跑步是最不花錢的嗜好之一。

13 One of my favorite pastimes is watching theatrical performances.
我最喜歡的休閒活動之一就是看劇場表演。

14 In his pastime, John likes to go fishing.
約翰喜歡在閒暇之餘去釣魚。

15 Tom tried to get to know the girl by asking her about her hobbies.
湯姆試著以詢問對方興趣的方式來了解這個女孩。

16 I am good at linguistics and specialize in it.
我擅長語言學，並專精於此。

17 My dad has a great appreciation for wine tasting.
我爸在品酒這個領域很有鑑賞力。 appreciation 欣賞；鑑賞

18 Our professor is an expert in economics.
我們的教授是經濟學專家。

19 Jody has a great reputation in the fashion industry.
裘蒂在時裝界負有盛名。

20 I am proficient in seven different languages.
我精通七國語言。 proficient 精通的；熟練的

21 My uncle masters in English.
我的舅舅精通英文。

22 My grandfather is very influential in the publishing industry.
我爺爺在出版界很有影響力。

23 My mom is capable of taking care of her kids and working efficiently at the same time.
我媽很有能力，能兼顧小孩與工作。

Part 1 自我介紹

Part 2 日常雜務

Part 3 職場應對

Part 4 休閒娛樂

Part 5 出國旅遊

Part 6 愛情來了

對話情境① 休閒時刻來塊麵包

A : I like to read **science fiction** in my free time. What about you?

B : I have been into **baking** lately.

A : **Good for you**. Is there any chance I can try some of your baking?

B : Sure! When will you have free time?

A : Anytime!

A：我閒暇時喜歡閱讀科幻小說，你呢？
B：我最近喜歡上烘焙。
A：真好，我有機會品嚐到你的作品嗎？
B：當然有！你什麼時候有空？
A：隨時都有空！

science fiction 名
科幻小說 / 電影

baking [`bekɪŋ] 名
烘焙

good for sb. 片
做得好

對話情境② 不想花錢買嗜好

A : Can you think of any hobbies that don't cost anything?

B : How about hiking?

A : I thought so too in the beginning, but then I realized the **expenditure** of the **gear** is shockingly high.

B : Well, then, what about **spacing out**?

A : That's not a hobby at all!

A：你能想到完全不用花錢的嗜好嗎？
B：登山怎麼樣？
A：我一開始也這樣想，但是後來發現購買裝備的花費高得驚人。
B：那發呆呢？
A：那根本稱不上是嗜好！

expenditure
[ɪk`spɛndɪtʃɚ] 名
消費；經費

gear [gɪr] 名 配備；
裝置

space out 片
精神恍惚

對話情境 3 語言達人

A : Now that you have mentioned your weaknesses, tell me more about your strengths.

B : I master in two different languages. My proficiency in English and Spanish can hold up to any test.

A : How did you manage to pull it off?

B : I listen to English and Spanish songs on the radio every day.

A：既然你剛剛提到自己的弱點，現在說說你的長處吧。

B：我精通兩種語言，英文和西班牙文的程度都經得起任何考驗。

A：你是怎麼辦到的？

B：我每天都用廣播聽英文和西文的歌曲。

proficiency
[prəˋfɪʃənsɪ] 名 熟練；精通

hold up 片 支撐；堅持

pull off 片 成功完成

對話情境 4 多元強項

A : The new guy in my department specializes in Internet security.

B : Sounds professional. I thought that's your specialty.

A : Well, that's one of my specialties.

B : So you're saying you're better than him?

A : I'm just saying I have multiple strengths.

A：我們部門的新人專精於網路安全。

B：聽起來好專業，我以為那是你的專長。

A：嗯，那的確是我其中一項專長。

B：所以你的意思是，你比他強囉？

A．我只是在說我的強項很多。

security [sɪˋkjʊrətɪ]
名 安全；防護

professional
[prəˋfɛʃənl] 形 專業的

multiple [ˋmʌltəpl]
形 多樣的

便利三句開口說

I am sorry. Please accept my apology.
▶ 很抱歉，請接受我的道歉。

替換句 ▶ I apologize. 我很抱歉。

☑ ➔ **句型提點** Using It Properly!

I am sorry 後面可接「for+ 名詞」，也可以接「that+ 子句」，意指對某件事深感抱歉。例如：I am sorry for the trouble I made the other day. 我對前幾天造成的麻煩感到抱歉。

I didn't mean to make you mad.
▶ 我不是故意要惹你生氣的。

替換句 ▶ It's not my intention to hurt you. 我沒有要傷害你的意思。

☑ ➔ **句型提點** Using It Properly!

「某人 +don't/doesn't mean to+ 原形動詞」表示某人並非故意做出後面的行為。mean 指意圖、打算，使用此句型表示說話者並非有意，且內心懷有歉意。

I appreciate it.
▶ 謝謝。

替換句 ▶ I am really grateful. 真的很感激。

☑ ➔ **句型提點** Using It Properly!

為單純表達感謝的句子。若要詳細描述感謝的內容，可在 appreciate 後面加上名詞或是「that+ 子句」。例：I appreciate your help. 感謝你的協助。

/ I appreciate that you fed my cats. 感謝你幫我餵貓。

Part 1 自我介紹

 有來有往的必備回應

Q   I am sorry. Please accept my apology.

       Never mind. *A*
       沒關係。

Q   I didn't mean to make you mad.

       That's all right. *A*
       沒事。

Q   I appreciate it.

       Anytime. *A*
       不客氣。

Part 2 日常雜務

Part 3 職場應對

Part 4 休閒娛樂

小知識補給站   *Some Fun Facts*

I'm sorry 也可以表達同情、遺憾；例如當好友的親人因病去世，你可以說 I'm sorry 來表達惋惜。另外，道歉時也可以說 I apologize，但此用法較為正式，且只單純地針對事情或行為道歉。Excuse me 的使用時機則是在引起別人的注意、造成別人不便的當下、需要別人借過一下時使用，例如，問路時的開場白通常都用 Excuse me，表達「不好意思打擾了」。Pardon (me) 則是 Excuse me 較為正式的用法；而 I beg your pardon 通常是在「沒有聽清楚別人講的話，希望對方重複一遍」的時候用，或表達強烈的不同意。

Part 5 出國旅遊

Part 6 愛情來了

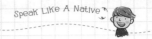
01 I'm truly sorry.
真的很抱歉。

02 Sorry, my bad.
對不起,我錯了。

03 I'm sorry to interrupt, but the bell is ringing.
抱歉打擾,電鈴響了。 `interrupt 打斷`

04 I did not intend to break your heart.
我不是故意要傷你的心。 `intend 想要;打算`

05 We apologize for all the inconvenience we caused.
我們為我們所造成的不便道歉。

06 If you'll excuse me, I have a meeting to attend.
我還有會議要參加,恕我先離席。

07 Will you forgive me?
你會原諒我嗎?

08 It's my fault. What can I do to fix this?
這是我的錯,我該怎麼彌補? `fix 修理;挽救;補償`

09 Is there any way that I could make it up to you?
有沒有任何方法可以補償你?
`make it up to sb. 對某人做出補償`

10 Apology accepted.
我接受道歉。

11 Forget it!
算了!

12 Don't worry. It's no trouble at all.
沒關係,沒有問題的。

13 It doesn't matter at all.
真的沒關係。

⑭ I am so grateful for your assistance.
非常感謝你的協助。

⑮ I can't thank you enough.
實在太感謝你了。

⑯ I just don't know how to express my gratefulness.
我真的不知道要如何表達我的感激之情。

⑰ Much obliged!
非常感激！ obliged 感激的

⑱ I'd like to say thank you to those who have supported me along the way.
我想要對一直以來支持我的人表達感謝。

⑲ Could you please express my gratitude to your parents?
可否請你將我的謝意轉達給你的父母？
gratitude 感激之情；感謝

⑳ I'll never forget what you have done for me. Thanks a million.
我永遠不會忘記你為我做的事，萬分感謝。

㉑ I really appreciate your generosity, but I can't take it.
我真的很感謝你的慷慨，但我不能收下。
generosity 寬宏大量；慷慨

㉒ That's very sweet of you to say so.
你這樣說真的很貼心。

㉓ The pleasure is all mine.
不用客氣，這是我的榮幸。 pleasure 愉悅；歡樂；滿意

㉔ Don't mention it.
別謝了。

㉕ It's no big deal.
這只是小事。

㉖ That's nothing to speak of.
沒什麼，不足掛齒。 speak of 談到

Part 1 自我介紹
Part 2 日常雜務
Part 3 職場應對
Part 4 休閒娛樂
Part 5 出國旅遊
Part 6 愛情來了

雙人實境對話 ‹oh!›

對話情境 ① 尋找座位

A : Excuse me, this seat is taken.
B : I am really sorry. I didn't **notice**.
A : I think there's one **available** down the hall.
B : Thanks a lot! I'll **give it a shot**.
A : You're welcome.

A：不好意思，這位子有人了。
B：真的很抱歉，我沒有注意到。
A：我記得沿著走廊下去還有一個空位。
B：非常感謝！我去看看。
A：不客氣。

notice [`notɪs] 動
注意
available [ə`veləbl]
形 可用的；有空的
give it a shot 片
試試看

對話情境 ② 溫馨小趴踢

A : Thank you for coming! Just make yourself at home.
B : Thanks. You have done a great job on your front **porch**!
A : Thank you for noticing that. Here, try some of the **hors d'oeuvres**.
B : Yummy. I'm in heaven.
A : I'll take that as a **compliment**.

A：謝謝你來參加，別拘束，當自己家吧。
B：謝謝，你的前廊佈置得真棒！
A：謝謝你注意到。來，嚐嚐這些開胃菜吧。
B：好吃，如同置身天堂呢！
A：我會把這話當作是讚美。

porch [portʃ] 名
門廊
hors d'oeuvres 片
（法）開胃菜
compliment
[`kɑmpləmənt] 名
讚美

對話情境 3 下班後聚餐

A : I am sorry for being this late. I was **stuck** in traffic.
B : Don't worry. The table isn't ready anyway.
A : This restaurant is always **crowded** during this time of the day.
B : That's why I ordered some drinks for us so that we won't get bored waiting.
A : That's so **thoughtful** of you!

A：抱歉遲到這麼久，我卡在車陣中。
B：沒什麼，反正桌子還沒準備好。
A：這家餐廳在這個時段總是座無虛席。
B：所以我先點了些飲料，免得等得很無聊。
A：你設想得真周到！

stick [stɪk] 動
被困住
crowded [`kraʊdɪd]
形 擁擠的
thoughtful [`θɔtfəl]
形 考慮周到的

對話情境 4 食言而肥

A : I can't go to the movie with you tonight. I'm terribly sorry.
B : You always make **promises** that you can't keep.
A : I never mean to! Something just **came up**!
B : Forget it. I'll go with someone else.
A : Please don't be **mad** at me. We'll do it next time.

A：我今晚不能跟你去看電影了，真的很抱歉。
B：你老是食言而肥。
A：我從來都不是有意的啊！就突然有事情。
B：算了，我跟別人去。
A：拜託不要生我的氣，我們下次再一起去吧。

promise [`prɑmɪs]
名 諾言 動 承諾
come up 片 出現；
發生
mad [mæd] 形 惱火
的；發瘋的

便利三句開口說

Which school do you go to?
▶ 你上哪一間學校？

替換句 Which school do you attend? 你就讀哪所學校？

✓ ➔ **句型提點** Using It Properly!

「Which+ 地點 / 場合 +do/does+ 人名 / 代名詞 +go+to」用來詢問對方「去哪一個地點或場合」。例如：Which gym does your brother go to? 你哥哥是去哪一間健身房啊？

Do you live on campus or off campus?
▶ 你住校還是住外面？

替換句 Do you live in a dormitory? 你住學校宿舍嗎？

✓ ➔ **句型提點** Using It Properly!

「Do/does+ 人名 / 代名詞 +live+ 介係詞 + 地點」用於詢問對方「住在哪裡」。campus 指校園，on campus 就是指住校，off campus 則表示外宿。

What is your major?
▶ 你主修哪一科？

替換句 Which department do you study in? 你是哪個系所的？

✓ ➔ **句型提點** Using It Properly!

此句型專門用於詢問對方的「主修科系為何」，特別是指大學生及專科院校的學生。major 指主修科系，副修科系則為 minor。

有來有往的必備回應

Part 1 自我介紹

Q Which school do you go to?

> I go to New York University. **A**
> 我就讀紐約大學。

Part 2 日常雜務

Q Do you live on campus or off campus?

> I live off campus. **A**
> 我住校外。

Part 3 職場應對

Q What is your major?

> I study in the School of Law. **A**
> 我唸法律系。

Part 4 休閒娛樂

小知識補給站
Some Fun Facts

　　各國的教育學制大不同，像美國的國中只有 2 年，而高中有 4 年；雖然台灣講「上 / 下學期」，國外大都用季節來分，例如秋季 (fall semester) 約九月時入學，對照台灣的學期制，就是上學期，而開學時間大約在二月的春季 (spring semester) 就是下學期；學期制度也有可能和台灣不同，大致上，各國最常採用的包括學期制 (semester)、三學期制 (trimester)、以及學季制 (quarter)，學期制包含春、秋兩學期，三學期制包括春、秋、冬，而學季制則是分成春、夏、秋、冬四個學期。聊天的時候，也可以多認識一下不同的教育制度。

Part 5 出國旅遊

Part 6 愛情來了

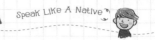
01 What grade are you in?
你讀幾年級？

02 I am sending my girl to a kindergarten this summer.
我今年夏天準備要送我女兒上幼稚園。 kindergarten 幼稚園

03 We have a transfer student in the class today.
今天我們班上來了一位轉學生。 transfer student 轉學生

04 I have been bad at English since day one.
我從一開始英文就很差。

05 Elementary school teachers often call the roll before class begins.
國小老師常常在上課前點名。 call the roll 點名

06 The teacher announced that the final exam begins a week from today.
老師宣布期末考在一週後開始。

07 Time's up. Put down your pens and hand in your papers.
時間到了。把筆放下、考卷交上來。

08 Tim scored a hundred on this chemistry exam by cheating.
提姆藉著作弊在化學考試上獲得滿分。

09 I pulled an all-nighter last night for my social report.
我昨晚為了我的社會報告挑燈夜戰。 all-nighter 通宵的工作

10 William is studying hard for the college entrance examination.
威廉正在為大學入學考試苦讀中。

11 I'd like to apply for several post-graduate programs, and I am wondering if you could write a recommendation letter for me.

我想要申請研究所，不知道您可否幫我寫推薦信？

⑫ My favorite subject is PE because I like sports.
我最喜歡的科目是體育課，因為我愛運動。

⑬ I major in sociology and minor in education.
我主修社會學，副修教育。 `minor in 副修`

⑭ I have a double major in accounting and journalism.
我雙主修會計學跟新聞學。 `double major 雙主修`

⑮ Chloe is working her way through college, meaning that she does not have any financial support from her family.
克蘿伊大學半工半讀，也就是說她沒有家中的經濟支持。
`work one's way through 半工半讀`

⑯ I feel like auditing this class before I decide whether or not to take it.
我想在決定修這堂課之前先旁聽。 `audit 旁聽`

⑰ Will you take any second foreign languages when you enter your sophomore year?
你升大二會選修第二外語嗎？
`sophomore 大學或高中的二年級學生`

⑱ To complete her master's degree, my niece is working on her dissertation arduously.
為了拿到碩士學位，我姪女努力撰寫她的碩士論文。

⑲ Our mid-term is going to be an open-book exam.
我們的期中考將會是開卷式考試。

⑳ Dylan skipped so many courses that he flunked out of school at the end of the semester.
狄倫翹太多課，所以在學期末被退學。 `flunk 考試不及格`

㉑ How many credits did Dad take in college to be able to graduate?
爸在大學的時候總共要修多少學分才能畢業啊？
`credit 學分`

Part 1 自我介紹

Part 2 日常雜務

Part 3 職場應對

Part 4 休閒娛樂

Part 5 出國旅遊

Part 6 愛情來了

對話情境 1 上學如同中樂透

A : It is so hard to get into a **private** elementary school these days.

B : Why is that?

A : **Enrollment** is not guaranteed even if you are financially capable.

B : How come?

A : You have to **draw lots** to see if you are allowed to enroll!

A：這年頭要上私立小學還真難。

B：為何？

A：即使你經濟富裕，也不一定能就學。

B：為什麼？

A：能否入學還得看有沒有抽到籤呢！

private [`praɪvɪt] 形
私人的；私有的

enrollment
[ɪn`rolmənt] 名 註冊；
入學

draw lots 片 抽籤

對話情境 2 運動非人人愛

A : PE is a **mandatory** class in university.

B : I am totally okay with that **arrangement**. I do well in all kinds of sports.

A : I am bad at sports! I wish I could **avoid** taking the class.

B : You can run, but you can't hide!

A : I'll just try and do my best, I guess.

A：體育課在大學是必修。

B：我覺得這樣安排很好，我運動方面很強。

A：我很差啊！真希望可以避開這堂課。

B：逃得了一時，躲不了一世！

A：那我只好盡力而為了。

mandatory
[`mændə‚torɪ] 形
義務的；強制的

arrangement
[ə`rendʒmənt] 名
安排

avoid [ə`vɔɪd] 動
避免；避開

對話情境 3 翹課事不過二

A：Do you think the Chinese teacher will take **attendance** tomorrow?

B：I can't say for sure.

A：I want to **skip** the class but don't want to get caught.

B：Haven't you learned your lesson?

A：Alright. I'll **attend** the class.

A：你覺得國文老師明天會點名嗎？
B：不知道耶。
A：我想翹課，但又不想被抓包。
B：你還沒記取教訓啊！
A：好啦，我會去上課的。

attendance
[ə`tɛndəns] 名 出席

skip [skɪp] 動 跳過；省略

attend [ə`tɛnd] 動 出席；參加

對話情境 4 校園八卦

A：Have you heard that Daniel was kicked out of school last semester?

B：No! Do tell!

A：He skipped a lot of courses, **cheated** during the **finals** and didn't turn in any **assigned** reports.

B：That explains it.

A：No wonder nobody feels sorry for him.

A：你有聽說丹尼爾上學期被退學了嗎？
B：沒有！快說怎麼回事！
A：他翹了很多堂課、考試作弊又連一份報告都沒交。
B：那也難怪了。
A：怪不得沒有人覺得他可憐。

cheat [tʃit] 動 作弊；欺騙

final [`faɪnl] 名 期末考 形 最後的

assign [ə`saɪn] 動 分配；指定

 Part 1 自我介紹

 Part 2 日常雜務

 Part 3 職場應對

 Part 4 休閒娛樂

 Part 5 出國旅遊

 Part 6 愛情來了

便利三句開口說

What ambition do you have regarding your career?

▶ 對於職涯，你有什麼樣的抱負？

替換句 Do you long to get ahead in your career?
你渴望在職場上領先他人嗎？

✓ ⌐**句型提點** Using It Properly!

句型「What+ 名詞 +do/does+ 人名 / 代名詞 +動詞」
可套用不同的動詞、名詞來做變化。例句： What
languages does he speak? 他說什麼語言？

- -

What do you want to be when you grow up?

▶ 你長大後想要成為什麼樣的人？

替換句 Where do you see yourself in ten years?
你十年後會在哪裡呢？

✓ ⌐**句型提點** Using It Properly!

「What+do/does+ 人名 / 代名詞 +want+to+be」
詢問某人「想要成為什麼」，be 也可用 become
代替，回答時要在 be/become 後面加名詞。例：I
want to be a ballerina. 我想要成為一名芭蕾舞者。

- -

Are you an ambitious person?

▶ 你是個有野心的人嗎？

替換句 Are you strongly motivated? 你深受激勵嗎？

✓ ⌐**句型提點** Using It Properly!

用來詢問別人是不是個有野心的人，ambition 為名
詞，意指野心。而 ambitious 為形容詞，故也可用「Is/

Are+ 人名 / 代名詞 +ambitious?」這個句型來問是
否有野心。

Part **1** 自我介紹

💬 有來有往的必備回應

Part **2** 日常雜務

Q What ambition do you have regarding your career?

> I want to open up a firm and practice law in the near future. *A*
>
> 我希望能在不久的將來開一間事務所,從事法律業務。

Part **3** 職場應對

Q What do you want to be when you grow up?

> I want to be a nurse when I grow up. *A*
>
> 我長大後想要當護士。

Q Are you an ambitious person?

> Yes, I believe so. *A*
>
> 是的,我認為我是。

Part **4** 休閒娛樂

💡 **小知識補給站**   *Some Fun Facts*

Part **5** 出國旅遊

　　美國對於自由平等、人人都能成功的思想提倡,讓許多人都抱持著美國夢 (American dream)。而美國夢的由來,是因為美國獨立之後至 19 世紀末,廣大的土地供人自由開墾、投資,讓大家都可以因自己的專業、努力、及價值倍受肯定。提到夢想,小時候不免會幻想著長大後的情景,現今,小朋友們嚮往成為的角色不外乎是體育明星、歌星、醫生、以及企業家,而近年來大數據 (big data) 的發展,更讓數據科學家 (data scientist) 成為最吃香的夢想職業之一。

Part **6** 愛情來了

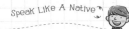
01 Do you consider yourself to be an ambitious person?
你認為自己是一個很有抱負的人嗎？

02 Darrel is very ambitious when it comes to eating.
戴洛在吃這方面相當有雄心壯志。

03 How would you define ambition?
你會如何定義「抱負」？ ambition 雄心；抱負

04 I think ambition is a powerful desire that drives you to be successful and achieve your goals.
我認為抱負是一種驅使你想要成功與達成目標的強大欲望。
desire 慾望 achieve 實現；完成

05 What if I don't have any ambition?
如果我沒什麼雄心壯志呢？

06 Do you think that ambition can be taught or do you think we are born with it?
你覺得有抱負是可以後天培養的，還是與生俱來的特質？

07 Does ambition always bring success?
有抱負絕對可以帶來成功嗎？

08 What are the positive results of being ambitious?
有雄心壯志會帶來哪些正面的影響？

09 His ambition was to win a gold medal at the Olympics.
他的志向是贏得奧運金牌。

10 I picture myself as a doctor fifteen years from now and feel greatly motivated.
我想像十五年後的自己會成為一位醫生，也因此充滿幹勁。

11 What kind of sacrifices would you make to have your dreams come true?
為了實現夢想，你會做什麼樣的犧牲呢？ come true 實現

⑫ What do you think is the difference between an ambition and a dream of doing something?

你覺得志向跟夢想的差別在哪裡？

⑬ Why are some people determined to succeed at any cost, yet others seem to lack any drive whatsoever?

為什麼有些人不擇手段、堅持要成功，而有些人則是無論如何都喪志？ `at any cost 不惜代價`

⑭ The company screened out applicants motivated only by money.

這間公司將只看重金錢的應徵者刷掉。

⑮ Sally wants to be a productive writer when she finishes her bachelor degree.

莎莉拿到大學文憑後，想要成為一位多產的作家。

⑯ My long-term goal is to run my own business, which is to open up a small café.

我的遠程目標是經營自己的事業，也就是開一間小咖啡店。

⑰ I've already planned out my short-term goal, and I am going to carry that out at my own pace.

我已規劃好我的近程目標，且會依自己的步調來實現它。

⑱ I want to be a freelancer because working 9 to 5 doesn't suit me.

我想要成為自由作家，因為朝九晚五的工作不適合我。

`freelancer 自由作家`

⑲ She was so career-driven that she doesn't allow any interruption from work.

工作至上的原則導致她無法接受工作以外的干擾。

⑳ Nick is trying so hard to get ahead in his career that he doesn't have time to get into a serious relationship.

尼克太致力於在職場上拔得頭籌，以至於沒時間認真談感情。 `get ahead 領先；進步`

Part 1 自我介紹

Part 2 日常雜務

Part 3 職場應對

Part 4 休閒娛樂

Part 5 出國旅遊

Part 6 愛情來了

雙人實境對話 oh!

對話情境 ① 含著金湯匙出生又怎樣？

A : Do you think one's **social status** as a child, whether rich or poor, affects his/her ability to **succeed** later in life?

B : I'd say there's no **definite** answer.

A : What makes you think that?

B : Throughout history, we've seen poor kids become millionaires and rich ones go bankrupt.

A : Makes a lot of sense.

A：你覺得一個小孩的背景，有錢或貧困，是否會影響他（她）在未來成功的能力？

B：我覺得很難說。

A：你為什麼這麼覺得？

B：綜觀古今，有許多窮小孩成為百萬富翁，有錢小孩卻破產的例子。

A：有道理。

social status 片
社會地位

succeed [sək`sid]
動 成功；實現目標

definite [`dɛfənɪt]
形 明確的；一定的

對話情境 ② 長大的志向

A : Our teacher wanted us to write an **essay** on "What do you want to be when you **grow up**?"

B : How did you do?

A : The teacher gave me an A+!

B : Wow! What did you write?

A : I wrote that I want to be an English teacher just like ours.

A：我們老師要我們寫一篇主題是「你長大後想做什麼」的文章。

B：你寫得如何？

A：老師給我 A+ 的成績！

B：哇！你寫了些什麼呢？

A：我寫我想要當跟他一樣的英文老師。

essay [`ɛse] 名
論文；文章

grow up 片 長大

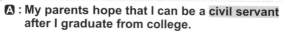

對話情境 3 爸媽的冀望

A : My parents hope that I can be a **civil servant** after I graduate from college.

B : I've heard it's hard to be one since you have to pass the **notoriously** difficult exam first.

A : The **bottom line** is that I don't see myself as a civil servant.

B : What do you see yourself then?

A : I want to be a contemporary dancer!

A：我父母希望我大學畢業後去當公務員。

B：我聽說要當公務員很難，因為你得先通過相當有難度的考試。

A：重點是我不覺得我適合當公務員。

B：那你覺得你適合做什麼？

A：我想要當現代舞的舞者！

civil servant 片
公務員

notoriously
[no`tɔrɪəslɪ] 副
惡名昭彰地

bottom line 片
重要事實

對話情境 4 人各有志

A : Will you attend the company lecture on "How to get a promotion in a year"?

B : No, I think I'll pass.

A : Why? I think it's a great opportunity to learn something and get **motivated**.

B : I am not as **ambitious** as you are.

A : Alright, just **suit yourself**.

A：你會參加公司有關「如何在一年內獲得升遷」的座談會嗎？

B：不，我想我不去了。

A：為何？我覺得這是很好的學習機會，同時還能被激勵。

B：我不像你這麼有雄心壯志。

A：好吧，隨便你。

motivate
[`motə‚vet] 動 給⋯動機；激起

ambitious
[æm`bɪʃəs] 形 有野心的；野心勃勃的

suit oneself 片
自便；隨（某人的）便

NOTE

日常雜務

趴趴走少不了這句

走跳國外要走得順、跳得高，
怎麼可以不顧到這些日常！

Let's go to the
supermarket!

* 從日用採買、租屋、銀行
  辦事都超順利！

名 名詞	動 動詞	形 形容詞
副 副詞	介 介係詞	助 助詞
連 連接詞	限 限定詞	縮 縮寫

銀行辦事去
Banking and finances

便利三句開口說

I would like to open a bank account.
▶ 我想要開立一個銀行帳戶。

替換句 What kind of account can I open here? 我可以在這裡開哪種帳戶？

✓ **句型提點** 〈 Using It Properly! 〉

「would like to + 原形動詞」為禮貌性用法，表達想要進行、辦理的事情，較「I want…」更為婉轉有禮。would 雖然也可當 will 的過去式，但在此句是表達客氣請求的語氣。

I'd like to deposit some money.
▶ 我想要存錢。

替換句 I'd like to make some deposits. 我想要辦理存款的業務。

✓ **句型提點** 〈 Using It Properly! 〉

此句型同「I would like to...」，只是將 I would 縮寫成 I'd。不論是電話上要求、商店裡購物、餐廳點菜，只要是表達自己想要的東西或想法，都可以用「I'd like to」開頭。

I need to withdraw some money.
▶ 我需要領錢。

替換句 I want to make some withdrawals. 我想辦理提款的業務。

✓ 句型提點 **Using It Properly!**

「人名 / 代名詞 +need+to+do something」，表示某人「為了個人因素而需要做某件事情」。例：I need to go to the bank this afternoon. 我今天下午需要去一趟銀行。

有來有往的必備回應

Q I would like to open a bank account.

What kind of account do you want, a checking or a savings account? *A*

您想要開哪一種戶頭，支票存款還是儲蓄存款？

Q I'd like to deposit some money.

How much are you depositing? *A*

您要存多少金額呢？

Q I need to withdraw some money.

How much would you like to take out? *A*

您想要提領多少金額呢？

小知識補給站 Some Fun Facts

在美國申請帳戶，若無社會安全號碼，通常可準備雙證件來證明身分，以及租屋契約，讓銀行將卡片寄到正確的住宿地點。一般來說，銀行會提供利息較高的 savings account（存款帳戶），主要用來存款；以及機動性較高、且有提款功能的 checking account（支票帳戶），後者利率雖低，但可隨時動用裡面的資金，常用於信用卡與支票的扣款。

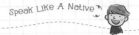
01 **I am heading to a local bank to open a checking account.**

我正要去本地銀行開支票存款戶頭。

02 **My husband and I want to buy a house, so we decide to apply for a mortgage.**

我先生跟我想要買房子，所以我們決定去申請貸款。

03 **Please take the number ticket first and fill out a deposit slip.**

請先領取號碼牌，並填寫存款單。 `deposit slip 存款單`

04 **The teller asked the man if he wanted to set up a savings account.**

櫃員詢問男子他是否想要開存款戶頭。

05 **Can I open an account if I am a foreign student of ABC school without a social security number?**

我是 ABC 學校的外籍學生，而且我沒有社會安全碼，請問我可以開戶嗎？

06 **I would like to open a checking or savings account that requires no minimum balance and with which I can use ATM cards.**

我想要開一個不需要最低存額、而且有自動櫃員機提款卡的支票帳戶或儲蓄存款帳戶。

07 **The account comes with a bank card so you can withdraw your money at any time.**

這個帳戶會附一張提款卡，你可以隨時用這張卡提領現金。

08 **I have never gotten a bank statement for the fees that I owe.**

我從來沒有收到有關我欠繳費用的銀行通知。
`bank statement 銀行結單`

09 **I want to deposit it into my checking account.**

我想要將錢存入我的支票存款帳戶。 `deposit 把（錢）儲存`

⑩ You need to deposit at least $50 into both accounts.
你需要存至少 50 元到這兩個帳戶裡。

⑪ I will be depositing $300 today.
我今天會存 300 元。

⑫ How do I order checks?
我要怎麼申請支票？

⑬ What's your interest rate for your checking accounts?
你們的支票存款利率是多少？ interest rate 利率

⑭ Could you sign the back of the check, please?
可否請你在支票背面簽名？

⑮ Give it about a week, and you should get your checks in the mail.
大約等一週，你就會收到含支票的郵件。

⑯ I wrote a check for $100, and it bounced.
我開了一張 100 元的支票，但跳票了。
bounce（支票）被拒付而退還給開票人

⑰ Do you have enough money in your account?
你帳戶裡有足夠的錢嗎？

⑱ I would like to transfer some money.
我想要轉帳。 transfer 轉帳

⑲ You have to hand in a written remittance slip to the teller to transfer your money.
你必須要將寫好的匯款單交給行員去轉帳。
remittance 匯款

⑳ I want it transferred into my checking account.
我想要把這筆錢轉到我的支存戶頭裡。

㉑ Slide your card into the machine, type your PIN in, click on whichever option you want, and you're done.
將你的卡片插入機器、輸入密碼，再點選你要的服務就可以了。

Part 1 自我介紹

Part 2 日常雜務

Part 3 職場應對

Part 4 休閒娛樂

Part 5 出國旅遊

Part 6 愛情來了

對話情境 1 房屋貸款

A：We'd like to apply for a **mortgage**.

B：How much would you like to borrow?

A：Well, we are interested in a **property** which costs \$180,000, but we have a **down payment** of only \$50,000.

B：So you need a \$130,000 **loan**. Do you have an account with this bank?

A：No, neither of us does.

A：我們想要申請貸款。

B：你們希望的貸款額度是多少呢？

A：這個嘛，我們對於一間要價 180,000 元的房子很感興趣，但我們只有 50,000 元的頭期款。

B：所以你們需要貸款 130,000 元，請問你們在本行有帳戶嗎？

A：我們都沒有。

mortgage
[`mɔrgɪdʒ] 名 貸款

property [`prɑpətɪ]
名 房地產

down payment 片
頭期款

loan [lon] 名 動
貸款

對話情境 2 留學生開戶

A：I just opened an account at this local bank.

B：Is the application **complicated** for foreign students?

A：Not at all! Just bring your passport, your **residence permit** and **fill out** some forms.

B：Doesn't sound that difficult.

A：我剛剛在這間本地銀行開戶了。

B：對外籍學生來說，申請帳戶會不會很麻煩？

A：一點都不會！只要準備好你的護照，居留相關證件，填寫表格就行了。

B：聽起來不難。

complicated
[`kɑmplə.ketɪd] 形
複雜的

residence permit
片 居留證

fill out 片 填寫（表格、申請書等）

對話情境 3 刷卡異常

A: There were **charges** on my credit card that I never made.

B: Do you have a **statement** for your credit card?

A: I do.

B: Which charges are you talking about?

A: They are the last four charges. Please **freeze** this card before you look into it.

A：我的信用卡上有我不曾消費過的扣款記錄。

B：請問你有帶資料來嗎？

A：有的。

B：你說的是哪幾筆呢？

A：最後四筆，在你們查明之前，請先暫停扣款。

charge [tʃɑrdʒ] 名
費用；價錢

statement
[`stetmənt] 名（銀行）
對帳單

freeze [friz] 動
凍結；結冰

對話情境 4 取消支票

A: I would like to cancel a check.

B: Is there a problem?

A: I **wrote out** the check for too much. It **was supposed to** be for $100, but I put $150 instead.

B: I'll cancel that check for you.

A: I really **appreciate** your help.

A：我想要取消一張支票。

B：請問有什麼問題嗎？

A：我金額寫太多了，應該只有 100 元，我卻寫成 150 元。

B：我會幫你取消。

A：非常感謝你的幫忙。

write out 片 寫下；
寫出

be supposed to
片 應該；應當

appreciate
[ə`priʃɪ.et] 動 感激；
賞識

自我介紹

日常雜務

職場應對

休閒娛樂

出國旅遊

愛情來了

Unit 12 尋找溫馨小窩
Searching for a cozy nest

便利三句開口說

Are there any apartments for rent?
▶ 有沒有公寓要出租？

替換句 Do you know how I could find an apartment for rent? 你知道我該如何找到要出租的公寓嗎？

✓ **句型提點** Using It Properly!

「Is/are+there+any+ 名詞」，用來詢問「某種狀態、事物有或沒有」的問句。例：Is there any water in this bottle? 這水瓶裡有沒有水？ / Are there any parking lots near the museum? 博物館附近有停車場嗎？

What kind of apartment would you like to rent?
▶ 你想要租什麼樣的公寓？

替換句 What are your criteria for renting an apartment? 你在租公寓方面有哪些條件？

✓ **句型提點** Using It Properly!

「What+kind+of+ 名詞 + 疑問句」用來詢問「類型」。例：What kind of exercise do you usually do? 你平常都做什麼樣的運動？ / What kind of girls does John like? 約翰喜歡什麼類型的女生？

When can I see the apartment?
▶ 我什麼時候可以看看公寓？

替換句 When can you show me around the apartment? 你什麼時候可以帶我參觀一下公寓？

☑ 句型提點 **Using It Properly!**

「When+ 助動詞 + 人名 / 代名詞 + 原形動詞」，目的是要問「什麼時候可以進行某件事情」。此句的 when 是詢問大範圍的時間，像是季節、年份、時間、時段等，都可以用 when 來做疑問句開頭。

有來有往的必備回應

Q Are there any apartments for rent?

> I am afraid there is none at the moment. *A*
> 不好意思，目前沒有。

Q What kind of apartment would you like to rent?

> I want to rent an apartment with two *A*
> bedrooms.
> 我想要租有兩房的公寓。

Q When can I see the apartment?

> Anytime. I would suggest you go in *A*
> the daytime.
> 隨時都可以，但我建議白天來看。

小知識補給站

Some Fun Facts

短期住宿想省住宿費，除了尋找青年旅館，也可以善用 Couchsurfing 或是 AirBnB 等網站來尋找便宜的住宿地點；若是長期租屋，務必先查好地點、房型、租金，根據需求及考量，尋找套房 (studio apartment)、大樓公寓 (condo)、或是雅房 (room)，同時也要注意押金 (deposit)、水電瓦斯 (utilities)、洗衣設備 (laundry facilities)、以及如何繳交租金等等。

Part 1 自我介紹

Part 2 日常雜務
Part 3 職場應對

Part 4 休閒娛樂

Part 5 出國旅遊

Part 6 愛情來了

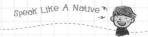
01 I'd rather rent a studio than stay in the dormitory on campus.

我寧願租套房也不要住學校宿舍。 studio 套房

02 As an overseas student, it took me quite some time to find accommodations.

身為一位海外學生，找住處花了我不少時間。
overseas 海外的；國外的

03 People often look for cheap apartments or condominiums to rent when going off to college.

上大學的時候，很多人會找便宜的公寓或套房來租。
condominium 公寓大樓

04 They moved down from upstairs because the rent was cheaper.

因為房租較便宜，所以他們從樓上搬下來住。 rent 租金

05 I decided to move out of my parents' place and start living on my own.

我決定從父母家裡搬出來自己住。

06 The monthly rent for a two-bedroom apartment would be $800.

含兩間臥室的公寓每月租金是八百元。

07 The rent is $650 a month, and electricity, water and gas are not included.

一個月的租金是 650 元，沒有包含水電及瓦斯。
included 被包括的

08 The rent is NT$100,000, but I believe the owner would be willing to accept an offer.

租金是新台幣十萬元，但我相信屋主願意接受講價。

09 The landlord showed me around the apartment.

房東帶我參觀公寓。 landlord 房東

10 The apartment has three bedrooms and one

bathroom.
這間公寓內有三間臥室和一間浴室。

⑪ **There is no air conditioner and heater in the bedroom.**
臥室裡面沒有冷氣跟暖氣。 heater 暖氣機

⑫ **The apartment complex I am about to rent doesn't allow any pets.**
我要租的這間公寓大樓禁止住戶養寵物。 complex 綜合設施

⑬ **My condo looks empty because it's not furnished.**
因為沒有附設傢俱，我的公寓看起來很空。
furnish 給（房間）配置傢俱

⑭ **My landlord renovated the whole apartment right before I moved in.**
就在我搬進來之前，我房東才替公寓做了一次大整修。

⑮ **All the furniture comes with the apartment. The kitchen is quite large, with a gas stove and a big fridge.**
公寓有附傢俱。廚房滿大的，有一個瓦斯爐跟大冰箱。

⑯ **The studio meets my requirements, so I signed the rental agreement.**
這間套房符合我的需求，所以我簽了租約。

⑰ **The tenant signed a one-year lease with the landlord.**
這個房客與房東簽了為期一年的租約。 tenant 房客；承租人

⑱ **Should I contact my landlord if the washing machine breaks down?**
如果洗衣機壞了，我是不是應該聯絡房東？
break down 故障

⑲ **Rent should be paid every month through wire transfer.**
房租每個月以電匯的方式繳納。 wire transfer 電匯

Part 1 自我介紹
Part 2 日常雜務
Part 3 職場應對
Part 4 休閒娛樂
Part 5 出國旅遊
Part 6 愛情來了

對話情境 ❶ 電話詢問空房

A : I'm calling about the apartment you **advertised**.
B : Yes. When do you need it?
A : Sometime around next week. What can you tell me about this apartment?
B : Well, it's a two-bedroom apartment, well **furnished**. Gas and water are included.
A : Thanks! May I come over to **take a look**?

A：我看到你的公寓出租廣告，想詢問細節。
B：是，你什麼時候需要呢？
A：大概下個星期，你可以先介紹一下這間公寓嗎？
B：這間公寓有兩間臥房，附全套傢俱，瓦斯和水費都包含在租金中。
A：謝謝你！我可以過去看看嗎？

advertise
[`ædvɚˌtaɪz] 動
登廣告
furnished [`fɜnɪʃt]
形 附傢俱的
take a look 片
看一看

對話情境 ❷ 租屋找仲介

A : How many rooms do you want?
B : Two bedrooms and one drawing room.
A : Do you have any floor **preference**?
B : I prefer an apartment on the first floor.
A : OK. I will show you a nice apartment **according to** your **requirements**. Let's go.

A：你們想要找幾房的房子？
B：兩間臥房以及一間畫室。
A：你們有偏好住哪一層樓嗎？
B：我喜歡住在公寓的一樓。
A：沒問題，我帶你們看一間符合你們需求的公寓，走吧！

preference
[`prɛfərəns] 名 偏好
according to 片
根據
requirement
[rɪ`kwaɪrmənt] 名 要求

對話情境 ③ 東西壞了找房東

A : The water **heater** is not working properly.
B : I'll contact the **plumber** to have a look.
A : Could you please ask him to check on the **air conditioner** as well?
B : What about it?
A : It has been making a lot of noise recently.

A：熱水器沒辦法正常運作。
B：我再連絡水電工過去看看。
A：可不可以也請他看看冷氣呢？
B：冷氣怎麼了？
A：它最近常發出噪音。

heater [`hitɚ] 名
加熱器
plumber [`plʌmɚ]
名 水電工
air conditioner 片
空調設備；冷氣機

對話情境 ④ 簽訂租約

A : The rent is **reasonable** and the location is **ideal**. I'll take it.
B : Great! Let's sign the contract now. Do you have your ID with you?
A : Here you go. Let's take a few minutes to **go over** the lease, shall we?
B : Absolutely. And be sure to sign it.
A : OK, will do.

A：房租很合理，地點也很理想，我要租這間。
B：太棒了！那就現在簽約吧，你有帶身分證嗎？
A：在這裡。我們可以花個幾分鐘，再看一遍合約吧？
B：當然沒問題，記得要簽名。
A：好，會的。

reasonable [`riznəbl] 形 合理的
ideal [ar`diəl] 形 理想的；非常合適的
go over 片 查看
lease [lis] 名 租約

Part 1 自我介紹
Part 2 日常雜務
Part 3 職場應對
Part 4 休閒娛樂
Part 5 出國旅遊
Part 6 愛情來了

主廚就是我

Here comes the master chef

便利三句開口說

What's your favorite food?

▶ 你最喜歡的食物是什麼？

替換句▶ What kind of food do you like the most? 你最喜歡什麼類型的食物？

☑ **▶ 句型提點** Using It Properly!

「What's+ 人名 / 代名詞（所有格）+favorite+ 名詞」用於詢問某人最喜歡的東西為何。例：What's Jimmy's favorite NBA team? 吉米最喜歡的 NBA 球隊是哪一支？

Do you know how to cook?

▶ 你會做菜嗎？

替換句▶ Can you cook? 你會做菜嗎？

☑ **▶ 句型提點** Using It Properly!

「Do/does+ 人名 / 代名詞 +know+how+to+ 原形動詞」用來詢問某人是否知道如何做某事。例：Does Joan know how to drive? 瓊知道怎麼開車嗎？/Do you know how to use a smartphone? 你知道如何使用智慧型手機嗎？

I am on a diet.

▶ 我正在節食。

替換句▶ I am trying to lose weight. 我在減肥。

☑ **▶ 句型提點** Using It Properly!

「人名 / 代名詞 +is/are+on a diet」表示某人正在節食。diet 是指日常飲食的總稱；be on a diet 為片

語，意指節制飲食，動詞也可搭配 go，變成 go on a diet。

有來有往的必備回應

Q What's your favorite food?

A My favorite food is Italian.
我最喜歡義大利菜。

Q Do you know how to cook?

A Of course I do!
當然會啦！

Q I am on a diet.

A Try to stay away from junk food.
試著遠離垃圾食物吧。

小知識補給站

　　描述食物，不一定只有 delicious，讚嘆美味還可以用 delightful、yummy、finger licking（令人食指大動的）、exquisite（精緻的）、mouthwatering（垂涎三尺的）；口感方面，喝到搶手的燈泡珍珠奶茶，QQ 的口感可以用 chewy（有嚼勁的）來表示，牛排軟嫩的肉質可以用 tender（嫩的）形容；至於味道，除了基本的酸、甜、苦、辣、鹹，還有巧克力那種又苦又甜的味道 (bittersweet)、薑汁的辛辣 (gingery)、白醬燉飯的濃濃奶油味 (creamy) 等等；下次與國外友人用餐時，不妨試著精準形容感受到的味道吧。

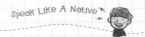
01 **There is a growing number of vegetarians around the world.**
全球吃素的人口有逐漸增長的趨勢。 `vegetarian 素食者`

02 **Rice is the staple food of more than half the world's population.**
全球人口當中，有超過半數的人以白米為主食。
`staple 主要的`

03 **Many youngsters love eating junk food.**
很多年輕人喜歡吃垃圾食物。 `junk food 垃圾食物`

04 **It is not good for your health to skip breakfast.**
不吃早餐對身體不好。 `skip 略過`

05 **It is not our custom to eat desserts after dinner.**
我們沒有晚餐後吃甜點的習慣。 `custom 習俗`

06 **It is quite ordinary for most Europeans to drink wine during meals.**
對大多數歐洲人來說，吃飯配紅酒是很平常的事。

07 **I am so hungry that I could eat a horse.**
我餓壞了！

08 **My sister is allergic to seafood.**
我妹妹對海鮮過敏。 `allergic 過敏的`

09 **Margaret has been so obsessed with losing weight that she is now struggling with an eating disorder.**
瑪格麗特太執著於減重，導致她現在患了飲食失調症。

10 **There are generally three to four courses in Western-style cuisine.**
西餐通常包含三到四道菜餚。 `cuisine 菜餚`

11 **First, there's an appetizer, then a salad, a soup of the day, a main course and a dessert to wrap it up.**

首先有開胃菜，再來是沙拉、當日湯品、主餐，最後以甜點作結。 wrap up 總結

⑫ In order to make this dish, you need to slice the onions, smash some garlic, cut the carrots in chunks and blanch the beef.

要做出這道菜，你必須先將洋蔥切絲、剁碎大蒜，將胡蘿蔔切塊，然後將牛肉以沸水燙過。 blanch 汆燙

⑬ At home, my father is the main chef, whereas my mom the sous chef.

在家裡，我爸爸是主廚，我媽反而是副主廚。 sous chef 副主廚

⑭ I have been cooking over ten years and can cook traditional Chinese food very well.

我煮菜的經驗超過十年，而且我擅長烹煮傳統中式料理。

⑮ My brother likes to call for pizza delivery every weekend and asks for the same toppings every single time.

我哥每週末都喜歡叫外送披薩，還每次都點一樣的配料。

⑯ Let's go eat a spicy hotpot! It's on me!

我們一起去吃麻辣鍋吧！我請客！

⑰ Are you going to bring homemade cooking to a potluck lunch next week?

下週的百樂餐聚會，你會帶自家做的料理去嗎？（potluck 是一種由參加者各自準備菜餚，並帶到指定地點的聚會。）

⑱ Do you like food from other countries?

你喜歡來自其他國家的料理嗎？

⑲ When I travel to a foreign country, I always eat at local diners or food stands because I think it's the best way to know the culture of a country.

當我到國外旅遊，我總是會嚐嚐當地的餐館或小吃攤，因為我認為這是認識當地文化最好的方式。

⑳ In some countries, animal organs are considered delicacies.

在某些國家，動物的內臟被視為佳餚。 delicacy 美味；佳餚

Part 1 自我介紹

Part 2 日常雜務

Part 3 職場應對

Part 4 休閒娛樂

Part 5 出國旅遊

Part 6 愛情來了

087

對話情境① 美味關鍵

A : Why is this dish **tasteless**?
B : I think the problem may be that you didn't **marinate** the pork.
A : Was that necessary?
B : Yes. Through this process, you let the meat soak up the sauce, and it will **unleash** the entire flavor of the dish.
A : Alright, lesson learned.

A：這道菜怎麼淡而無味？
B：我想問題出在你沒有先將豬肉滷過。
A：這是必要的嗎？
B：當然，經由這道手續，豬肉會吸收醬汁，而後將味道釋放於菜餚中。
A：好吧，學了一課。

tasteless [`testlɪs]
形 沒味道的

marinate
[`mærə.net] 動 醃泡；
浸於滷汁中

unleash [ʌn`liʃ] 動
釋放

對話情境② 不可信的廚藝

A : What's for dinner tonight?
B : Whatever meal that you plan on making.
A : Do you trust my cooking skills?
B : I'm so **done** for the day. I'll eat whatever is put in front of me.
A : **In that case**, let's order **takeout**.

A：晚餐吃什麼？
B：你打算煮什麼，我就吃什麼。
A：你信得過我的烹飪技術？
B：我今天超累，放在我眼前的我都吃得下去。
A：這樣的話，我們叫外送好了。

done [dʌn] 形
累壞的

in that case 片
既然如此

takeout [`tek.aut]
名 外賣食物 / 餐館

對話情境 **3** 烹飪門外漢

A : Do you want to join a cooking class with me?

B : What do they teach?

A : Well, just some basic stuff like how to cut and prepare ingredients, season them, and know the differences among frying, deep frying, steaming, grilling and so on.

B : It's all Greek to me!

A : Then you should definitely go with me!

A：你要不要跟我一起去上烹飪課？

B：他們會教些什麼？

A：這個嘛，就一些基礎的東西，像是如何切菜跟準備食材、調味，和分辨煎、炸、蒸、烤等料理方式。

B：有聽沒有懂！

A：那你更應該要跟我一起去啦！

deep fry [ˋdipˋfraɪ] **⑩** 炸

steam [stim] **⑩** 蒸

grill [grɪl] **⑩** 燒烤

be all Greek to sb. **片**
（某人）完全不懂的

對話情境 **4** 烹飪課堂上

A : You are here today to learn basic cooking skills.

B : Excuse me. What if I don't know how to peel or slice ingredients? Is this the place to be?

A : You've come to the right place.

B : What if I also want to learn how to cook some French cuisine?

A : No rush. One step at a time.

A：你們今天是要來學習基礎的烹飪技巧。

B：請問，如果我不會削皮或切食材，來這邊適合嗎？

A：你來這就對了。

D：如果我還想要學法式料理呢？

A：別急，一步步來吧。

peel [pil] **⑩** 削皮

slice [slaɪs] **⑩** 切片

ingredient
[ɪnˋgridɪənt] **名** 原料；
成分

自我介紹

日常雜務

職場應對

休閒娛樂

出國旅遊

愛情來了

歡樂過慶典
Celebrating holidays

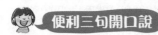
便利三句開口說

What holidays do you celebrate?
▶ 你們會慶祝哪些節日？

替換句▶ What are the major holidays in your country?
你們國家的主要節慶有哪些？

✓ **句型提點 Using It Properly!**

「What+ 名詞 +do/does+ 人名 / 代名詞 + 動詞」用
以詢問某人對於某件事的做法或看法。要注意的是，
助動詞 do/does 後面的動詞必須為原形。

- -

What is the biggest holiday of the year in your country?
▶ 你們國家一年之中最盛大的節日是什麼？

替換句▶ Name one holiday that's emphasized in your
country. 說一個你們國家很看重的節日。

✓ **句型提點 Using It Properly!**

詢問某物之最，可用「What+is+the+ 形容詞最高級
+ 名詞」。例：What is the most expensive dish
in this restaurant? 這間餐廳最貴的一道菜為何？

- -

Do you have a favorite holiday? What is it?
▶ 你有最喜歡的節日嗎？是什麼節日？

替換句▶ What's your favorite holiday? 你最喜歡的節日
為何？

✓ **句型提點 Using It Properly!**

以助動詞 Do/Does 開頭的問句，為 Yes/No 疑問句，

即單純問對方是或不是。例：Do you go to work by bus? 你搭公車上班嗎？

 **有來有往的必備回應**

Q What holidays do you celebrate?

> We celebrate Chinese New Year and Dragon Boat Festival. *A*

我們會慶祝春節和端午節。

Q What is the biggest holiday of the year in your country?

> It should be Chinese New Year. *A*

應該就是春節了。

Q Do you have a favorite holiday? What is it?

> Yes. My favorite one is Valentine's Day. *A*

有啊，我最喜歡的是情人節。

 小知識補給站 Some Fun Facts

　　因應文化、歷史的不同，各國都發展出自己獨特的節日以及慶祝方式。美國最常見的節日不外乎是聖誕節、感恩節、萬聖節、國慶日（又稱獨立紀念日）；義大利有威尼斯嘉年華、巴西的里約嘉年華、德國啤酒節、印度灑紅節、泰國天燈節等等，都是國際極富盛名的幾個慶典。另外，西班牙甚至還有番茄節，在街頭上演互砸番茄的大戰；而墨西哥在亡靈節，會與家人朋友同聚，為去世的家人或朋友祈福，街上還可以看到裝扮成骷髏頭的人們在遊行。

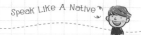
01 It's traditional in America to eat turkey on Thanksgiving Day, which usually falls on the last Thursday in November.

在十一月的最後一個星期四，也就是感恩節當天，吃火雞是美國的一項傳統。

02 Halloween is a holiday when adults dressed in costume to attend parties and children knock on doors, yelling "Trick or treat!"

萬聖節是個大人變裝參加派對，而小孩敲門大喊「不給糖就搗蛋」的節日。

03 Santa Claus and Christmas trees always come to mind when we talk about Christmas.

提到聖誕節，就會想到聖誕老公公跟聖誕樹。

04 There are some traditions when celebrating Christmas. For example, decorating Christmas trees, unwrapping Christmas presents, kissing under the mistletoe and so many more.

慶祝聖誕節時總有一些傳統，像是佈置聖誕樹、拆聖誕禮物、在槲寄生下親吻等等。

05 Easter, one of the religious holidays, is to celebrate the resurrection of the Lord, Jesus Christ.

宗教節日之一的復活節，是為了要紀念耶穌基督復活的那一天。

06 Is there any special food connected with holidays in your country?

在你們國家，有什麼特殊的食物是和節慶有關的嗎？

07 Eating rice dumplings on Dragon Boat Festival is a Chinese custom passed down for centuries.

端午節吃粽子是流傳了好幾個世紀的中國習俗。

08 How do you usually celebrate Chinese New

Year?

你通常怎麼慶祝春節？ celebrate 慶祝

⑨ People get together and have family reunion dinner on Chinese New Year's Eve.
人們在除夕夜的時候都會團聚，一起吃年夜飯。

⑩ On the day before Chinese New Year, parents give children red envelopes with money inside.
春節的前一天，父母親會發裝有壓歲錢的紅包給小孩。

⑪ I have mixed feelings about Chinese New Year. I like the festive atmosphere but don't like the weight I put on.
我對春節的感覺很複雜，我喜歡節慶的氣氛，但不喜歡變胖的結果。

⑫ Are holidays approved by the government in your country, or are they based on traditions?
節慶在你們國家是經由政府允許，還是依據傳統而訂？

⑬ We now celebrate some holidays that have come from other countries, such as Valentine's Day, Halloween, Christmas and so on.
我們現在會慶祝一些外來的節慶，例如西洋情人節、萬聖節、聖誕節等。

⑭ Does Mother's Day fall on the second Sunday of May in your country as well?
你們國家的母親節也是在五月的第二個禮拜天嗎？

⑮ There's no school and work on most of the national holidays in Taiwan.
台灣大部分的國定假日都放假。 national holiday 國定假日

⑯ I would rather stay indoors than be stuck in traffic during holidays.
假日期間，我寧願待在室內也不想塞在車陣中。

⑰ I couldn't care less about some holidays. I think they are way too commercialized.
我對於某些節慶真的再無感不過，我覺得它們都被操作得太商業化了。

Part 1 自我介紹
Part 2 日常雜務
Part 3 職場應對
Part 4 休閒娛樂
Part 5 出國旅遊
Part 6 愛情來了

雙人實境對話 oh!

對話情境 ① 團圓過節

A : How will you celebrate this coming Chinese New Year?
B : I'm flying back to the States.
A : Why is that?
B : Most of my relatives are there, so it would be lonely to stay here all by myself.
A : That's very true.

A：你打算怎麼過即將來臨的春節？
B：我要飛回美國。
A：為什麼？
B：我大部分的親戚都在那邊，所以我一個人待在這邊會很寂寞。
A：這倒是。

coming [`kʌmɪŋ] 形
即將到來的
relative [`rɛlətɪv]
名 親戚
all by oneself 片
單獨地

對話情境 ② 單身情人節

A : What's your plan today?
B : Am I supposed to have one?
A : Well, just asking. It's Valentine's Day!
B : Whatever. I am so going straight home after work. I can't bear seeing all the love birds on the street.
A : Poor you. Here, hope my homemade chocolate can cheer you up.

A：你今天有什麼計畫？
B：我應該要有嗎？
A：只是隨便問問，今天是情人節啊！
B：隨便啦，我今天下班後鐵定要直接回家，我受不了看到街上成雙成對的閃光。
A：真可憐，來，希望我親手做的巧克力能讓你開心點。

bear [bɛr] 動 忍受
love birds 片 情侶
homemade
[`hom`med] 形
自製的

對話情境 ③ 月餅節流變

A: Is there any special food you eat on Mid-Autumn Festival?

B: Traditionally, we eat moon cake, which is a kind of Chinese pastry.

A: Does the younger generation follow the tradition?

B: No. Having a BBQ on Mid-Autumn Festival has become a trend.

A: Sounds like fun!

A：你中秋節會吃什麼特別的食物嗎？
B：傳統上，我們會吃一種叫做月餅的中式甜點。
A：年輕一輩的也照著傳統嗎？
B：沒有，中秋節烤肉已經變成年輕一代的主流趨勢。
A：聽起來很有趣！

moon cake 片 月餅
pastry [`pestrɪ] 名 糕點
trend [trɛnd] 名 趨勢；傾向

對話情境 ④ 萬聖節變裝

A: I am going to dress up as Spider-Man on Halloween. And you?

B: I still haven't decided.

A: It's only three days away. You have to come up with something.

B: Help me! I haven't got the slightest idea.

A: Since you are below-average height, I think dressing up as a Hobbit shouldn't take too much effort.

A：我萬聖節要裝扮成蜘蛛人，你呢？
B：還沒決定。
A：只剩三天了，你得要想出些什麼才行。
B：快幫幫我！我一點主意都沒有。
A：既然你身高偏矮，我想你裝扮成哈比人應該不會太費力。

dress up 片 打扮
come up with 片 想出
slight [slaɪt] 形 少量的，輕微的

095

Unit 15 開趴眾樂樂

Party time

便利三句開口說

I will dress up for the party tonight.
▶ 我將為今晚的派對盛裝打扮。

替換句 ▶ I will dress nicely for the party tonight. 我將為今晚的派對特別打扮。

✓ ➔ **句型提點** Using It Properly!

片語「dress up for+ 場合」指為了某個場合盛裝打扮。例：She dressed up for her first date. 她為了她的初次約會精心打扮。

Who is invited to the party?
▶ 有誰受邀參加派對呢？

替換句 ▶ Who else is going to the party? 還有誰會去派對？

✓ ➔ **句型提點** Using It Properly!

片語 be invited to 意指受邀至某個場合，例如：Debby was invited to an international conference last week. 黛比上週受邀參加一場國際會議。

Should I bring anything to the party?
▶ 我該帶些什麼去參加派對嗎？

替換句 ▶ What should I bring to the party? 我該帶什麼去派對呢？

✓ ➔ **句型提點** Using It Properly!

以助動詞 should 開頭，可用來詢問他人的建議，而

片語 bring something to+ 地點，指帶某樣東西去某個地方。例：Should I bring my boyfriend to your wedding reception? 我該不該帶我男友去參加你的婚禮呢？

 有來有往的必備回應

Q I will dress up for the party tonight.

A Me, too. I'm so excited!

我也是，真是太令人興奮了！

Q Who is invited to the party?

A I have no idea. The only guest I know is you.

不清楚，我認識的賓客就只有你了。

Q Should I bring anything to the party?

A No. The hostess said in particular that all guests should come empty-handed.

不用，女主人特別說客人要兩手空空地去。

小知識補給站 *Some Fun Facts*

　　身在國外一定要去體會一下國外的派對風情，各種常見派對有：喬遷派對 (housewarming party)、歡送會 (farewell party)、泳池派對 (pool party)、大型狂歡派對 (rave party)、睡衣派對 (slumber party)、雞尾酒派對 (cocktail party)、變裝派對 (costume party) 等等。參加派對之前，問問有無著裝要求 (dress code)，也可更加融入派對的氣氛當中。

 Part 1 自我介紹

 Part 2 日常雜務

Part 3 職場應對

 Part 4 休閒娛樂

 Part 5 出國旅遊

 Part 6 愛情來了

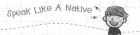
01 **Who is going to throw a birthday party for Rita?**
誰要幫芮塔辦慶生派對？ `birthday party 慶生會`

02 **What do you say we plan a surprise party for Mom's coming birthday?**
我們來為媽媽即將到來的生日規劃驚喜派對吧？

03 **R.S.V.P. at the end of an invitation stands for "Please reply" in English.**
邀請函最後的 R.S.V.P. 在英文裡代表「請回覆」的意思。

04 **Tom is thinking about a simple BBQ party at his backyard to celebrate his promotion.**
湯姆想要在他家後院辦一個簡單的 BBQ 派對，來慶祝他的升遷。

05 **John partied hard in his college years and now he seldom goes to parties.**
約翰在大學時期玩得很瘋，現在他很少參加派對了。

06 **Are you going to invite a DJ to this party or haven't you thought about it yet?**
你這次派對打算邀請 DJ 嗎？還是你還沒想過這件事？

07 **You have to invite Jason. He's always the life of the party, and he keeps things exciting.**
你一定要邀請傑森，他是派對的開心果，能炒熱氣氛。

08 **I'd like to invite you to my housewarming party this weekend.**
我想邀請你來參加我這週末舉辦的新居落成派對。
`housewarming 慶祝喬遷聚會`

09 **I'd love to go, but I already have another appointment on that day. Terribly sorry!**
我很想去，但是我那天已經有約了，真的很抱歉！

10 **We're having Ted's birthday party this Saturday at 8:00 at my house.**

本週六八點開始，我們會在我家舉辦泰德的生日趴。

⑪ Please make yourself at home.
請別拘束，就當自己家吧。

⑫ I am not attending if it's a "BYOB" party.
(BYOB=Bring your own bottle)
如果這是一個「請自備飲料」的派對，我就不去了。

⑬ The dress code for the party is polka dot. Try to think outside the box, guys!
這次派對的服裝主題是「點點風」。各位，請盡情發揮創意吧！

⑭ Are you a party starter, goer or pooper?
你是一個派對主辦人、參加者還是砸派對的人？

⑮ Throwing a potluck party isn't as simple as I expected. As an organizer, you have to plan ahead and assign dishes to the guests.
舉辦一個百樂趴並沒有想像中容易。身為主辦人，你必須事先規劃好，分派每位客人該準備的料理。

⑯ Sarah even made a to-do list for the party she is going to hold this month.
莎拉甚至還為這個月要舉辦的派對列待辦清單。
[to-do list 執行表]

⑰ You could create a beverage stand with a variety of drinks where guests can help themselves.
你可以設置飲料檯，上面放各種飲料讓賓客自助飲用。

⑱ I want to show off my new house and also get a chance to meet my new neighbors by throwing a housewarming party.
我想要辦個新居落成派對，秀一下我的新住所，也可藉機認識新鄰居。

⑲ As the host of Mary's baby shower, I am carefully selecting the guests and making name tags for all of them.
身為瑪麗的準媽媽派對主辦人，我很小心地挑選賓客名單，並為每一位客人製作名牌。

Part 1 自我介紹

Part 2 日常雜務

Part 3 職場應對

Part 4 休閒娛樂

Part 5 出國旅遊

Part 6 愛情來了

099

雙人實境對話

對話情境 1　音樂美食趴

A : Are you going to the party on Saturday?

B : I am still thinking about it. Are you?

A : Yeah, I heard it's going to be a lot of fun. This party is going to have a **DJ**, food, and **drinks**.

B : Really? That does sound like fun. What time does it start?

A : It starts at 8:00, and I really think you should go.

A：你會參加週六的派對嗎？
B：我還在考慮，你呢？
A：我會去，聽說會很好玩。這次的派對有 DJ，還會提供食物跟飲料。
B：真的假的？聽起來的確很好玩，幾點開始？
A：八點開始，真心覺得你一定要去。

DJ (Disk Jockey)
名 唱片或音樂電台廣播員

drink [drɪŋk] 名
飲料；酒

對話情境 2　邀請來同樂

A : Listen, I'm going to have a party this Sunday. Would you like to come?

B : Oh, I'd love to go. Who's going?

A : **A number of** people haven't told me yet. But, Peter and Mark are going to **help out** with the **cooking**.

B : Hey, I'll help, too!

A : Would you? That would be great!

A：聽著，我禮拜天要辦一場派對，你想來嗎？
B：喔！我當然要去，還有誰會去啊？
A：有些人還沒回覆我，不過彼得跟馬克會幫忙料理食物。
B：嘿，我也要幫忙！
A：你也要來嗎？那太好了！

a number of 片
一些

help out 片 幫忙

cooking [`kʊkɪŋ]
名 飯菜；烹調

對話情境 ③ 出席確認

A : It's Dan. I just received the **invitation** to your party.

B : Can you **make it**?

A : Well, let's see. It's next Saturday night, right? Should I bring anything?

B : Just yourself.

A : **Fantastic**! I'll be there.

A：我是丹，我剛剛有收到你的派對邀請函。

B：你能來嗎？

A：我看看，下星期六晚上對吧？我要帶什麼東西去嗎？

B：人來就好。

A：太好了！我會過去的。

invitation
[ˌɪnvəˈteʃən] 名 邀請；請帖

make it 片 到達；成功

fantastic
[fænˈtæstɪk] 形 極好的

對話情境 ④ 規劃派對

A : Do you have a minute?

B : Sure, what's it about?

A : It's about Kathy's **bridal shower**. I had made a **guest list**, and I think we should go over it and see if everything's **in order**.

B : I'd love to, but what could possibly go wrong?

A : Anything could happen!

A：你有時間嗎？

B：當然，什麼事？

A：是關於凱西的準新娘派對。我擬了一張賓客清單，我想我們應該看一遍，確定事情都已安排妥當。

B：我很樂意，不過，會有什麼不妥的安排嗎？

A：任何事情都有可能發生！

bridal shower 片 婚前派對

guest list 片 賓客名單

in order 片 情況良好

 Part 1 自我介紹

 Part 2 日常雜務

 Part 3 職場應對

 Part 4 休閒娛樂

 Part 5 出國旅遊

 Part 6 愛情來了

101

馬路如虎口
Safety on the road

便利三句開口說

Do you have a driver's license?
▶ 你有駕照嗎?

替換句 Do you know how to drive a car? 你會開車嗎?

✓ ⌐▸ **句型提點** ⟨Using It Properly!⟩

「Do/does+ 人名 / 代名詞 +have+ 名詞」為詢問某人有沒有某物的問句。例:Does your sister have any sense of humor? 你妹有沒有一點幽默感啊? / Do your neighbors have enough food? 你們鄰居有足夠的食物嗎?

- -

Do you drive a manual or an automatic car?
▶ 你是開手排車還是自排車?

替換句 Is your car a stick shift or automatic? 你的車是手排還是自排?

✓ ⌐▸ **句型提點** ⟨Using It Properly!⟩

「Do/does+ 人名 / 代名詞 +drive+ 名詞」可用來詢問對方是開哪一種車子。manual car 指手動排檔車,automatic car 則是指自動排檔車。例如:Does your boyfriend drive a Mercedes? 你男友開賓士車嗎?

- -

John got into a car accident last night.
▶ 約翰昨晚發生車禍。

替換句 John hit a car that stopped in front of him. 約翰撞到停在他前方的車子。

✓ 二、句型提點 Using It Properly!

「人名／代名詞＋get(依時態變化)＋into＋某件事情」
表示某人與後面所述的事情扯上關係。片語 get into
即表示「陷入某種處境」。

🗨 有來有往的必備回應

Q Do you have a driver's license?

Yes, I do. I've had one since I turned eighteen. *A*

我有，我從滿十八歲那年就有駕照了。

Q Do you drive a manual or an automatic car?

I drive an automatic. *A*

我開自排車。

Q John got into a car accident last night.

Is he alright and what about the people in the other car? *A*

他還好吧？另外一車的人也還好吧？

💡 小知識補給站　Some Fun Facts

　　在美國，各州對於駕駛的法令不一定都相同，所
以上路前務必先熟悉交通規則，像是限速、看到校車
要讓校車先行，此外，保持行車距離也是非常重要的。
停車時，還需注意停車位是公用的還是他人的專屬停
車位……等等。除了法規之外，美國有 22 州開放「申
請換發當地駕照」的服務，旅居美國的國人也視需求
申請，以免除筆試及路考。

 自我介紹
 日常雜務
 職場應對
 休閒娛樂
 出國旅遊
 愛情來了

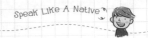
01 Buckle up and let's hit the road.
繫好安全帶，準備上路。 hit the road 上路；出發

02 If there are no traffic lights, I never stop at a zebra crossing even if there are people waiting to cross.
如果沒有交通號誌，即使有行人等過馬路，我也絕不停在斑馬線後方。 zebra crossing 斑馬線

03 Running through a red light may cost you a fortune if you get caught.
如果你闖紅燈被逮到，罰鍰可是很重的。

04 Driving under the influence is not allowed here in Taiwan.
在台灣，酒駕是被禁止的。 influence 影響；作用

05 You will run the risk of having your driver's license revoked.
你會冒著被吊銷駕照的風險。 revoke 撤銷；廢除

06 People in Japan drive on the left side of the road whereas people in Taiwan do the opposite.
在日本，大家開車都靠左側的路上，在台灣則是相反的。

07 Have you heard that there's no speed limit on highways in Germany?
你知道德國的高速公路沒有速限嗎？ speed limit 速度限制

08 She went over the speed limit and was pulled over by the police.
她的車速超過速限，被警察攔了下來。
pull over 把…開到路邊

09 Your license expired three months ago.
你的駕照已經逾期三個月了。

10 You're driving the wrong way on a one-way street.
你在單行道上逆向開車。 one-way 單行道的

⑪ You cut off another car.
你超了其他車。

⑫ Step on it! Don't you feel annoyed that the car behind you is tailgating?
快加速！你不覺得後面那台車貼那麼緊很煩嗎？
`tailgate 緊跟著前車行駛`

⑬ Duncan's personality changes every time he is behind the wheel.
鄧肯只要一握到方向盤，就變了個人。
`personality 人格；個性`

⑭ Ken's car broke down and he was stranded on the side of the road.
肯的車子壞了，所以只好先擱在路邊。`stranded 擱淺的`

⑮ Amy slammed on the brakes before she almost ran over a dog.
愛咪在差點碾過一隻狗之前緊急踩下煞車。`slam 猛推`

⑯ There are special devices on the market that can detect the location of speed cameras.
現在市面上有特殊的儀器可以偵測出測速照相機的位置。

⑰ A truck flipped over on the highway and caused a traffic jam.
一輛卡車在高速公路翻覆，造成交通堵塞。`flip over 翻轉`

⑱ I had a flat tire and couldn't start my engine. I needed to have my car towed.
我輪胎爆胎，而且無法發動車子，我需要找人來拖吊。
`flat tire 爆胎`

⑲ Do you know how to change a tire on your car?
你知道怎麼換車子的輪胎嗎？

⑳ This man in a coma was the victim of a hit-and-run.
這位昏迷的男人是那場肇事逃逸車禍的受害人，
`coma 昏迷` `hit-and-run 肇事逃逸`

Part 1 自我介紹

Part 2 日常雜務

Part 3 職場應對

Part 4 休閒娛樂

Part 5 出國旅遊

Part 6 愛情來了

雙人實境對話 *oh!*

對話情境 1　酒駕付出代價

🅐 : Can I see your driver's license, please?

🅑 : Here you go, officer. May I ask why you pulled me over?

🅐 : Have you been drinking tonight, Mr. Davidson?

🅑 : I had one or two drinks. I'm okay to drive, though. I know my limit.

🅐 : I'm afraid that we have zero tolerance for drinking and driving.

A：我可以看你的駕照嗎？

B：警官，請看，我可否請問你為何攔下我嗎？

A：你今晚是不是有喝酒，戴維森先生？

B：是有喝一兩杯，但我還可以開車，我知道自己的酒量。

A：很抱歉，酒後駕車是被禁止的。

know one's limit
片 知道某人的極限

tolerance
[`tɑlərəns] 名 寬容；忍受

drinking and driving 片 酒駕

對話情境 2　路考

🅐 : Good morning. Let's see how you start your vehicle.

🅑 : Okay, I'm done.

🅐 : Good job. Now, tell me how you leave the curb.

🅑 : First, I need to look back for passing cars. Also, I need to signal before entering traffic.

🅐 : Very nice! It's a good start.

A：早安，我們來看看你如何發動車子。

B：好了。

A：相當好。現在，告訴我你要怎麼開出車道。

B：首先，我必須確認有無往來車輛，開進車道前，還必須打方向燈。

A：非常好！這是個很好的開始。

curb [kɜb] 名 路邊

signal [`sɪgnl] 動 發出信號（此指打方向燈）

traffic [`træfɪk] 名 交通行列；交通

對話情境 ③ 爆胎這樣做

A : Oh, boy, I think we have a flat tire.
B : What should we do? Do you think we can make it to the nearest **exit**?
A : I think we need to pull over on the **shoulder**.
B : And what next?
A : Then we call the **towing** service.

A：哇，我覺得輪胎好像爆了。
B：我們該怎麼辦？你覺得我們有辦法撐到最近的匝道出口嗎？
A：我覺得我們得要停靠在路肩了。
B：那接下來呢？
A：接下來就連絡拖車服務囉。

exit [`ɛksɪt] 名 出口
shoulder [`ʃoldə] 名 路肩
tow [to] 動 拖；拉

對話情境 ④ 養車花費大

A : It's time again for my car's regular **tune-up**.
B : I just had mine. I have to say that having a car is like raising a kid.
A : I couldn't agree with you more.
B : In order to **cut down on** car maintenance expenses, I do some basic car **maintenance** myself.
A : Same here. I buy engine oil from retailers and change my oil and **filter** on my own.

A：又到了我保養車子的時間了。
B：我才剛保養過我的，我必須要說，養車跟養小孩一樣。
A：非常認同。
B：為了要節省車子的保養費，我會自己做一些基本的保養。
A：我也是，我會跟零售商購買機油和燃料過濾器，自行更換。

tune-up [`tjun͵ʌp] 名 調整
cut down on 片 削減
maintenance [`mentənəns] 名 維修
filter [`fɪltə] 名 過濾器 動 過濾

Part 1 自我介紹
Part 2 日常雜務
Part 3 職場應對
Part 4 休閒娛樂
Part 5 出國旅遊
Part 6 愛情來了

聊天氣開啟話題

Talking about weather never gets old

便利三句開口說

How's the weather today?
▶ 今天天氣如何？

替換句 How is it today? 今天天氣如何？

✓ ~●句型提點 Using It Properly!

此句是詢問當下天氣狀況的基本問句。若要詢問過去某個時間點的天氣狀況，可用「How was the weather+ 過去時間」。

It looks like it's going to rain.
▶ 看起來快要下雨了。

替換句 It is cloudy. 天色烏雲密佈。

✓ ~●句型提點 Using It Properly!

以 It looks like (看起來…) 開頭，表示猜測語氣；be going to... (將要…) 後面則須接原形動詞。此句「It looks like it's going to+ 天氣狀況的動詞」可以表示說話者經由天色等因素判斷天氣將有什麼變化。

What kind of weather do you like?
▶ 你喜歡什麼樣的天氣？

替換句 What's your favorite weather? 你最喜歡的天氣為何？

✓ ~●句型提點 Using It Properly!

kind 為「種類」，搭配固定介係詞 of、之後接名詞，而「What kind of…」後面接疑問子句，即可表示想詢問的種類。例：What kind of music do you like to listen to? 你喜歡聽什麼樣的音樂？

💬 有來有往的必備回應

Q　How's the weather today?

　　　　　It's cloudy today.　A

　　　　　今天是陰天。

Q　It looks like it's going to rain.

　　　　　No surprise. It's the rainy season.　A

　　　　　不驚訝，現在是雨季。

Q　What kind of weather do you like?

　　　　　I like it when it's warm and sunny.　A

　　　　　我喜歡溫暖又晴朗的天氣。

💡 小知識補給站　Some Fun Facts

　　收聽英語新聞與氣象預報時，經常會聽到主播用以下關鍵字來播報未來天氣：晴朗 (clear)、晴時多雲 (mostly clear)、多雲時晴 (partly clear)、多雲 (partly cloudy)、多雲時陰 (mostly cloudy)、陰天 (cloudy)。而夏秋之際常出現的颱風 (typhoon)，大西洋區域的國家稱之為颶風 (hurricane)，太平洋南邊及印度洋區域則稱旋風 (cyclone)。傾盆大雨常用片語 raining cats and dogs 來形容，此片語的緣起，其中一說是因為英國早期地下道發展不完善，所以每次下大雨，路上都會看到貓狗屍體，另外一說，也有人覺得是在比喻下大雨的混亂，就像是貓狗喧囂的情況。

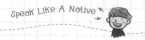
01 **Lovely day, isn't it?**
今天天氣很棒，對吧？ lovely 美好的；令人愉快的

02 **We couldn't ask for a nicer day, could we?**
這天氣真是再好也不過了，對吧？

03 **Isn't it a beautiful day for a walk?**
今天真是個適合散步的好天氣！

04 **It sure would be nice to be in Hawaii right about now.**
此刻若可以在夏威夷，就太棒了。

05 **I cannot imagine life without air-conditioning in summer in Taiwan.**
我無法想像在台灣夏天沒有冷氣的日子。

06 **It's going to rain by the looks of it.**
這天色看起來像是要下雨了。

07 **I didn't expect any thunderstorm this afternoon and didn't bring an umbrella when I went out.**
我沒料到今天下午會有暴雨，所以出門沒有帶傘。
thunderstorm 大雷雨

08 **It was pouring rain, so Jessie was soaking wet.**
因為這場傾盆大雨，潔西全身都溼透了。 pour 傾注；倒；灌

09 **Terrible weather, isn't it?**
這天氣真糟，對吧？

10 **Can you believe all of this rain we've been having?**
這陣子下不停的雨是不是令人難以置信？

11 **Cold and gloomy weather makes me depressed.**
又冷又陰暗的天氣讓我感到沮喪。

12 **It's turned out nice again.**
天氣又轉好了。 turn out 結果成為

⑬ **I hear it'll clear up later.**
我聽說天氣晚點就會轉晴。 `clear up 放晴`

⑭ **The sun's trying to come out.**
太陽嘗試著探出頭。 `come out 露出；出現`

⑮ **What's the average low temperature in Taiwan?/ It's approximately ten degrees Celsius.**
台灣最低溫平均幾度？/ 大概是攝氏 10 度。

⑯ **We have not had any rain for several weeks.**
我們這裡已經好幾個星期沒下雨了。

⑰ **It finally decided to rain!**
終於天降甘霖啦！

⑱ **What's the weather forecast for the rest of the week?**
這整週的天氣預報為何？ `weather forecast 氣象預報`

⑲ **I hear they're calling for thunderstorms all weekend.**
我聽他們說整個週末都會有暴風雨。

⑳ **They're saying we will have blue skies for the rest of the week.**
他們說本週剩下的幾天會是大晴天。

㉑ **They're expecting snow in the north.**
他們預期北邊會下雪。 `expect 預期…可能發生`

㉒ **We're in for frost tonight.**
今天晚上的溫度會冷到結霜喔。 `frost 霜；結霜`

㉓ **I hear that showers are coming our way.**
我聽說不久後就會下陣雨。

㉔ **I heard a cold front is approaching soon.**
我聽說會有冷鋒接近。 `cold front 冷鋒面`

㉕ **What strange weather we're having!**
最近的天氣真的很奇怪！

自我介紹

Part 2 日常雜務

職場應對

休閒娛樂

出國旅遊

愛情來了

111

對話情境 ① 一起去海邊

A: It would be nice to go to the beach sometime this weekend.

B: What's the weather going to be like? I may want to go, too.

A: The weather this weekend is supposed to be warm.

B: Will it be good beach weather?

A: I think it will be.

A：這週末找時間去海邊應該很好。
B：天氣如何？我可能也想去走走。
A：這週末的天氣應該很溫暖。
B：會是個好的沙灘日嗎？
A：我覺得會喔！

go to the beach
片 去海邊

sometime
[`sʌm,taɪm] 副
某一時候

be supposed to
片 應該；理應

對話情境 ② 颱風快消失吧

A: The weatherman on tonight's news said a powerful typhoon will lash Taiwan soon.

B: I am looking forward to a day off.

A: You should be worrying about heavy rain, flooding, and possible landslides!

B: You're right. Let's hope it changes its course then.

A: I hope it vanishes into thin air.

A：晚間新聞的氣象播報員說即將會有強大的颱風侵襲台灣。
B：我好期待颱風假。
A：你應該要擔心豪雨、淹水跟可能發生的土石流吧！
B：你說的對，那希望它轉向。
A：我希望它徹底消失。

weatherman
[`wɛðə,mæn] 名
氣象預報員

lash [læʃ] 動
猛烈打擊；鞭打

vanish into thin air 片 完全消失

對話情境 3 惡性循環

A : Don't you think it's getting hotter in summer here in Taiwan?

B : I wonder if it's because of global warming.

A : Most definitely. Global warming has caused gradual increase in the average temperature of the Earth's atmosphere.

B : Even if I were willing to save energy and create less pollution, I couldn't survive without air conditioning.

A : It's a vicious circle.

A：你不覺得台灣的夏天愈來愈熱嗎？

B：我在想是不是因為全球暖化的關係。

A：八九不離十，全球暖化已經造成地球大氣層的平均氣溫升高了。

B：即便我很想要節約能源跟減少污染，但不開冷氣的話，我根本撐不下去。

A：這是惡性循環。

global warming
 全球暖化

atmosphere
[`ætməs.fɪr]
大氣層；氣氛

vicious circle
惡性循環

對話情境 4 會咬人的風

A : It's freezing cold out there.

B : I think it's minus five degrees Celsius.

A : Are you sure you're going for a run right now?

B : I'll put my hi-tech windbreaker on.

A : Be careful! The wind in this season bites!

A：外面冷得刺骨。

B：我覺得這是零下五度的天氣。

A：你確定要在這種天氣出去跑步？

B：我會穿上我的高科技防風外套。

A：小心點！這季節的寒風可是會咬人的！

freezing cold
極冷的

hi-tech [`haɪ`tɛk]
 高科技的

windbreaker
[`wɪnd.brekɚ]
防風上衣

自我介紹

日常雜務

職場應對

休閒娛樂

出國旅遊

愛情來了

113

揪團喝一杯
Let's go for a drink

便利三句開口說

How about going for a drink after work?
▶ 下班後去喝一杯如何？

替換句 Let's go get a drink. 去喝一杯吧。

✓ 句型提點 Using It Properly!

若想提出邀約或是建議、詢問意見，常用「How about+ 名詞 / 現在分詞 (V-ing)」，以 How about 開頭，後面加上邀約或是提議內容。

When is Happy Hour at XYZ bar?
▶ XYZ 酒吧的暢飲時間是幾點？

替換句 Are there any discounts on the drinks from 4 to 7 p.m.? 飲料下午四點到七點有沒有折扣？

✓ 句型提點 Using It Properly!

「When + be 動詞 + (詢問內容) + at + 地點」用來詢問在某地的某事是什麼時候。疑問詞 When 不僅可問時間，也可問星期、月份、季節、年份等等。

Hi, there, what can I get you today?
▶ 嗨，今天要點什麼？

替換句 Can I take your orders? 需要點單了嗎？

✓ 句型提點 Using It Properly!

get 在這裡表示提供、準備之意。是在餐廳中最常聽到店員使用的問句之一，當店員問此句，可以直接回答想要點什麼菜。

Part
1
自我介紹

Part
2
日常雜務

Part
3
職場應對

Part
4
休閒娛樂

Part
5
出國旅遊

Part
6
愛情來了

有來有往的必備回應

Q How about going for a drink after work?

A Sure, let's go.

當然好，走吧。

Q When is Happy Hour at XYZ bar?

A No idea. We can ask around.

不清楚，我們可以問問。

Q Hi, there, what can I get you today?

A I'd like a beer and a whisky on the rocks, please.

我要一杯啤酒跟一杯威士忌加冰塊。

小知識補給站 Some Fun Facts

　　Happy Hour（暢飲時間）的緣起其中一說，是來自於數十年前紐約的一家酒吧，老闆將每天下午五點到六點訂為 happy hour，讓人們在下班回家的路上，可以享受半價飲料，吸引不少顧客上門，之後，餐飲業者為了吸引消費者，更把時間延長，通常為星期一到五、從黃昏一直到晚上 8、9 點，依照各個餐廳自行訂定不同的時段，有時甚至連餐點也減價。另外，點酒時，想要加冰塊可說（酒名）+on the rocks，不加冰塊是 neat，不含酒精的其他飲料是 mixer，調酒則是 cocktail；下班之餘不妨趁著happy hour 的時段，認識新朋友、放鬆一下，還可以省下不少荷包！

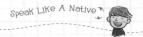

01 What a day! What do you say we go out for a drink?

好累的一天！我們去喝一杯如何？

what do you say 你覺得…怎樣？

02 Awesome! I could use a drink!

太棒了！我需要喝一杯。 awesome 很好的

03 What I need now is nothing but a drink.

我現在最需要的就是一杯酒。

04 Let's make sure who's going to be the designated driver before we go to the bar tonight.

今天晚上我們去酒吧前，先確定誰要負責開車吧！

designated driver 指定司機

05 "Bartender, a glass of Chardonnay, please."

「酒保，請給我一杯白葡萄酒。」 bartender 酒保

06 We have stout, ale, draft, bitter, and light beers.

我們有黑麥啤酒、麥芽啤酒、生啤酒、苦啤酒跟淡啤酒。

07 I want some beer. Make it a pitcher.

我想要喝啤酒，來個一壺好了。 pitcher 水壺

08 I'd like a cocktail/a beer/a Scotch.

我要一杯雞尾酒／啤酒／蘇格蘭威士忌。

09 The wine list is on the second page of your menu.

酒單在菜單的第二頁。 wine list 酒類一覽表

10 Would you like to order anything off the appetizer menu?

你想要在開胃菜單裡點些什麼嗎？ appetizer 開胃菜

11 I don't drink. Do you offer any kind of non-alcoholic beverages?

我不喝酒，你們有提供不含酒精的飲料嗎？ beverage 飲料

⑫ **Cheers! Here's to us!**
敬我們！ cheers 大家乾杯！

⑬ **I spent too much money on wining and dining this month.**
我這個月花太多錢在吃喝上面了。 wine and dine 吃喝

⑭ **All the drinks are half price during happy hour.**
所有的飲料在暢飲時間內都半價。
happy hour 快樂時光（酒類促銷時段）

⑮ **All the beers are on the house tonight.**
今晚所有啤酒都由本店招待。 on the house 店家招待

⑯ **It's ladies' night tonight, meaning free entry for ladies.**
今晚是淑女之夜，所有女性可免費入場。 entry 入場

⑰ **It's free entry for anyone wearing a mini-skirt tonight.**
所有穿迷你裙的人今晚入場一律免費。

⑱ **Drink with discretion. I hope you know your limit.**
謹慎飲酒，希望你清楚自己的酒量。 discretion 謹慎

⑲ **I feel a bit tipsy.**
我有點微醺。 tipsy 微醉的

⑳ **John was drunk with only a shot of tequila and a chaser.**
約翰只喝了一小杯龍舌蘭跟一杯淡酒就醉了。
chaser 飲烈酒後喝的飲料

㉑ **That guy over there is seriously wasted.**
那邊的那傢伙已經醉得不成樣了。 wasted 喝醉的

㉒ **You'll get drunk easily if you mix drinks.**
如果你混酒喝，很容易就醉了。

㉓ **He was short and fat, with a large beer belly.**
他又矮又胖，還有著大大的啤酒肚。 beer belly 啤酒肚

自我介紹 Part 1

日常雜務 Part 2

職場應對 Part 3

休閒娛樂 Part 4

出國旅遊 Part 5

愛情來了 Part 6

對話情境① 光顧新酒吧

A : Good evening, Sir. What would you like to drink today?

B : Do you have any Belgian beers?

A : You have come to the right place! We happen to have a great selection.

B : Then I'll have a Stella Artois.

A : Sure. Coming right up!

A：先生晚安，今天想要喝點什麼？

B：你們有賣比利時啤酒嗎？

A：你來對地方了！我們正好有些上選。

B：那給我來瓶時代啤酒吧。

A：好的，馬上來！

Belgian [ˋbɛldʒən]
形 比利時的 名
比利時人

selection
[səˋlɛkʃən] 名
選擇；選集

對話情境② 借酒澆愁

A : Bottoms up!

B : Dude, slow down! It's not water you're drinking.

A : I had a bad day. I need this.

B : Alright then. Here's to a better tomorrow!

A : That's the spirit!

A：乾杯！

B：老兄，喝慢點！你又不是在喝白開水。

A：我今天過的不順，我需要這樣喝。

B：好吧，那就敬明天會更好！

A：沒錯，就是要這樣！

bottoms up 片 乾杯

that's the spirit 片
做的對（表示贊同）

對話情境 ③ 在酒吧約會

A : This bar is quaint. How did you find this place?

B : I saw the ads on Facebook and thought we might as well check it out ourselves.

A : (Flipping through the menu) And the price is fairly reasonable.

B : Let me buy you a drink first while you decide on the appetizers.

A : You're the sweetest!

自我介紹

日常雜務

A：這酒吧好特別，你怎麼找到這裡的啊？

B：我在臉書看到廣告，想說乾脆我們一起來看看。

A：（翻菜單的同時）而且價錢也相當合理。

B：那我先幫你點杯飲料，你就慢慢決定開胃菜要點什麼吧。

A：你最好了！

quaint [kwent] 形
古老別緻的；古怪的

fairly [`fɛrlɪ] 副
相當地；簡直

appetizer
[`æpə͵taɪzə] 名
開胃菜

職場應對

對話情境 ④ 喝醉窘境

A : OK, I think you've had enough.

B : What? No!!! It's still happy hour. Let's carry on!

A : Listen to yourself! You're stone drunk! It's midnight.

B : Seriously? I'm not feeling well...

A : Let's get you a cab.

休閒娛樂

A：好了，我覺得你該停止了。

B：什麼？不行！現在還是暢飲時間，繼續喝吧！

A：看看你！你醉了吧！都已經半夜了。

B：真的嗎？我不太舒服…

A：我幫你叫台計程車吧。

carry on 片
繼續下去；進行

stone drunk 片
醉酒而精神恍惚的

cab [kæb] 名（英）
計程車

出國旅遊

愛情來了

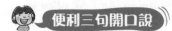

Unit 19 頭上多作怪
Getting a fancy hairstyle

便利三句開口說

Did you get a haircut?
▶ 你剪頭髮了嗎？

替換句 ▶ Did you have your hair cut? 你把頭髮剪了嗎？

✓ 句型提點 〈 Using It Properly!〉

詢問某人是否得到或拿到某樣東西，可用「Do/did+ 人名 / 代名詞 +get+ 受詞（名詞）」。get 在口語經常用到，不只可以指得到，還可指變成、理解、說服…等等，可根據前後語意判斷意思。

How would you like your hair cut?
▶ 你想要剪什麼樣的髮型？

替換句 ▶ What kind of hairstyle do you want? 你想要什麼樣的髮型？

✓ 句型提點 〈 Using It Properly!〉

「How would+ 人名 / 代名詞 +like+ 名詞＋動詞」，詢問某人「想用什麼方式達到某樣事情」。例：How would you like your steak cooked? 你的牛排想要幾分熟？

What do you want to do with your hair?
▶ 你想要怎麼用你的頭髮？

替換句 ▶ What can I do for you today? 今天可以幫您做什麼呢？

✓ 句型提點 〈 Using It Properly!〉

「What+do/does+ 人名 / 代名詞 +want+to+ 動詞」

為詢問他人想做什麼事情時用的句型。例：**What does he want to eat on his birthday?** 他生日的時候想要吃什麼？

 有來有往的必備回應

Q Did you get a haircut?

A Yes. You noticed!
是啊！你注意到了。

Q How would you like your hair cut?

A I only want a trim.
我只想稍微修剪一下。

Q What do you want to do with your hair?

A I want to perm and color my hair.
我想要燙髮跟染髮。

小知識補給站 *Some Fun Facts*

　　美國理髮店可以直接走進店裡、不一定要事先預約；剪髮時，首重與設計師之間的溝通，常用的關鍵字不外乎是層次 (layer)、打薄 (thin out)、旁分 (side parting)、中分 (central parting)、剪瀏海 (bang trimming)、鬢角 (side burn)、燙髮 (perm)、波浪大捲 (waive)、捲髮 (curling)、染髮 (dye)、挑染 (highlights)、護髮 (hair treatment) 等等。國外也有很多複合式的美容院，同時提供美髮、美甲、甚至美妝的服務，還可以自己選擇設計師，不過這就需要事前預約了。

01 I made a reservation at the hair salon I usually go to.

我在常去的那家美容院預約了時間。 hair salon 美容院

02 Do you have a regular hairdresser, or should we assign one for you?

你有指定的美髮師嗎？還是我們幫你選定一個？
hairdresser 美髮師　assign 指派

03 I have had my hair long and curly for the past five years and feel like a change now.

我留長捲髮已經五年了，現在在想要改變。 curly 捲髮的

04 Melody cut her hair short because she can't stand the summer heat.

美樂蒂因為無法忍受夏天的酷熱而把頭髮剪短。

05 Do you think I would look okay with bangs?

你覺得我留瀏海適合嗎？ bang 前瀏海

06 What kind of female hair style is most trendy this year?

哪一種女性髮型今年最流行？ trendy 時髦的；流行的

07 We discussed the hairstyles with the hairstylists first, and then we had our hair shampooed.

我們先跟設計師討論髮型，然後才去洗了頭髮。
hairstyle 髮型　hairstylist 髮型設計師

08 The stylist will usually wash my hair, towel dry it, and comb my hair out before starting to cut my hair.

設計師通常會先幫我洗頭、用毛巾擦乾、梳理整齊後才開始剪頭髮。

09 One of the best things about going to a hair salon is that we can have our heads massaged and enjoy the newest treatments on the market.

去美容院最棒的事情之一就是可以享受頭皮按摩跟市面上最新的美髮產品。

⑩ Are you in for a haircut or a perm?
你想要剪還是燙頭髮？ perm 燙髮

⑪ Do you want to color your hair today?
你今天想要染頭髮嗎？

⑫ Making an appointment is generally recommended, but not required because they take people on a first-come, first-serve basis.
基本上，建議您先打電話預約，但並非必要，因為他們採取先來先服務的機制。

⑬ I usually ask my hairdresser to cut a little off the top and sides, and trim off any split ends.
我通常會要求我的理髮師修剪我的髮尾，並修掉分岔。

⑭ Jerry only wanted a trim, so he went down to a barber shop near his place.
傑瑞只想要修剪一下頭髮，所以他去家裡附近的理髮院。

⑮ Can you cut about two inches off the length?
你可否剪掉大約兩吋的長度？

⑯ I want one inch off the top and the sides shaped.
我想要剪掉一吋上面的頭髮，並將側邊頭髮剪出個型。

⑰ I would like a straight perm today.
我今天想要離子燙。 straight 平直的

⑱ Can you color my hair to brown?
可否幫我把頭髮染成咖啡色？

⑲ Can you thin out my hair a little bit?
可否幫我把頭髮打薄一點？ thin out 變稀薄

⑳ In addition to paying at the front desk, Claire always tips her hairdresser because she is always satisfied with her new look.
除了去櫃檯結帳，克萊兒總會給設計師小費，因為她對新造型總是很滿意。

Part 1 自我介紹
Part 2 日常雜務
Part 3 職場應對
Part 4 休閒娛樂
Part 5 出國旅遊
Part 6 愛情來了

123

雙人實境對話 oh!

對話情境 1 急需剪髮

A : I need to get my haircut. Do you have any **openings** today?
B : Do you have a **regular** hairstylist?
A : No. Any **hairdresser** will do.
B : If that's the case, you can come anytime you want.
A : Great, I'll come right over.

A：我需要剪髮，你們還有空出來的時間嗎？
B：你有指定的設計師嗎？
A：沒有，任何一個都可以。
B：若是這樣的話，你隨時可以過來。
A：太好了，我這就過去。

opening [ˋopənɪŋ]
名 空檔；空位
regular [ˋrɛgjələ]
形 固定的；經常的
hairdresser
[ˋhɛr͵drɛsə] 名
理髮師

對話情境 2 新造型

A : I like your new look!
B : Is it that obvious? I just had my hair cut.
A : You look good in short hair.
B : Are you sure I'm not looking **weird**?
A : Take it easy. You look **fabulous**!

A：我喜歡你的新造型！
B：這麼明顯嗎？我才剛剛剪了頭髮。
A：你剪短髮很適合。
B：你確定看起來不會很怪嗎？
A：放輕鬆，你看起來很棒！

weird [wɪrd] 形
奇怪的
take it easy 片
放輕鬆
fabulous [ˋfæbjələs]
形 驚人的；極好的

對話情境 3 救星出手

A: I'm in desperate need of your help.
B: Wow. You do look like it.
A: I got this very bad haircut while traveling. Look at these excessive layers!
B: I'll curl your ends toward your face to add volume. You'll look great.
A: You're my savior!

A：我急需你的幫忙。
B：哇，你看起來的確很需要。
A：我出國玩的時候剪壞了頭髮，你看看這些過度的層次！
B：我會將髮尾朝臉部內捲，增加厚度，你看起來會很美的。
A：你真是我的救星！

desperate
[`dɛspərɪt] 形 非常的；極度渴望的

excessive
[ɪk`sɛsɪv] 形 過度的

volume [`vɑljəm]
名 總數；體積

對話情境 4 美容院服務

A: Morning. What would you like to do with your hair today?
B: I'd like to have it trimmed and a straight perm.
A: Got it. So how much do you want to cut off your hair?
B: Just within an inch would be enough.
A: OK. Let me get you a glass of water first.

A：早安，你今天想要怎麼用你的頭髮？
B：我想要稍微修剪，然後離子燙。
A：知道了，你想要剪多少？
B：一吋以內就夠了。
A：好的，我先幫你倒一杯水。

trim [trɪm] 動 修剪

perm [pɝm] 名
燙髮；捲髮 動 燙髮

within [wɪ`ðɪn] 介
不超過

Part 1 自我介紹
Part 2 日常雜務
Part 3 職場應對
Part 4 休閒娛樂
Part 5 出國旅遊
Part 6 愛情來了

美容院紓壓
Spa and facial treatments

 便利三句開口說

I have a facial once a month.
▶ 我一個月做一次臉。

替換句 I go to a beauty parlor every month. 我每個月去一次美容院。

☑ →句型提點 **Using It Properly!**

頻率用語 once 為一次、兩次 twice、三次 three times、四次 four times，以此類推。後可接時間，例：once a day/week/month/season，分別表示一天一次、一週一次、一個月一次以及一季一次。

Have you ever had a massage?
▶ 你有給人按摩過嗎？

替換句 Have you tried a massage before? 你以前有試過按摩嗎？

☑ →句型提點 **Using It Properly!**

「have+ 動詞過去分詞」為現在完成式，若放在疑問句，可以用來詢問某人是否曾經有過後述的經驗。例：Have you ever been to Japan? 你曾經去過日本嗎？

What kind of service do you have here?
▶ 你們這邊提供哪些服務？

替換句 What kind of treatment do you have here? 你們這邊有什麼療程？

☑ 句型提點 **Using It Properly!**

「What kind of+ 名詞 + 完整疑問句」，表示在詢問哪一類。例：What kind of food do you like? 你喜歡吃什麼樣的食物？

有來有往的必備回應

Q I have a facial once a month.

A Does it cost much?

做臉會很貴嗎？

Q Have you ever had a massage?

A No, I've never had one.

不，我從沒給人按過。

Q What kind of service do you have here?

A We have massage, facials, aromatherapy and sauna.

我們這邊提供按摩、做臉、芳香療法跟桑拿服務。

小知識補給站 *Some Fun Facts*

美容項目五花八門，從早期著重臉部清潔保養的 facial、新興的 spa、芳療 (aromatherapy) 等等，設備、知識也愈來愈發達、多元。像是讓身體接觸零下 110℃ 液態氮的冷桑拿 (cold sauna) 及冷療 (cryotherapy)，利用低溫抑制發炎，有放鬆肌肉、甚至有加速傷口恢復的功效；對歐美人來說，因古銅色皮膚說明常去度假的習慣、象徵地位，甚至還發展出 tanning salon，讓顧客不去海灘也能擁有令人稱羨的古銅膚色。

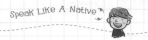
01 Do I have to make a reservation in advance?
我需要先預約嗎？ `in advance 預先`

02 I try to go for a massage and a facial once a month.
我試著每個月做一次按摩跟臉部保養。 `facial 臉部美容`

03 What kind of service are you interested in?
你對什麼樣的服務感興趣呢？

04 We have traditional Thai massage, oil massage, body scrub, and facial massage with aromatic oil.
我們這裡提供傳統的泰式按摩、精油按摩、身體磨砂（去角質）、使用芳香精油的臉部按摩等服務。

05 Do you do body wrapping here?
你們有提供身體裹敷嗎？
`body wrap 身體裹敷（一種身體美容療程）`

06 We offer a Thai body herbal wrap, tomato-and-honey body wrap, detox body wrap, and seaweed body wrap.
我們提供泰式草本裹敷、番茄跟蜂蜜裹敷、排毒身體裹敷以及海藻身體裹敷。 `detox 排毒的`

07 What does a body package include?
請問身體套組包含什麼內容？

08 It includes a body scrub, body massage, herbal sauna and body wrap.
有包含身體磨砂（去角質）、全身按摩、草本沐浴以及身體裹敷。

09 A nice massage can relieve stiffness and help improve your blood flow.
好的按摩可以減輕僵硬，並促進血液循環。
`relieve 緩和；減輕`

10 Oil massage is a kind of aromatherapy. The

aromatic **oil can help you relax, and it reduces stress.**

精油按摩是一種芳香療法，芳香精油可以幫助你放鬆，並減緩壓力。 aromatic 芳香的

⑪ **The herbal sauna helps open your pores and thus release toxins. The body scrub improves blood circulation and removes dead cells.**

草本沐浴能打開你的毛孔，進而排出毒素。身體磨砂促進血液循環並去除角質。 pore 毛孔

⑫ **The body wrap warms up your body and boosts the release of body toxins.**

身體裹敷溫熱你的身體，並加速身體毒素的釋放。
boost 促進；增加 release 釋放

⑬ **Body and facial massage help rid you of your muscle tension. You will feel totally relaxed.**

身體與臉部按摩能去除肌肉緊繃的狀態，你將會感到通體舒暢。 tension 繃緊；緊張

⑭ **Be careful not to eat a heavy meal before the session.**

切記不要在療程之前吃大餐。

⑮ **Wait about one hour before taking a shower. This is to let your body absorb the effects of the treatment.**

要等一小時之後再洗澡，這是為了讓身體吸收療程效果。

⑯ **The price will be 15% off if you pay for the annual package.**

如果您購買一年份的服務，我們將替您打 85 折。

⑰ **The session will begin in three minutes. Please relax and feel free to give us some feedback.**

療程將在三分鐘後開始，請放鬆，歡迎隨時向我們反應。

⑱ **The masseuse will start to massage your head and then go all the way down to your toes.**

按摩師將會開始按摩你的頭部，然後一路按到腳指頭。
masseuse 女按摩師

Part 1 自我介紹

Part 2 日常雜務

Part 3 職場應對

Part 4 休閒娛樂

Part 5 出國旅遊

Part 6 愛情來了

對話情境 ① 抓住青春的尾巴

A : My facial skin is becoming loose. Can you suggest some **treatments** for it?

B : Sure! We do have some facial treatments that will **tighten** your skin.

A : Are these treatments safe?

B : Don't worry. We only use **certified** and tested products.

A : Great. Where can I start?

A：我的臉部皮膚有點鬆垮，可不可以建議我一些療程？

B：當然沒問題！我們的確有一些臉部的療程可以緊緻您的肌膚。

A：這些療程安全嗎？

B：別擔心，我們只使用檢驗合格並經過認證的產品。

A：太棒了，我可以怎麼開始？

treatment
[`trirmənt] 名 治療；對待

tighten [`taɪtṇ] 動 使變緊

certified
[`sɝtə,faɪd] 形 認證合格的

對話情境 ② 耳根子軟的客人

A : What does this promotional package include?

B : It includes body scrub, **essence** oil massage, **manicure** and **pedicure**.

A : It does sound like a bargain.

B : Yes, it does! And the promotion will end this week.

A : Make sure I get one, please!

A：這個促銷的組合包含什麼？

B：包含身體磨砂、精油按摩、手部跟足部護理。

A：聽起來蠻划算的。

B：沒錯！而且促銷活動只到這禮拜喔。

A：我要買一份！

essence [`ɛsṇs] 名 精油

manicure
[`mænɪ,kjʊr] 名 指甲護理

pedicure
[`pɛdɪk,jʊr] 名 足部護理

對話情境 3 做臉時間

A : Welcome to ABC Beauty **Parlor**. How can I help you?

B : My name is Vicky Chang. I **made a reservation** the other day.

A : Oh, yes. You are having a facial today.

B : How long does it normally take?

A : It takes about an hour.

A：歡迎來到 ABC 美容院，有什麼可以幫您服務的？

B：我叫做張薇琪，我前幾天有打電話預約。

A：喔是的，您今天要做臉。

B：通常要做多久？

A：大約一個鐘頭。

parlor [`pɑrlɚ] 名
店舖

make a reservation 片
預約

對話情境 4 按摩服務

A : Hello, Madame. Have you ever tried Thai **therapy** before?

B : No. It's my first time.

A : Before we begin, there's something you need to know in advance.

B : OK, I'm listening.

A : If you feel pain or any **uncomfortableness**, please **feel free to** let me know.

A：夫人您好，您有試過泰式療法嗎？

B：沒有，這是我初次嘗試。

A：在我們開始之前，有件事先要告訴您。

B：好的，我在聽。

A：如果您感到疼痛或任何不適，請不用客氣，隨時讓找知道。

therapy [`θɛrəpɪ] 名 療法

uncomfortableness [ʌn`kʌmfətəblnɪs] 名 不舒適

feel free to 片 請便；請隨意

NOTE

Part 3

職場應對

許你一個順風順水

找工作、離開公司從頭到尾都順利，
職場上不被當小白就得這麼說！

Wish me great
success!

* 問公司福利、加薪、轉職可以
這樣說！

名 名詞	動 動詞	形 形容詞
副 副詞	介 介係詞	助 助詞
連 連接詞	限 限定詞	縮 縮寫

飯碗何處去
Go get a job

便利三句開口說

I am looking for a job.
▶ 我正在找工作。

替換句 I'm trying to find a job. 我正試著找工作。

✓ **句型提點** Using It Properly!

片語 look for 意指尋找，後面可接想找的人或物。
若後面接動詞，則必須使用「現在進行式」，因為找
工作通常會持續一段時間。例：She is looking for
her cat. 她正在尋找她的貓。

Do you know if there are any job openings?
▶ 你知道有任何職缺嗎？

替換句 Do you know if the company is hiring? 你知
不知道那間公司是否有在徵人？

✓ **句型提點** Using It Properly!

「Do/Does+ 人 / 代名詞 +know+if+ 子句」用以詢
問某人知不知道後述的狀況。例：Do you know if
she is coming to the prom? 你知道她是否會來參
加畢業舞會嗎？

How's the job hunting going?
▶ 工作找得怎麼樣呢？

替換句 Have you landed a good job yet? 你找到好工
作了嗎？

✓ **句型提點** Using It Properly!

「How+be 動詞 + 人 / 事 +going」用來詢問、

關心某人或某事的狀況如何。例： How are your
parents doing lately? 你的父母親最近如何？

 有來有往的必備回應

Q I am looking for a job.

I am not trying to scare you, but the
unemployment rate has reached the
highest point these days. A

我不想嚇你，不過這陣子的失業率才創了新高。

Q Do you know if there are any job openings?

Not that I am aware of. A

就我所知是沒有。

Q How's the job hunting going?

I've just posted my resume online. A

我才剛在網站上登錄了我的履歷。

小知識補給站　　Some Fun Facts

　　在美國，常常見到人們上傳自己的履歷到求職網
站 LinkedIn，LinkedIn 雖然主要是為被動求職者而
設計的，但不僅有獵頭 (headhunter) 在上面尋找合
適的候選人，還能運用其公開推薦的功能建立人脈與
口碑，其社群的功能則可以和全世界不同國家、不同
領域的人交換意見，甚至有創業家運用 LinkedIn 的
人脈，成功募集到創業基金。網路以及各種平台的興
起，提供許多更多新穎的求職方式，讓人們可以借助
網路的力量增加效率，不再漫無目的地疲於面試。

右側邊欄：
自我介紹 Part 1
日常雜務 Part 2
職場應對 Part 3
休閒娛樂 Part 4
出國旅遊 Part 5
愛情來了 Part 6

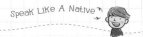
01 Finding the ideal job often takes a lot of research and patience.

找到理想工作之前，通常會花不少時間，還要有耐心。

ideal 理想的；完美的

02 In order to get ahead in job hunting, I need to go over my resume several times and make sure there are no typos and errors.

為了成功求職，我必須檢查履歷表很多次，確定沒有拼錯字或其他錯誤。

03 Attending job fairs held at colleges might provide leads to job openings.

參加學校所辦的就業博覽會，說不定可以取得應徵職缺的機會。

04 Looking in the local newspaper under the classified ads to see if there are any job postings is considered old-fashioned nowadays.

如今，在地方報紙分類廣告找職缺已被視為老派作法了。

old-fashioned 過時的；老派的

05 Are there many good job vacancies in your company?

你公司有沒有好的職缺呢？ vacancy 空缺

06 I have connections with a guy who works for a computer company, and he might be able to pull a few strings and line you up with an interview.

我認識一個在電腦公司上班的人，他或許能夠幫忙牽線、幫你安排面試。 pull strings 通過私人關係

07 I am a fresh graduate and I am worried that I won't be qualified for many opportunities.

我是社會新鮮人，真擔心自己不符合很多工作機會的標準。

qualified 合格的

08 **It is getting harder for fresh graduates to locate a job because of the dwindling opportunities in the job market.**

對於社會新鮮人來說，要找到工作愈來愈難，因為就業市場一直萎縮。 dwindling 愈來愈少的

09 **I think I am qualified for all the requirements of the job description posted on this website.**

我認為這網站所列的應徵條件我都符合。
job description 工作說明

10 **Any fresh graduate is welcome to apply for this position.**

歡迎所有應屆畢業生來應徵這個職位。 position 職位

11 **Sam is looking for a job in the IT industry.**

山姆在找跟資訊產業有關的工作。
IT=information technology 資訊科技

12 **I've always wanted to apply for a job as a publicist.**

我一直都想應徵公關人員這個職位。 apply for 申請

13 **How long have you been looking for a new job?**

你找新工作找多久了？ look for 尋找

14 **Jamie has been looking for a job for over a month on his own, and now he is turning his head towards some recruiting agencies.**

傑米已自行找了一個多月的工作，現在他轉向一些徵才機構尋求協助。 on one's own 獨自；主動

15 **My sister has sent dozens of resumes to different companies and is now anticipating some replies.**

我妹已寄出十幾份履歷表給不同公司，現在在等候回音。

16 **The government has set up a job hunting unit for assisting the unemployed to get a job.**

政府成立了求職小組來協助失業者找工作。
unemployed 失業的

自我介紹 · Part 1

日常雜務 · Part 2

職場應對 · Part 3

休閒娛樂 · Part 4

出國旅遊 · Part 5

愛情來了 · Part 6

137

雙人實境對話 〈oh!〉

對話情境 ① 求職 ING

A: So how's the **job hunt** going?
B: I have gone to five interviews so far.
A: Wow! You're **on a roll**! Any word from that consulting job for the cosmetics company?
B: Not yet. They said they'd get back to me, but I haven't heard from them.
A: Well, make sure you **follow up**. It shows **initiative**.

A：工作找得如何？
B：我已經去面試過五次了。
A：哇！你很有進展啊！上次那個化妝品公司的顧問職缺回覆你了嗎？
B：還沒耶，他們說會通知我，但到現在都還沒有任何消息。
A：總之記得主動詢問，展現你的積極態度。

job hunt ● 求職
be on a roll ● 好運連連
follow up ● 跟蹤；追查
initiative [ɪ`nɪʃətɪv] ● 主動性

對話情境 ② 非走不可

A: Do you know if there are any job **openings**?
B: No, Why? Did you leave your last job?
A: Yes. My boss treated me badly, and I didn't like my chances for **advancing** in the company.
B: That's too bad.
A: Please **keep your eyes open** for me.

A：你知道有任何職缺嗎？
B：不清楚，為什麼問這個？你離職了？
A：嗯，我老闆對我很不好，而且我不看好在那邊升遷的機會。
B：太糟了。
A：麻煩幫我多注意一下。

opening [`opənɪŋ] ● 空缺
advance [əd`væns] ● 晉升；發展
keep one's eyes open ● 注意；留心

對話情境 3 電話詢問職缺

A: Hi, my name is Joe Smith. I've learnt there's a **vacancy** for a sales **executive** in your company.

B: That's right. We are looking for an **experienced** salesperson.

A: Sounds good. I have got four years of sales experience.

B: Great! What sort of products have you sold?

A: I've sold computers.

A：您好，我叫做喬·史密斯。我得知貴公司有一個業務主管的職缺。
B：是的，我們在找有經驗的業務人員。
A：聽起來很棒，我有四年的業務經驗。
B：太好了！你之前販售什麼樣的商品？
A：我是賣電腦的。

vacancy [`vekənsɪ]
名 空缺；空白

executive
[ɪg`zɛkjutɪv] 名 主管

experienced
[ɪk`spɪrɪənst] 形 有經驗的

對話情境 4 來電約面試

A: Hello. Is that Mr. Mark Anderson?

B: Yes. May I ask who's calling?

A: I am calling from ABC Corp. You've applied for a job with us. We **received** your resume.

B: Oh yes! I am interested in your vacancy for a computer **programmer**.

A: Can you come in for an interview?

A：您好，請問是馬克·安德森先生嗎？
B：是的，請問你是？
A：我這裡是 ABC 公司。您有來應徵本公司的職缺，我們收到了你的履歷。
B：對！我對貴公司電腦工程師的職缺有興趣。
A：您可以過來面談嗎？

receive [rɪ`siv] 動
收到；接受

programmer
[`progræmə] 名 程式設計師

 自我介紹 Part 1

 日常雜務 Part 2

 職場應對 Part 3

 休閒娛樂 Part 4

 出國旅遊 Part 5

 愛情來了 Part 6

面試定生死
Nail a job interview

便利三句開口說

I am here for my interview.
▶ 我是來這裡面試的。

替換句 I have an appointment for an interview today. 我今天有預約面試。

✓ **句型提點** Using It Properly!

「人名／代名詞＋be 動詞＋here＋for＋某事」，for 後面接理由、目的，表示某人是為了某事而來。例：Lucas is here for a concert. 盧卡斯是為了看演唱會而來的。

- -

Can you tell us about yourself?
▶ 你能自我介紹一下嗎？

替換句 Can you introduce yourself? 你能不能做個自我介紹？

✓ **句型提點** Using It Properly!

「Can＋人名／代名詞＋tell＋受詞＋about＋人／事／物」，詢問可否能夠說明一下某人／事／物。

- -

How much do you know about our company?
▶ 你對我們公司了解多少？

替換句 Do you know what our company does? 你知道我們公司是做什麼的嗎？

✓ **句型提點** Using It Properly!

「How much＋do/does＋人名／代名詞＋know

about+ 人 / 事 / 物」，詢問某人對於某事的了解程度。而 How much 所問的是對之後所接的人 / 事 / 物了解多少，是一種不可數的「抽象概念」。

有來有往的必備回應

Q I am here for my interview.

A Take a seat. The interviewer will be here shortly.

請稍坐一下，面試官馬上就來了。

Q Can you tell us about yourself?

A I have a master's degree in computer science.

我是資訊工程碩士。

Q How much do you know about our company?

A Your company has been in the leading position in the industrial design industry.

貴公司一直都引領工業設計業界的潮流。

小知識補給站

在履歷上面，最好提供實際的數據、相關資料或推薦人來佐證你的能力；一般而言，在尋求正職職位時，會同時附上一封求職信 (cover letter)，簡短說明申請此公司的原因、自己的專長、以及能為公司帶來怎樣的效益。好不容易取得面試機會後，不管形式為現場面試、電話面試、或網路面試，都要誠實以對，展現自信！

Part 1 自我介紹
Part 2 日常雜務
Part 3 職場應對
Part 4 休閒娛樂
Part 5 出國旅遊
Part 6 愛情來了

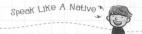
01 Showing calmness and modesty during a job interview helps you make a great impression.
面試時展現出鎮定及謙遜的態度可以幫你的第一印象加分。

02 Dressing up as a professional for any job interview demonstrates that you take the job seriously.
在面試時穿著正式服裝，能展現出你認真看待這份工作的態度。

03 Are you most interested in a good, steady job with benefits or one that will allow you to quickly advance?
你對於穩定、福利佳的工作最有興趣，還是一份可以讓你迅速升遷的工作？

04 I really appreciate the opportunity to interview for this position.
我對於能夠面試這份工作感到相當感激。 interview 面試

05 What do you know about our organization?
你對於我們的組織有什麼樣的認知？
know about 知道關於…的情形

06 I think I have a pretty good understanding of the job. I believe that I can handle it with ease, and I hope to have the opportunity to work for you.
我認為我對這份工作有相當程度的了解，相信我可以輕鬆勝任，希望能有機會為您工作。 with ease 容易地；從容地

07 Can you tell me something about yourself?
你可否談談你自己？

08 I have a bachelor's degree in English Literature, and I am hoping to find a job in which I could make the full use of the language.
我有英語文學的學士文憑，希望做一份能發揮我文學專才的工作。 bachelor's degree 學士學位

09 **Do you feel that you are exceptionally good at anything in particular?**

你覺得你在哪方面特別有優勢？ `good at 精於；擅長`

10 **What can you do for us that someone else can't?**

有哪些事情是別人做不到，唯獨你能替我們辦到的？

11 **I am proficient in three different languages, and I have nothing but enthusiasm to do the job well.**

我精通三國語言，而且我對於把工作做好有著強烈的熱誠。

12 **Though I may be a fresh graduate with no work experience, I am passionate about learning new things.**

雖然我是沒有任何工作經驗的社會新鮮人，但我對於學習新事物充滿熱情。 `graduate 大學畢業生`

13 **I am confident in my managerial potential because I am a good listener and can always put myself in others' shoes.**

我對於我的管理潛力很有信心，因為我很善於傾聽，總是能將心比心。 `potential 潛力`

14 **Do you have any practical experience in teaching?**

你在教書這方面有任何實務經驗嗎？ `practical 實際的`

15 **I have over ten years of experience in this field, and I think you will like what my references have to say about me.**

我在這領域有超過十年的經驗，而且我認為你會喜歡我的推薦人對我所下的評語。

16 **Your resume suggests that you may be over-qualified or too experienced for this position. What's your opinion?**

你履歷上的經驗非常豐富，來應徵這份工作有點大材小用，你覺得呢？

17 **My long-range goal is to achieve an executive position and to lead a team of my own.**

我的長期目標是做到管理階級，並能夠領導屬於我自己的團隊。 `executive 主管級的`

Part 1 自我介紹

Part 2 日常雜務

Part 3 職場應對

Part 4 休閒娛樂

Part 5 出國旅遊

Part 6 愛情來了

143

對話情境① 面試問題

A : Good morning. Thank you for the interview.

B : No problem. Now, do you prefer working with others or flying **solo**?

A : Actually, I enjoy both.

B : Would you be able to **relocate**?

A : I am **open** to relocating.

A：早安，謝謝安排面試。

B：不會。那麼，請問你偏好團隊合作還是單打獨鬥？

A：其實兩種我都喜歡。

B：你能接受外派嗎？

A：我對外派抱持接受的態度。

solo [ˋsolo] 副
單獨地

relocate [riˋloket]
動 使遷移；調動

open [ˋopən] 形
願意接受的

對話情境② 面試前的閒聊

A : Good morning. I am here for my interview.

B : Hello, nice to meet you. Did you have any trouble finding the place?

A : No problem.

B : How did you get here?

A : I go everywhere with **public transportation**. I'm used to **commuting**.

A：早安，我是來面試的。

B：很高興認識你，這邊會不會很難找？

A：沒問題的。

B：你怎麼來的呢？

A：我出門都搭大眾運輸工具，很習慣通勤。

public transportation 片
大眾交通工具

commute [kəˋmjut]
動 通勤

對話情境 3 向面試官提問

A: May I ask you how much this position pays per year?

B: This job pays sixty-five thousand dollars per year.

A: What kind of **benefits** does this job have?

B: This job provides full medical and **disability**.

A: Thanks for the details.

A：可否請問這個職位的年薪是多少？
B：這份工作的年薪是六萬五千美元。
A：那這份工作有提供什麼福利嗎？
B：這份工作提供完整的醫療險和失能險。
A：謝謝你提供的詳細資訊。

benefit [`bɛnəfɪt]
名 利益；優勢
disability
[dɪsə`bɪlətɪ] 名
傷殘保險

對話情境 4 面試改期

A: Hello, may I speak to Mr. Chang?

B: Yes, this is he.

A: I am calling from Market Corp. You have an interview **scheduled** with us for the 5th.

B: Yes, I know. I will be there as **required**.

A: Well, I am sorry, but we need to **shift** it to the 6th. You see, the person who is supposed to interview you will be out of town.

A：你好，請問張先生在嗎？
B：我就是。
A：這裡是市場公司，你跟我們約在五號面試。
B：我知道，我會依照指定時間抵達。
A：很抱歉，因為你的面試官那天剛好出差，我必須跟你改到六號。

schedule [`skɛdʒʊl]
動 安排；預定
require [rɪ`kwaɪr]
動 要求；命令
shift [ʃɪft] 動 轉換

自我介紹

日常雜務

職場應對

休閒娛樂

出國旅遊

愛情來了

145

職前訓練一把罩
Rookie in orientation

便利三句開口說

It's my first day at work.
▶ 今天是我第一天上班。

替換句▶ Hello, I am new here. 嗨，我是新來的。

✓ **句型提點** Using It Properly!

「It's+ 所有格 +first+day+at+ 地點」用來表示某人在新階段的第一天，通常指的是求學或工作的新階段。例如：It's Maggie's first day at university and she is so excited about it. 今天是瑪姬進大學的第一天，她非常興奮。

. . . .

Welcome aboard!
▶ 歡迎加入！

替換句▶ Pleased that you are here. 很高興你能來。

✓ **句型提點** Using It Properly!

「aboard」原意指「在船 / 飛機 / 火車上」，Welcome aboard 表示歡迎搭乘本船次 / 航班 / 車次。在歡迎新人的場合，就衍生出「歡迎加入我們」的意思。

. . . .

Let me show you around the office.
▶ 我來帶你參觀一下公司。

替換句▶ I'll give you a tour of our facility. 我帶你認識一下公司的設施。

✓ **句型提點** Using It Properly!

「Let+ 人名 / 受格 + 原形動詞」，使役動詞 let 可表

達建議、請求、命令。要注意的是，使役動詞後方的動詞必須使用原形動詞。例：Let us finish this together! 讓我們一起來完成這事吧！

有來有往的必備回應

Q It's my first day at work.

A Looking forward to working with you.
很期待與你共事。

Q Welcome aboard!

A Thanks! It's an honor to be here.
謝謝！能來這裡是我的榮幸。

Q Let me show you around the office.

A I really appreciate it!
真的很感謝！

小知識補給站

Some Fun Facts

「orientation」有定位、方向之意，不只是學校的新生訓練用此字代表，職場的新人培訓也是用 orientation。企業的新進人員職前訓練 (Orientation Training, O.T.) 被視為是教導 (indoctrination) 或指導訓練 (induction training)，通常由人力資源部門介紹各種職位所承辦的業務、福利政策和運作程序，新人藉此建立對職場的第一印象，同時也是幫助職場新人熟悉工作環境、建立歸屬感、了解企業以及公司的目標的一種方式。

147

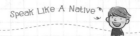
01 **Try to get to the office fifteen minutes earlier than you're supposed to on your first day of work.**

第一天上班，建議你比公司規定的時間再早到十五分鐘。

02 **Don't get too stressed out on your first day and remember to relax so that you can optimize your productivity.**

第一天上班不用太過緊張，記得要放鬆心情以將自己的產能最大化。 `stress out 感到焦慮` `optimize 使完美`

03 **You should also pay attention to the clothing and appearance on the first day of work.**

第一天上班你也應該要注意服裝儀容。

`pay attention to 注意；關心`

04 **The best thing anyone can do in the first few days of a new job is listen and observe.**

一位新進員工到職的前幾天，最重要的事情是傾聽與觀察。

`observe 觀察`

05 **Continue to arrive at work early and don't rush out the door at the end of the day.**

保持上班準時，並且不要在第一時間趕著下班。

`rush out 衝出`

06 **First impressions matter, so please wear a smile on your face every time you meet new people in the office.**

第一印象相當重要，所以在辦公室看到新面孔時，請面帶微笑。

07 **No need to try too hard to impress people.**

沒有必要為了要讓人印象深刻而過於做作。

`impress 給…極深的印象`

08 **It is highly suggested that you put your cell phone on silent to show you are 100% attentive.**

強烈建議你把手機關靜音，表示對工作百分百專注。

09 A senior colleague gave me a tour of our office so that I would know my way around here.

資深同事帶我參觀了辦公室，好讓我了解這裡的環境。

10 Your supervisor is the one with grey hair who is now sitting in his corner office.

你的主管是那位坐在大辦公室的灰髮男子。

`supervisor 監督人` `corner office 公司高層的辦公室`

11 Let me take you to your cubicle and then you can get familiar with the environment.

我先帶你去你的位子，再讓你熟悉環境。 `cubicle 隔間`

12 First of all, you'll need to report to the Human Resources Department.

首先，你要向人資部門報到。 `human resources 人力資源`

13 Although the first day of work really is more about listening, you can and should ask questions when necessary.

雖然第一天上班主要是在聽人介紹，不過你可以、也應該在必要的時機發問。

14 Don't hesitate to come to me if you encounter any questions.

如果你遇到任何問題，不要遲疑，馬上來問我。

`hesitate 躊躇；猶豫` `encounter 遇到`

15 Do I need to clock in and out?

我上下班需不需要打卡？ `clock in/out 打卡上班 / 下班`

16 Do I need to stay in the office all day or do I get to go out and about?

我需要一整天待在辦公室，還是要常常出去跑？

17 I notice that the fax machine and the copier are in the next room, aren't they?

我注意到傳真機跟印表機在隔壁房間，對吧？

18 Use your lunch hours to get together with your co-workers.

利用你的午休時間與同事相處。 `lunch hour 午餐時間`

Part 1 自我介紹
Part 2 日常雜務
Part 3 職場應對
Part 4 休閒娛樂
Part 5 出國旅遊
Part 6 愛情來了

149

雙人實境對話

對話情境 1 辦公室文具申請

A : Excuse me. I was wondering how to order office **supplies**.

B : We have a **requisition** form on the company website. What type of supplies do you need?

A : I need paper, ink **cartridges**, and paper clips.

B : How quickly will you need your supplies?

A : I need all of my supplies right away.

A：不好意思，我想請問一下該如何申請文具。

B：公司網站有線上的申請表格。你需要什麼樣的文具？

A：我需要紙、墨水匣以及迴紋針。

B：你多快需要用到這些東西？

A：我馬上就要了。

supply [səˋplaɪ] **名**
用品；補給品

requisition
[͵rɛkwəˋzɪʃən] **名**
申請單；正式請求

cartridge
[ˋkɑrtrɪdʒ] **名** 墨水匣

對話情境 2 新人報到

A : Good morning, Mr. Lake.

B : Good morning, Ms. Green. Welcome to your first day in our company. Joanna will **introduce** you to the team.

A : Thank you very much, Mr. Lake.

B : **Glad** to have you on our team.

A：雷克先生，早。

B：格林小姐，早，歡迎加入本公司。喬安娜將會向團隊介紹你。

A：謝謝你，雷克先生。

B：很高興本團隊多了你一員生力軍。

introduce
[͵ɪntrəˋdjus] **動** 介紹

glad [glæd] **形**
高興的；樂意的

150 MP3 ▶ 069

對話情境 3 公司內規

A : Hi, I'll be **assisting** you with your training **assignment**.

B : Hi, nice to meet you. So where should we start?

A : Well, you've got to learn about our **practices**. We have rules for everything in this company.

B : Oh. That's interesting.

A : Don't worry. I am just talking about the rules for handling customers. We like to make sure that our customers are happy here.

A：你好，我會協助你進行訓練工作。

B：很高興認識你，我們該從哪裡開始呢？

A：你要先了解我們的執業方式。公司裡的每個環節都有規矩的。

B：喔，挺有趣的。

A：別擔心，我是說對於處理客戶的規矩，我們希望確保客戶的滿意度。

assist [ə`sɪst] 動
協助；支持
assignment
[ə`saɪnmənt] 名 任務；
工作
practice [`præktɪs]
名 慣例；練習

對話情境 4 巧遇主管

A : Could you show me the accounting department?

B : Sure. Are you new here?

A : I've just joined as the **payroll clerk**. I need to meet the **CFO**.

B : Well, it's good that I ran into you here. I am the CFO.

A : Really? Nice to meet you, Ma'am.

A：可否請您告訴我會計部怎麼走？

B：當然，你是新來的嗎？

A：我是剛加入擔任發放薪資的人員，需要拜見財務長。

B：那我在這邊遇到你還真好，我就是財務長。

A：真的？很高興見到您，長官。

payroll [`pe.rol] 名
薪水帳冊
clerk [klɜk] 名
職員；記帳員
**CFO (Chief
Financial Officer)**
縮 財務部長

151

Unit 24 基本電話禮儀
Basic phone etiquette

便利三句開口說

Hello, this is Susan Chang calling.
▶ 你好，我是張蘇珊。

替換句▶ Hello, it's Susan Chang. 嗨，我是張蘇珊。

✓ **句型提點** Using It Properly!

講電話時，因為電話中只能聽見聲音而不見其人，故用 This is 開頭，表示自己的身分，而不用 I am... 或 My name is...。

. . . .

Thank you for calling ABC Corp. Carol speaking. How can I help you?
▶ 感謝您來電 ABC 公司，我是凱倫。請問您需要什麼協助呢？

替換句▶ You've reached ABC Corp. How may I be of help to you? 這裡是 ABC 公司，能幫您什麼樣的忙呢？

✓ **句型提點** Using It Properly!

接電話時，可用「人名 +speaking」告訴來電者自己是誰。如同第一句便利句，因只聞其聲不見其人，故不用 I am...，也不用 My name is...。

. . . .

May I speak with Mr. Wang, please?
▶ 請找王先生。

替換句▶ Would Mr. Wang be available? 王先生方便講電話嗎？

✓ **句型提點** Using It Properly!

當對方接起電話，禮貌性的開場可以用「May I

152 🎧 MP3 ▶ 070

speak with 某人 , please?」，介係詞 with 後接要找的對象。回答時可說 This is he/she. What's it about? 我就是，有什麼事嗎？

有來有往的必備回應

自我介紹

Q Hello, this is Susan Chang calling.

Could you please repeat your name? *A*

能不能請你再說一次姓名？

日常雜務

Q Thank you for calling ABC Corp. Carol speaking. How can I help you?

May I speak to anyone from the accounting department? *A*

可否幫我轉會計部？

職場應對

Q May I speak with Mr. Wang, please?

I'll put you through. Please hold. *A*

我幫您轉接，請稍等。

休閒娛樂

小知識補給站　　Some Fun Facts

　　撥打一通電話可概括為三大部分：問候、報出自己的身分、詢問問題。若欲尋找的對象不在，可以請代接者留言，留下自己的姓名、電話、詢問事項；等待轉接時，對方會請你 hold，表示等一下、先別掛斷電話。代接別人的電話時，則應詢問來電者姓名，並告知對方自己是誰，再請對方留言。若透過電話推銷產品，則要注意地域，和美國相比，歐洲較難接受長時間用電話談生意。此外還要注意撥打時間，如美國人通常不會在晚上九點半後打電話。

出國旅遊

愛情來了

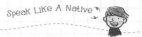
01 May I speak with Olivia Morgan, please?

麻煩找奧莉薇雅‧摩根。

02 Please hold, and I'll put you through to his/her office.

請稍等，我為您轉接。 put...through 為…接通電話

03 Hello, Mr. Lin, I've got Michelle Watson on the phone for you. Are you going to take this?

哈囉，林先生，蜜雪兒‧華生在線上說要找你，你現在方便接嗎？

04 All of our operators are busy at this time. Please hold for the next available person.

所有的接線生都在忙線中，請稍候，我們將盡快為您服務。

05 I'm afraid he's stepped out. Would you like to leave a message?

很不巧，他剛剛離開辦公室，您要不要留言呢？

step out 暫時外出

06 I'm sorry, Lisa's not here at the moment. Can I ask who's calling?

很抱歉，麗莎現在不在，請問您哪裡找？

07 I've written down your message and your name. Would you mind spelling your last name for me?

我將您的訊息及姓名都記下了，能否麻煩您再拼一次您的姓氏？

08 I'll make sure she gets the message.

我會確保她有收到留言。 message 口信；訊息

09 Can you tell him his wife called, please?

能否請你告訴他，他老婆來電呢？

10 That's okay. I'll call back later.

沒關係，我晚點再打一次。

⑪ It's James from Yoyo Inc. When do you expect her back in the office?

我是優優公司的詹姆士，她大概什麼時候會回辦公室呢？

Inc. = incorporated 股份有限公司

⑫ Could you ask him to call his mom when he gets in?

可不可以請他進公司的時候，打電話給他母親？

⑬ Do you have a pen handy? I don't think he has my number.

你現在方便抄嗎？我想他應該沒有我的電話號碼。

handy 手邊的；近便的

⑭ My number is 222-3456, extension 12.

我的電話是 222-3456，分機 12。extension 電話分機

⑮ Sorry, wrong number.

抱歉，我打錯了。

⑯ The signal is breaking up. Can you call me back later?

訊號不穩定，你能否晚點再回電給我？ call back 回電

⑰ I have another call coming through. I'd better run.

我有插撥，得先掛了。 come through 接通

⑱ Well, I guess I'd better get going. Talk to you soon.

嗯，我想我得先掛電話了，我們再聊。 get going 出發

⑲ Thanks for calling. Bye for now.

謝謝來電，先這樣。

⑳ I have to let you go.

我得掛電話了。（禮貌的講法，意思是不佔用對方時間，好讓對方掛電話去做別的事。）

㉑ Hello. You've reached 222-6789. Please leave a detailed message after the beep. Thank you.

您好，這裡是 222-6789 的電話，請在嗶聲後留下詳細的留言，謝謝。

155

雙人實境對話

對話情境 ① 基本辦公室電話對應

Ⓐ：Hello, you've reached ABC Corp. How can I help you?

Ⓑ：Yes, can I speak to Rosa Wilson, please?

Ⓐ：Who's calling, please?

Ⓑ：It's Richard Davis here.

Ⓐ：**Certainly. Please hold, and I'll put you through.**

A：您好，這裡是 ABC 公司，請問有什麼事？
B：是，請找蘿莎·威爾森。
A：請問您哪裡找？
B：我是李察·戴維斯。
A：好的。請稍等，我幫您轉接。

certainly [`sɜtənlɪ] 圖 當然；可以

hold [hold] 圖 保持；握著（此指不要掛斷電話）

put sb. through 圖 替某人轉接電話

對話情境 ② 請幫我留言

Ⓐ：Hello, ABC Company.

Ⓑ：Hi, this is Janet from AT&T. May I speak with Alex, please?

Ⓐ：He's in a meeting right now. Would you like to **leave a message**?

Ⓑ：Yes. Can you have Alex **call me back** when he is available?

Ⓐ：Certainly. I'll **make sure** he gets the message.

A：您好，這裡是 ABC 公司。
B：你好，我是 AT&T 的珍妮特，請問亞力士在嗎？
A：他現在正在開會，您要留言嗎？
B：好，請亞力士有空的時候回我個電話。
A：好的，我會替您轉達。

leave a message 圖 留言

call sb. back 圖 回電給某人

make sure 圖 確定

對話情境 ③ 打錯電話

A : Hi, this is Mason. May I talk to Patricia?
B : There's no one here by that name.
A : Um, is this 2555-9999?
B : No. You dialed the wrong number.
A : Sorry about that.

A：哈囉，我是梅森，請問派翠西亞在嗎？
B：這裡沒有這個人。
A：喔，請問這裡電話是 2555-9999 嗎？
B：不是，你打錯電話了。
A：不好意思。

by name 名叫…
dial [`daɪəl] 撥號

對話情境 ④ 收訊不良

A : Hello, hello, still there? Can you hear me?
B : Um, I'm sorry. There seems to be some problem with our connection.
A : Do you want me to call you back later?
B : No, it's fine. Could you repeat what you just said?
A : OK. Here it comes.

A：哈囉，哈囉，還在嗎？聽得到嗎？
B：很抱歉，我覺得線路有點問題。
A：要不要我晚點再打來？
B：不用，沒關係，可不可以請你再重覆一次剛剛講的事情？
A：好，聽好了。

seem [sim] 似乎；看起來好像
connection [kə`nɛkʃən] 連接
repeat [rɪ`pit] 重說；重複

Part 1 自我介紹
Part 2 日常雜務
Part 3 職場應對
Part 4 休閒娛樂
Part 5 出國旅遊
Part 6 愛情來了

157

會議大小事
Attending meetings

便利三句開口說

We're here today to discuss the marketing campaign.
▶ 我們今天開會的目的是要討論行銷活動。

替換句 I called this meeting to discuss the marketing campaign. 我之所以召開本次會議，是為了討論行銷活動。

✓ **句型提點** **Using It Properly!**

「人名 / 代名詞 +be 動詞 +here+to+ 動詞」，to 後面接「目的」，表示某人於此時此地要進行某事；在集會上，發表演說者經常用此句型表明目的。

- -

First, let's go over the report from the last meeting.
▶ 首先，我們先來瀏覽一下上次的會議紀錄。

替換句 Here are the minutes from our last meeting. 這是上次的會議紀錄。

✓ **句型提點** **Using It Properly!**

片語 go over 指從頭瀏覽到尾；用使役動詞 Let's 開頭，表達邀請、建議。要注意使役動詞後面的動詞，一定是接原形動詞。

- -

Shall we get down to business?
▶ 是否就進入正題了呢？

替換句 I'd like to move on to today's topic. 我想要進入今天會議的主題。

☑ ➥ 句型提點 ◁ **Using It Properly!**

用 shall 當問句的開頭，表示禮貌性地徵求意見。
shall 常常用於未來式，並且僅限於用在第一人稱，
也常會出現在正式的規章中。

💬 **有來有往的必備回應**

Q　We're here today to discuss the marketing
campaign.

> Let me summarize the main points of　*A*
> the last meeting.
>
> 讓我概述一下上次會議的重點。

Q　First, let's go over the report from the last
meeting.

> Excuse me, but I haven't received a　*A*
> copy of the report yet.
>
> 不好意思，但是我還沒有拿到紀錄的影本。

Q　Shall we get down to business?

> > Yes, please.　*A*
> >
> > 好的，麻煩你了。

💡 **小知識補給站**　Some Fun Facts

　　常見的會議說法有：conference 為大型會議，
通常為期多日；meeting 指小型會議，像是公司內部
的會議與討論；seminar 具學術性質，與會人數不多，
能與講者有較多互動；在 symposium 則會有專業人
士演講，並提供食物或飲料；congress 則偏向政治
商或專業領域的大型正式會議。

159

01 We're pleased to welcome the new vice president to say a few words before we get started.
在會議開始前，我們很榮幸邀請到新任副總裁來說幾句話。

02 Who will be the chair of the meeting?
誰要當這次會議的主席？ chair 會議的主席

03 I skimmed over the document before the meeting.
我已經在開會前瀏覽過這份文件了。 skim over 瀏覽；略讀

04 By the end of this meeting, I'd like to have a tangible conclusion.
會議結束前，我希望能有具體的結論。
tangible 明確的；實際的

05 I'm afraid Dr. Lee can't be with us today. She is doing research overseas at this time.
李博士目前在海外做研究，她今天恐怕沒辦法參與了。

06 Sandra, can you tell us how the charity project is progressing?
珊卓，可否請你告訴我們慈善計畫目前進行到哪個階段？

07 There are three items on the agenda.
今日議程有三件事項要討論。 agenda 議程；待議事項

08 We don't have all day, so could you please cut to the chase?
我們的時間不多，所以請講重點。 cut to the chase 切入正題

09 So, if there is nothing else we need to discuss, let's move on to today's agenda.
如果沒有其他需要討論的，我們就直接進行今天的議程。

10 Let's brainstorm about some solutions.
我們一起腦力激盪出解決方案吧。
brainstorm 腦力激盪；集思廣益

11 Elsa has agreed to take the minutes.

艾莎同意當會議紀錄。 minutes 會議紀錄

⑫ We will hear a short report on each point first, followed by a discussion round the table.
針對每件要項，我們會先聽簡報，然後才是與會的討論。

⑬ We'll have to keep each item to ten minutes. Otherwise we'll never get through.
每項報告請控制在十分鐘之內，不然我們會討論不完。

⑭ I don't see eye to eye with Sherry on this matter.
針對這個議題，我跟雪莉的意見不合。
see eye to eye with... 與…看法一致

⑮ I think we can leave this point aside for now.
我想我們可以先將這點擱著，晚點再討論。
leave aside 不考慮

⑯ We may need to vote on item 5 if we can't get a unanimous decision.
如果我們沒有辦法達成一致的決定，我們就必須針對議案 5 投票表決。 unanimous 一致同意的

⑰ Let's come back to this point at the end.
我們最後再回來討論這一點。 come back 回來

⑱ Before we close, let me just summarize the main points.
結束前，讓我將要點做個總整理。 summarize 總結

⑲ It looks as though we've covered the main items. Is there any other business?
看起來我們每一點都討論到了，還有什麼事項要處理嗎？

⑳ Can we fix the date for the next meeting, please?
可不可以敲定下次的會議時間呢？ fix 確定；決定

㉑ The next meeting will be on Wednesday, the third of June in this same room.
下次會議就在這個地點，時間是六月三號，星期三。

㉒ Thank you all for attending.
感謝各位參與會議。 attend 出席；參加

自我介紹 Part 1

日常雜務 Part 2

職場應對 Part 3

休閒娛樂 Part 4

出國旅遊 Part 5

愛情來了 Part 6

161

雙人實境對話 ◆ oh!

對話情境 ① 確認會議時間及主題

Ⓐ: We're having a meeting tomorrow. Can you make it?

Ⓑ: When is it taking place?

Ⓐ: We're planning on 10 o'clock. Is that OK?

Ⓑ: Yes, that'll be fine.

Ⓐ: We're going to go over last quarter's sales figures.

A：我們明天要開會，你有辦法參加嗎？
B：幾點開始？
A：我們預計從上午十點開始，可以嗎？
B：可以，時間沒問題。
A：我們將討論上一季的銷售額。

take place 發生；舉行

quarter [`krɔrtɚ] 名 一季；四分之一

figure [`fɪgjɚ] 名 金額；數量

對話情境 ② 會議前的回顧

Ⓐ: I assume that everyone has a copy of the agenda of today's meeting?

Ⓑ: Sorry, chairman, but I think there are some latecomers.

Ⓐ: In that case, I'd like to ask you to skim over the minutes of the previous meeting first.

Ⓑ: Could we quickly go over the conclusion of the last meeting just to keep in the loop?

Ⓐ: Sure, let's do that.

A：我想每個人都有拿到今天會議的議程吧？
B：抱歉，主席，我想有些人還沒到。
A：既然這樣，我想請你們先瀏覽上次的會議紀錄。
B：請問能否快速地講一遍上次會議的結論，好進入狀況？
A：當然可以，就這麼辦。

assume [ə`sjum] 動 認為；假定

latecomer [`let.kʌmɚ] 名 遲到者

keep in the loop 得知相關資訊

對話情境 ③ 會議中介紹成員

A : I'd like you to join me in welcoming Robert Dickenson, our **northeast** area sales **vice** president.

B : Thank you. I'm looking forward to today's meeting.

A : I'd also like to introduce Jessica Quinn, who recently joined our team.

B : May I also introduce my **assistant**, Bob Thompson.

A : Well, since everyone is here, we should **get started**.

A：我想請各位跟我一同歡迎羅伯‧狄克森，我們東北區的業務副總裁。

B：謝謝大家，我很期待今天的會議。

A：我也想藉此機會，介紹最近加入我們團隊的潔西卡‧昆恩。

B：同時我也介紹一下我的助理，包柏‧湯普森。

A：既然人都到齊了，就開始開會吧。

northeast
[`nɔrθ`ist] 形 東北的

vice [vaɪs] 形 副的

assistant
[ə`sɪstənt] 名 助理

get started 片 開始

對話情境 ④ 會議紀錄

A : Before we go into details, I'd like to ask Danny to **lead** point 1. Will someone take the notes?

B : I'll do it.

A : Be sure to **record** all the results and conclusions.

B : Shall I email the notes to all the **attendees** later?

A : Not before I check them.

A：進入詳細的報告之前，我想要請丹尼主持第一點，誰願意幫忙做紀錄？

B：我來。

A：記得要紀錄所有的結果跟結論。

B：會議紀錄之後要寄發給所有與會的人員嗎？

A：在給我檢查之後才寄。

lead [lid] 動 帶領

record [rɪ`kɔrd] 動 記錄

attendee [ə`tɛndi] 名 出席者

便利三句開口說

I need to get an estimate before deciding to place an order.

▶ 我要先拿到估價單，才會決定是否下單。

替換句 I need to know the quoted price before I make the purchase. 我需要知道報價才能下訂。

✓ → **句型提點** Using It Properly!

片語 place an order 意指下訂單。before 連接兩個有時間順序的句子，要注意前後兩句時態須一致，且 before 之後的句子須用現在式或接動詞 V-ing 形式。

This price is way beyond my budget.

▶ 這價錢超出我預算太多了。

替換句 The price is above my limit. 價格超出我的限度。

✓ → **句型提點** Using It Properly!

片語 way beyond 指遠遠超出，後面可加名詞。例：The movie was way beyond my expectations. 這部電影遠超出我的預期。

Do you ship door-to-door?

▶ 你們有幫忙送貨到府嗎？

替換句 Can you deliver to the designated address? 你可以運送到指定地點嗎？

✓ → **句型提點** Using It Properly!

door-to-door 在國際貨運業方面，就是從發貨人工廠或倉庫發貨，貨品清關後，送至收貨人指定配送地點，通常有包含進出口的手續。

有來有往的必備回應

Q　I need to get an estimate before deciding to place an order.

> You'll have it by the end of the week. *A*

這禮拜會給你（估價單）。

Q　This price is way beyond my budget.

> It's the best I can offer. *A*

這是我能給的最低價了。

Q　Do you ship door-to-door?

> Yes, all shipments are door-to-door. *A*

是，我們所有的運送都送貨到府的。

小知識補給站

Some Fun Facts

　　敲定生意的方式各有特色，而酒吧早已成為美國人談生意的場所選擇之一，但在挑選合適的酒吧時，必須注意店內的氣氛，例如：最好是挑有隱私的座位或包廂來談生意、周遭可有適度的交談聲、不過於暗的燈光、合宜的裝飾…等等，如果酒吧的酒單符合對象的國籍和習慣，當然更好，甚至於在點單時，也可以適度地配合對方；與客戶建立良好的關係，為談生意的其中一項基礎，在酒吧的放鬆氣氛裡，也有幫助建立信任感；在談生意時，當然也需要注意措辭，不宜過度謙卑或不禮貌，許多專業術語也須事先熟知，以顯示專業度。

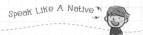
01 **I'd like to place an order for a number of your standard bookshelves.**
我想要下訂單購買你們的標準型書櫃。
place an order 下訂單

02 **How many are you interested in ordering for purchase?**
你想要下訂多少量呢？ purchase 買；購買

03 **I need to know the quantity before quoting you a more precise price.**
在提供報價給你之前，我需要知道確切的下訂量。
quote 報價；開價 precise 精確的

04 **The price is not what I expected. Is there any way that you could lower it?**
這價錢跟我預期的有出入，你可以再降價嗎？ lower 降下

05 **Where are your products manufactured?**
你們的商品是在哪裡生產的？ manufacture 製造

06 **Do you have many available in the warehouse?**
你倉庫裡的現貨還有很多嗎？ warehouse 倉庫

07 **I keep a large supply in stock.**
我存有大量現貨。 in stock 有庫存；有現貨

08 **What does the estimate include?**
這個報價包含哪些項目？ estimate 估價；估計

09 **Estimates include merchandise, packaging and shipping, duty if required, any taxes and insurance.**
這個報價包含商品單價、包裝、運送費，若有稅金也會記載，還有保險費用。 duty 稅；關稅

10 **Delivery dates depend on your location, but we can usually deliver within fourteen business days.**

送達日期端看你的所在地而定，但我們通常在十四個工作天內會送達。

⑪ **I'm concerned about the delays we're experiencing with some of our suppliers.**
我對於最近供應商交貨的延期感到擔憂。 `supplier 供應商`

⑫ **What type of logistical structure do you have?**
你們的物流配送的方式為何？ `logistical 物流的`

⑬ **What type of distribution services do you provide?**
你們提供什麼型態的配送服務？ `distribution 分配；分發`

⑭ **We distribute to both wholesale and retail outlets.**
我們的配送從批發端到零售端都有。 `retail 零售的`

⑮ **The bill of lading lists the merchandise shipped. It's included with every shipment or delivery.**
海運提單列出了運送的商品清單，每次運送都一定會附上。
`bill of lading 提貨單；貨運單`

⑯ **What are the terms of your payment?**
你們的付款條件為何？ `term 條件；條款`

⑰ **The payment terms are 90-day net.**
付款條件是貨到九十天付清。

⑱ **Our attorney is still going through the terms and conditions.**
我們的法務正在審核合約條款。 `condition 條件`

⑲ **We both see eye to eye on this agreement.**
我們雙方對於這份合約的看法相同。

⑳ **Deal! Let's sign a contract.**
一言為定！簽約吧。 `sign a contract 簽合約`

㉑ **It's a two-year contract. We need to be extra careful before signing it.**
這是個為期兩年的合約，我們簽約之前一定要格外謹慎。

167

對話情境 1 訂購文具

A: I need to order some more supplies. I need three **dozen** ballpoint pens, as well as six black markers.

B: Did you want six dozen black markers or six?

A: Oh, it was six each.

B: Would you like this order delivered, or will you pick it up?

A: Please deliver it to our **headquarters** and send it **COD**.

A：我還需要訂購文具。我要三打原子筆，六支黑色麥克筆。

B：你的麥克筆是要六打還是六支？

A：喔，六支。

B：商品需要配送嗎？還是自取呢？

A：麻煩送到我們總公司，貨到付款。

dozen [`dʌzn] 名
一打

headquarters
[`hɛd`kwɔrtɚz] 名
總部

COD (Cash On Delivery) 縮
貨到付款

對話情境 2 訂單殺價

A: I am not sure I am satisfied with the price you **quoted**.

B: It's not the first time we have done business together. You know that's the best I can **offer**.

A: What do you say if we increase the purchase **quantity** to thirty thousand pieces?

B: I will get back to you with a new price tomorrow.

A: That's what I'm talking about!

A：我不太滿意你給我的報價。

B：我們又不是第一次合作，你知道我已經給你很多優惠了。

A：如果我們將訂單量增加到三萬件呢？

B：我明天會重新擬一份報價單給你。

A：這才像話！

quote [kwot] 動
報價；引用

offer [`ɔfɚ] 動 開價；
提供

quantity
[`kwɑntətɪ] 名 數量

對話情境 3 email 訂購

A: I am attracted to some of the items in your catalogue.

B: Do you need any samples before purchasing?

A: It's not necessary. How do I place the order?

B: You can email the service account printed on the cover of the catalogue. We will handle the order as soon as the email is received.

A: OK, that sounds convenient.

A：我對你們型錄上的一些產品有興趣。
B：購買前您需要看樣品嗎？
A：不需要，我要怎麼下訂呢？
B：您可以寄電子郵件到型錄封面所標示的地址，我們會在收到信後立即處理訂單。
A：了解，聽起來滿便利的。

catalogue
[`kætəlɔg] 名 型錄
sample [`sæmpl]
名 試用品
as soon as 片
一…就…

對話情境 4 付款條件

A: We'd like to order three cartons of watermelons and please have them delivered tomorrow.

B: We only accept half the total payment as a deposit and the balance is paid off within fifteen days.

A: Can the payment terms be more flexible?

B: Sorry. It's agricultural produce we are dealing with here.

A: Alright, I understand.

A：我們想要訂購三箱西瓜，請於明天出貨。
B：我們只接受先預付一半的訂金，而且尾款要在十五天內付清。
A：付款條件能再有彈性一些嗎？
B：抱歉，這些是農產品呢。
A：好吧，我了解。

carton [`kɑrtn̩] 名
一箱；紙盒
deposit [dɪ`pɑzɪt]
名 訂金
balance [`bæləns]
名 尾款；結餘
pay off 片 付清

Part 1 自我介紹

Part 2 日常雜務

Part 3 職場應對

Part 4 休閒娛樂

Part 5 出國旅遊

Part 6 愛情來了

便利三句開口說

What kind of benefits does the company offer?
▶ 公司提供什麼樣的福利？

替換句 Are the benefits at your new job any good?
你新公司的福利好嗎？

✓ **句型提點** Using It Properly!

「What kind of+ 名詞 +do/does+ 子句」用來詢
問後方子句具體的種類為何。例：What kind of
service does the company provide? 這間公司提
供什麼類型的服務？

Do I get any bonus?
▶ 我會得到分紅嗎？

替換句 Is there any year-end bonus? 有年終獎金嗎？

✓ **句型提點** Using It Properly!

「Do/does+ 人名 / 代名詞 +get+any+bonus」用
來詢問會不會有分紅。bonus 為名詞，意指分紅、
額外的收穫；get 為得到；any (任何) 則常用於疑
問句或否定句中。

The company covers labor and health insurance.
▶ 公司提供勞健保。

替換句 Labor and health insurance are included in
the benefit plan. 勞健保包含在福利制度中。

✓ **句型提點** **Using It Properly!**

cover 有許多意思，而在此句意為涵蓋，可以想像保險就像是一把無形的保護傘，將我們覆蓋在裡面。

有來有往的必備回應

Q What kind of benefits does the company offer?

A We cover health and labor insurance.

我們提供勞健保。

Q Do I get any bonus?

A It depends on the increase of company's profits.

這要視公司的獲利成長情況而定。

Q The company covers labor and health insurance.

A Is there any other medical insurance included?

還有包含其他的醫療保險嗎？

小知識補給站　Some Fun Facts

美國是已開發國家中唯一一個把帶薪假期作為一項額外福利、而非員工基本權利的國家，所以像是年假有多少天，必須跟雇主先談好。此外，美國的企業常提供的額外福利還包括住房補助、養老金、教育培訓計畫、及醫療保險。員工福利方面，最令人眼紅的不外乎 Google，內部設立遊戲室、健身房、且父母都有育嬰假…等等，以人至上的工作文化，讓員工能更好地發揮自己的創意。

171

01 **I will take a day off tomorrow.**
我明天要請一天假。 take a day off 請假休息一天

02 **June is taking her maternity leave now and won't be back in the office until next month.**
瓊恩現在正在請產假，下個月才會回公司。
maternity 產婦的；孕婦的

03 **The law in Taiwan requires employers to provide employees with certain benefits, such as labor and health insurance.**
台灣法律規定雇主要提供員工基本福利，例如勞保及健保。

04 **Health insurance is an important benefit; it is less expensive through the employer at group rates than when taking it out on one's own.**
健保是個很重要的福利，公司團體加保的費率會比單一人加保來得實惠。 rate 費率；費用

05 **Joey is a salesman who gets a minimum wage plus some commission.**
喬伊是個領基本薪資外加佣金的業務員。
minimum wage 基本薪資

06 **I think my company is offering a good benefits package.**
我認為我公司的福利制度很好。 benefit 利益；津貼

07 **Our company offers free, unlimited training courses to all the full-time employees.**
公司提供所有正職員工免費的訓練課程，不限次數。
unlimited 無限量的

08 **I think we have a health and dental plan.**
我記得我們有提供健保以及牙醫保險。 dental 牙科的

09 **We provide paid vacations for full-time employees who have been in the company over five years.**

對於年資超過五年的正職員工，公司提供有薪假給他們。

⑩ Should the employee become ill or have an accident, his or her medical treatment is adequately covered.
若有員工生病或發生意外，他 / 她的部分醫療費用將由保險負擔。 `adequately 足夠地；適當地`

⑪ Many US employers now help cover the expense of childcare facilities in their communities.
許多美國的雇主現在都會協助支付社區內兒童保育設施的費用。 `childcare 兒童保育；兒童照管`

⑫ Another important benefit our company offers is flextime, which allows the employees to vary their working hours, within limits, each day.
我們公司另外一項重要的福利就是提供彈性工作時間，讓員工可以在一定的限度內，調整自己每天的工作時段。
`flextime 彈性工作時間` `vary 變更；修改`

⑬ Employees with flextime tend to be happier at work.
享有彈性工時的員工上班時的心情會比較愉悅。
`tend to 傾向；易於`

⑭ My cousin's company is offering pension plans that guarantee a fixed monthly sum to retirees.
我表哥的公司提供退休金，保證退休員工每月有定額的退休金可領。 `pension 退休金` `sum 金額`

⑮ There is the stock ownership plan in my company, which permits the employees to buy shares of the company's stock at subsidized prices.
我們公司有員工持股的福利制度，讓員工以補助價認購公司的股票。 `subsidize 補貼；資助`

⑯ When considering an offer, the candidate should examine the benefits offered by the prospective employer.
在考慮是否要接下工作時，應徵者應該要檢視未來雇主所提出的福利。 `prospective 將來的；未來的`

173

對話情境 ① 臨時請假

🅰 : Where is Alice? I haven't seen her all morning.
🅑 : She is taking a day off today.
🅰 : What happened to her? Is everything alright?
🅑 : She called in sick.
🅰 : Oh, I see.

A：愛麗絲呢？一整個早上都沒看到她。
B：她今天請一天假。
A：怎麼了？都還好吧？
B：她臨時打來請病假。
A：喔，我知道了。

happen to 片
使遭遇；發生於
call in sick 片
臨時請病假

對話情境 ② 詢問福利

🅰 : Before ending this interview, are there any questions you might want to ask?
🅑 : I am quite concerned about the company's benefits.
🅰 : Our company covers basic insurance, such as labor and health insurance.
🅑 : How many days of annual leave will I have?
🅰 : You will have a one-week annual leave after your probation period.

A：面試結束前，你有沒有任何問題想問我們？
B：我對於公司的福利滿關心的。
A：我們公司提供基本的保險，例如勞保及健保。
B：我會有幾天的年假？
A：試用期過後，你一年會有七天的年假。

concerned
[kənˋsɝnd] 形 關心的
annual leave 片
年假
probation
[proˋbeʃən] 名 試用期

對話情境 ③ 薪資機密

Ⓐ : What's your starting salary?

Ⓑ : That is rather personal. I'd like to keep it to myself.

Ⓐ : Come on, I am your mom. I have the right to know!

Ⓑ : Let's just say that I get the minimum wage plus commission and year-end bonus.

Ⓐ : Sounds promising!

A：你的起薪是多少？
B：這個問題很私人，我不想告訴別人。
A：拜託，我是你媽耶，我有權利知道！
B：反正就是基本薪資加佣金，再加上年終啦。
A：聽起來大有可為喔！

commission
[kə`mɪʃən] 名 佣金

year-end bonus
片 年終獎金

promising
[`prɑmɪsɪŋ] 形 有前途的

對話情境 ④ 辦公室硬體福利

Ⓐ : Where do you normally work out?

Ⓑ : I usually work out at my office if I arrive early.

Ⓐ : At your office? Or near your office?

Ⓑ : We have a state-of-the-art gym on the top floor of my company.

Ⓐ : Wow, I envy you!

A：你通常在哪裡健身？
B：如果提早進公司，我通常會在公司運動。
A：你是指在公司裡，還是公司附近啊？
B：我們公司頂樓有一個頂級的健身房。
A：哇，真羨慕你！

state-of-the-art
[`stetəvðɪ`ɑrt] 形 最先進的

envy [`ɛnvɪ] 動 忌妒；羨慕

175

職場甘苦談

Promotions and layoffs

 便利三句開口說

I got a promotion last week.
▶ 我上禮拜升官了。

替換句▶ I was promoted last week. 我上禮拜升官了。

☑ ➔ 句型提點 ◀ Using It Properly!

promotion 為名詞，意為提拔，常搭配動詞 get，故
get a promotion 是指在職場上受到提拔、升官。be
promoted 也指被升官、升職，而此處的 promote
為動詞。

Dan got laid off because of the downsizing.
▶ 因為縮編，丹被解雇了。

替換句▶ Dan was let go because of the downsizing.
因為縮編，丹被解雇了。

☑ ➔ 句型提點 ◀ Using It Properly!

get laid off 指被解雇；downsizing 為企業縮編。
because of 可以顯示前後句子的因果關係，前面加
有一般動詞的完整句子 (結果)，後面加上名詞 (原
因)。

I don't know how to ask for a raise.
▶ 我不知道該怎麼要求加薪。

替換句▶ I have no clue as to how to negotiate a
raise. 我不知道該怎麼談加薪。

☑ ➔ 句型提點 ◀ Using It Properly!

片語 ask for 指要求、索取某樣東西或事情。若想加

上是向「誰」請求，可在 ask 後面加上請求對象，變成「ask + 某人 + for + 某事 / 物」。

 有來有往的必備回應

Q I got a promotion last week.

This is great news! *A*

這真是好消息！

Q Dan got laid off because of the downsizing.

That's too bad. *A*

太糟糕了。

Q I don't know how to ask for a raise.

You need to plan ahead what you are going to address. *A*

你必須事先計劃要說的內容。

 小知識補給站

　　若想要加薪，不妨列出自己過去在公司的成就，提出具體的數據 (statistics)、業績成長 (sales increase)、同性質的工作薪水範圍…等等，來證明自己的能力，並且尋找適當的時間點提出要求，來增加升遷的機會。而升職相關用語除了 promotion 之外，也可以用 advancement 表示，pay raise 則為加薪。相反地，雖然大家都不樂見被減薪 (pay cut)、降職 (demotion)，也可以先反思自己的缺點，並適時改進，藉機增加自己的專業度。

自我介紹

日常雜務

職場應對

休閒娛樂

出國旅遊

愛情來了

01 I want to move up the corporate ladder.

我想要在公司沿職務位階晉升。 corporate 公司的

02 A high position means more responsibility. Are you sure you're ready for that?

職位愈高，責任愈重，你確定你準備好了嗎？

03 I hope I will be able to cope with all the new responsibilities.

我希望自己能處理之後所要面臨的新責任。
cope with 處理；解決

04 Sometimes being promoted doesn't guarantee you a raise.

有時候升官不代表加薪。 promote 晉升

05 Being a supervisor means building a good team where members work well with each other.

擔任主管意味著要建立好的團隊，讓成員們能良好地與彼此共事。

06 Before bringing up the subject of a raise to your boss, it is best to consider if the department is currently functioning well.

在跟老闆談加薪前，最好先考量你的部門現階段是否運作良好。

07 How long has it been since your last pay increase?

你上次加薪是多久以前的事？ pay increase 加薪

08 As an employee, you sometimes need to ask yourself whether you are worth the price the company pays.

身為員工，你有時該想想自己是否無愧於你領的薪水。

09 Rosa didn't succeed in asking for a raise because she didn't request a meeting with her manager and caught him off guard.

蘿莎要求加薪未果，因為她沒有事先跟經理安排面談，反而冒失地去找他。 `catch sb. off guard 使某人措手不及`

⑩ Our company is facing a financial crisis, so you have no grounds to ask for a raise.
我們公司面臨財務危機，所以你沒有要求加薪的理由。

⑪ May I apply to be transferred to another department?
我可否要求轉調其他部門？ `transfer 調任；調動`

⑫ This is my old business card. I just got transferred to another department.
這是我之前的名片，我才剛轉調至新部門。

⑬ Due to the organizational restructuring, I have to let go some of the senior employees.
由於組織重整，我必須要請一些資深的員工離開公司。

⑭ Layoffs are extremely tough because they can happen to loyal and productive employees who have done nothing wrong.
資遣很難，因為有些忠誠、有產能又沒做錯事的員工也會受到衝擊。

⑮ My boss needed to tighten the budget since the business had slowed down due to the recession.
因為經濟蕭條導致生意成長緩慢，所以老闆需要縮減開支。

⑯ Steven is now jobless because his former company was forced to liquidate the business.
史蒂芬前一個公司被迫結束營業，所以他目前失業。

⑰ The factory workers are going on a strike because of the overdue wages.
因為工廠積欠的薪水，所以工人們準備罷工。 `strike 罷工`

⑱ Make sure you get your severance pay if you are let go.
若遭解雇，請確保你有拿到資遣費。 `severance pay 遣散費`

⑲ His company is going bankrupt and is being forced to shut down.
他的公司即將破產，而且要被迫關閉。 `shut down 關閉；停工`

179

自我介紹 Part 1

日常雜務 Part 2

職場應對 Part 3

休閒娛樂 Part 4

出國旅遊 Part 5

愛情來了 Part 6

對話情境 ① 要求升官

A : I have been working in this company for over a **decade**. I think it's about time to ask for a promotion.

B : Do you think you've got what it takes to be a supervisor?

A : Sure. Who has better experience than I have?

B : I suggest that you **outline** your point and be **rational**.

A : Thanks for your suggestions. I will.

A：我在這間公司已經服務超過十年了，也該是時候要求升遷了。

B：你覺得你有資格擔任一位主管嗎？

A：當然啦。有誰比我還有經驗呢？

B：我建議你先立個大綱，並且要合情合理。

A：謝謝你的建議，我會的。

decade [`dɛkɛd] 名 十年

outline [`aut. lain] 動 概述

rational [`ræʃən!] 形 有理的；理性的

對話情境 ② 通報好消息

A : I have really good news today.

B : What is your good news?

A : I got a promotion today. You are looking at the new **supervisor** of the marketing **department**.

B : Wow, this is great news! I am so glad for you.

A : I will probably start my new job a week from Monday.

A：我今天有個大好消息。

B：是什麼呢？

A：我今天升官了，你正在跟未來的行銷部主管講話呢！

B：哇，真是個好消息！真為你開心。

A：下週一開始，我可能就要忙新業務了。

supervisor [ˌsupə`vaɪzə] 名 主管；管理人

department [dɪ`pɑrtmənt] 名 （企業）部門

對話情境 3 加薪失敗

A : Boss, got a minute?

B : What is it?

A : It's about my salary. You see, I got so tied up by the house mortgage lately and...

B : I know what you're getting at, but it's not appropriate to bring up a subject like this.

A : Alright, I was just trying my luck.

A：老闆，有空嗎？

B：什麼事？

A：是關於我的薪水，我最近被房貸壓得喘不過氣，所以…

B：我知道你要講什麼，但是突然提這種要求並不妥當。

A：好吧，只是想說說看。

get tied up 片 被纏住；無法脫身

get at 片 試圖說明

bring up 片 提起

try one's luck 片 碰運氣

對話情境 4 進行解雇

A : Boss, you wanted to see me?

B : Yes. It seems to me that you've been coming late recently.

A : Um...guilty as charged.

B : Punctuality is what the company values most. I am afraid I have to let you go.

A : What? Don't I deserve a second chance?

A：老闆，你找我嗎？

B：是的，你最近似乎一直遲到。

A：嗯…我錯了。

B：準時是公司最看重的，很遺憾，我必須請你離開公司。

A：什麼？不能再給我一次機會嗎？

guilty as charged 片 有罪；有過錯

punctuality [ˌpʌŋktʃʊˋælətɪ] 名 準時

let sb. go 片 解雇某人

181

再見了公司
Leaving the company

 便利三句開口說

I want to quit my job.
▶ 我想要辭職了。

替換句▶ I am considering a career change. 我在考慮
轉換跑道。

✓ **➔句型提點** ⟨ Using It Properly! ⟩

quit one's job 指辭職。「人 +want to+ 動詞」是指
某人想要做某事。不定詞（to+ 原形動詞）使用時機
為一句中若有兩個動詞，第二個動詞的形式須用不定
詞；如同此句已出現動詞 want（想要），故後面用
不定詞來表示想要達成的事情。

My colleague is going to retire this week.
▶ 我的同事這禮拜準備要退休。

替換句▶ My colleague is preparing for his retirement.
我同事準備要退休了。

✓ **➔句型提點** ⟨ Using It Properly! ⟩

「人名 / 代名詞 +be+going+to+retire」表示某人即
將要退休。be going to 雖然跟 will 一樣是未來式，
但通常是指已有計畫的決定，且發生時間點是離現在
較近的未來。

I don't know how to write a resignation letter.
▶ 我不知道該怎麼寫辭呈。

替換句▶ Can you show me how to write a resignation
letter? 可否教我怎麼寫辭呈？

☑ ⊃ 句型提點 ⟨ Using It Properly! ⟩

「人名 / 代名詞 +don't/doesn't+know+how+to+動詞」，意即某人不知道該怎麼做或完成某件事情。

例：She doesn't know how to cook. 她不會下廚。

有來有往的必備回應

Q I want to quit my job.

     How come? A

     為什麼？

Q My colleague is going to retire this week.

     Who will be taking over his work after A
     he retires?

     他退休後誰來接他的工作呢？

Q I don't know how to write a resignation letter.

     You can find several references online. A

     你可以在網路上找到範本。

小知識補給站   *Some Fun Facts*

　　人才流動不可避免，若需離職或轉職，一般來說會先口頭告知主管、並提出清楚的辭呈、再來完成交接等事項；離職原因 (reasons for leaving) 也需要話術，並事先做好準備，大部分說法有：組織變動 (organizational changes)、缺乏升遷機會 (lack of advancement)、期望更高的薪資待遇 (better pay)…等，而離職之時最好避免抱怨現任工作，注意禮貌，並以高 EQ 來表達自己的請求，並且別忘了偶爾跟原來的同事聊聊，保留人脈囉。

Part 1 自我介紹
Part 2 日常雜務
Part 3 職場應對
Part 4 休閒娛樂
Part 5 出國旅遊
Part 6 愛情來了

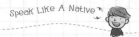
01 I can't stand my boss anymore, so I quit.
我再也無法忍受我老闆，所以辭職了。 `quit 辭職`

02 I have been getting a bit sick and tired of my job recently.
我最近對我的工作逐漸心生厭倦。
`sick and tired of 厭惡；厭倦`

03 I no longer have any passion toward this job anymore.
我對這份工作已經毫無熱忱了。 `passion 熱情`

04 Jimmy is not sure whether she could put up with this unbelievable workload anymore.
吉米不確定自己是否能繼續忍受這難以置信的工作量。
`put up with 忍受` `workload 工作量`

05 I don't get along well with my coworkers and feel like leaving this job.
我跟我的同事處不來，所以想要離職。
`get along well 和睦相處`

06 David finds that he is not cut out for being a salesperson and wants a career change.
大衛發現自己不適合當業務，所以想要轉換跑道。
`be cut out for 適合從事…工作`

07 A new opportunity is being offered and I want to further my career.
有一個新的機會，而我也想藉此更精進我的職涯。
`further 促進；助長`

08 I enjoyed my time here, but I shouldn't pass this opportunity up.
我很喜歡待在這邊的時光，但我不想要錯失這個大好機會。

09 I have a wonderful opportunity to work at a different company. I am putting in my two-week notice.

別家公司提供了一個很棒的工作機會給我，我現在要正式提出辭呈了。

⑩ Most companies would ask for a two-week notice before the resigning employees step down from their positions.
很多公司會要求員工提前兩週告知離職一事。
`step down 辭職`

⑪ You need to give a resignation letter to your current employer.
你需要向現在的雇主提出辭呈。 `resignation 辭職`

⑫ You'll need at least a month to pass down your duties before you leave this job.
在你離職之前，需要至少一個月的時間來交接你的工作。

⑬ He retired at the age of 68.
他在 68 歲的時候退休。 `retire 退休`

⑭ She vacated her position when she got pregnant.
她懷孕的時候就離職了。 `vacate 辭職；離開`

⑮ My supervisor is not yet mentally ready for going into retirement.
我的主管在心態上還沒有準備好要退休。

⑯ The financial consultant topped out at age forty because he was burned out.
那名財務顧問在四十歲就停止晉升，因為他已經身心俱疲。
`top out 不再上升；達到頂點` `burn out 筋疲力竭`

⑰ That publicist resigned over a financial scandal.
那位公關因為一樁金融弊案而辭職。 `resign 辭職`

⑱ My mom left her position with the New York Times.
我媽離開了紐約時報的工作。

⑲ I am very willing to help train a replacement during the transition.
我很樂意協助交接工作給接任者。 `transition 過渡期；轉變`

對話情境 1 茶水間聊離職

A: Hey, just between you and me. I've had it with this job and want to leave ASAP.

B: Hold your horses. It's standard to give a two-week notice.

A: I know. But do you know how to write a resignation letter?

B: I am an expert of writing letters.

A: Great! Let me get a pen and my notebook.

A：跟你講一件事，不要跟別人說，我已經受夠這份工作，想馬上離開。

B：別急，一般來說要提前兩週告知。

A：我知道，但你知道怎麼寫辭呈嗎？

B：我可是寫信專家呢。

A：太好了！我去拿一支筆跟筆記本。

ASAP (As Soon As Possible) 縮 盡快

hold one's horses 慣 別急；等一下

expert [`ɛkspɚt] 名 專家

對話情境 2 與主管談離職

A: Alex, I received an offer from a different company. This is a great opportunity for me, so I accepted it.

B: I see. Is there anything wrong with your current job?

A: My decision has nothing to do with my duties here. I really enjoyed working with you.

A：亞力士，我接到其他公司的邀約，我覺得是相當好的機會，所以我接受了。

B：了解。現在的工作有什麼問題嗎？

A：我的決定跟現在的工作情況無關，我真的很喜歡與你共事。

offer [`ɔfɚ] 名 錄取 通知；提議

duty [`djutɪ] 名 義務；職責

對話情境 3 離職及交接

Ⓐ: I got your resignation letter. You didn't **state** a specific date for leaving.

Ⓑ: I think I can work for another month and wait for a **replacement** to take over.

Ⓐ: OK, it **makes sense**.

Ⓑ: And if you want, I can **train** the new employee.

Ⓐ: Yes, that would be necessary.

A：我收到你的辭呈了，你沒有提到確切的離職時間。

B：我想我可以再待一個月，等接任者接手。

A：嗯，這樣很合理。

B：如果需要的話，我可以幫忙訓練新員工。

A：好，這是需要的。

state [stet] 動 說明

replacement [rɪˋplesmənt] 名 接替者；代替

make sense 片 合理；說得通

train [tren] 動 訓練

對話情境 4 與退休同仁道別

Ⓐ: Henry has been like a father to me, and he is going to retire soon.

Ⓑ: What do you say we hold a **farewell party** for him?

Ⓐ: That's an awesome idea!

Ⓑ: What do you want this party to be like?

Ⓐ: Let's just keep it **warm** and simple.

A：亨利一直像爸爸一樣照顧我，而如今他即將要退休了。

B：我們幫他辦一場歡送會怎麼樣？

A：這主意太棒了！

B：你想要辦什麼樣的派對？

A：辦得溫馨、簡單就好。

farewell party 片 歡送會

warm [wɔrm] 形 熱情的；溫暖的

自我介紹

日常雜務

職場應對

休閒娛樂

出國旅遊

愛情來了

187

Part 4

休閒娛樂
朝 A 咖級玩家邁進

教你貼近、融入國外生活，
不小心就變成半個外國人！

It's my vacation!

* 血拚、運動、放鬆身心，
各種說法看這篇！

名 名詞	動 動詞	形 形容詞
副 副詞	介 介係詞	助 助詞
連 連接詞	限 限定詞	縮 縮寫

Unit 30 百貨公司血拼一場
In the department store

 便利三句開口說

QQ Mall is having a big sale this weekend. Do you want to go?

▶ QQ 百貨這週末有特惠，你想去嗎？

替換句▶ Are you having a sale right now? 你們現在有打折嗎？

✓ ▶句型提點 Using It Properly!

片語 have a big sale 就是舉辦大拍賣的意思，主詞須為商家而非商品。例：The store had a big sale last month to clear old stocks. 那間店上個月有減價大甩賣。

Are you looking for something in particular?

▶ 有特別在找什麼樣的商品嗎？

替換句▶ Can I help you find something or are you just looking? 需要我幫你找什麼嗎？還是你只想先看看？

✓ ▶句型提點 Using It Properly!

片語 look for 意為「尋找」；in particular 的意思為「特定地」，一般放在要強調的字後面。例：Alison likes to read novels, sci-fi in particular. 艾莉森喜歡看小說，特別是科幻小說。

Just browsing.

▶ 只是逛逛。

替換句▶ I am just looking. 我只是看看而已。

自我介紹

✓ **句型提點** **Using It Properly!**

完整句子為 I am just browsing，口語上，只要不致於引起誤解，一般動詞之前的主詞可省略。像此句，就省略了一般動詞 (browse) 之前的主詞及 be 動詞。browse 意指瀏覽，表示隨意看看，並沒有特別要買什麼東西。

日常雜務

有來有往的必備回應

Q QQ Mall is having a big sale this weekend. Do you want to go?

　　　　Sure. I'll go with you. *A*
　　　　好啊，我跟你去。

職場應對

Q Are you looking for something in particular?

　　　　I am looking for the latest running shoes. *A*
　　　　我在找最新的跑步鞋。

Q Just browsing.

　　　　OK. If you need me, just shout! *A*
　　　　好的，如果有什麼需要，就喊一聲吧！

休閒娛樂

小知識補給站

Some Fun Facts

大拍賣中看到 20% off 的標誌，是指從總價去掉 20%，換句話說，就是打八折，可別誤會成打兩折而大買特買囉。美國的折扣季節通常有感恩節、黑色星期五 (感恩節隔日)、聖誕節、元旦等等；而英國特別在聖誕節後的節禮日 (Boxing Day)、夏季的六月以及七月、以及換季清倉才有比較多打折活動。

出國旅遊

愛情來了

191

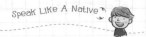
01 Do you have these shoes in size seven?
你這雙鞋有七號的嗎？

02 If you can't find them on the rack, they may be out of stock.
如果你在架上找不到的話，那可能就是沒貨了。
`out of stock 無庫存；無現貨`

03 Let me check in the stockroom first, and I'll be right back.
讓我確認一下庫存，馬上回來。 `stockroom 倉庫`

04 Do you think it's possible to get a discount?
有沒有可能打折呢？ `discount 折扣`

05 If there's a flaw in this vacuum machine, can I return it?
如果吸塵器有瑕疵，我可以退貨嗎？ `return 退回`

06 If a problem with it comes up, you can show it to us and we'll give you a refund.
如果產品有問題，你可以先拿來給我們看，之後我們會退款給你。 `refund 退款`

07 Would you like to use the fitting room to try it on?
你想要去試衣間試穿嗎？ `fitting room 試衣間`

08 There's a discount of 30% on this blouse.
這件女用襯衫打七折。 `blouse 短衫`

09 This jumper goes well with my trousers.
這件針織上衣跟我的褲子很搭。 `jumper 針織上衣`

10 Have you got this in another color?
你這件還有別的顏色嗎？

11 We have a good range of jogging shoes from all the major brands.
我們有各大品牌的全系列慢跑鞋。

⑫ **Shall I gift-wrap it?**
請問要幫您包裝嗎？ gift-wrap 用包裝紙包裝

⑬ **I think I'll take it! It's a bargain.**
我想我會買這個，真的很划算！ bargain 特價商品；便宜貨

⑭ **How would you like to pay?**
您要如何付款呢？

⑮ **Do you take credit cards?**
你們收信用卡嗎？

⑯ **I'm almost maxed out on my credit card, so I think I'll pay with a check.**
我的信用卡快超支了，我會用支票付款。 check 支票

⑰ **You don't happen to have any change, do you?**
您沒有零錢，對吧？ change 零錢；找零

⑱ **That's NT$2,000 altogether.**
總共是新台幣兩千元。 altogether 全部；合計

⑲ **Are you a price-conscious shopper?**
你是個買東西很注意價位的人嗎？
price-conscious 留意價格的

⑳ **The department's annual sale is coming up, and we're expecting a crowd of excited female consumers in the cosmetics section.**
百貨公司的週年慶快要到了，我們預期化妝品區將會有一群興奮的女性消費者聚集。 annual sale 週年慶

㉑ **Don't throw the receipt away too quickly, in case that there's something wrong with the purchase.**
收據不要太早丟掉，以防你買的東西有問題。 receipt 收據
purchase 購買的物品

㉒ **If you don't know your way around a huge department store, ask directions at the information desk on the first floor.**
如果你搞不清楚大型百貨公司內的方位，可以到一樓的服務台詢問。

Part 1 自我介紹

Part 2 日常雜務

Part 3 職場應對

Part 4 休閒娛樂

Part 5 出國旅遊

Part 6 愛情來了

193

雙人實境對話

對話情境 ① 被敲竹槓

🅐 : How much did you pay for it?
🅑 : 200 bucks.
🅐 : 200 bucks for a piece of **junk** like that? That's a **rip-off**!
🅑 : What do you mean?
🅐 : It's not **worth** it. You can get the same item in a supermarket for only 20 bucks!

A：這東西花了你多少錢？
B：兩百塊。
A：用兩百塊買一個這樣的垃圾？真是被坑了！
B：什麼意思？
A：這東西根本不值這個價錢。在超級市場，同樣的東西只賣二十元而已！

junk [dʒʌŋk] 名 垃圾
rip-off 片 剝削；詐騙
worth [wɜθ] 形 值⋯錢的

對話情境 ② 購物諮詢

🅐 : Excuse me. Could you help me?
🅑 : Of course. How can I help you?
🅐 : I am looking for a **sweater**.
🅑 : What **size** do you wear?
🅐 : Medium, I think.

A：不好意思，可以幫我個忙嗎？
B：當然，請問您需要什麼？
A：我想找一件毛衣。
B：您穿什麼尺寸？
A：應該是 M 號。

sweater [`swɛtɚ] 名 毛衣
size [saɪz] 名 尺寸；尺碼

對話情境 ③ 想買圍巾

A : Hi, are you being helped?
B : No, I'm not. I'm interested in some scarves.
A : Let's see. What do you think of this one here? It's made of silk.
B : It looks nice, but I'm looking for something for the winter.
A : Maybe you would like a heavy wool scarf. Let me show you some.

A：您好，請問有人招呼您嗎？
B：沒有，我想看看圍巾。
A：我看看，這件您覺得如何？這是絲製的。
B：看起來不錯，但我想找適合冬天的圍巾。
A：也許您會比較喜歡厚重的羊毛圍巾，我挑幾款給您看看。

scarf [skɑrf] 名 圍巾
be made of 片 由…製成
silk [sɪlk] 名 絲
wool [wʊl] 名 羊毛

對話情境 ④ 人擠人煩死人

A : Let's do some window shopping at the mall this weekend.
B : I'll pass. I can't stand lining up for the elevator.
A : We can take the escalator, silly!
B : Still, it's such a waste of time.
A : I'll go myself then.

A：週末我們去百貨公司逛逛吧！
B：我就不去了，我受不了排隊等電梯。
A：我們可以搭手扶梯啊，傻瓜！
B：我還是覺得很浪費時間。
A：那我自己去好了。

window shopping 片 逛街（通常只是瀏覽商品而無意購買）
line up 片 排隊
escalator [ˋɛskə͵letə] 名 電扶梯

自我介紹

日常雜務

職場應對

休閒娛樂

出國旅遊

愛情來了

195

再戰血拚超級市場

At the supermarket

便利三句開口說

I am going grocery shopping.
▶ 我要去採買了。

替換句 I need to do some shopping. 我需要做些採買。

✓ 句型提點 Using It Properly!

grocery 指食品、日常生活用品;所以買菜或是日用品時,就可以用 go grocery shopping 來表示,其中的動詞 go 須根據採買的時間來調整時態。

Do you go to big supermarkets or small grocery stores?
▶ 你是去大型超市還是小型雜貨店?

替換句 Where do you usually go grocery shopping? 你通常都去哪邊採買?

✓ 句型提點 Using It Properly!

supermarket 為超級市場,通常占地較大、商品較多。而 grocery store 則為雜貨店,通常指位於住宅區附近且較小型的店面,大多為私人經營,雖然規模比較小,但極具便利性。

We are running out of rice.
▶ 我們的米快吃完了。

替換句 I am short of rice. 我現在缺米。

✓ 句型提點 Using It Properly!

片語 run out of 意指用完、耗盡。使用現在進行式可表示「快要用盡」。例:He is running out of money. 他身上快沒錢了。

有來有往的必備回應

Q I am going grocery shopping.

> *A* Get some frozen food for me.
>
> 幫我買些冷凍食品。

Q Do you go to big supermarkets or small grocery stores?

> *A* I shop mostly at big supermarkets.
>
> 基本上，我都在大型超市買。

Q We are running out of rice.

> *A* Be sure to put it on your shopping list.
>
> 記得把這一項放入你的購物清單。

小知識補給站   Some Fun Facts

美國有許多連鎖超市 (supermarket)，而這些超市因為大都設在土地較便宜的郊區，常用大量購買但價格低廉的方式，吸引顧客上門。反之，市區因為寸土寸金，通常有較多小型的雜貨店 (grocery store) 販賣食物、飲料、報紙…等等；市區雖然也有便利商店 (convenience store) 的蹤跡，卻不像台灣 24 小時全天營業，也不一定包含影印、代收繳費等功能，在治安不好的國家，便利商店甚至會僱用保全，以防半夜遭遇歹徒搶劫。另外，大型量販店也可以稱為 hypermarket，占地比 supermarket 更大，商品也更加齊全，讓顧客 次就能在裡面買齊所有需要的東西。

自我介紹 Part 1

日常雜務 Part 2

職場應對 Part 3

休閒娛樂 Part 4

出國旅遊 Part 5

愛情來了 Part 6

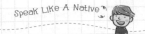
01 **Can you stop by the grocery store on your way home?**

你回家的時候可以順道去一下雜貨店嗎？

grocery store 雜貨店

02 **We're out of soy sauce. Can you run to the nearest grocery store and get some for me?**

我們沒醬油了，你可不可以跑一趟最近的雜貨店，幫我買一瓶？

03 **Please get two loaves of bread and a box of vanilla ice cream.**

請買兩條麵包跟一盒香草冰淇淋。 loaf（一條或一塊）麵包

04 **I am used to bringing my own reusable bags while doing grocery shopping.**

我去採買的時候習慣自己帶環保袋。 reusable 可多次使用的

05 **Do you need a coin to get a shopping cart?**

你需要零錢去拿購物推車嗎？ shopping cart 購物手推車

06 **Look at my shopping list! I guess by the time I get to the cashier, I will probably have a full shopping cart.**

看看我的購物清單！我猜我去結帳時，我的購物車應該會全滿。 cashier 收銀員

07 **You can find milk, dairy and yogurt in the dairy section.**

在奶製品區你可以找到牛奶、乳製品跟優格。

dairy 牛奶製的

08 **Do you have more flour in the back? I see the shelf is empty.**

你們倉庫裡面還有麵粉嗎？我看貨架上都是空的。

shelf 架子；貨架

09 **Where can I find some detergent?**

哪邊可以找到清潔劑？ detergent 洗潔劑

⑩ Can you tell me where the produce section is?

可不可以告訴我生鮮食品區在哪裡？ `produce 農產品`

⑪ Pasta is in aisle 5. Just go straight down and you'll see it.

義大利麵在第五條走道，繼續直走你就會看到了。
`pasta 義大利麵食` `aisle 走道`

⑫ Really sorry, but our canned tuna is out of stock for now.

很抱歉，我們的鮪魚罐頭目前缺貨。 `canned 罐頭裝的`

⑬ Wait for me in the checkout line! I forgot to get some bags of chips.

在結帳隊伍那邊等我！我忘了買洋芋片。 `checkout 結帳`

⑭ Let's go to the express checkout. We are only buying five items.

我們去快速結帳櫃檯吧，我們才買五樣東西。 `express 快的`

⑮ That will be \$100 dollars. How would you like to pay?

一共是 100 元，請問您要怎麼付款？

⑯ Do you need any plastic bags? They cost one cent each.

你需要塑膠袋嗎？一個一分錢。 `plastic 塑膠的`

⑰ Son, place that divider after our items so that the lady behind us can start placing her groceries down, too.

兒子，把分隔棒放在我們買的商品後面，這樣排在我們後面的女士也能把東西放在輸送帶上。 `divider 分隔物`

⑱ If you find any problems with anything you've bought, you have 14 days from today to return them or exchange them for something else.

商品有十四天的鑑賞期，如果這期間有任何問題，您可以拿來退貨或換貨。

⑲ You can have a full refund if you keep your receipt.

如果您有保留收據，就可以全額退款。 `full refund 全額退款`

Part 1 自我介紹
Part 2 日常雜務
Part 3 職場應對
Part 4 休閒娛樂
Part 5 出國旅遊
Part 6 愛情來了

雙人實境對話 〈oh!〉

對話情境 ① 幫忙採買物資

A: I am only **halfway** through my assignment and cannot go to the supermarket.

B: I can do that for you. What do you need?

A: Some toilet paper, **deodorant**, fruits and meat.

B: I need more details.

A: Here's my shopping list.

A：我功課才做了一半，沒辦法去超市買東西。

B：我可以幫你跑一趟，你要買什麼？

A：衛生紙、芳香劑、水果跟肉。

B：我需要商品的詳細資訊。

A：這是我的購物清單。

halfway [`hæf we]
形 中途的

deodorant
[diˋodərənt] 名
除臭劑

對話情境 ② 為週末大菜做準備

A: I will make a **roast** chicken on Sunday. Let's go grocery shopping first.

B: What ingredients do you need?

A: I need to buy a whole chicken, some onions, apples, a **stick** of butter and some fresh **herbs**.

B: What's for dessert?

A: Let's buy some pastries there.

A：我週日要做烤雞，我們先去買菜吧。

B：你需要哪些材料？

A：我需要一隻全雞、一些洋蔥、蘋果、一條奶油跟新鮮香草。

B：那甜點呢？

A：我們就直接在那裡買些糕點吧。

roast [rost] 動 烤

stick [stɪk] 名 棒狀物；枝條

herb [hɝb] 名 香草；藥草

對話情境 3 詢問東西哪裡買

A : Excuse me, where can I find some ketchup?

B : It's in the condiments section in aisle 2. Just go down towards the canned food section first, and then you'll see it on your left side.

A : And do you have any chewing gum?

B : You will find it at the checkout counter.

A : Great, that's convenient.

A：請問，番茄醬在哪裡？
B：在醬料區，第二道道那邊。你可以先往罐頭區走，它會在你的左手邊。
A：你們有賣口香糖嗎？
B：你在結帳櫃檯就可以看到。
A：太好了，真方便。

condiment
[`kɑndəmənt] 名 調味品；佐料

section [`sɛkʃən]
名 部分；區域

checkout [`tʃɛk. aut]
名 收銀台

對話情境 4 排隊等結帳

A : You can go ahead of me. You're just buying a few things.

B : Wow, that's very nice of you.

A : No problem. Besides, my husband is getting some steak at the deli.

B : Oh, that's a bit far. It might take a few minutes given that it's the weekend.

A : Exactly! So, please go ahead.

A：你先吧，你買的東西比較少。
B：哇，你人真好。
A：沒什麼，而且我先生正在生鮮區買牛排。
B：喔，那有點遠，而且又是週末，可能要等好幾分鐘。
A：沒錯！所以別客氣，你先請吧。

ahead [ə`hɛd] 副
在前面

deli [`dɛlɪ] 名 熟食店

given [`ɡɪvən] 介
考慮到

Part 1 自我介紹
Part 2 日常雜務
Part 3 職場應對
Part 4 休閒娛樂
Part 5 出國旅遊
Part 6 愛情來了

201

Unit 32 電影院聲光氣氛佳
Enjoying the movies

便利三句開口說

How about going to a movie theater on Saturday night?

▶ 禮拜六晚上去看部電影怎麼樣？

替換句 What do you say we go to the cinema on Saturday night? 禮拜六晚上去看電影，你覺得如何？

✓ **句型提點** Using It Properly!

以 How about 開頭，表示「提議」或是「邀請進行某事」，How about 後面須加動名詞 (V-ing) 或是名詞，表示「提議的事情」。例：How about a drink? 要來喝一杯嗎？

What is your all-time favorite movie?

▶ 你最喜歡的電影是哪一部？

替換句 What is the movie that you like the best? 哪部電影是你最愛看的？

✓ **句型提點** Using It Properly!

all-time favorite 意為「一直以來都喜愛的」。例如：My all-time favorite talk show would be The Oprah Show. 我一直以來都很喜歡歐普拉脫口秀。

Do you usually watch movies at home or at a movie theater?

▶ 你通常會在家看電影，還是去電影院？

替換句 Where do you prefer watching movies? 你喜歡在哪裡看電影？

Part 1 自我介紹

Part 2 日常雜務

Part 3 職場應對

Part 4 休閒娛樂

Part 5 出國旅遊

Part 6 愛情來了

☑ ㄧ、句型提點 **Using It Properly!**

詢問對方是否經常做某事，可用「Do/Does+ 人名 / 代名詞 +usually+ 原形動詞」。其中 usually 為頻率副詞，常放在主要動詞前面，表示動作發生的頻率。

 **有來有往的必備回應**

Q How about going to a movie theater on Saturday night?

Excellent idea! *A*

好主意！

Q What is your all-time favorite movie?

My all-time favorite movie is Gone With The Wind. *A*

一直以來，我最喜愛的電影是《亂世佳人》。

Q Do you usually watch movies at home or at a movie theater?

I prefer going to a movie theater. *A*

我比較喜歡去電影院。

💡 **小知識補給站** *Some Fun Facts*

只要提到電影、影星，就會想到位於美國加州的好萊塢 (Hollywood)，精細的分工、雄厚的財力…等等，都造就了好萊塢在電影工業中屹立不搖的地位。好萊塢還有一條星光大道 (Walk of Fame)，道路上面嵌滿了鑲有名星姓名的星形獎章，甚至連虛構的角色像是米老鼠、小熊維尼也有獎章呢。

01 Do you know that Spiderman III will be coming out in theaters this weekend?
你知道《蜘蛛人 3》這週末要上映嗎？ come out 出版；發表

02 My sister goes to see movies on a regular basis.
我妹經常去看電影。

03 What is your favorite genre of movie?
你最喜歡的電影類型是哪種？ genre 文藝作品之類型

04 My favorite genres are action and horror movies.
我最喜歡的類型是動作片和恐怖片。 horror movie 恐怖片

05 I'm glad that they didn't have any love scenes. Sometimes a love scene destroys a good movie.
我很開心這部片沒有感情戲，有時候，感情戲會毀了一部好電影。 scene（電影）鏡頭；場面

06 Let's definitely go see this Oscar-winning film.
我們一定要去看這部奧斯卡得獎影片。

07 This movie is the best comedy of the year.
這部電影是今年度最佳喜劇。 comedy 喜劇

08 I couldn't stop laughing throughout the entire movie.
這部電影讓我從頭笑到尾。

09 Every time my boyfriend asks me to see a sci-fi movie with him, I make up excuses to turn him down.
每次我男友要我陪他去看科幻電影，我都會找藉口拒絕他。 make up 編造

10 My brother is going to see a chick flick because he is going on a date tomorrow night.
我哥明天晚上的約會要去看劇情片。
chick flick 主要吸引女性觀眾的電影

11 I will definitely see that movie again when it

comes out on DVD.
這片子出 DVD 的時候，我一定還要再看一遍。

⑫ Don't forget to switch off your cell phone before the movie begins.
電影開始前，別忘了要將手機關機。 switch off 關上

⑬ It's too bad that I can't take my kids to see this hit movie because it is R-rated.
這部強檔片被歸在限制級實在很可惜，我不能帶我的孩子一起去看。

⑭ That motion picture is said to be breaking box office records this year.
據說那部院線片將會打破今年的票房紀錄。
box office 票房收入

⑮ What do you think about all the special effects in that 3D movie we just saw?
你覺得我們剛剛看的 3D 電影的特效如何？
special effects 特殊效果

⑯ Name three movies that you like to watch over and over again.
舉出三個你會一直反覆看的電影。

⑰ I felt really annoyed by the guy sitting next to me who couldn't stop talking during the movie.
坐我隔壁的傢伙整場電影講話講不停，真是煩死人了。

⑱ The movie didn't have many cheesy or stupid scenes.
這部電影沒有太多俗氣或白癡的鏡頭。 cheesy 下等的

⑲ I regret reading the review of the movie I am about to see.
我後悔在我看那部電影之前先讀了它的影評。 review 評論

⑳ The Transformers series immediately became blockbusters once they hit the theaters.
《變型金剛》系列一上映，就馬上成為票房冠軍。
blockbuster 賣座電影

自我介紹

日常雜務

職場應對

休閒娛樂

出國旅遊

愛情來了

205

雙人實境對話 oh!

對話情境 1 週末電影院人潮

A: I'm going to the movies with a friend this weekend. How about you?

B: I'm not sure yet.

A: Well, do you want to go to the cinema with us?

B: Tempting, but I don't like the crowds.

A: Don't worry. We'll go to the least crowded one.

A：我這個週末要跟朋友去看電影，你呢？

B：還不確定。

A：那你想要跟我們一起去看電影嗎？

B：滿想的，但我不喜歡人擠人的感覺。

A：別擔心，我們會去最不擠的那間戲院。

cinema [`sɪnəmə]
名 電影院

tempting [`tɛmptɪŋ]
形 吸引人的

crowd [kraud] 名 人群

對話情境 2 好電影值得一看

A: What's your favorite movie?

B: That would be The Sound of Music. It's my favorite movie of all time!

A: Oh, why is that?

B: All the actresses and actors sing beautifully and the dialogue is touching.

A: I should go see it as well.

A：你最喜歡的電影是哪一部？

B：應該是《真善美》。我一直以來都很喜歡這部電影！

A：喔，為什麼？

B：裡面演員的歌聲優美，對白又感人。

A：我也應該看看。

beautifully
[`bjutəfəlɪ] 副 出色地；美麗地

dialogue [`daɪə,lɔg]
名 對話；對白

touching [`tʌtʃɪŋ]
形 感人的；動人的

對話情境 3　邀約一同看電影

A: Hey, I'm going to see a movie with Brad and Jason. Do you want to come?

B: When are you guys going?

A: We're going to see the eight o'clock showing.

B: That would be great. Where are you guys meeting?

A: We're meeting at the theater at seven thirty. Make sure to be there on time, or we won't have time to buy popcorn. See you later!

A：嘿，我要跟傑森還有布萊德去看電影，你要來嗎？
B：你們什麼時候要去？
A：我們要看八點那場。
B：太好了，你們約在哪碰面？
A：我們七點半要在戲院集合。一定要準時到喔，要不然會沒時間買爆米花。等一下見！

guy [gaɪ] 名 朋友；人；男人

showing [`ʃoɪŋ] 名 放映

對話情境 4　喜愛的電影大不同

A: What kind of movies do you like?

B: I like documentary films.

A: Wow, you're deep. I like comedies because I don't want to use my brain while watching movies.

B: I was just kidding. I like romance films.

A: Oh, same here. Let's go see one!

A：你喜歡哪一種類的電影？
B：我喜歡紀錄片。
A：哇，你好有深度。我喜歡喜劇，因為我看電影的時候不想用大腦。
B：開坑笑的，我喜歡愛情電影。
A：喔，我也是，那我們找一部去看吧！

documentary [ˌdɑkjə`mɛntərɪ] 形 文件的

deep [dip] 形 深奧的；深的

romance [ro`mæns] 名 愛情故事；戀愛

入境隨俗瘋球賽
Crazy about sport games

便利三句開口說

Basketball is a popular game here in Taiwan.
▶ 籃球比賽在台灣很受歡迎。

替換句 There are many people who are into basketball in Taiwan. 台灣有很多人喜歡籃球。

☑ **句型提點** Using It Properly!

「運動 +is+a popular game+in+ 地點」用來介紹
「某地最受歡迎的體育運動」。popular 為受歡迎的；
game 則是指體育方面的比賽。

- -

Who's your favorite soccer player?
▶ 你最喜歡的足球員是誰？

替換句 Which soccer player are you interested in following? 有哪個足球員是你有興趣關注的？

☑ **句型提點** Using It Properly!

詢問對方最喜歡的人是誰，可用「Who+is+ 人名
（所有格）+favorite+ 人」。例：Who is Emily's
favorite singer? 艾蜜莉最喜歡的歌手是誰？

- -

Have you ever watched games at a baseball field?
▶ 你有到棒球場看過比賽嗎？

替換句 Have you ever been to Yankee Stadium? 你
去過洋基體育場嗎？

☑ **句型提點** Using It Properly!

「Have/Has+ 人名 / 代名詞 +ever+ 動詞 (過去分

詞)」，詢問某人是否曾經做過某事。ever 用來表示「曾經有過類似經驗」，除了疑問句，也常在肯定句中看到，且後面接的動詞須為過去分詞形式。

💬 有來有往的必備回應

Q　Basketball is a popular game here in Taiwan.

　　　　I am a big fan of it myself!　*A*

　　　　我自己也是個球迷！

Q　Who's your favorite soccer player?

　　　　Definitely Beckham!　*A*

　　　　鐵定是貝克漢啊！

Q　Have you ever watched games at a baseball field?

　　　　No. I hope I will have a chance in the future.　*A*

　　　　沒耶，希望以後有機會去。

💡 小知識補給站　　Some Fun Facts

在美國，有許多不同的職業賽事，像是最常見的 NBA（職業籃球比賽）、MLB（職棒大聯盟）、NFL（國家美式足球聯盟）、以及 MLS（足球大聯盟）。而歐洲則以足球為主要風行的運動，賽事包含足球五大聯賽及世界盃足球賽。賽季時，親朋好友常常相約一起在家或酒吧看比賽，大家還爭相為自己支持的球隊應援，並穿上球隊衣服、帽子以示支持；甚至有因為支持隊伍不同而打架鬧事的事件，由此可見大家對運動比賽的瘋狂程度。

自我介紹　日常雜務　職場應對　休閒娛樂　出國旅遊　愛情來了

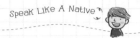
01 My boyfriend always gets too carried away during the NBA season.

我男友在 NBA 賽季時，總是變得魂不守舍。

`carry away 吸引住`

02 I am so excited by the slam dunk contest coming up this weekend!

我對這週末要舉辦的灌籃大賽感到非常興奮。

`slam dunk 灌籃；扣籃`

03 Michael Jordan is a legendary NBA player.

麥可‧喬丹是美國職籃的傳奇人物。 `legendary 傳奇的`

04 It was clearly a blocking foul!

這明顯是個阻擋犯規。 `foul (比賽中的) 犯規`

05 The athlete finished the game with a layup shot.

這名球員上籃得分，結束了這場比賽。 `layup 上籃`

06 His three-pointer shot in the last second changed the whole outcome of the game.

他最後關頭的三分球改寫了比賽的結果。 `shot 投籃`

07 What a game!

真是精彩的比賽！

08 Watching games makes me want to shoot some hoops.

看著比賽讓我也想打籃球了。 `shoot hoops 投籃；打籃球`

09 Americans are crazy about Major League Baseball.

美國人很瘋職棒大聯盟。

10 If you ever have a chance to go to America, you have to see a ball game at a stadium.

如果你有機會去美國，一定要去球場看場球賽。

`stadium 球場`

11 Many people in Taiwan are baseball fanatics.

台灣人很多都是棒球狂熱份子。 `fanatic 狂熱者`

⑫ There are usually nine innings in a baseball game.
一場棒球比賽通常有九局。 `inning ( 棒球 ) 局`

⑬ Baseball is so much fun. I like to slide into the bases.
棒球好有趣，我最喜歡滑壘了。 `slide 滑壘`

⑭ The pitcher on the mound is the ace of the team.
投手丘上那位投手是隊上的王牌。 `ace 王牌；能手`

⑮ He struck out!
他遭到三振出局！ `strike out 三振出局`

⑯ He hit a home run and ended the game!
他擊出一支全壘打，比賽結束！ `home run 全壘打`

⑰ Let's go to a sports bar and watch the World Cup final.
我們去運動酒吧看世界盃決賽吧！ `final 決賽`

⑱ I don't want to miss out on the game the German goalkeeper is playing in tonight.
我不想錯過今晚德國門將即將出場的這場比賽。
`goalkeeper 守門員`

⑲ Who do you think will win the World Cup?
你覺得誰會贏得世界盃冠軍？

⑳ What country are you following in the World Cup?
你支持哪一支世界盃隊伍？ `follow 密切注意`

㉑ How many goals has he scored so far?
他目前已經射門得分多少球了？ `score 得分`

㉒ Who is your favorite World Cup player?
誰是你最喜歡的世界盃球員？

㉓ Some fans think of soccer games as a matter of life and death.
有些球迷覺得足球比賽的結果就如同生死大事般重要。

Part 1 自我介紹

Part 2 日常雜務

Part 3 職場應對

Part 4 休閒娛樂

Part 5 出國旅遊

Part 6 愛情來了

對話情境 ① 網球界重要賽事

A : Do you watch The Wimbledon Championships?

B : Yes. I like tennis very much, and I watch the games on TV.

A : Me, too. I never **miss a single** game.

B : Which tennis player is your favorite?

A : That would be Maria Sharapova.

A：你有看溫布頓網球賽嗎？

B：有，我很喜歡網球，會看電視轉播。

A：我也是，我不會錯過任何一場比賽。

B：你最喜歡哪個網球球員？

A：當然是瑪麗亞‧莎拉波娃。

miss [mɪs] 動 錯過

single [`sɪŋgl] 形
（用於否定句）連一個
也沒有的

對話情境 ② 現場看球賽

A : I bought two tickets to the baseball game this Saturday. Do you want to come with me?

B : Sure. Where are the seats?

A : Two **infield**-reserved tickets behind the **home plate**.

B : Wow! That must have **cost you a fortune**.

A : Never mind.

A：我買了兩張本週六棒球賽的票，想
　　不想跟我去？

B：當然，座位在哪裡？

A：本壘板後方的內野保留票。

B：哇！應該花不少錢吧。

A：沒關係的。

infield [`ɪn. fild] 名
（棒球）內野

home plate 片
本壘板

cost sb. a fortune
片 （某人）花了一大
筆錢

對話情境 ③ 看球賽何必去酒吧

Ⓐ : I bet all the sports bars **downtown** will be **packed** tonight.

Ⓑ : Is it because of the World Cup final?

Ⓐ : Duh.

Ⓑ : Why don't we just watch it at home? We can lie on the couch, get giant bags of snacks, and even call some friends to join us.

Ⓐ : That's what I was going to say.

A：我跟你賭今天晚上市區的運動酒吧一定爆滿。

B：是因為世界盃總決賽吧？

A：不然咧。

B：我們何不乾脆在家裡看轉播就好？我們可以躺在沙發上面、吃大包大包的零食，還可以叫一些朋友來加入我們呀。

A：我正準備這麼說。

downtown
[ˌdaʊn`taʊn] 形 市中心的

packed [pækt] 形 塞滿的

對話情境 ④ 看球賽就是要配洋芋片

Ⓐ : Did you get some chips at the supermarket?

Ⓑ : No. What for?

Ⓐ : What? How could you not prepare some chips at home when it's the NBA **playoffs**?

Ⓑ : Who the heck knows what that is!

Ⓐ : Argh... It is the **postseason tournament**, and it is very important.

A：你去超市有買洋芋片嗎？

B：沒有，為什麼需要？

A：蛤？現在是美國 NBA 季後賽耶，怎麼能不準備幾包洋芋片在家啊？

B：誰曾知道那是什麼東西啊！

A：呃…這是美國職籃整季最終的決賽啦，非常重要！

playoff [`ple͵ɔf] 名 季後賽

postseason
[ˌpost`sizn] 形 （體育比賽）季後的

tournament
[`tɝnəmənt] 名 比賽

213

Unit 34　跑出你的一片天
Go from zero to marathon

便利三句開口說

Let's go for a run!
▶ 我們去跑步吧！

替換句 How about going out for a run? 去跑個步如何？

✓ ⤷ **句型提點** ❰ Using It Properly! ❱

用 Let's 開頭可表達「提議、邀約」，「Let's+ 原形動詞」即表示「提議一同進行某件事」。例：Let's order some takeout. 我們叫些外賣吧！

- -

Have you ever run a marathon?
▶ 你有參加過馬拉松嗎？

替換句 What kind of running events have you been to? 你參加過什麼樣的跑步比賽？

✓ ⤷ **句型提點** ❰ Using It Properly! ❱

run a marathon 表示「參加馬拉松比賽」。
marathon 也可代表需耗費比一般多的時間及耐力的賽事或活動，例如：dance marathon (舞蹈馬拉松；是比賽時間連續好幾天的舞蹈比賽)。

- -

Are there any running guides for a beginner like me?
▶ 有沒有給像我這種初學者的跑步指南？

替換句 Are there any beginner's running programs I could take? 有沒有專為跑步初學者開設的課程？

☑ **句型提點** Using It Properly!

詢問某樣東西或某種狀態是否存在，可用「Is/Are+there+any+ 名詞」。例：Are there any further questions you would like to ask me? 你還有什麼問題想要問我嗎？

💬 **有來有往的必備回應**

Q　Let's go for a run!

　　I'd rather stay at home.　*A*
　　我寧願待在家裡。

Q　Have you ever run a marathon?

　　No. But I am training for the one in the end of this year.　*A*
　　沒有，不過我正在為今年年底的馬拉松訓練。

Q　Are there any running guides for a beginner like me?

　　Yes, there are countless online guides to choose from.　*A*
　　有的，網路上有很多的指南可挑選。

💡 **小知識補給站** Some Fun Facts

　　距離為 42.195 公里的跑步賽事，即稱為馬拉松；從最早的奧林匹克運動會裡，就有馬拉松這項比賽。甚至還有距離超過 42 公里的超級馬拉松 (Ultramarathon)，在公認最艱苦的撒哈拉馬拉松當中，參賽者必須在撒哈拉沙漠中露宿 6 晚，完成長度 254 公里的總距離，也就是一般馬拉松的 6 倍之多。

Part 1 自我介紹

Part 2 日常雜務

Part 3 職場應對

Part 4 休閒娛樂

Part 5 出國旅遊

Part 6 愛情來了

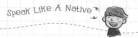
01 **I go to an elementary school across from my house and jog a few laps around the playground every night.**
我每天晚上都在我家對面的小學操場慢跑幾圈。 `lap 一圈`

02 **I go jogging in the morning when the air is still fresh.**
我趁早上空氣還新鮮的時候慢跑。 `jogging 慢跑`

03 **Some people find jogging stressful, but I see it as a way to relieve some of my stress.**
有些人覺得慢跑壓力很大，但我覺得這是一個可以紓壓的管道。

04 **I usually jog on a treadmill because it's convenient.**
跑步機很方便，所以我通常都用它練跑。 `treadmill 跑步機`

05 **Running on a treadmill is the last resort for me, and I only do it if it's raining.**
如果一直下雨，萬不得已我才會在跑步機上跑步。
`the last resort 最後手段`

06 **I decided to start jogging one day and fell for it right away.**
我有天決定開始跑步，後來就愛上了這項運動。
`fall for 對⋯傾心`

07 **I find it hard to catch my breath when running.**
跑步的時候，我感覺自己快喘不過氣了。
`catch one's breath 喘氣`

08 **Running has become a trendy exercise in Taiwan in the past few years.**
近幾年，跑步在台灣成為一項主流的運動。 `trendy 流行的`

09 **There are hundreds of running events held each year in Taiwan.**
每年有幾百場的跑步賽事在台灣舉辦。

⑩ Don't try too hard in your first race, or you might end up getting disappointed.

初次參加賽事的時候別太勉強，否則你會以失望收場。

⑪ I am training for my first half marathon this winter.

我在為今年冬天的半程馬拉松做訓練。 `marathon 馬拉松賽跑`

⑫ I think most people can run as long as they set their minds to it.

我覺得只要有心，每個人都可以跑步。
`set one's minds to 有心想…`

⑬ Some people think they are not capable of running because they don't have the habit of working out on a regular basis.

有些人因為沒有固定運動的習慣，所以會覺得自己無法跑步。 `be capable of 有能力做…的`

⑭ Don't overtrain yourself, or you might experience unexpected injuries.

不要訓練過度，否則你會導致意想不到的運動傷害。
`overtrain 訓練過度` `injury 傷害`

⑮ Learn correct form before you even hit the pavement.

上路開跑之前，要先學習正確的姿勢。 `pavement 人行道`

⑯ You need to keep a steady pace in order to endure a longer run.

你需要維持一定的速度，才能跑更久。 `pace 步速`

⑰ I try to exhale and inhale with a fixed tempo so I don't pant like a dog.

我試著以穩定的節奏吸吐氣，才不至於喘得跟隻狗一樣。

⑱ I invest a big sum of money in all kinds of running gear.

我花了很多錢在各種跑步配件上。 `gear 工具；設備`

⑲ I find that the only two important gear I need are shoes and shirts.

我發覺兩件最重要的跑步配件是鞋子跟上衣。

217

雙人實境對話 〈oh!〉

對話情境 1 慢跑來減肥

A : There are more and more people running in the park.

B : I know. I just don't understand what makes them start?

A : **Losing weight** may be among the top three reasons.

B : **Speaking of which**, I think I need to lose some myself.

A : What do you say we join the crowd in the park as well?

A：有愈來愈多人在公園跑步了。
B：是啊，但我不懂他們怎麼想跑？
A：減肥應該是排行榜前三名。
B：說到減肥，我覺得我也該減一些。
A：那我們也加入公園的群眾，如何？

lose weight 片
減輕體重；減肥

speaking of which 片 說到這個

對話情境 2 跑步何必化妝

A : Come on, just put on your shoes and let's get going.

B : Wait, I need to **powder my nose** first.

A : Are you insane? We're out for a run, not a beauty contest!

B : I can't **stand** going out without **make-up**.

A : Suit yourself. Wait till you see that big zit on your face.

A：快點穿上鞋子，我們該出發了。
B：等等，我要先補個妝。
A：你瘋了嗎？我們是出去跑步，又不是參加選美！
B：我不能忍受素顏出門啦！
A：隨便你，等著看你臉上長出痘痘吧。

powder one's nose 片 補妝

stand [stænd] 動
忍受

make-up [`mek.ʌp]
名 妝容

對話情境 3 慢跑小撇步

A : You've been running for so many years. Can you give me some tips on running?

B : First of all, you need to get a pair of **high-impact** running shoes.

A : Got it. Anything else?

B : Never skip **warm-ups**.

A : Thanks for the **tips**.

A：你已經跑步好幾年了，可否告訴我一些撇步呢？

B：了解，還有呢？

A：首先，你要去買一雙能吸收高衝擊的跑步鞋。

B：千萬不可省略暖身運動。

A：謝謝你和我分享這些撇步。

high-impact
[haɪ`ɪmpækt] 形 能承受高衝擊的
warm-up
[`wɔrm.ʌp] 名 暖身
tip [tɪp] 名 提示

對話情境 4 跑步還是戶外好

A : What's the difference between running outdoors and running on a treadmill?

B : **For starters**, you can't enjoy the fresh air by running indoors.

A : Makes sense.

B : Also, your body will **adapt** to all kinds of **terrain** if you run outdoors.

A : Sounds like you are for running outdoors.

A：在室外跑步跟在室內用跑步機跑有什麼差別？

B：首先，你在室內跑是呼吸不到新鮮空氣的。

A：有道理。

B：而且，如果在戶外跑，你的身體就能適應各種地形。

A：聽起來你是贊成到戶外跑步的人。

for starters 片
首先；第一
adapt [ə`dæpt] 動
適應
terrain [`tɛrən] 名
地形；地域

游泳招式學起來
Swim like a fish

便利三句開口說

Do you know how to swim?
▶ 你會游泳嗎？

替換句 ▶ Can you swim? 你會游泳嗎？

✓ 句型提點 Using It Properly!

「Do/does+ 人名 / 代名詞 +know+how+to+ 動詞」，詢問某人是否知道如何進行某件事情。例：Do you know how to pick a lock? 你知道怎麼把鎖撬開嗎？

What style of swimming do you specialize in?
▶ 你游泳專精哪一式？

替換句 ▶ What style of swimming are you familiar with? 你熟悉哪種游法？

✓ 句型提點 Using It Properly!

「What+style+of+ 名詞 +do/does+ 人名 / 代名詞 +specialize+in」可用來詢問「某人擅長的運動 / 事情是哪一種」。片語 specialize in 意為「專精」。

How often do you swim?
▶ 你都多久游一次泳？

替換句 ▶ Do you go swimming often? 你常常去游泳嗎？

✓ 句型提點 Using It Properly!

用 How often 開頭來詢問「做某件事情的頻率」。常見的頻率副詞從高到低依序是：always（總是）、usually（經常）、often（經常）、sometimes（有時）、seldom（甚少）、never（從未）。

有來有往的必備回應

Q Do you know how to swim?

> No, I know nothing about swimming. *A*
> 不，我完全不會游泳。

Q What style of swimming do you specialize in?

> I specialize in the butterfly stroke. *A*
> 我最擅長蝶式。

Q How often do you swim?

> I swim twice a week. *A*
> 我一個禮拜游兩次。

小知識補給站

　　泳式種類有自由式（freestyle）、蛙式（breaststroke）、仰式（backstroke）、蝶式（butterfly stroke）、甚至還有狗爬式（dog paddle/doggie paddle）。講到游泳，就不可不知美國運動員麥可‧弗雷德‧菲爾普斯二世 (Michael Fred Phelps II)，他是目前拿下最多游泳項目金牌的紀錄保持者，不但有 23 塊奧運金牌，比賽時還多次刷新世界紀錄。與游泳有關的運動還有奧運比賽常見到的水上芭蕾 (synchronized swimming)、雙人跳水 (synchronized diving)、以及鐵人三項 (triathlon)；之後還發展出水中有氧 (water aerobics)，需要在水深及腰的深度，身體保持垂直，並且在水裡進行跑、跳等的有氧運動。

Part 1 自我介紹
Part 2 日常雜務
Part 3 職場應對
Part 4 休閒娛樂
Part 5 出國旅遊
Part 6 愛情來了

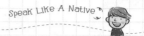
01 I'm not a good swimmer. The only style I know is the dog paddle.
我不擅長游泳，我唯一會的是狗爬式。
`dog paddle 狗爬式游泳`

02 I can't hold my breath long enough to be an effective swimmer.
我沒辦法憋氣太久，所以無法成為優秀的游泳健將。
`swimmer 游泳者`

03 I can hold my breath for a minute and a half.
我可以憋氣一分半鐘。 `hold one's breath 暫時屏住呼吸`

04 I believe swimming is very healthy, especially for the joints.
我認為游泳有益健康，尤其是對關節很好。 `joint 關節`

05 Swimming can increase your cardiovascular performance as well as your muscle strength.
游泳可以強化你的心肺功能與肌耐力。
`cardiovascular 心血管的`

06 My kids are taking swimming lessons at a local swimming pool during summer vacation.
我孩子暑假的時候去本地的游泳池上游泳課。

07 Learning how to float on your back is one of the basic skills acquired in the first few swimming lessons.
學習如何利用自己的背部漂浮是在前幾堂游泳課程中必學的基本技巧。 `acquire 習得；取得`

08 Younger students are allowed to dive off the side of the pool or from the diving board.
年輕的學員可以從泳池旁邊跳水，或選擇從跳板跳水。
`dive 跳水` `diving board 跳板`

09 If you are a beginner, please stay in the shallow end and practice.

如果你是初學者，請待在淺水區練習。 shallow 淺的

⑩ I've been swimming ever since I was six years old.
我六歲就開始游泳了。

⑪ I'm on the swimming team.
我是游泳隊的一員。

⑫ I made the varsity swimming team.
我進了大學的游泳校隊。 varsity 大學代表隊

⑬ Are there any lifeguards at your community swimming pool?
你家社區的游泳池有沒有救生員？ lifeguard 救生員

⑭ I like freestyle swimming, but I'm better at the butterfly.
我喜歡游自由式，但我擅長的是蝶式。 freestyle 自由式的

⑮ I'm pretty quick at the backstroke.
我的仰式游得滿快的。 backstroke 仰泳

⑯ I've done my ten laps for the day.
我已經游完今天的十圈了。

⑰ Get your goggles and swimming suit ready. Let's go for a swim!
把你的蛙鏡跟泳衣準備好，我們去游泳吧！ goggle 護目鏡

⑱ Some people go to the beach not to swim but to sunbathe.
有些人去海邊不是為了游泳，而是為了享受日光浴。
sunbathe 沐日光浴

⑲ Be sure to put on some sunscreen if you don't want to get burned.
如果你不想被曬傷的話，記得擦防曬乳。 sunscreen 防曬乳

⑳ Danny fell asleep under the sun with only trunks on and got a sunburn.
丹尼只穿了泳褲在太陽底下睡著，結果就被曬傷了。
sunburn 曬傷

對話情境 1　游泳機

A: Is there a swimming pool in this hotel?

B: We don't have a full-sized swimming pool, but we do have individual swim stations.

A: What exactly does that mean?

B: Well, it is like a treadmill, except instead of running, you swim.

A: That sounds really cool.

A：這家飯店有游泳池嗎？

B：我們沒有游泳池，但我們有供個人使用的游泳機。

A：那是什麼東西啊？

B：它就像跑步機一樣，只是你用它來游泳，而不是跑步。

A：聽起來很酷耶。

full-sized [`fʊl`saɪz] 形 全尺寸的

station [`steʃən] 名 地方；站

instead of 片 而不是；代替

對話情境 2　不想曬太黑

A: Have you got dressed yet? Don't forget your goggles.

B: I am almost ready. Have you applied some suntan lotion?

A: I don't want to get too tanned this summer, so I put on some sunblock lotion.

B: Can I have some of that as well?

A: Sure. Here you go.

A：你換好衣服了沒？別忘了帶蛙鏡。

B：我快好了，你有塗助曬乳嗎？

A：我今年夏天不想要曬太黑，所以我擦了防曬乳。

B：我可以也借用一點嗎？

A：當然，拿去吧。

suntan lotion 片 助曬劑

sunblock lotion 片 防曬乳

對話情境 ③ 專業級的練習

A : How often do you guys go swimming?
B : We set a goal of swimming five times a week.
A : Wow. And how long do you swim each time?
B : I don't really keep track, but we swim 50 laps, which equals 2,500 meters every time.
A : My goodness; that's hard-core!

A：你們多久去游一次泳？
B：我們立下一週要游五次泳的目標。
A：哇，那你們一次都游多長？
B：我沒有特別記錄，不過我們每次大概都游 50 趟，大約有 2,500 公尺。
A：天啊，真厲害！

keep track 片 紀錄；密切關注
hard-core [ˋhɑrd.kɔr] 形 信念堅定的

對話情境 ④ 自由式教學

A : What style of swimming are you most familiar with?
B : Freestyle.
A : Oh, can you show me how to swim this stroke correctly?
B : I suggest you surf the internet first. There are a lot of how-to clips you can start right away on your own.
A : Sure, I will. But will you still demonstrate it for me in the water?

A：你最熟悉哪一種游泳姿勢？
B：自由式。
A：喔，那你可以教我怎麼游標準的自由式？
B：建議你先上網找資料。網路上有很多教學影片，你回家馬上就能自學了。
A：我回去當然會找，但你還是能在水裡示範給我看吧？

stroke [strok] 名 泳姿；划水動作
how-to [ˋhɑuˋtu] 形 入門的；提供指南的
clip [klɪp] 名 片段

自我介紹

日常雜務

職場應對

休閒娛樂

出國旅遊

愛情來了

225

乘風單車行
Traveling by bike

便利三句開口說

Can you ride a bike?
▶ 你會騎腳踏車嗎？

替換句 Do you know how to ride a bike? 你知道怎麼騎單車嗎？

✓ **句型提點** **Using It Properly!**

若要詢問「對方的能力」、「能不能做某事」，可用助動詞 can 開頭，後面必須接原形動詞。例：
Can she swim? 她會游泳嗎？ / Can he play the piano? 他會彈鋼琴嗎？

Do you own a bike or do you use a rental bike?
▶ 你自己有腳踏車還是用租的？

替換句 Do you have a bike of your own? 你有自己的腳踏車嗎？

✓ **句型提點** **Using It Properly!**

連接詞 or 用於連接兩個子句，常用在疑問句中表示「或者」、「還是」，提供聽者兩個選項，所以結果不是子句一就是子句二。

I love riding on the bike path along the river.
▶ 我喜愛在沿著河畔的腳踏車道騎行。

替換句 I enjoy riding along the coastline. 我喜歡沿著海岸線騎車。

☑ ➔ **句型提點** ⟨ *Using It Properly!* ⟩

「喜愛做某事」可以用「love+V-ing」表示，love 後面必須接動名詞 (V-ing) 或是不定詞 (to+ 原形動詞)。例：Mia really loves baking cookies by herself. 米雅很喜歡自己手做餅乾。

💬 **有來有往的必備回應**

Q Can you ride a bike?

Yes, I can. *A*

我會騎車。

Q Do you own a bike or do you use a rental bike?

I always rely on the bike rental service in Taipei. *A*

我都仰賴台北市的腳踏車租賃服務。

Q I love riding on the bike path along the river.

Take me with you next time, please. *A*

拜託下次帶我一起去吧！

💡 **小知識補給站**

Some Fun Facts

提到單車，就可以聯想到單車賽事，最著名的比賽莫過於環法自行車賽 (Le Tour de France)：比賽一場為期 21 天，主要在法國舉辦，參賽者須組成 9 人的隊伍參加比賽，還要挑戰各種坡度和地形，而主要獎項有黃衫 (總排名冠軍；總騎乘時間最短的冠軍)、綠衫 (衝刺王；在每段衝刺點的積分累計最高者)、紅點衫 (爬坡王；登山積分累積最高者)、以及白衫 (最佳新人；25 歲以下總騎乘時間最短者)。

自我介紹 日常雜務 職場應對 休閒娛樂 出國旅遊 愛情來了

01 I think riding a bike is more eco-friendly than taking any other type of transportation.

我覺得騎腳踏車比其他任何交通工具都要來得環保。

02 I learned how to ride a bike when I was seven.

我七歲的時候就學會騎腳踏車。 `ride a bike 騎腳踏車`

03 Have you ever ridden racing bikes, mountain bikes, BMX bikes or other recreational bikes?

你有騎過賽用腳踏車、越野腳踏車、小輪賽車或其他休閒用腳踏車嗎？

04 Cycling around Taiwan has been one of the popular pastimes for the past several years.

騎車環島在近幾年成為台灣最熱門的休閒活動之一。

`cycling 騎腳踏車`

05 Cyclists pedaled at their own pace and shared their experiences after the ride.

騎士按自己的步調踩踏前進，並在騎完之後分享經驗。

`pedal 踩踏板`

06 There are more and more people cycling to work thanks to the public rental bikes all around Taipei.

由於台北公共腳踏車的租賃愈來愈普及，有愈來愈多人騎腳踏車上班。 `thanks to 幸虧；由於`

07 I went on a cycling tour this summer and rode 900 kilometers in total.

我這個夏天參加了單車之旅，總共騎了 900 公里。

08 I've decided to start mountain biking to get in shape.

為了雕塑身形，我決定開始騎越野自行車。

`in shape 處於良好的健康狀況`

09 In order to train myself for the triathlon, I have to set a four-week cycling program of over 200

km per week.
為了要訓練鐵人三項的競賽，我制定了四週計畫，每週要騎超過 200 公里的自行車。

⑩ I took my bike into a cycling shop to get a tune-up.
我把腳踏車拿去自行車行檢查。 `tune-up 調整`

⑪ This bike has 12 gears.
這台腳踏車有 12 段變速。 `gear 排檔`

⑫ My bike was in pretty bad shape, so I wasn't sure if it would serve my needs.
我的腳踏車狀態相當差，所以我不確定是否能符合我的需求。 `serve 適用；供應`

⑬ The mechanic at the shop adjusted my brakes, oiled the chain, fixed my flat tire, and adjusted the spokes in my wheels.
自行車行的技師調整了我的剎車、幫鍊條上油、修好洩氣的輪胎，並調整好車輪的輪輻。 `spoke 輪輻`

⑭ I'm thinking about getting a lighter bike, but my current bike will have to do for now.
我有考慮要買一台輕一點的腳踏車，但我現在這台暫時也還堪用。

⑮ I need a new bike helmet to protect my head in case I fall off the bike.
我需要一頂新的安全帽來保護我的頭部，以免我從腳踏車上摔下來。 `fall off 落下`

⑯ Make sure your brakes are functioning normally.
一定要確定你的煞車運作正常。 `brake 煞車`

⑰ Cyclists should always wear protective gear.
騎士上路應該要全程配戴護具。 `protective 防護的`

⑱ For your own safety, when riding a bike in the dark, be sure to dress in a bright-colored outfit.
安全起見，在天黑後騎腳踏車時，一定要穿亮色系衣服。

自我介紹

日常雜務

職場應對

休閒娛樂

出國旅遊

愛情來了

對話情境 ① 腳踏車諮詢

A : What kind of bike are you looking for?
B : I'm really not sure.
A : We carry road bikes, mountain bikes, beach cruisers, and racing bikes.
B : I'll be riding mainly to work, but I want something versatile enough for anything.
A : I would either go for a road bike or a mountain bike.

A：你在找什麼樣的腳踏車？
B：我不太確定。
A：我們有公路車、越野車、沙灘自行車以及比賽用自行車。
B：我主要是騎去上班，但希望它的功能盡量多一點。
A：如果是我的話，我會選擇公路車或越野車。

carry [ˋkærɪ] 動
商店備有（某貨品）
beach cruiser 片
沙灘自行車
versatile [ˋvɝsət!]
形 多功能的

對話情境 ② 放手一搏

A : Can you ride a bike?
B : I can't and don't think I will ever learn.
A : Everyone can learn! Let me teach you.
B : I am afraid of getting hurt, and I have poor balance.
A : How do you know the results if you never try?

A：你會騎腳踏車嗎？
B：我不會，而且也不覺得我學得起來。
A：每個人都學得會！讓我來教你。
B：我很怕受傷，而且我平衡感很差。
A：如果你不試，怎麼會知道結果呢？

poor [pʊr] 形 不足
的；缺乏的
balance [ˋbæləns]
名 平衡
result [rɪˋzʌlt] 名
結果

對話情境 ③ 代步工具

🅐 : Can you tell me a little bit about the difference among the various bikes?

🅑 : The mountain bikes are very **sturdy** for **off-road** cycling. Beach cruisers have just one speed, so you won't be shifting any gears.

🅐 : I just want a simple tool for transportation.

🅑 : Just go for a **utility** bike, then. The gears are simple without many complicated functions.

A：可不可以跟我說明一下這些腳踏車的差別呢？

B：越野車在非一般道路上使用也很穩健。沙灘自行車只有一個定速，所以不用換檔。

A：我只想要一個簡單的代步工具而已。

B：那就挑選萬用的工具腳踏車吧。檔速很單純，沒有太多複雜的功能。

sturdy [`stɝdɪ] 形
堅固的

off-road [`ɔf͵rod]
形 越野的

utility [ju`tɪlətɪ] 形
多用途的

對話情境 ④ 單車環島

🅐 : What's your plan for the five-day national holiday?

🅑 : My best buddy and I are going to cycle around Taiwan, along the sea coast.

🅐 : Wow, you are so **adventurous**. Have you ever done that before?

🅑 : No. I am a **first-timer**.

🅐 : Oh, you'd better start to plan the entire **route**.

A：五天的國定假日你有什麼計畫？

B：我跟我最好的朋友要一起沿著海岸線環島台灣。

A：哇，你好有冒險精神，你以前環島過嗎？

B：沒有，我第一次參加。

A：喔，那你最好開始規劃全程路線了。

adventurous
[əd`vɛntʃərəs] 形
愛冒險的

first-timer
[`fɝst͵taɪmə] 名 新手

route [rut] 名 路線

Part 1 自我介紹
Part 2 日常雜務
Part 3 職場應對
Part 4 休閒娛樂
Part 5 出國旅遊
Part 6 愛情來了

野炊露營樣樣通

Become a camping professional

便利三句開口說

Have you ever been camping?

▶ 你有露過營嗎？

替換句 Have you ever been on a camping holiday?
你放假時有去露營過嗎？

✓ 句型提點 Using It Properly!

詢問對方「是否有做過某事的經驗」，可用「Have/ has+ 人名 / 代名詞 +ever+ 動詞 (過去分詞)」句型表示。要記得第三人稱單數須用 has，其他則用 have，且後面的動詞須為過去分詞。

I don't know how to pitch a tent.

▶ 我不會搭帳篷。

替換句 I can't pitch a tent. 我不會搭帳篷。

✓ 句型提點 Using It Properly!

「人名 / 代名詞 +don't/doesn't+know+how+to+ 動詞」，表示「某人不知道怎麼做某件事」。do/ does 加上否定的 not，變成 do not/does not，在口語中常省略說成 don't/doesn't。

Let's build a campfire!

▶ 我們來升營火吧！

替換句 Let's start a campfire! 一起來升火吧！

✓ 句型提點 Using It Properly!

campfire 指營火，常搭配的動詞有 build, start, set up，指搭建營火、生火。而句子若用 Let 開頭，可

表示「提出建議」。例：Let's take a short break.
我們稍微休息一下吧。

有來有往的必備回應

Q Have you ever been camping?

A Yes, I have.
是的，我有露營過。

Q I don't know how to pitch a tent.

A Let me show you how.
讓我來示範給你看。

Q Let's build a campfire!

A Let me catch my breath first.
先讓我喘口氣再說。

小知識補給站 Some Fun Facts

常見的露營方式包括使用露營車 (recreational vehicle; RV)，車內有床、廚房、洗手間…等，如同一個移動式的家，設備一應俱全；也有可以伴隨蟲鳴鳥叫入睡的野外露營 (adventure camping)，不過生火、搭帳篷，樣樣都要自己來；國外甚至發展出「glamping」(glamorous 與 camping 的複合字)，雖然睡在野外，卻不必忍受傳統露營的各種不便，且住宿種類繁多，像是樹屋、木屋、蒙古包…等等，讓人們可以徜徉在大自然中度過美好的露營假期。

自我介紹 Part 1

日常雜務 Part 2

職場應對 Part 3

休閒娛樂 Part 4

出國旅遊 Part 5

愛情來了 Part 6

233

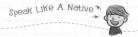
01 Before going camping, I went to the sporting goods store to get some new gear.
去露營之前，我跑了一趟運動用品店，買了新的配件跟用具。 `gear 工具；設備`

02 Modern tents are very light and very easy to pitch.
現代化的帳篷很輕，也很容易搭建。

03 I bought a new sleeping bag, one that was waterproof for the camping trip.
我買了一個具有防水功能的新睡袋，露營時可以使用。

04 I will only go camping with you if you have a camping trailer. I can't stand sleeping in a tent.
除非你有露營車，我才跟你去露營，實在無法忍受睡在帳篷裡。

05 What are the advantages and disadvantages of camping out?
在野外露營有什麼優缺點？ `camp out 搭帳篷露營`

06 Some campsites are non-reservable and are available on a first-come, first-served basis.
有些露營區不接受預約，而是以「先到先服務」的機制營運。 `campsite 露營地`

07 I usually reserve a campsite at a campground in the canyon.
我通常會在峽谷的露營地預約一個露營區。 `canyon 峽谷`

08 Are there shower facilities at this campsite?
這個露營區有淋浴設備嗎？ `facility 設施；設備`

09 The campsite overlooks the whole lake.
露營區俯瞰整個湖區。 `overlook 眺望；俯瞰`

10 The view around the site was breathtaking!
營區附近的景緻真是美不勝收。 `breathtaking 驚人的`

⑪ It's better to arrive at the site before it gets dark. I don't want to pitch a tent in the dark.

最好在天黑前抵達露營區，我不想要摸黑搭帳篷。

pitch a tent 搭帳篷

⑫ We always look for a campsite that has a lot of shade from the sun, is near a water source, has a good fire pit, and has a good spot to pitch a tent.

找營區的時候，我們總是注重要有很多遮陽處、靠近水源、有好的火坑，而且是個好搭帳篷的地點。

pit 坑洞 spot 地點

⑬ What do you say we unload our gear from the car, set up our tent, and start a fire to prepare dinner?

你覺得我們先從車上卸下裝備、搭帳篷，然後升火準備晚餐如何？

⑭ Building a fire isn't difficult if you have the right tinder and wood to get it going.

要升火並不困難，如果你有適合的火種跟助燃的木頭就很容易。

⑮ I like to roast marshmallows after setting up the campfire.

升好營火後，我喜歡烤棉花糖。 campfire 營火

⑯ The least interesting thing during a camping trip is taking down the tent.

露營之旅最無趣的就是拆帳篷的時候了。 take down 拆掉

⑰ Besides bringing all the camping gear, a first aid kit shouldn't be ignored.

除了攜帶全套的露營配備之外，急救箱也別忘了帶。

first aid kit 急救藥箱

⑱ After dinner, we sometimes sit around the fire and tell stories or sing songs.

用過晚餐後，我們有時會圍著營火坐一圈，說故事跟唱歌。

Part 1 自我介紹
Part 2 日常雜務
Part 3 職場應對
Part 4 休閒娛樂
Part 5 出國旅遊
Part 6 愛情來了

對話情境① 手機充當手電筒

A : Two sleeping bags, a **gas stove**, and some **canned food**.
B : **Check**, check, check.
A : Ah, you must have forgotten the flashlight.
B : That wouldn't be necessary. We all have smartphones, don't we?
A : Oh, you mean using the flashlight app as a **substitute**?

A：兩個睡袋、一個瓦斯爐、還有一些罐頭。
B：打勾、打勾、打勾。
A：啊，你一定忘了要帶手電筒。
B：不需要，我們不是都有智慧型手機嗎？
A：喔，你是說用手電筒應用程式來取代嗎？

gas stove 片 瓦斯爐
canned food 片 罐頭食品
check [tʃɛk] 名 動 打鉤
substitute [`sʌbstə.tjut] 名 替代物；代替者

對話情境② 你到底會什麼

A : Go and **pitch** the tent.
B : I don't know how.
A : Then, go and **set up** a campfire.
B : Um, you'll have to show me how.
A : What **exactly** can you do?

A：去搭帳篷。
B：我不會。
A：那去生火。
B：喔，那你必須示範給我看。
A：你到底會做什麼？

pitch [pɪtʃ] 動 搭（帳篷）
set up 片 搭建；設置
exactly [ɪg`zæktlɪ] 副 確切地；究竟

對話情境 3　露營定義大不同

A : Do you want to go camping next month?
B : Are we going to sleep in a real tent?
A : Duh. Where else are we going to sleep?
B : I thought there would be some trailers so that we could sleep indoors.
A : Well, my kind of camping involves staying in the woods and sleeping in the open air.

A：你下個月想不想去露營？
B：我們要睡在真的帳篷裡嗎？
A：不然呢？還有哪裡可以睡？
B：我以為會有露營車，這樣就可以睡在室內了。
A：嗯，我所謂的露營是要待在森林裡，睡在大自然中的。

trailer [`trelɚ] 名
拖車
woods [wʊdz] 名
森林
in the open air 片
在戶外

對話情境 4　沒有輕便旅行這回事

A : Do we need to buy a tent and some sleeping bags?
B : I think we can rent everything at the campsite we are going to.
A : Great. So we can travel light this time.
B : There's no such thing as traveling light. I am bringing lots of food and drinks.
A : Brilliant idea!

A：我們需不需要買帳篷跟睡袋？
B：營區那裡應該都有得租。
A：太棒了，那我們這次可以享受輕便旅行了。
B：沒有輕便旅行這回事，我要帶很多食物跟飲料。
A：好主意！

sleeping bag 片
睡袋
light [laɪt] 副 輕裝地
brilliant [`brɪljənt]
形 絕妙的；出色的

自我介紹
Part 1

日常雜務
Part 2

職場應對
Part 3

休閒娛樂
Part 4

出國旅遊
Part 5

愛情來了
Part 6

237

便利三句開口說

What kind of music do you like?
▶ 你喜歡什麼類型的音樂？

替換句 What musical genres do you like? 你喜歡什麼種類的音樂？

☑ ➜ **句型提點** Using It Properly!

「What+kind+of+ 名詞 + 主要問句」可用來詢問「某物的類型」。例：What kind of book are you reading? 你在讀什麼書？ / What kind of person is she? 她是個怎樣的人？

Can you play a musical instrument?
▶ 你會演奏樂器嗎？

替換句 Do you know how to play a musical instrument? 你知道怎麼彈奏樂器嗎？

☑ ➜ **句型提點** Using It Properly!

助動詞 can 不只能詢問「能力」，還可以表達「徵求許可」以及「要求幫忙」。表能力的例句：Can he cook? 他會煮飯嗎？ / 表徵求許可，例如：Can I come in? 我可以進去嗎？

Do you prefer oldies or new hits?
▶ 你喜歡老歌還是新曲？

替換句 Do you like listening to oldies or new hits? 你喜歡聽老歌還是新曲？

✅ 🜲 **句型提點** ❰ Using It Properly! ❱

prefer 表示偏好，後面須接名詞或動名詞；另外，因為 prefer 是以表現「狀態」為主，所以大多用現在式。若想強調兩者之中比較喜歡某一個，也可以說 prefer A to/over B，就表示兩者之中比較喜歡 A。

💬 **有來有往的必備回應**

Q What kind of music do you like?

> I like classical music best. *A*
>
> 我最喜歡古典音樂。

Q Can you play a musical instrument?

> Yes, I can. I've been playing piano since *A*
> I was six.
>
> 我會，我六歲就開始彈鋼琴，一直到現在。

Q Do you prefer oldies or new hits?

> I like both, actually. *A*
>
> 其實我兩種都喜歡。

💡 **小知識補給站** *Some Fun Facts*

時下最受歡迎的流行樂都可以稱為 pop music，其他常見的音樂種類還有：DJ 操刀製作的電子舞曲 (EDM)、純人聲合唱 (A Cappella)、抒情輕快的鄉村音樂 (country music)、傳統的民歌 (folk)、憂鬱的藍調 (blues)、融合即興演奏技巧的爵士樂 (jazz)、節拍及歌唱強勁的搖滾音樂 (Rock and Roll)、節奏感強烈的放克音樂 (funk)…等等。

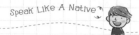

01 I think music is indispensable and the spice of life.
我認為音樂是生活中不可或缺的調味品。
`indispensable 必需的`

02 I can't work without music, which means I listen to music practically everyday.
我工作的時候不能沒有音樂,也就是說,我基本上是天天聽音樂。

03 The Billboard charts are the major indication of the popularity of songs and albums in the United States.
告示牌排行榜是美國音樂或專輯受歡迎程度的主要指標。

04 I enjoy listening to Broadway musicals.
我喜歡聽百老匯的音樂劇。 `musical 歌舞劇`

05 My brother's favorite type of music is heavy metal, and he is also a member of an amateur band.
我哥最喜歡的音樂類型是重金屬,他同時也是業餘樂團的成員。 `amateur 業餘的`

06 I like jazz music in general, be it ragtime, blues, big band swing, bebop and so many other types.
幾乎所有種類的爵士樂我都喜歡,不論是拉格泰姆、藍調、大樂團、咆勃爵士樂或其他種類,我都喜愛。

07 When I hear the music from the '80s, I always feel like dancing to the beat.
當我聽到 80 年代 (1980-1989) 的音樂時,我總是會想要跟著節奏起舞。

08 My brother misses the old-school hip-hop of his college years.
我哥懷念他大學時期的老式嘻哈音樂。 `old-school 老派的`

09 Did you hear the new song by Coldplay on the

radio yesterday?
你昨天有聽到廣播放的酷玩樂團的新歌嗎？ `radio 收音機`

⑩ **I will most definitely buy the CD when the new album is released.**
這新專輯的光碟一出，我一定會去買。 `release 發行；發表`

⑪ **He is the most old-fashioned guy I've ever met! He still listens to music on a cassette player!**
他真的是我見過最老派的人了！他現在還在用卡帶播放器聽音樂。 `cassette player 卡帶式播放器`

⑫ **I download most of the music online and listen to it on my iPod.**
我的音樂幾乎都是線上下載，再存到 iPod 上面聽。

⑬ **There are now several smart phone apps, which provide diversified music services.**
現在有一些智慧型手機的應用程式提供多元化的音樂服務。

⑭ **I have a long workout playlist in my phone that I cannot do without!**
我手機裡有一長串的健身專用音樂，萬萬不能缺少它們！

⑮ **I am watching Adele's live performance on YouTube. Her voice is amazing!**
我在 YouTube 上看愛黛兒的現場演唱會，她聲音超迷人！

⑯ **There are more and more live concerts being held in the Taipei Arena these days.**
台北小巨蛋近期舉辦的演唱會愈來愈多。

⑰ **My mom was invited to a classical concert performed in a concert hall.**
我媽受邀參加在音樂廳表演的古典音樂會。
`concert hall 音樂廳`

⑱ **I am trying to make up my own music by playing the ukulele.**
我嘗試用烏克麗麗來創作音樂。 `ukulele 烏克麗麗琴`

⑲ **Can you memorize the lyrics of all the songs you like?**
你可以記得所有你喜愛歌曲的歌詞嗎？ `lyric 歌詞`

自我介紹 日常雜務 職場應對 休閒娛樂 出國旅遊 愛情來了

241

雙人實境對話 〈oh!〉

對話情境 ① 音樂配美食

A : What kind of music do you think we should play during the dinner party this Saturday?

B : I am thinking about something upbeat and mellow.

A : I happen to have several CDs of jazz music.

B : What types of jazz?

A : Mostly female vocal jazz and bossa nova.

A：這週六的晚餐聚會，你覺得我們應該播放什麼樣的音樂啊？

B：我覺得輕快溫和的音樂比較好。

A：我剛好有一些爵士音樂的 CD。

B：什麼種類的爵士樂？

A：大部分是女伶演唱的爵士跟巴薩諾瓦。

upbeat [`ʌp͵bit] 形
歡快的

mellow [`mɛlo] 形
柔和的

bossa nova 名 巴薩諾瓦（爵士樂的一種）

對話情境 ② 支持正版

A : Are you downloading music from the Internet?

B : Yeah, I have a huge collection of pop music in my computer.

A : I thought it was illegal.

B : Well, who would know? Everybody is doing it.

A : I'd rather spend extra money buying the originals to show my respect to the composers and singers.

A：你都從網路上下載音樂來聽嗎？

B：對，我電腦裡有一整套流行音樂。

A：這樣是違法的吧。

B：沒有人會知道啦，而且大家都這麼做。

A：我寧願多花點錢買正版，來表達我對作曲者跟演唱者的尊重。

illegal [ɪ`ligl] 形
非法的

original [ə`rɪdʒən!]
名 原版；原作

composer
[kəm`pozə] 名
作曲者

對話情境 ③ 舒心禪樂

A : Why do you call the file "Zen music"?

B : Oh, this file contains all the music I play when I do Yoga.

A : Can I listen to some songs?

B : Go ahead. You can download them if you want.

A : That's very generous of you!

A：你為什麼把這個檔案夾取名「禪樂」？

B：喔，這裡面存了所有我做瑜珈時候要聽的音樂。

A：我可以聽幾首嗎？

B：可以啊，如果你想要的話，也可以下載。

A：你真大方！

---

file [faɪl] ② 資料夾

contain [kən`ten] ⑩ 包含；含有

generous [`dʒɛnərəs] ⑭ 慷慨的；大方的

對話情境 ④ 年度頒獎大典

A : Are you going to watch the Grammy Awards tonight?

B : Oh, I totally forgot! I'm going to cancel my dinner date.

A : Wow, you take the Grammy's seriously.

B : Absolutely. My favorite singer, Lady Gaga, will be performing at the Grammy's.

A : We must not miss out on that!

A：你今天晚上要看葛萊美頒獎典禮嗎？

B：喔，我完全忘記了！我得取消晚餐約會。

A：哇，你真看重這場頒獎典禮。

B：當然，我最愛的歌手女神卡卡會在典禮上表演呢。

A：那我們可絕對不能錯過！

---

take sth. seriously ⑮ 認真對待某事

miss out on ⑮ 錯過；錯失

自我介紹

日常雜務

職場應對

休閒娛樂

出國旅遊

愛情來了

243

健身訓練樣樣行

Working out in a gym

便利三句開口說

Where do you work out?
▶ 你都在哪裡健身？

替換句 Are you a member of a gym? 你是健身房的會員嗎？

✓ **句型提點** Using It Properly!

「Where+do/does+人+動詞」用來詢問對方「在哪裡做某事」，回答時可以直接說出地點就好。片語 work out 的意思是健身、運動。

I joined ABC Health Club a couple of months ago.
▶ 我幾個月前加入了 ABC 健身俱樂部。

替換句 I work out at ABC Gym. 我在 ABC 健身房運動。

✓ **句型提點** Using It Properly!

join 為「加入」，常指加入某個已經成立的團體或組織。此句的 join a club 即表示加入某俱樂部而成為會員。health club、gym 則都是指健身房。

I've been working out a lot lately.
▶ 我最近經常去健身。

替換句 I've been exercising for the past few weeks. 我過去幾個禮拜以來都在運動。

✓ **句型提點** Using It Properly!

「have/has+been+V-ing」是完成進行式，表示「從

過去一直到現在，且未來也都會持續進行」，後接時間副詞 lately，強調「最近」一直有在做這件事。

有來有往的必備回應

Q　Where do you work out?

　　　　　I work out at QQ Gym.　*A*
　　　　　我在 QQ 健身房健身。

Q　I joined ABC Health Club a couple of months ago.

　　　　　How much does a gym membership cost?　*A*
　　　　　健身房的會員費怎麼算？

Q　I've been working out a lot lately.

　　　　　No wonder you look fit.　*A*
　　　　　難怪你的身材看起來很健美。

小知識補給站　Some Fun Facts

　　對於美國人，健身不只是名星們保持體態的方式，同時也是大眾維持健康的一種方式，不但有愈來愈好的健身設備，還有愈多的健身方式可供選擇，像是基礎的有氧舞蹈 (aerobics)、肌耐力訓練 (muscular endurance)、 重訓 (weight training)、 核 心 肌 群訓練 (core conditioning)，到近期的新式有氧訓練 (cardiovascular training)、 飛輪 (spinning)、 階梯有氧 (step aerobics)，新興起的還有懸吊訓練 (TRX suspension training)、 空中瑜珈 (aerial yoga)、 間歇運動 (tabata training)…等各式各樣的運動。

245

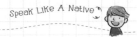
01 I go to a health club around three times a week to stay in shape and stay fit.
我一周去健身房三次左右以保持身形、維持健康體態。

02 I will take a day off from exercising, because my muscles need rest.
我會找一天休息不去運動，因為肌肉也需要休息。
`muscle 肌肉`

03 Exercise also lets me burn off stress from work.
運動也能舒緩工作帶給我的壓力。 `burn off 燒掉（某物）`

04 My gym pal and I are a little bit too obsessed with workouts, for we hit the gym almost every single day.
我的健身房夥伴跟我有點太沉迷於健身，我們幾乎每天都去健身房報到。 `be obsess with 沉迷於…`

05 I started lifting weights about two years ago.
我兩年前開始練舉重。 `lift weights 舉重`

06 They say it's much more effective if you work out over an hour.
他們說健身超過一個鐘頭比較有效果。 `effective 有效的`

07 I ran several miles on a treadmill and did some stretching on a yoga mat.
我在跑步機跑了幾哩，接著在瑜珈墊上做伸展操。
`stretch 延伸；拉長`

08 My brother trains on machines and then relaxes in the Jacuzzi for a few minutes to alleviate his muscle pain.
我弟先用機器鍛鍊，再去按摩浴池泡幾分鐘，來減緩肌肉酸痛的現象。 `alleviate 減輕；緩和`

09 I love doing aerobics to improve my cardiovascular fitness.
我喜歡上有氧課程來增強我的心肺功能。

cardiovascular 心血管的

⑩ I need to work on my biceps and triceps. What kind of exercise do you recommend?

我需要加強二頭肌跟三頭肌，你建議我做什麼樣的運動？

⑪ When you bench press, how many reps and sets do you do?

當你做臥推的時候，你都做幾下？共做幾組？

bench press 臥推　rep = repetition 重複

⑫ I squat 400 pounds and curl 90 pounds.

我深蹲可承受 400 磅，二頭舉啞鈴可到 90 磅。

squat 深蹲

⑬ Do you do low reps with heavy weights, or many reps with light weights?

你都用很重的訓練用具做少量訓練，還是減輕重量但增加訓練次數？

⑭ I'm trying to gain bulk, so I'm doing low reps with heavy weights.

我想要練肌肉，所以我用強力的重量搭配少量訓練。

bulk 巨大；大塊

⑮ I'm trying to get ripped, so I'm doing a lot of repetitions.

我想要練出肌肉線條，所以我做很多次的訓練。

⑯ Besides cardio workouts, I do lunges and squats, and I lift free weights every other day.

除了心臟功能的訓練，我每隔一天還會做弓箭步、深蹲及舉重。 cardio 心臟的

⑰ Alvin lifts weights and discusses nutrition with his personal trainer at the gym.

亞文在健身房舉重，並與他的健身教練討論營養的話題。

⑱ I do jumping jacks, run in place, and jump rope on the balcony.

我會在家裡的陽台做交互蹲跳、原地跑步和跳繩等運動。

jumping jack 交互蹲跳

Part 1 自我介紹

Part 2 日常雜務

Part 3 職場應對

Part 4 休閒娛樂

Part 5 出國旅遊

Part 6 愛情來了

247

對話情境 ① 來去健身

Ⓐ : When I have some time, I like to exercise.
Ⓑ : Do you go jogging or do you go to a health club?
Ⓐ : I joined Happy Gym a couple of months ago.
Ⓑ : How do you exercise?
Ⓐ : I usually spend 30 minutes on the bicycle for the cardio, and then I lift weights for about 45 minutes.

A：如果有時間，我喜歡去運動。
B：你會到外面慢跑，還是去健身房？
A：我幾個月前加入了快樂健身房。
B：你都做什麼運動？
A：我通常花半小時在腳踏車上做有氧運動，然後舉重約四十五分鐘。

health club 🖱
健身房
a couple of 🖱 幾個
lift weights 🖱 舉重

對話情境 ② 有規劃的重訓

Ⓐ : Let's go work out later today.
Ⓑ : Sure. What time do you want to go?
Ⓐ : How about at 3:30?
Ⓑ : That sounds good. We can work on legs and forearms.
Ⓐ : I just played basketball earlier, so my legs are a little sore. Let's work out on arms and the stomach today.

A：我們晚點去健身吧。
B：當然好，你幾點要去？
A：三點半如何？
B：聽起來很棒，我們來鍛鍊腿和手臂的肌肉吧。
A：我剛剛去打籃球，腳有點酸，我們今天還是鍛鍊手臂跟肚子吧。

work on 🖱 忙於；
從事
forearm [`for.ɑrm]
🖲 前臂
sore [sor] 🖲 疼痛的

對話情境 ❸ 久久不見你變了

A : Wow, You got big. You must have **put a lot of effort into bulking up**.

B : Yeah, I've been working out a lot.

A : How long have you been lifting weights?

B : For a year and a half.

A : Yeah. Last time I saw you, it was like two years ago.

A：哇，你變的好大隻。你一定花了很多心血增重吧。

B：對啊，我最近很常健身。

A：你舉重舉多久啦？

B：一年半。

A：對喔，上次見到你大概是兩年前了。

put effort into 片 努力

bulk up 片 增重

對話情境 ❹ 新的訓練課程

A : Have you seen anyone doing the latest training program at the gym?

B : No. What's the program like?

A : I think it's called TRX, and I saw people working out with some sort of **flexible** rubber **tubing** attached to a machine.

B : Sounds very **up-to-date**.

A : Let's join the program next time!

A：你在健身房有看到誰在做最新的訓練課程嗎？

B：沒有，那是什麼課程？

A：好像叫 TRX，我看到有人使用一條從機器拉出來的彈力繩做訓練。

B：聽起來好先進。

A：我們下次也去參加吧！

flexible [`flɛksəbl] 形 有彈性的

tubing [`tjubɪŋ] 名 管子

up-to-date [`ʌptə`det] 形 最新的；流行的

Part 1 自我介紹

Part 2 日常雜務

Part 3 職場應對

Part 4 休閒娛樂

Part 5 出國旅遊

Part 6 愛情來了

NOTE

Part 5

出國旅遊
愈玩愈樂的必備句

打破一個人出國的恐懼不安，
用語言加深你的旅遊豐富度！

Where am I ??

★ 迷路、旅途中遇到問題？
　這樣解決！

名 名詞　　　動 動詞　　　形 形容詞

副 副詞　　　介 介係詞　　　助 助詞

連 連接詞　　　限 限定詞　　　縮 縮寫

出入機場
In and out the airport

 便利三句開口說

Where's the check-in counter for American Airlines?

▶ 請問美國航空的櫃台在哪裡？

替換句 I am flying with AA. Where do I check in? 我搭乘美國航空，請問我應該要到哪邊登記劃位？

✓ → **句型提點** Using It Properly!

「辦理登記手續」為 check in，而不管是在機場辦理登機手續或是在旅館辦理入住手續，都可以用 check in 來表示。若做名詞使用，中間須加連字號 (hyphen)，變成 check-in。

- -

Here are my passport and my e-ticket.

▶ 這是我的護照跟電子機票。

替換句 (May I have your passport and ticket, please?) Here you go. （麻煩出示您的護照跟機票。）在這裡。

✓ → **句型提點** Using It Properly!

當拿給對方東西時，可用「Here+is/are+ 名詞」。例：Here's the book you asked for. 你要找的書在這裡。替換句的「Here you go.」則為此句簡略的講法。

- -

I'd like an aisle seat, please.

▶ 我想要坐靠走道的位子。

替換句 I prefer an aisle seat. 我喜歡坐在走道旁邊。

☑ ○ **句型提點** 〈 **Using It Properly!** 〉

禮貌地表示需要某項物品或請求的事項，可以用「人名／代名詞 +would+like+ 名詞」，would 可與主詞一起縮寫成「I'd」。aisle seat 指靠走道的座位，window seat 則是靠窗座位。

有來有往的必備回應

Q　Where's the check-in counter for American Airlines?

　　Go straight. You'll see a sign marked G5, and there it is.　*A*

往前直走，你會看到一個寫著 G5 的標誌，就在那邊。

Q　Here are my passport and my e-ticket.

　　Are you checking any bags?　*A*

你有要拖運行李嗎？

Q　I'd like an aisle seat, please.

　　Noted.　*A*

知道了。

小知識補給站　Some Fun Facts

　　上機之前，一定要事先確認好起飛時間 (departure time)、航廈 (terminal)、登機門 (boarding gate/ departing gate)、班機號碼 (flight number)、行李限額 (baggage allowance)；在機場裡面，有些航空公司也會提供旅客自助報到的機器 (kiosk)，只要掃瞄護照、輸入訂位資訊就能取得登機證，再去櫃檯托運行李後，就可以完成報到。

自我介紹　日常雜務　職場應對　休閒娛樂　出國旅遊　愛情來了

01 **Most people nowadays book their airline tickets online.**
現在很多人都上網買機票。 airline ticket 機票

02 **Even though you bought your ticket online, you will need a boarding pass to get on the plane.**
即使是在網路上購票，還是得有登機證才能登機。
boarding pass 登機證

03 **What time do we take off?**
我們的班機幾點起飛？ take off (飛機)起飛

04 **What time are we going to board?**
我們幾點要登機？ board 登機；上飛機

05 **Is there a shuttle bus that goes between terminals?**
航廈之間有沒有接駁公車？ terminal 航廈；航空站

06 **Where are you flying today?**
您今天要飛往哪裡呢？

07 **I am placing you in 25A. The gate number is D3. It is on the bottom of the ticket. They will start boarding twenty minutes before the departure time.**
您的位子在 25A，登機門是 D3，資料都註明在票的最下方。起飛前二十分鐘開始登機。

08 **We got to the airport really early, so I decided to try and get on an earlier flight as a stand-by passenger.**
我們太早抵達機場，所以我試著登記早班航空的候補機位。

09 **This airline allows two carry-on bags per passenger.**
這家航空公司允許一位乘客攜帶兩件登機袋。
carry-on 可隨身攜帶的

10 **Please lay your bags flat on the conveyor belt,**

and use the bins for small objects.
請將你的袋子平放在運輸帶上，並將小型物品置於籃中。

⑪ **You'll have to go through security before arriving at your gate. I hope you don't have any metal in your pockets!**
前往登機門之前，你必須先通過安檢。希望你口袋裡面沒有放什麼金屬物喔！ security 安檢；保護措施

⑫ **Be sure to take coins and keys out of your pocket, so that the alarm won't go off.**
記得要將零錢跟鑰匙拿出口袋，警報器才不會響。
alarm 警報器 go off 響起

⑬ **There has been a gate change.**
登機門有異動。 gate 登機門

⑭ **United Airlines flight 880 to Miami is now boarding.**
美國聯航前往邁阿密的 880 班機現在可以開始登機。

⑮ **Please have your boarding pass and identification ready for boarding.**
請將您的登機證以及證件準備好，以便登機。

⑯ **We would like to invite our first and business class passengers to board first.**
我們先邀請頭等艙以及商務艙的旅客登機。
first/ business class 頭等艙／商務艙

⑰ **We are now inviting passengers with children and any passengers requiring special assistance to begin boarding.**
我們現在邀請攜帶小孩的旅客，以及需要特別協助的旅客開始登機。

⑱ **We would now like to invite all passengers to board.**
我們現在邀請所有旅客進行登機。 passenger 乘客；旅客

⑲ **This is the final boarding call for United Airlines flight 880 to Miami.**
這是美國聯航 880 班機前往邁阿密的最後登機廣播。

雙人實境對話 ⟨oh!⟩

對話情境 ① 早班航班

A : Can you drive me to the airport? I'm **heading off** to Japan for business tomorrow morning.

B : Sure. What time is your **flight**?

A : The plane takes off at 8:00 a.m. I'd like to get to the airport by 6:00.

B : Yeah, arriving 2 hours early is considered **standard** for international flights.

A : So, we'll have to wake up really early tomorrow morning!

A：可以載我去機場嗎？我明天早上要去日本出差。

B：當然可以，你飛機幾點？

A：飛機是早上八點的。我想早上六點就到機場。

B：嗯，提早兩個鐘頭是國際航班標準的規定。

A：所以明天我們得起個大早了！

head off 動身去⋯

flight [flaɪt] 名 班機

standard [`stændəd] 形 標準的 名 標準

對話情境 ② 辦理登記劃位

A : Good afternoon. Where are you flying to today?

B : Los Angeles.

A : Your passport, please. Are you **checking** any bags?

B : Yes, I am checking one bag.

A : OK, please place your bag on the **scale**.

A：午安，您今天飛往哪裡呢？

B：洛杉磯。

A：請出示護照，您要託運行李嗎？

B：要，我要託運一件行李。

A：好的，請將您的袋子放在秤上。

check [tʃɛk] 動 托運行李

scale [skel] 名 磅秤

對話情境 3 通過安檢

A : Please **lay** your bags **flat** on the **conveyor belt**, and use the **bins** for small objects.
B : Do I need to take off my shoes, too?
A : Yes, you do. And make sure you take out everything in your pockets.
B : OK. I am done.
A : Okay, come on through.

A：請將您的袋子平放在運輸袋上,並將小型物品放在籃子裡。
B：鞋子也需要脫掉嗎?
A：是的,並請確認您口袋裡的東西都拿出來了。
B：好,我好了。
A：好的,請過去吧。

lay [le] 動 放;擺
flat [flæt] 副 平地
conveyor belt 片 輸送帶
bin [bɪn] 名 容器

對話情境 4 入境

A : Here it is. (Handing his passport to **Customs officer**)
B : Where are you coming from?
A : I'm coming from Seoul, South Korea.
B : What is the **purpose** of your **visit**?
A : I'm here **on business**.

A：都在這了。(將護照相關資料交給海關)
B：您從哪裡過來的?
A：我從南韓首爾過來的。
B：您這次旅行的目的是?
A：我是來出差的。

Customs officer 片 海關人員
purpose [`pɝpəs] 名 目的;意圖
visit [`vɪzɪt] 名 參觀;拜訪
on business 片 出差;辦事

Part 1 自我介紹
Part 2 日常雜務
Part 3 職場應對
Part 4 休閒娛樂
Part 5 出國旅遊
Part 6 愛情來了

257

上機之後
Please fasten your seatbelt

便利三句開口說

I am traveling first class/economy class.
▶ 我搭乘頭等艙 / 經濟艙。

替換句 I am flying first class/economy class. 我搭乘頭等艙 / 經濟艙。

✓ **句型提點** Using It Properly!

「人名 / 代名詞 +is/are+traveling/flying + 某艙等」可以表示搭乘某種艙等。first class =頭等艙、business class =商務艙、economy class/tourist class =經濟艙。

Could you tell me where 12D is?
▶ 可以告訴我座位 12D 在哪裡嗎？

替換句 Could you tell me where I can find my seat?
可否告訴我如何找到我的座位？

✓ **句型提點** Using It Properly!

問句用 could 開頭，表示禮貌性的請求對方協助。若需要再更加禮貌，可以在主要動詞前面加上 kindly。例如：Could you kindly email me the details? 可以麻煩您將細節 email 給我嗎？

Could I get something to drink, please?
▶ 請問我可以點些飲料嗎？

替換句 Could you please get me a Coke? 可否給我一杯可樂呢？

✅ 句型提點 **Using It Properly!**

使用 could 當問句開頭較為禮貌，句尾加上 please 又再更禮貌的表示「請、請問」，當然也可以把 please 置於句中。例如：Could somebody please answer the phone? 請問誰可以去幫忙接個電話嗎？

有來有往的必備回應

Q I am traveling first class/economy class.

Have a nice flight! *A*
祝您旅途愉快！

Q Could you tell me where 12D is?

It's the third row, on your right hand side. *A*
在您右手邊的第三排。

Q Could I get something to drink, please?

Sure. What would you like to drink? *A*
沒問題，請問您想要喝點什麼？

小知識補給站 *Some Fun Facts*

空服人員最常使用的英文不外乎是安全解說、點餐、詢問需不需要其他服務…等等，別再怕自己聽不懂，而不敢向空服員詢問事情了！你可以善用 "could" 來當開頭，提出需求之後更別忘了感謝空服員的幫忙；而快抵達目的地時，也要記得向空服員索取入境單 (arrival card/ disembarkation card) 來填寫，並於入境時繳交給海關人員。

Part 1 自我介紹
Part 2 日常雜務
Part 3 職場應對
Part 4 休閒娛樂
Part 5 出國旅遊
Part 6 愛情來了

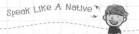
01 **Could you help me put this bag in the overhead compartment?**

可否幫我將這袋子放進上方的行李箱置物中？

overhead 在頭上的 compartment 隔層

02 **We'll have a layover in Denver, and then we will continue to Los Angeles.**

我們在丹佛會短暫地停留一下，然後就會繼續飛往洛杉磯。

layover 臨時滯留

03 **It's the exit row, the second row past the first-class cabin. You're in Seats A and B, which are on the right side of the plane behind the lavatory.**

這在緊急出口那一排，也就是過了頭等艙後的第二排。
你們的位子是 A 跟 B，在飛機右邊、廁所的後面。

cabin 客艙 lavatory 廁所

04 **I always watch the safety instructions at the start of the flight.**

每次飛機起飛前，我都會看安全指南。

safety instruction 安全介紹

05 **Please direct your attention to the flight attendants throughout the first-class and economy-class cabins for a few safety announcements.**

請將您的注意力轉向在頭等艙以及經濟艙的空服員，聆聽
有關安全須知的說明。 direct 將 (注意力) 轉向

06 **Please fasten your seatbelt. You insert the buckle into the latch and adjust the belt so it fits low and firmly.**

請繫好您的安全帶。請將扣環扣入座位的插梢，並調整綁
帶使其穩固。 buckle 扣上 latch 扣環

07 **Please make sure to switch off any electronic devices during take-off and landing.**

飛機起飛及降落時，請確保您的電子儀器關機。
switch off 關閉　electronic 電子的

08 Once the pilot announces that we've reached our cruising altitude, you can get up to go to the bathroom.

當機長廣播說我們到達巡航高度時，你就可以起身去廁所了。 altitude 高度；海拔

09 I get a little nervous when there is turbulence. I'm always convinced that the plane is going down!

一遇到亂流我就會開始緊張，總覺得飛機要掉下去了！

10 I get motion sickness easily. Any turbulence will get me sick as a dog.

我容易暈機，任何一點亂流都能讓我變得跟條病狗一樣。

11 Grab the barf bag. He's going to puke!

快點拿嘔吐袋來，他要吐了！ barf bag 嘔吐袋

12 Hopefully, they will have some good in-flight entertainment, and I will be too distracted to get sick.

希望他們在機上有提供有趣的娛樂節目，這樣就能分散我的注意力，而不會覺得不舒服了。 in-flight 飛行過程中的

13 Will they be showing an in-flight movie?

他們會在機上播放電影嗎？

14 Please push the call button if you need anything.

若您需要任何服務，請按服務鈴。

15 Could I get another blanket, please? I'm a little cold.

可以再多給我一條毯子嗎？我有點冷。 blanket 毛毯

16 Could I have a pillow and a headset?

可以給我一個枕頭跟一副耳機嗎？ headset 雙耳式耳機

17 Could you also lend me a pen to fill out this immigration form?

可否也借我一支筆，讓我填寫入境表格？
immigration form 入境表格

Part 1 自我介紹

Part 2 日常雜務

Part 3 職場應對

Part 4 休閒娛樂

Part 5 出國旅遊

Part 6 愛情來了

對話情境 ① 機上餐點

A : Would you like chicken or **pasta**?
B : I'll have the chicken.
A : Anything to drink?
B : What kind of **soft drinks** do you have?
A : Coke, Diet Coke, Sprite, and Juice.

A：您想吃雞肉還是義大利麵？
B：我要雞肉。
A：要喝點什麼嗎？
B：你們有提供哪些不含酒精的飲料？
A：可樂、健怡、雪碧跟果汁。

pasta [`pɑstə] 名
（總稱）義大利麵食

soft drink 片 不含
酒精的飲料

對話情境 ② 還有供餐嗎？

A : Excuse me, how long will it take to **reach**
Seattle?
B : It's a long **journey**. We still have five hours
before landing.
A : Will there be any more meals before we land?
B : Yes, another meal will be **served** in two hours,
but I can get you some snacks now, if you like.
A : Yes, that would be great.

A：請問，到西雅圖大概要多久？
B：這路程滿長的，降落前還有五個小
　時的飛行時間。
A：降落前還會提供餐點嗎？
B：有的，兩個小時後會提供另外一餐。
　需要的話，我現在可以拿些點心給
　您。
A：嗯，太好了。

reach [ritʃ] 動 抵達
journey [`dʒɝnɪ] 名
旅程
serve [sɝv] 動 供應

對話情境 3 填寫入境表格

Ⓐ : Here's an arrival card for **immigration**, Ma'am.

Ⓑ : Thanks. Could you **lend** me a pen, please?

Ⓐ : Another **cabin crew** member will be bringing pens around in a moment.

Ⓑ : Great. I need to fill out this immigration form before we land.

Ⓐ : Sure. Someone will bring you a pen shortly.

自我介紹

日常雜務

A：女士，這是入境單。

B：謝謝，可以借我一支筆嗎？

A：等等會有另外一位機組人員拿筆給您。

B：太好了，我必須在降落前填好這表格。

A：沒問題，馬上就會有人拿筆給您了。

immigration
[ˌɪməˋgreʃən] 名 入境審查；移民入境

lend [lɛnd] 動 借（出）

cabin crew 片 機組人員

對話情境 4 與空服員的對話

Ⓐ : Can I ask you some questions about the in-flight **instructions**?

Ⓑ : I would be happy to help you **clarify** anything you need help with.

Ⓐ : Could you help me find out where my nearest exit is?

Ⓑ : There is a card in your seat pocket that shows you where. Yours is two **rows** in front of you.

Ⓐ : Thanks for your explanation.

職場應對

休閒娛樂

出國旅遊

愛情來了

A：可不可以問你有關飛機內的介紹？

B：我很樂意為您解答。

A：可否告訴我，離我位子最近的緊急逃生口在哪裡？

B：您座位前方的口袋中有一張卡片有標明。在您座位前兩排就有一個。

A：謝謝你的說明。

instruction
[ɪnˋstrʌkʃən] 名 指南；操作說明

clarify [ˋklærəˌfaɪ] 動 使清楚；澄清

row [ro] 名 （一排）座位

入住旅館
Checking in at the hotel

便利三句開口說

Hi, my name is Wilson, and I have a reservation for tonight.

▶ 你好，我姓威爾森，我今天晚上有預約訂房。

替換句▶ Hi, my name is Wilson. I booked a room for tonight. 你好，我姓威爾森，我之前有預約今天晚上的房間。

✓ **句型提點** Using It Properly!

「have a reservation for」表達已有預約訂位，for 後面接預約時間或人數，表示預約的內容。

- -

I'd like a room for two people for three nights, please.

▶ 我需要一間兩人房，待三個晚上。

替換句▶ I need a double room for three nights. 我需要一張雙人床的房間，共三個晚上。

✓ **句型提點** Using It Properly!

「would like + 請求事項」為「表達需求」較禮貌的方式。雙人房可以說 double/twin room，兩者差別為：double room 只有一張雙人床，而 twin room 則有兩張單人床。

- -

How much is the charge per night?

▶ 房價一個晚上是多少呢？

替換句▶ How much does a room cost? 一間房間怎麼計費？

Part 1 自我介紹
Part 2 日常雜務
Part 3 職場應對
Part 4 休閒娛樂
Part 5 出國旅遊
Part 6 愛情來了

✓ ⌐ 句型提點 < Using It Properly!

此句可用來詢問價錢，「How much」後面須接不可數名詞。介係詞 per 表示「每…」，例：per person 每人；per year 每年；per meter 每公尺。

有來有往的必備回應

Q Hi, my name is Wilson, and I have a reservation for tonight.

A Let me check. Yes. A twin room for one night.

我幫您查一下，有的，一間雙床房，待一個晚上。

Q I'd like a room for two people for three nights, please.

A Do you have a reservation?

請問您有先訂房嗎？

Q How much is the charge per night?

A The rate I can give you is USD$90 with tax.

含稅價我可以給你 90 美元。

小知識補給站 *Some Fun Facts*

在美國住宿，像是幫忙提行李的行李小弟 (hotel porter)、泊車人員 (valet)、以及客房清理服務 (housekeeping service)，通常都需要給小費；給清潔人員的小費可放在床頭，而給泊車人員小費可於取車時再給；若有請門房 (concierge) 代訂餐廳、票券等等，也可視難度高低給予小費。

265

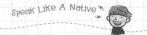
01 I'd like to make a reservation for next week.
我想要預訂下週的房間。 reservation 預約；預訂

02 I'd appreciate it if you could give me a room with a view of the lake.
如果你可以幫忙安排能俯瞰湖景的房間，那就太感謝了！

03 How long will you be staying?
您要停留多久呢？

04 I will be needing the room until the 1st of September.
我將會住在此房間至九月一號。

05 We recommend that you make a reservation, though. It's still considered peak season then.
我們還是建議您先預訂房位，現在這期間還算是旺季。
peak season 旺季

06 There are only a few vacancies left.
現在只剩下幾間空房而已了。

07 Do you have any rooms with two double beds? We're a family of four.
你們有兩張雙人床的房型嗎？我們一家四口同行。

08 Do you do group bookings?
你們接受團體訂房嗎？ group booking 團體預約

09 We do require a fifty dollar credit card deposit to hold the room.
我們規定要先用信用卡扣款 50 元的押金來預訂房位。
deposit 押金 hold 保留

10 Do you take credit cards?
你們收信用卡嗎？

11 Do I pay now or when I check out?
我是現在付款還是等退房的時候再付呢？

⑫ Is there anything else we can do to help you enjoy your stay?
還有什麼需要服務的地方，可以讓您待得更開心？

⑬ Enjoy your stay, and please do not hesitate to contact me at any time if you ever need any assistance.
祝您住宿愉快，若需要任何服務，請不用客氣，隨時都可聯絡我。

⑭ The elevator is just around the corner. Do you need any help with your bags?
電梯就在轉角處，您需要協助拿行李嗎？ `elevator 電梯`

⑮ How much should I tip a hotel porter?
我該給行李小弟多少小費？ `porter 搬運工`

⑯ I'd like to order room service, please.
我想要叫客房服務，謝謝。 `room service 客房服務`

⑰ Cable television is included, but the movie channel is extra.
有線電視包含在房間費用內，但電影頻道要額外付費。

⑱ Do the rooms come equipped with irons?
房間裡有熨斗可使用嗎？ `equip with 給…配備`

⑲ I'm in 408, and my hairdryer doesn't seem to be working.
我是 408 號的房客，我的吹風機不能用。
`hairdryer 吹風機`

⑳ Can you give me a wake-up call at 7:00?
你明早七點可否用電話叫醒我？ `wake-up call 電話叫醒服務`

㉑ Does this hotel have a shuttle bus to the airport?
這間旅館有沒有接駁車到機場？ `shuttle bus 接駁車`

㉒ I'd like to check out, please.
我要退房，謝謝。 `check out 退房`

雙人實境對話

對話情境 1 辦理入住

> **A : Hi, I am Connery. I have a reservation for tonight.**
> **B : Good afternoon, sir. Yes, a single room for two nights.**
> **A : That is correct.**
> **B : Your room number is 1511, on the 15th floor. Here is your key card.**
> **A : Thanks a lot!**

A：嗨，我是康納力，我有預訂今天晚上的房間。

B：先生，午安。有的，一間單人房，待兩個晚上。

A：是的。

B：您的房號是 1511，在 15 樓。這是您的房卡。

A：感謝！

single room 名 單人房

key card 名（電子）房卡

對話情境 2 現場訂房

> **A : I'd like to have a room for four people for three nights.**
> **B : Do you have a reservation?**
> **A : No, I don't.**
> **B : That would be $200 including continental breakfast.**
> **A : Can I pay with a credit card?**

A：我想要一間四人房，住三個晚上。

B：您有預訂嗎？

A：沒有。

B：這樣總共是兩百元，有包含歐陸早餐。

A：我可以刷卡嗎？

continental breakfast 名 歐陸式早餐（通常包含麵包、果醬 / 奶油、沙拉、飲料）

pay with 片 用…付費

對話情境 3 總統套房

A : How much is the charge per night?

B : For the **presidential suite**, the **rate** I can give you is $3,000, tax included.

A : The **rate** is not my major concern. I want to make sure the room has a view **overlooking** the lake.

B : That I can **assure** you!

A : Good, I'll take it.

A：一個晚上多少錢呢？

B：若是總統套房，我可以給您含稅價 3000 元。

A：價錢不是我主要考量。我想要確定 這房間可以俯瞰湖面的風景。

B：這點我可以跟您保證。

A：很好，那我要了！

presidential suite
片 總統套房

rate [ret] 名 價錢

overlook [ˌovɚˋluk]
動 俯瞰

assure [əˋʃur] 動
向⋯保證

對話情境 4 房型確認

A : I would like to **make a reservation**.

B : What day will you be arriving, and how long will you be staying?

A : I will be arriving on May 14 and will be needing the room for three nights.

B : Would you like a smoking or **non-smoking** room?

A : A non-smoking room, please.

A：我想要預約訂房。

B：請問您哪一天抵達，打算停留多久 呢？

A：我五月十四日抵達，需要住三個晚 上。

B：您要要可吸煙的還是禁煙的房型？

A：麻煩給我禁煙房。

make a reservation 片
預約

non-smoking
[ˌnɑnˋsmokɪŋ] 形
禁止吸煙的

Part 1 自我介紹
Part 2 日常雜務
Part 3 職場應對
Part 4 休閒娛樂
Part 5 出國旅遊
Part 6 愛情來了

269

選擇交通工具
Means of transportation

便利三句開口說

Where can I find a bus stop?
▶ 我在哪裡可以找到公車站牌？(公車站牌在何處？)

替換句▶ Where can I catch a bus? 我要在哪邊搭公車？

✓ **句型提點** Using It Properly!

「Where+can+ 人 +find+something」主要在詢問「某人可以在哪裡找到某物」或問「某物在哪裡」。

Would you like a round-trip ticket or a one-way ticket?
▶ 您要來回票還是單程票？

替換句▶ One way or return ticket? 單程還是來回票？

✓ **句型提點** Using It Properly!

對話中使用 would 可表達禮貌，而 would like 後面可以接名詞或是不定詞 (to+ 原形動詞)。例如：Would you like to order something to eat? 你想要點些什麼來吃嗎？ / Would you like some samples? 你想要一些試用包嗎？

Do you know where I can get a taxi?
▶ 你知道我要在哪裡招計程車嗎？

替換句▶ Could you organize a taxi for me this evening, please? 可否幫我安排今天傍晚的計程車？

✓ **句型提點** Using It Properly!

在探聽消息時可以使用「Do/does+ 人 +know+ 子句」，來詢問對方是否知道後面的事情。

有來有往的必備回應

Q Where can I find a bus stop?

A Go straight ahead and you'll see the bus stop.

往前直走,你就可以看到公車站牌了。

Q Would you like a round-trip ticket or a one-way ticket?

A A round-trip ticket, please.

請給我來回票。

Q Do you know where I can get a taxi?

A You can catch one anywhere on the street.

你可以沿路隨意招計程車。

小知識補給站　Some Fun Facts

　　遊玩時,交通工具的選擇不僅會影響預算、也會影響時間安排;從機場到市中心,通常可搭機場接駁公車 (airport shuttle) 或是計程車 (美式 taxi/ 英式 cab),當然也可以直接找租車公司 (car rentals),大部分租車公司只需要客人提供國際駕照以及台灣駕照即可。進市區之後最常用的交通工具則莫過於公車、捷運 (metro) 以及地下鐵 (subway);而在港灣景點,除了渡輪 (ferry) 之外,甚至有水陸兩用的 land and water bus 和水上計程車 (water taxi)。不妨根據自己的預算及時間考量,選擇最適宜的交通工具吧!

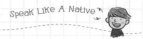
01 I just arrived and need help getting transportation to my hotel.

我剛剛才到，需要能夠帶我去飯店的交通方式。

02 How long does it take to get to Central Station from my hotel?

從我飯店到中央車站大概要花多久時間？

get to 抵達；把…送到

03 This bus goes all the way to the Lille Museum, right?

這公車一路會到里爾博物館，對嗎？ all the way 整個途中

04 There is one thing that one must do when traveling by bus and that is, keep change handy with you.

有一件事情是使用公車代步的人需要注意的，那就是隨時將零錢準備好。

05 There are shuttles, taxis, and buses that go all over the city.

這城市有接駁車、計程車跟公車穿梭往來。 all over 到處

06 Does this bus stop at the National Museum?

這公車在國立博物館有設停靠站嗎？

07 Excuse me, where can I get a bus for Market Street?

請問要往市場街去的公車在哪邊等？

08 Where is the ticket office?

請問售票處在哪裡？ ticket office 售票處

09 I hitchhiked my way across the United States last year.

我去年用路邊搭便車的方式穿越美國本土。

hitchhike 搭便車旅行

10 The car rental agencies are next to the information counter as you exit.

租車公司在服務台旁邊，你出去的時候就會看到。
rental 出租；租賃的

⑪ I want to be able to get around easily, so I'm looking into buying a cheap train pass or tickets to make travel in Europe a little easier.

我想要到處遊走，所以在找便宜的火車通行套票，這樣可以讓在歐洲的旅程輕鬆些。 pass 通行證；憑證

⑫ I bought a kind of pass that allowed me to get on and off the train at any stop during my trip last year.

我去年買了一種通行票，讓我可以在不同的火車站上下車。
get on and off 上下車

⑬ My friend who went to Europe two months ago suggests looking online for Internet specials on train passes.

兩個月前去歐洲的朋友建議我上網找特殊優惠的火車套票。

⑭ You can find the car number and the seat number on the ticket.

你可以在票上找到車廂編號以及座位號碼。

⑮ Can I check my luggage instead of carrying it on the train?

我可以託運我的行李、就不用拿上火車嗎？ luggage 行李

⑯ Let's wait at the platform. I think our train will be arriving in 10 minutes.

我們去月台等吧，我想我們的火車十分鐘內就要到了。
platform 月台

⑰ How much is the typical taxi fare to downtown New York?

去紐約市中心的標準計程車價位是多少？ fare 車資

⑱ I'm really in a hurry, so can you take the quickest route, please?

我趕時間，可以麻煩你走最快抵達的路線嗎？ route 路線

⑲ Keep the change.

不用找錢了。

273

雙人實境對話 ⟨oh!⟩

對話情境 ① 詢問公車資訊

A : Where can I find a bus stop near my hotel?
B : There's one **right across** the street.
A : Which bus should I take to get to Central Park?
B : You can **catch** the 12. It comes every eight minutes.
A : Thanks a lot!

A：在我住的飯店附近有公車站嗎？
B：正對面就有一個。
A：我要搭哪一班車才會到中央公園？
B：可以搭乘 12 路，每隔八分鐘就有一班。
A：感謝！

right [raɪt] 副 恰好；正好
across [əˋkrɔs] 介 在…那邊；穿過
catch [kætʃ] 動 趕上；搭上

對話情境 ② 購買來回火車票

A : Would you like a **round-trip ticket** or a **one-way ticket**?
B : I am coming back soon, so I want a round-trip ticket.
A : When are you leaving and when will you be **returning**?
B : I am leaving tomorrow, Thursday. Please give me a return ticket for Friday.
A : Sure. Right away.

A：您要購買來回車票還是單程車票？
B：我很快就會回來，所以要來回票。
A：你什麼時候要出發？回程是什麼時候呢？
B：我明天週四離開，回程麻煩給我週五的票。
A：好的，馬上好。

round-trip ticket 片 來回票
one-way ticket 片 單程票
return [rɪˋtɜn] 動 返回；歸還

對話情境 3 飯店叫車服務

A : Do you know where I can get a taxi?

B : You can get one on the main street. Or, I can book one for you if you want.

A : That would save me a lot of trouble.

B : When will you need to be picked up?

A : Around 7 p.m. I need to go out for a business dinner.

A：請問我要在哪裡招計程車呢？

B：您可以在主街攔到計程車，或者如果您需要，我可以幫您預約。

A：那會省下我很多麻煩。

B：您需要計程車幾點來接？

A：晚間七點左右。我需要外出參加商務晚會。

save [sev] 動 節省

pick up 片 搭載；（用汽車）接

對話情境 4 下錯車站

A : Is this our bus stop?

B : I think it is. Let's hop off.

A : Dude, where are we at?

B : I have absolutely no idea.

A : I think you made us get off early. We should have waited till we pass the bridge.

A：我們在這站下嗎？

B：好像是耶，快下車。

A：老兄，我們現在是在哪啊？

B：我完全不知道。

A：我覺得你剛剛讓我們提早下車了。我們應該等到過橋之後才下車的。

hop off 片 下車

have no idea 片 不知道

absolutely [`æbsə,lutlɪ] 副 完全地

自我介紹

日常雜務

職場應對

休閒娛樂

出國旅遊

愛情來了

275

人生地不熟
Asking for directions

 便利三句開口說

Could you tell me how to get to Central Park?

▶ 可否請你告訴我該怎麼去中央公園嗎？

替換句 Can you give me the directions to Central Park? 你可以告訴我往中央公園的方向嗎？

✔ ➔ **句型提點** **Using It Properly!**

如果對方是不熟悉的談話對象，在詢問的時候可以用助動詞 could 開頭，較為禮貌。例：Could you tell me where the train station is? 可否請你告訴我火車站在哪裡？

I am looking for the Holiday Inn.

▶ 我在找假日飯店。

替換句 I don't know where the Holiday Inn is. 我不知道假日飯店在哪裡。

✔ ➔ **句型提點** **Using It Properly!**

問路時，必須要清楚表達目的地，用句型「look for+地點」，可以幫助對方了解你「想去哪裡」而為你指路；動詞可以使用現在進行式 (V-ing) 表示你「正在」尋找那個地點。

Let's ask for directions then.

▶ 我們還是來問路好了。

替換句 Let's get someone to give us directions. 我們向別人問路吧。

✓ ⊃ **句型提點** **Using It Properly!**

ask for (詢問) + direction (方向) 意指問路。then 放在句尾可強調「現在」。例如:Come on then!

💬 有來有往的必備回應

Q Could you tell me how to get to Central Park?

> Turn right at the next block, and you'll see it right away. *A*

在下個路口右轉,你馬上就會看到了。

Q I am looking for the Holiday Inn.

> There's one right across the street. *A*

對面就有一間。

Q Let's ask for directions then.

> Let's do that! *A*

就這麼辦吧!

小知識補給站 Some Fun Facts

身在國外人生地不熟,難免會走錯路。迷路時,可以先到附近的遊客中心 (visitor center)、商家、或是警察局詢問,當然也可以問問路人,但記得先用 Excuse me 當開場白,以免顯得唐突;若有地圖,也可以在地圖上面將路線記下來,路線上如果有任何明顯的地標,都能幫助你更快找到你的目的地。問路時,務必要注意禮貌、感謝別人的幫助,別再呆看著地圖,因為不敢開口問路而錯失許多時間了!

Part 1 自我介紹
Part 2 日常雜務
Part 3 職場應對
Part 4 休閒娛樂
Part 5 出國旅遊
Part 6 愛情來了

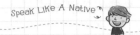
01 I think I might be lost. I need to ask for directions.
我擔心會迷路，我需要問個路。 direction 方向；方位

02 Could you give me directions to the nearest post office?
可以告訴我郵局在哪個方向嗎？ post office 郵局

03 Can you tell me how to get to the city library?
可否告訴我要如何去市立圖書館？ library 圖書館

04 Excuse me. Is there a grocery store around here?
請問，這附近有雜貨店嗎？ excuse me 請問；請原諒

05 Excuse me. I'm afraid I can't find a bank. Do you know where one is?
不好意思，我似乎找不到銀行，你知道哪裡有嗎？

06 What's the best way to get to the neighboring town?
要到鄰近的城鎮，最佳方式為何？ neighboring 鄰近的

07 Which way is the museum?
博物館要往哪個方向走呢？

08 Hi, I am looking for a café named Deja vu. Have you ever heard of it?
嗨，我在找一間咖啡廳，叫做似曾相識，你有聽過這間店嗎？

09 Where is the historic site mentioned in this brochure?
這張傳單上面提到的歷史遺跡在哪裡？ brochure 小冊子

10 How do I get to the museum from here?
我要怎麼從這裡到達博物館呢？

11 Could you show me the way?
可不可以請你指引方向？

12 The museum is right opposite Central Park.

博物館就在中央公園的對面。

⑬ It's a 20-minute drive.
大概是二十分鐘的車程。 drive (開車) 車程

⑭ Go straight ahead on this street to the second traffic light.
這條街直走，到第二個紅綠燈那邊。 traffic light 紅綠燈

⑮ Go straight ahead on this street until the third traffic light. Take a left there, and continue on until you come to a bus stop.
這條街往前直走，到第三個紅綠燈左轉，繼續走，直到你看到一個公車站。

⑯ You'll see the restaurant you're looking for on your left hand side, after 200 yards or so.
你將會看到你要找的餐廳在你的左手邊，大概離這 200 碼左右的距離。 or so 大約

⑰ I think it's just a few blocks away.
我記得只隔幾條街吧。 block 街區

⑱ It'll take you about fifteen minutes to get there on foot.
你步行大概要花十五分鐘左右才會到。 on foot 步行

⑲ I am not sure. You might need to ask someone else.
我不是很清楚，你可能需要再去問問別人。

⑳ Try going straight down the road for a couple of minutes and ask any passerby there.
試著沿路往下直走幾分鐘，然後再問附近的路人吧。
passerby 行人

㉑ It's a bit complicated. I might as well take you there myself.
有點複雜，乾脆我帶你去好了。

㉒ Thank you very much for taking the time to explain this to me!
很感謝您花那麼多時間解釋給我聽！

279

Part 1 自我介紹

Part 2 日常雜務

Part 3 職場應對

Part 4 休閒娛樂

Part 5 出國旅遊

Part 6 愛情來了

雙人實境對話

對話情境 ❶ 路邊問路

Ⓐ : Could you tell me how to get to the nearest post office?

Ⓑ : Go straight for a couple of minutes and turn left to a small alley.

Ⓐ : OK. Sounds easy so far.

Ⓑ : You'll have to walk for at least five minutes until you see a small statue right next to the post office.

A：可否請你告訴我，最近的郵局要怎麼去？

B：往下直走約幾分鐘後，左轉到一條小巷子。

A：好，目前聽起來還算容易。

B：你還必須再走至少五分鐘，之後會看到郵局旁邊的小雕像。

a couple of 片
一些；幾個

alley [`ælɪ] 名
小巷子

so far 片 目前

statue [`stætʃu] 名
雕像

對話情境 ❷ 旅遊書的推薦餐廳

Ⓐ : I am looking for this famous restaurant printed in this guidebook.

Ⓑ : Let me see the address first.

Ⓐ : Isn't this restaurant famous in town?

Ⓑ : Maybe the book isn't up-to-date. It doesn't seem far, though.

Ⓐ : If that's the case, I'll go try my luck then.

A：我在找這本旅遊書介紹的有名餐廳。

B：先讓我看看地址吧。

A：這間餐廳在這裡不有名嗎？

B：可能是這本書的內容沒有更新，不過看來似乎離這裡不遠。

A：這樣的話，那我去碰碰運氣吧。

guidebook
[`gaɪd͵bʊk] 名
旅遊指南

up-to-date
[`ʌptə`det] 形
最新的；含最新訊息的

try one's luck 片
碰運氣

對話情境 ③ 堅持不問路

🅐 : We are so lost! Let's ask for directions.
🅑 : Hold on! I think I can figure it out myself.
🅐 : What's up with you? We've been circling around for the past forty-five minutes.
🅑 : I am on it! Everything is under control.
🅐 : Whatever...

A：我們完全迷路了！來問路吧。
B：等等！我覺得我能找到路。
A：你到底是要怎樣？我們都已經在這裡繞圈繞了四十五分鐘了耶。
B：我在處理啊！全部都在我的掌控當中。
A：隨便啦。

hold on 🔃 等一下；停一停

figure out 🔃 想出；理解

be on it 🔃 正在辦

under control 🔃 在可控制範圍中

對話情境 ④ 同樣不熟悉

🅐 : Can you tell me where the closest police station is?
🅑 : You're asking the wrong person. I am new here, too.
🅐 : Oh, are you a tourist as well?
🅑 : No. I just moved into town very recently.
🅐 : That's OK. I'll ask someone else.

A：請問，最近的警局在哪裡？
B：你問錯人了，我對這一區也很不熟。
A：喔，你也是觀光客嗎？
B：不，我是最近才搬到這裡的。
A：沒關係，那我問別人吧。

tourist [ˋtʊrɪst] 🏷 觀光客

as well 🔃 也（用於句尾）

move into 🔃 搬進；遷入

自我介紹

日常雜務

職場應對

休閒娛樂

出國旅遊

愛情來了

老饕大開吃戒

Savoring delicious food and beverages

便利三句開口說

Do you have a reservation?

▶ 請問您有訂位嗎？

替換句▶ Have you got a reservation? 請問您有訂位嗎？

☑ **句型提點** **Using It Properly!**

「have a reservation+for+ 人數 / 時間」，可以清楚表示訂了「幾個人的位子」或「什麼時間的位子」。例：Sam has a reservation for two tomorrow night. 山姆訂了明晚、兩人的位子。

Are you ready to order?

▶ 請問可以點餐了嗎？

替換句▶ Can I take your order? 我可以幫您點餐了嗎？

☑ **句型提點** **Using It Properly!**

「be 動詞 +ready+to+ 動詞原形」意指「準備好進行某件事」。例：I am ready to go. 我準備好了，可以走了。/ Are you ready to jump? 你準備好要跳了嗎？

What are today's specials?

▶ 今日特餐有什麼？

替換句▶ What do you recommend? 你有什麼推薦的菜色嗎？

☑ **句型提點** **Using It Properly!**

「today's special」指餐廳的今日特餐。用 what 當問句開頭的「What+be 動詞 + 事 / 物」句型，可用

來詢問某事 / 物「是什麼」。例：What is that thing on your hair? 你頭髮上那個東西是什麼？

有來有往的必備回應

Q Do you have a reservation?

A Yes, I made a reservation the other day for tonight.

有，我之前已經訂了今天晚上的位子。

Q Are you ready to order?

A I'm still trying to decide.

我還沒決定好。

Q What are today's specials?

A One is poached salmon and the other is grilled shark.

水煮鮭魚，另一個是碳烤鯊魚。

小知識補給站   *Some Fun Facts*

　　在正式的西餐廳，通常會從開胃菜 (appetizer) 開始，再來是湯、前菜 (entrée)、主菜 (main course)、最後才是甜點 (dessert)。而在用餐禮儀方面，臨時離席時，可將餐巾擺於椅背或扶手上、刀叉放在餐盤兩側成八字形，而用餐完畢則將餐巾放在桌上、並將刀叉一起平放在同一側或盤內即可。另外，因美國的餐廳服務員主要收入來源為小費，結帳帳單上會列出建議小費金額 (Quick Gratuity Guide / Suggested Gratuity)，收取 15%~30% 不等的小費。

Part **1** 自我介紹

Part **2** 日常雜務

Part **3** 職場應對

Part **4** 休閒娛樂

Part **5** 出國旅遊

Part **6** 愛情來了

283

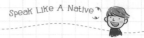
01 **Let's have something exotic for dinner.**
我們晚餐來吃點異國料理吧。 exotic 異國情調的

02 **I am not much of a fan of all-you-can-eat buffet meals.**
我不是很喜歡吃到飽的餐廳。 buffet 自助餐

03 **I would like to make a reservation for this Saturday night.**
我想要訂本週六晚餐的位子。

04 **I'm sorry, but we're fully booked on that day.**
很抱歉，那一天已經客滿了。 fully booked 訂位已滿的

05 **Would you like to reserve a private dining room?**
您想要預訂私人的用餐包廂嗎？

06 **Welcome to Giovani. Here are your menus. Today's special is grilled salmon. I'll be back to take your order in a minute.**
歡迎光臨喬凡尼，這裡是菜單。今日特餐是烤鮭魚，我稍後再過來為您點餐。

07 **Are you ready to order? What would you like with that?**
請問可以點餐了嗎？ 您要什麼來搭配主餐？ order 點菜

08 **Can you give us a few more minutes?**
能否讓我們再考慮一下？

09 **I'd like to have a glass of Chardonnay before I order.**
點餐前，請先幫我上一杯白酒。
Chardonnay 夏多內（白葡萄酒）

10 **Do you have any recommendations?**
你有沒有什麼推薦的菜色？

11 **Would you like a starter?**
您想要點一道開胃菜嗎？ starter 開胃菜

⑫ **I am thinking about a light appetizer, like a Nicoise salad.**
我想要清爽的開胃菜，例如尼斯沙拉。 `light 清淡的；清爽的`
`appetizer 開胃菜`

⑬ **The appetizers are on the house.**
開胃菜由本店招待。 `on the house 商家免費提供`

⑭ **What would you like for the main course?**
您的主餐要點什麼？ `main course 主菜`

⑮ **I'd like the seafood spaghetti.**
我想要海鮮義大利麵。 `spaghetti 義大利麵條`

⑯ **How would you like your steak?**
您的牛排要幾分熟？

⑰ **I like my steak rare/medium rare/medium/ medium well/well done.**
我的牛排要一分熟 / 三分熟 / 五分熟 / 七分熟 / 全熟。

⑱ **How would you like your eggs? Scrambled, sunny side-up, over-easy, or over-hard?**
蛋的熟度想要怎樣呢？炒蛋、太陽蛋、半熟蛋、還是熟蛋？

⑲ **Would you like anything to drink?**
您想要點什麼飲料嗎？

⑳ **Can I have a look at the wine list?**
可以看一下你們的酒單嗎？

㉑ **I'll have a glass of wine, please.**
我要一杯紅酒，謝謝。

㉒ **I'd like to have an iced coffee, easy on the ice, please.**
我想要一杯冰咖啡，少冰，謝謝。

㉓ **Here is your food. Enjoy your meal.**
您的菜來了，請慢用。

㉔ **You can take the rest of your chicken home in a doggie bag.**
你可以把剩下的雞肉打包帶回家。 `doggie bag 打包帶走`

自我介紹

日常雜務

職場應對

休閒娛樂

出國旅遊

愛情來了

285

對話情境 1 週末請訂位

A : Do you have a reservation?
B : No. Is it **necessary**?
A : We recommend you do that during weekends. Now, all the tables are **reserved**.
B : When will a table be **available**?
A : Not until 9 p.m.

A:您有訂位嗎?
B:沒有,一定要訂位嗎?
A:我們建議您週末還是要訂位,現在所有的桌子都被預訂了。
B:那什麼時候會有空位?
A:要到九點之後才有位子。

necessary
[ˋnɛsə͵sɛrɪ] 形 必要的

reserved [rɪ`zɝvd]
形 被預訂的

available [əˋveləbl]
形 有空位的

對話情境 2 訂包廂

A : I'd like to **reserve** a table for dinner.
B : How large a group are you **expecting**?
A : Eight people.
B : Would you like a **private** dining area?
A : That would be great!

A:我想要訂晚餐的位子。
B:您大概有多少人要用餐呢?
A:八個人。
B:您想要私人的包廂嗎?
A:那太好了!

reserve [rɪ`zɝv] 動
預約;預定

expect [ɪk`spɛkt]
動 預期

private [ˋpraɪvɪt] 形
私人的

對話情境 3 初嘗墨西哥菜

Ⓐ : Hi, it's my first time here and I'd like to try some local food. What do you recommend?

Ⓑ : Our nachos with beef and cheese is pretty good. Would you like to try it?

Ⓐ : Sure, I'll take those.

Ⓑ : Anything to drink?

Ⓐ : Sparkling water, please.

A：嗨，這是我第一次來這邊用餐，我想要試試看有本地特色的食物。你有什麼推薦嗎？

B：我們的玉米片配起司牛肉還不錯。您要吃吃看嗎？

A：好啊，那我點這道。

B：要什麼飲料嗎？

A：請給我氣泡水。

nachos [ˋnætʃoz]
名 墨西哥玉米片

sparkling water
片 氣泡水

對話情境 4 點菜

Ⓐ : Can I take your order now?

Ⓑ : Yes. I'll have the beef stew for starters, and my wife would like the tomato soup.

Ⓐ : What would you like for the main course?

Ⓑ : I'll have a sirloin steak and my wife would like the fried trout with mashed potatoes.

Ⓐ : Got it.

A：您準備好點餐了嗎？

B：好了，我的開胃菜要點燉牛肉，我太太要蕃茄湯。

A：您的主餐要點什麼？

B：我要一客沙朗牛排，我太太要炸鱒魚佐馬鈴薯泥。

A：好的。

stew [stju] 名 燉肉

sirloin steak 片
沙朗牛排

trout [traut] 名 鱒魚

mashed potatoes
片 馬鈴薯泥

287

開心觀光去
Organizing your itinerary

便利三句開口說

I enjoy visiting cathedrals.
▶ 我對參觀大教堂很有興趣。

替換句 Visiting cathedrals fascinates me. 參觀大教堂讓我沉醉不已。

✓ ➔ 句型提點 Using It Properly!

表示對某件事情樂在其中，可以用句型「enjoy+V-ing」。例：Olivia enjoys scuba diving. 奧莉薇亞很喜歡水肺潛水。/ He enjoys playing online games. 他很喜歡玩線上遊戲。

Do you go on package tours during holidays?
▶ 你假期出國都參加旅行團的行程嗎？

替換句 Do you usually travel with a tour group? 你出遊通常都跟旅行團嗎？

✓ ➔ 句型提點 Using It Properly!

package tours 是指套裝行程，通常由旅行社提供路線，並包含食衣住行；若是自己安排所有行程，則叫做 independent /self-guided tour；有領隊帶隊的團體旅遊則稱為 escorted tour。

What do you recommend that we see?
▶ 你會建議我們看些什麼？

替換句 Any suggestions on the attractions we should see? 有什麼景點是你推薦一定要參觀的嗎？

☑ **句型提點** Using It Properly!

詢問對方建議什麼，可以用「What+do/does/did+人 +recommend+that+ 子句」，要注意的是，子句的動詞必須是原形動詞。

有來有往的必備回應

Q I enjoy visiting cathedrals.

A I love outdoor scenic spots more.
我比較愛戶外風景。

Q Do you go on package tours during holidays?

A Yes. I still do.
是的，我還是跟團。

Q What do you recommend that we see?

A I recommend that you join the city tour.
我建議你們參加市區導覽的行程。

小知識補給站

　　許多觀光勝地針對觀光客，也提供一日票 (day tickets)、兩日或多日的觀光票券 (tourist pass)、或是 hop-on/off bus (同一張票在一天內，可無限制地在某段區域上下車)；當然，也可以到當地報名一日遊 (day tour)、野外探險類型的遊覽 (safari)、觀光巴士 (bus tour)、甚至是親近野外的獨木舟探險 (canoe adventures) 等等，不妨試試各種當地旅遊，欣賞當地最特別的地形、動物、生態，選擇最適合自己的行程以及方式，好好享受一下原汁原味的在地風情吧。

Part 1 自我介紹
Part 2 日常雜務
Part 3 職場應對
Part 4 休閒娛樂
Part 5 出國旅遊
Part 6 愛情來了

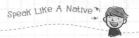
01 Does this package tour cover most of the must-see attractions?
請問這個套裝行程包含大部分必看的觀光景點嗎？
must-see 值得一看的　attraction 旅遊景點

02 I have been going on tours I have organized myself for a decade.
我走自己規劃的旅遊行程已經有十年了。

03 Do you enjoy museums and architecture, or would you rather hit some outdoor hotspots and venues?
你喜歡參訪博物館與建築物，還是喜歡戶外的景點和場合？

04 I love visiting churches and cathedrals, as well as other historic buildings.
我愛參觀教堂跟天主教大教堂，以及其他古蹟建築。

05 I do a lot of online research before going abroad and always bring guidebooks with me.
我會在出國前上網做很多研究，還會隨身攜帶旅遊書。

06 Let's go to the tourist information office to ask about the opening hours for the Uffizi Gallery.
我們去遊客服務中心詢問有關烏菲茲美術館的開放時間吧。

07 Do you have any free maps and information booklets of the city?
請問你有免費的地圖和市區導覽手冊嗎？ booklet 小冊子

08 We are only here for one day. What do you recommend that we see?
我們才在這裡待一天，你建議我們看些什麼好？

09 Do you have any information about local places of interest?
請問你有任何關於當地景點的資訊嗎？

10 Does the sightseeing tour leave from here?
請問觀光團是從這裡出發嗎？ sightseeing 觀光；遊覽

⑪ How much is the admission for the museum?

請問博物館的入場費多少？ `admission 入場費`

Part 1 自我介紹

⑫ What time does the art gallery close?

請問藝廊幾點關門？ `art gallery 美術館；畫廊`

⑬ Where can I find a souvenir shop?

哪裡可以找到紀念品專賣店？ `souvenir 紀念品`

Part 2 日常雜務

⑭ Other attractions include historical sites of interest, as well as parks, gardens, and stately homes and castles.

其他景點還有歷史遺跡、公園、花園、貴族莊園和古堡等。

⑮ Some palaces and parliament buildings are also open to visitors.

有些宮殿或國會建築也是對外開放的。 `palace 宮殿`
`parliament 議會；國會`

Part 3 職場應對

⑯ I am taking my kids to a theme park during the trip.

這趟旅行中，我要帶我的孩子去主題遊樂園。
`theme park 主題樂園`

⑰ I think that Christmas markets are one of the most joyful attractions all around Europe.

我覺得聖誕市集是歐洲最令人開心的景點之一了。

Part 4 休閒娛樂

⑱ What do you say that we join the beer festival in Germany?

我們去參加德國的啤酒節怎麼樣？ `festival 慶祝活動`

⑲ How can we miss out on the Statue of Liberty while we are in New York?

我們人在紐約，怎麼能錯過自由女神像呢？ `miss out 錯過`

Part 5 出國旅遊

⑳ If you want to go onto the Eiffel Tower, you can't avoid waiting in line.

如果你想要登上艾菲爾鐵塔，就免不了要排隊等候。

㉑ Some people suggest that we travel across France by TGV.

有些人建議我們搭乘法國高速列車穿越法國境內。

Part 6 委情來了

雙人實境對話 *oh!*

對話情境 ① 市區導覽

Ⓐ : Welcome to Seattle! How can I be of help?

Ⓑ : What do you recommend that we see?

Ⓐ : We have **tours** for all **interests**. What interests you?

Ⓑ : I want to see **a bit of** everything. Do you have a city tour?

Ⓐ : Yes, in fact, I usually suggest that to visitors.

A：歡迎來到西雅圖！我能幫您什麼忙呢？

B：你建議我們看些什麼呢？

A：我們有各種景點的行程，您對什麼感興趣呢？

B：我什麼都想看看，你們有市區導覽嗎？

A：有的，事實上，我通常都會推薦這個行程給遊客。

tour [tʊr] ❷ 旅遊；遊覽

interest [`ɪntərɪst] ❷ 興趣 ⓥ 使感興趣

a bit of ⓟ 一點點

對話情境 ② 購物行程

Ⓐ : What's your plan for today?

Ⓑ : I don't have anything in mind.

Ⓐ : What do you say we go to an **outlet**? You could get some **sneakers on sale**.

Ⓑ : Great! How do we get there?

Ⓐ : Let me check online.

A：你今天有什麼計畫？

B：沒特別的想法。

A：去暢貨中心如何？你可以趁特價買雙運動鞋。

B：太棒了！我們要怎麼去那裡？

A：讓我上網查查。

outlet [`aʊt.lɛt] ❷ 暢貨中心；商場

sneaker ❷ 運動鞋

on sale ⓟ 特價銷售

對話情境 ③ 動靜兼具

Ⓐ: Have you been to Central Park or the Museum of Modern Art?

Ⓑ: No, but I've heard a lot about both.

Ⓐ: Well, Central Park is **wonderful** for running. Afterwards, you should **head** to the museum to enjoy the art.

Ⓑ: Great! That **sounds like a plan**. Thanks a lot.

Ⓐ: I'm sure you'll have a good time there.

A：你有去過中央公園或現代藝術博物館嗎？

B：沒有，但我時常聽到這兩個景點。

A：中央公園很適合愛跑步的人，之後你還可以去博物館欣賞藝術。

B：太好了！不錯的計畫，謝謝。

A：我相信你會玩得很開心。

wonderful
[`wʌndəfəl] 形 極好的；驚人的

head [hɛd] 動 朝…出發

sounds like a plan 片 聽起來不錯

對話情境 ④ 巴黎景點

Ⓐ: We've seen Notre Dame and the Eiffel tower. Now what?

Ⓑ: There is so much to see in Paris. We should go to the Basilica of the Sacred Heart and Moulin Rouge, like most tourists.

Ⓐ: I want to see some **artistic exhibitions** as well.

Ⓑ: Oh, then we can most definitely not miss the Louvre Museum.

Ⓐ: I **couldn't agree with you more**!

A：聖母院跟巴黎鐵塔我們都看過了，現在要幹嘛？

B：巴黎有太多可以看的，我們應該跟其他遊客一樣，到蒙馬特的聖心堂和紅磨坊去看看。

A：我也想去看和藝術有關的展覽。

B：喔，那我們絕對不能錯過羅浮宮。

A：我舉雙手贊成！

artistic [ɑr`tɪstɪk] 形 藝術的

exhibition [ˌɛksə`bɪʃən] 名 展覽

couldn't agree with sb. more 片 完全同意某人意見

Part 1 自我介紹

Part 2 日常雜務

Part 3 職場應對

Part 4 休閒娛樂

Part 5 出國旅遊

Part 6 愛情來了

293

失物招領
Lost and found

便利三句開口說

Where can I find the lost-and-found counter?

▶ 這邊哪裡有失物招領的櫃檯？

替換句 Is there a lost-and-found counter in this building? 這棟大樓有沒有失物招領的櫃檯？

✓ ➔ **句型提點** Using It Properly!

用 where 開頭的 wh 問句，來詢問地點在哪裡。
lost-and-found 字面意思為失而復得，這個失去又
被找到的過程，就延伸成為失物招領；用 lost 而不用
loose 是因為東西已經不見了，故用過去式。

....

I lost my wallet!

▶ 我的皮夾不見了！

替換句 My wallet is missing! 我的皮夾不見了！

✓ ➔ **句型提點** Using It Properly!

動詞 loose 指遺失，後面直接加遺失的物品，因為東
西不見一定是已經發生的事情，所以大多用過去式。
例：He lost his iPhone. 他的 iPhone 不見了。

....

I've been pickpocketed!

▶ 我被扒了！

替換句 Someone stole my money! 有人偷了我的錢！

✓ ➔ **句型提點** Using It Properly!

用現在完成式「have+ 過去分詞」可以表示「曾經」。
pickpocket 為順手牽羊，可以當動詞，也可以當名
詞。例：Be careful of pickpockets! 小心扒手！

有來有往的必備回應

Q Where can I find the lost-and-found counter?

There is one on the ground floor. *A*

(失物招領)櫃檯在一樓。

Q I lost my wallet!

Where did you lose it? *A*

你在哪裡掉的？

Q I've been pickpocketed!

You'd better go down to the police station *A*
to report this crime.

你最好去警局報案。

小知識補給站   Some Fun Facts

　　出門在外，一定要小心安全、當心錢財。出國之前可以先做足功課，查查當地旅遊需要注意的事項，並且保持警覺，隨時注意周遭的人事物。錢包等重要物品最好放到包包裡面，包包也盡量不要離身；若發現東西被偷了，可以到附近的警察局報案，錢包裡面若有信用卡，也可撥打信用卡公司提供的國際專線，先報失、止付；而證件遺失則是令人最頭痛的，必須聯絡駐外使館，請使館人員協助補發護照或相關證件。偷竊手法日新月異，職業小偷更是防不勝防，最安全的方法，還是財不露白，並隨時注意自己身上的包包，將錢財證件分開放，對於周遭情況也要時時注意，以免變成竊賊眼中的肥羊。

自我介紹 Part 1
日常雜務 Part 2
職場應對 Part 3
休閒娛樂 Part 4
出國旅遊 Part 5
愛情來了 Part 6

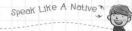
01 I lost my backpack in the shopping mall.
我的背包掉在購物中心裡了。 shopping mall 大型購物商場

02 I left my tote bag on the floor while putting on my jacket, and then I forgot to take it with me.
我為了穿夾克，就把手提包放在地上，結果忘記拿包包。

03 I was a passenger on a Sunny Airlines flight yesterday and I think I left my keys on the plane.
我是昨天搭乘晴天航空的乘客，我似乎把我的鑰匙忘在飛機上了。

04 Don't panic. Try to think of which places you have been to today.
別驚慌，試著回想你今天去過的地方。 panic 恐慌；驚慌

05 I must have dropped my wallet when I tried to take out my camera from my backpack.
我一定是在要從我背包拿相機的時候，不小心把錢包也拉出來了。

06 I've lost my wallet, and I was wondering if anybody has dropped it off here.
我錢包掉了，在想有沒有人把它送來這裡？
drop off 把⋯放下

07 To claim the item, you have to fill out a claim form.
想領回失物，你必須填寫失物招領的表單。
claim 要求；認領 fill out 填寫 (表格)

08 Be sure to hold on to your personal belongings at all times.
切記一定要隨時保管好個人財物。
personal belongings 私人攜帶物品

09 You should probably go to the police station and file a police report for your lost wallet.
你應該去警局報案，說明你的錢包遺失了。

⑩ Do you think they will be able to find it?
你覺得他們會找到嗎？

⑪ We don't have a policy of finders, keepers, so don't worry.
我們沒有誰撿到就是誰的這種制度，所以不用擔心。

⑫ I was lucky enough to have someone return my purse to the local police station.
我很幸運，因為有人撿到我的錢包，並送到警察局。

⑬ I can't seem to find my passport!
我好像找不到我的護照！ passport 護照

⑭ What should I do if I have lost my passport?
要是我護照掉了該怎麼辦？

⑮ You should find your embassy and have your passport re-issued.
你應該到你國家的領事館重新申辦護照。 embassy 大使館

⑯ You should be extra careful because this place is famous for pickpocketing.
你必須格外小心，因為這個地方的遭竊率高得出名。

⑰ I was mugged fifteen minutes ago on Main Street, outside the bank.
我十五分鐘前在美因街的銀行外面被搶了。 mug 行兇搶劫

⑱ I need to take a statement from you. Could you please describe to me exactly what happened?
我需要你的口供。可否請你確切描述到底發生了什麼事情？

⑲ Did you see the one who assaulted you?
你有看到攻擊你的人嗎？ assault 襲擊；攻擊

⑳ Did you see the mugger's face?
你有看到搶匪的臉嗎？ mugger 強盜

㉑ I haven't seen anyone turn in the handbag you just described.
我沒看到有人把你描述的那種手提包送過來。
turn in 交上；歸還

Part 1 自我介紹

Part 2 日常雜務

Part 3 職場應對

Part 4 休閒娛樂

Part 5 出國旅遊

Part 6 愛情來了

雙人實境對話 <oh!>

對話情境 ① 尋找失物

A: Where can I find a lost-and-found **counter**?
B: What's wrong?
A: I lost my **handbag** while holding too many shopping bags.
B: I think the counter is on the first floor.
A: Can you come with me? I need someone to **help** me **with** my bags.

A：請問哪裡有失物招領的櫃檯？
B：怎麼了？
A：我手上拿太多購物袋，結果手提包不見了。
B：櫃檯好像在一樓。
A：可不可以跟我一起去？我需要有人幫我看著袋子。

counter [`kaʊntɚ]
名 櫃檯
handbag
[`hænd.bæg] 名
手提包
help...with 片
幫忙…

對話情境 ② 處理搶劫

A: Are you okay?
B: No. I got **robbed**.
A: Oh my God! By who?
B: **Some** guy on the street just **mugged** me.
A: We should report this to the police **right away**!

A：你還好嗎？
B：不，我被搶了。
A：我的天啊！被誰搶啊？
B：被街上一個男性搶劫。
A：我們應該馬上報警處理！

rob [rɑb] 動 搶劫
some [sʌm] 限 某個
（修飾名詞單數）
mug [mʌg] 動 搶劫
right away 片 立刻；
馬上

對話情境 3 我被扒了

A : I've been pickpocketed!

B : Are you okay? At least you were not attacked and injured.

A : Well, **looking on the bright side**, you're right.

B : Let's go to the local police station and **report** your missing belongings.

A : I wouldn't **get my hopes up**. These days, people are less honest than they used to be.

A：我被扒了！

B：你還好吧？還好你沒有被攻擊。

A：嗯，樂觀點看，的確是這樣。

B：我們去附近警察局報失吧。

A：我不抱什麼希望，這些年人們愈來愈不誠實了。

look on the bright side ⏺ 往好處想

report [rɪˋport] ⓥ 舉報；報告

get one's hopes up ⏺ 抱很大的希望

對話情境 4 粉紅色錢包

A : I lost my wallet! Has anybody dropped it off here?

B : All right, I'll have a look. Could you tell me what it looks like?

A : Sure. It's a pink wallet with white **polka dots** on it.

B : I'm sorry, but it doesn't look like anybody has **picked it up**. Where did you leave it?

A : I think I left it on one of the **benches** upstairs.

A：我錢包掉了！請問有人將它拿到這邊嗎？

B：好，我看看。可以請你告訴我錢包的外觀嗎？

A：好的。是粉紅色的錢包，上面有白色點點的花樣。

B：很抱歉，看起來好像沒有人撿到，你在哪邊掉的呢？

A：我好像放在樓上的座椅上。

polka dots ⏺ 圓點花紋

pick...up ⏺ 將…撿起來

bench [bɛntʃ] ⓝ 長椅

自我介紹

日常雜務

職場應對

休閒娛樂

出國旅遊

愛情來了

299

Unit 48 身體不舒服
Feeling sick

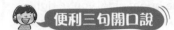 便利三句開口說

I am feeling a little sick.
▶ 我覺得有點不舒服。

替換句 I don't feel well. 我不舒服。

☑ **句型提點** Using It Properly!

身體不適的時候，可以用 feel sick 來表達。例：
Matthew feels sick whenever he smells a
stench of blood. 馬修每次聞到血腥味都會感到噁心
想吐。

I got food poisoning.
▶ 我食物中毒了。

替換句 I might have eaten some poisonous food. 我
可能吃到有毒的食物。

☑ **句型提點** Using It Properly!

這裡的 get 延伸出「感染、得到」的意思。food
poisoning 意為食物中毒。例：It's easy to get
food poisoning while traveling if you are not
careful enough with food and water. 旅遊時如果
不夠注意飲食和飲水，很容易就會食物中毒。

Don't get too carried away and be careful of heat stroke!
▶ 不要開心過頭了，小心中暑！

替換句 Drinking water in such heat can help avoid
sun stroke. 在如此高溫下補充水分能預防中暑。

✔ ➛句型提點 **Using It Properly!**

中暑為 heat stroke，也可以說 sunstroke。而片語 get carried away 指「得意忘形、做的過頭」。

🗨 有來有往的必備回應

Q　I am feeling a little sick.

　　Why don't you stay at the hotel and take 　*A*
　　a rest?

　　你何不待在旅館休息？

Q　I got food poisoning.

　　I ate the same thing as you did, but I am 　*A*
　　feeling fine.

　　我跟你吃的東西一樣，但我人覺得好好的。

Q　Don't get too carried away and be careful of
　　heat stroke!

　　　　Don't worry! I drink a lot of water. 　*A*

　　　　別擔心！我喝很多水。

💡 小知識補給站　*Some Fun Facts*

　　水土不服的時候，先別緊張，可以先到藥局 (pharmacy) 找成藥，小病痛也能去診所 (clinic) 就診；在醫院裡掛號，可以根據不舒服的部位，找牙醫 (dentist)、眼科醫師 (optometrist/eye doctor)、皮膚科醫師 (dermatologist)、耳鼻喉科醫師 (ENT doctor)、或是小兒科醫師 (pediatrician)。當然，若有常用的藥品，旅遊時也要記得隨身攜帶。

Part 1 自我介紹
Part 2 日常雜務
Part 3 職場應對
Part 4 休閒娛樂
Part 5 出國旅遊
Part 6 愛情來了

01 They have been traveling for two days and will need some time to acclimatize.
他們已經旅行了兩天，需要一些時間適應當地氣候。
`acclimatize 使適應`

02 It's hard for me to get adapted to the tropical weather while traveling in Indonesia.
在印尼旅遊時，我很難適應當地的熱帶型氣候。
`adapt 適應` `tropical 熱帶的`

03 Can you tell me how to treat food poisoning?
可否告訴我該如何處理食物中毒的情形呢？
`food poisoning 食物中毒`

04 I caught a severe cold and got a really high fever when traveling in Finland.
我去芬蘭旅遊時得了重感冒，並發高燒。 `severe 嚴重的`

05 I didn't know that Madrid was this hot in summer, and I accidentally got sunstroke on day one.
我不知道馬德里的夏天這麼熱，我才待了一天竟然就中暑了。 `accidentally 意外地`

06 My friend caught a cold due to the alternation between indoor heat and outdoor chill.
我朋友因為室內與室外的溫差而感冒。 `alternation 交替`

07 What have we eaten? I have had an upset stomach since yesterday!
我們吃了什麼嗎？從昨天開始，我就一直鬧肚子！
`upset stomach 腸胃不適`

08 I am not feeling well. I need to see a doctor.
我不太舒服，我要去看醫生。

09 What can I do to make you feel better?
我能幫你做點什麼，讓你舒服一點嗎？

⑩ I think I have a cold. Can you take my temperature? I hope it's not a high fever.
我覺得我感冒了，可不可以幫我量體溫？希望不是發高燒。
`temperature 體溫` `fever 發燒`

⑪ I need help right away. Can you take me to the emergency room of the nearest hospital?
我急需幫忙，可不可以帶我去最近的醫院掛急診？

⑫ I am feeling a little sick. Let's call it a day.
我覺得不太舒服，今天就到此為止吧。
`call it a day 今天到此為止`

⑬ I am wondering if they have a first aid kit at the hotel.
不知道飯店有沒有急救箱。 `first aid kit 急救箱`

⑭ Here, take some painkillers and let's continue on our itinerary.
來，吃些止痛藥就繼續我們的行程吧。 `painkiller 止痛藥`

⑮ Why don't you stay in the hotel and take some rest for the day?
你今天何不乾脆待在飯店休息呢？

⑯ I've had diarrhea since we ate that seafood soup.
自從我們喝了那個海鮮湯之後，我就開始拉肚子。
`diarrhea 腹瀉`

⑰ My head is spinning. I think I might have gotten an infection.
我頭昏，我覺得我感染疾病了。 `infection 傳染病`

⑱ I've got the flu.
我感冒了。 `flu 流行性感冒`

⑲ I tripped and fell on a rock, which left a deep cut on my knee.
我絆倒，跌在石頭上，結果膝蓋被割了很深的一道。

⑳ I feel like throwing up, and I have the cold sweats. I guess it's heat stroke.
我想吐，而且在冒冷汗，我猜我是中暑了。 `heat stroke 中暑`

自我介紹

日常雜務

職場應對

休閒娛樂

出國旅遊

愛情來了

雙人實境對話 〈oh!〉

對話情境 1 氣溫驟降不習慣

A：I am feeling a little sick.
B：What's the matter with you?
A：I'm not sure. It could be the snow last night.
B：Do you think you caught a mild cold?
A：I guess so. I am not used to the weather in this country!

A：我覺得不太舒服。
B：你是怎麼了？
A：我不確定，可能是昨天晚上下雪的關係。
B：你覺得有沒有可能是輕微感冒？
A：也許吧，我還不習慣這個國家的天氣。

mild [maɪld] 形 輕微的
catch a cold 片 感冒
be used to 片 習慣於（某事）

對話情境 2 食物中毒

A：I got food poisoning.
B：What kind of symptoms do you have?
A：I have diarrhea, and I have vomited several times.
B：Is it possible that your lunch is the cause of this?
A：You're right! I went to the central market, which attracts mainly tourists, and had a plate of raw oysters!

A：我食物中毒了。
B：你有那些症狀？
A：我拉肚子，還吐了好幾次。
B：有沒有可能是你的午餐有問題？
A：對耶！我去了大部分觀光客必去的中央市場，吃了一大盤生蠔！

symptom [ˋsɪmptəm] 名 症狀
vomit [ˋvɑmɪt] 動 嘔吐
raw [rɔ] 形 生的

對話情境 3 別中暑了

A : I am so excited by this **overseas** marathon **coming up** this weekend!

B : Don't get too carried away and be careful of heat stroke.

A : I know. That's why I am fully prepared.

B : How exactly are you prepared?

A : I have three water bottles **strapped** to my waist!

A：這週末的海外馬拉松真令我興奮！

B：不要太忘我，小心中暑。

A：我知道，所以我已經做好萬全的準備。

B：怎麼個萬全法？

A：我已經把三個水瓶綁在我的腰上了！

overseas [`ovɚˋsiz] 形 海外的

come up 片 即將發生；出現

strap [stræp] 動 用帶子捆綁

對話情境 4 扭傷腳踝

A : What happened to your **ankle**?

B : I **sprained** my ankle while traveling to Germany last week.

A : I am sorry to hear that. But, how did it happen?

B : I was wearing my **high-heeled shoes**.

A : Why am I not surprised?

A：你的腳踝怎麼了？

B：我上週去德國玩的時候不小心扭到腳。

A：真令人遺憾，但是，你是怎麼扭傷的啊？

B：我當時穿著高跟鞋。

A：這就難怪了。

ankle [`æŋkl] 名 腳踝

sprain [spren] 動 扭傷

high-heeled shoes 名 高跟鞋

自我介紹

日常雜務

職場應對

休閒娛樂

出國旅遊

愛情來了

NOTE

Part 6

愛情來了
情場得意 & 失意

搭訕、曖昧、求婚、訂終身，
抓準時機這樣說一定不被打槍！

Can I have your
number?

★ 小鹿亂撞？心動就要行動！

- 名 名詞
- 動 動詞
- 形 形容詞
- 副 副詞
- 介 介係詞
- 助 助詞
- 連 連接詞
- 限 限定詞
- 縮 縮寫

情聖大師
Flirting like a casanova

便利三句開口說

How is your drink? Do you suggest that I order the same?

▶ 你的飲料好喝嗎？你建不建議我點一樣的？

替換句 Any suggestions on the drink? 有沒有推薦什麼飲料？

✓ ➔ **句型提點** Using It Properly!

「Do/does+ 人名 / 代名詞 +suggest+that+ 子句」用以詢問某人的建議。要特別注意，that 子句所使用的動詞一律用原形。例：Does the doctor suggest that you bring your son for the review? 醫生建議你帶你兒子複診嗎？

Can I have your number?

▶ 可以給我你的電話嗎？

替換句 How can I get her number? 我要怎麼要到她的電話？

✓ ➔ **句型提點** Using It Properly!

電話號碼為 telephone number，而簡化後，口語上常常只說 number；have one's number 就表示要到某人的電話號碼。例：Did you get his number? 你有要到他的電話嗎？

Hi, what's up?

▶ 嗨，你好！

替換句 I just want to come over and say hi. 我只是想要過來打個招呼。

✅ ⇒**句型提點** Using It Properly!

年輕人之間常用此句來打招呼，相當於「最近過得怎樣？」；回答時，可答「Not much.」，或是以原句的「What's up?」回覆對方也可以。

自我介紹

有來有往的必備回應

Q How is your drink? Do you suggest that I order the same?

My drink is fine. If you need suggestions, you can ask the bartender. *A*

我的飲料還不錯。如果你需要建議，可以問問酒保。

日常雜務

Q Can I have your number?

I don't give my number to strangers. *A*

我不把電話隨便給陌生人。

職場應對

Q Hi, what's up?

Do I know you? *A*

我認識你嗎？

休閒娛樂

 Some Fun Facts

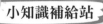

💡 **小知識補給站**

不尷尬的搭訕開場白，可以從稱讚別人、聊聊日常開始，電影或美劇情節中，也常常聽到用魔術師形容對方，或是利用雙關語、唸起來相近的詞語來比喻，像是「Are you from Memphis/Tennessee? Cause you're the only ten I see.」，曼非斯 (Memphis) 是田納西州 (Tennessee) 其中一個城市，而 ten I see 讀音很像 Tennessee，表示對方在你心目中是滿分的理想女神。

出國旅遊

愛情來了

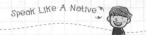
01 Hi! I like you. And I'd like to get to know you.
嗨！我喜歡你，想要進一步認識你。

02 That guy over there is super hot!
那邊的那個男生超級帥！

03 Wow, she is smoking hot!
哇，她超辣的！ smoking hot 身材正點的

04 If your boyfriend doesn't show up, I'll be right over there.
如果妳男友沒出現的話，我就坐在那邊。
show up 出現；露面

05 You look like someone I'd like to meet.
你看起來很像我想要認識的人。

06 Hi, I'm sure we've met before.
嗨，我很確定我們在哪裡見過。

07 Your smile is like sunshine.
你的笑容像陽光一般。

08 You have an incredible energy about you.
你散發出的能量很吸引人。 incredible 難以置信的

09 Shall we talk or continue flirting from a distance?
我們要不要聊個天，還是要繼續曖昧地遙望對方？
from a distance 從遠方

10 I never pass up the opportunity to say hello to a beautiful woman.
我絕不會白白錯失與漂亮女士打招呼的機會。
pass up 拒絕；放棄

11 Uh, hi, I'm really nervous.
呃、嗨，我真的很緊張。

12 Hi, my name is Joe. Can I buy you a drink?

嗨，我是喬。可以請妳喝杯飲料嗎？ buy...a drink 請…喝飲料

⑬ Your dog is so cute! What kind is it?
你的狗真可愛！是什麼品種的啊？

⑭ Is this seat taken?
這位子有人坐嗎？

⑮ Excuse me, I just wanted to say that you are really beautiful. What's your nationality?
打擾了，我只是想跟妳說，妳真的很漂亮，妳是哪國人啊？

⑯ How long have you lived here?
你住在這裡多久了？

⑰ Wow, you look exactly like a girl I went to school with.
哇，妳長得很像我以前的一位同學。 look like 看起來像…

⑱ I know this is really forward of me, but I just wanted to tell you that you're gorgeous.
我知道這樣講有點唐突，我只是想跟你說，你很可愛。
gorgeous 極其漂亮的

⑲ What's your view on this scenario? I need a female perspective.
這個情況在你看來怎麼樣？我需要參考女性的觀點。

⑳ Dude, I wouldn't talk about Star Trek if I were you. That might really freak a woman out.
老兄，如果我是你，就不會聊《星際大戰》，這話題可能會嚇跑女生。 freak...out 把…嚇壞

㉑ I suggest that you smile, be confident, and demonstrate positive energy, and she will pick up your vibe and be sucked into it.
我建議你面帶微笑、有自信一點、散發正面能量，她自然會感受到你的情緒，進而被影響。 demonstrate 顯示；表露

㉒ I don't want to use those cheesy pick-up lines to get to know girls anymore.
我再也不想用那些俗氣又老套的搭訕台詞來把妹了。
cheesy 庸俗的

311

對話情境 ① 以詢問來開啟對話

A : How is your drink?
B : Um, I haven't tried it yet.
A : Oh, I am just wondering what to order. Any **suggestions**?
B : I'd say you must try their coffee if you've never been here before.
A : Oh, I am a big **fan** of coffee. I **assume** you are, too?

A：你的飲料好喝嗎？
B：嗯，我還沒喝。
A：喔，我只是在想要點什麼。你有什麼建議嗎？
B：如果你以前沒來過，我建議你嚐嚐他們的咖啡。
A：我是咖啡愛好者，我猜你也是？

suggestion
[sə`dʒɛstʃən] 名 建議

fan [fæn] 名 粉絲；仰慕者

assume [ə`sjum]
動 認為；假定

對話情境 ② 白目搭訕

A : Can I have your number?
B : Uh, no. I don't **even** know you.
A : I am Peter. Now you **do** know me. What is your name?
B : I am not sure I want to answer any of your questions.
A : Why not?

A：可以給我你的電話嗎？
B：呢，不要，我根本就不認識你。
A：我叫彼得。你現在在認識我了，那你叫什麼名字呢？
B：我不確定我想要回答你的問題。
A：為什麼不？

even [`ivən] 副 甚至
（強調語氣）

do [du] 助 （用以加強語氣）

對話情境 3　順利搭訕

Ⓐ : Hi, what's up?

Ⓑ : Not much. Do I know you?

Ⓐ : No. I know this is really **forward** of me, but I just wanted to tell you that you're cute. And my name is Thomas.

Ⓑ : **I'm flattered**. I am Emily.

Ⓐ : I am wondering if I could buy you a drink?

A：嗨，你好。

B：嗨，我們認識嗎？

A：不，我知道這麼說很唐突，我只是想跟你說你很可愛，我的名字是湯瑪士。

B：過獎了，我是艾蜜莉。

A：不知道可否請你喝杯飲料？

forward [`fɔrwəd]
形 冒失的

I'm flattered 片
過獎了；受寵若驚

對話情境 4　圖書館毛遂自薦

Ⓐ : Excuse me. Can you **reach** that book for me? The one with the golden **spine**.

Ⓑ : Oh, sure. There.

Ⓐ : Thanks, that's very nice of you. Do you come here often?

Ⓑ : Not really. I just moved to this neighborhood.

Ⓐ : Oh, if you need someone to **show you around**, I'd be happy to help.

A：不好意思，可不可以幫我拿那本書呢？金色書背的那本。

B：喔，沒問題，拿去吧。

A：謝謝，你人真好，你常來嗎？

B：不太常，我才剛搬來這一區。

A：如果你需要人帶你認識環境，我很樂意幫忙。

reach [ritʃ] 動 伸手構到

spine [spaɪn] 名
書脊

show sb. around 片 帶某人到處參觀

嘗試約會創造機會
Attending all kinds of dates

便利三句開口說

I am going on a blind date.
▶ 我要去相親。

替換句 My friend set me up on a blind date. 我朋友設局讓我參加相親。

✓ **句型提點** Using It Properly!

blind date 直譯為盲目約會，約會之前男女雙方都沒有見過，類似中文的相親，但不一定如相親一樣以結婚為前提。例：She likes to set up blind dates for her single friends. 她很喜歡幫她的朋友安排約會。

What should I talk about on a blind date?
▶ 相親的時候我該聊些什麼？

替換句 I hope I won't run out of subjects to talk about. 我希望我不會沒有話題可以聊。

✓ **句型提點** Using It Properly!

詢問別人意見，可以用助動詞 should 來提問。例：How should I deal with that picky customer? 我應該怎麼應付那位奧客？ / Whom should I vote for? 我該投給誰呢？

They hooked up on a speed date.
▶ 他們在快速聯誼中相識。

替換句 They met in a speed dating event. 他們在快速聯誼的活動中認識。

✓ ⇒ 句型提點 ◁ Using It Properly!

片語 hook up 指相識、牽線、勾搭。speed date 則譯為快速約會。

💬 有來有往的必備回應

Q　I am going on a blind date.

　　　I hope you are well prepared.　*A*

　　　希望你準備好了。

Q　What should I talk about on a blind date?

　　　You should practice beforehand.　*A*

　　　在去之前，你應該要預先做準備。

Q　They hooked up on a speed date.

　　　I thought they were coworkers.　*A*

　　　我以為他們是同事。

小知識補給站　Some Fun Facts

　　除了最常見的一對一約會，其他的約會方式還有：團體約會 (group dating)，通常有兩對以上的情侶，大家一起約出來吃飯；聯誼則用 mixer 或稱 matchmaking event，參加者多，但不一定互相認識；盲約 / 相親 (blind date) 則為兩個陌生人的初次約會，通常由朋友介紹，是一場由第三方幫忙安排的約會；而在快速約會 (speed date) 中，參加者可在時間限制之內，與在場的所有異性交談，主持人通常會在交談時間結束時提醒大家換位子；當然也有更多人運用網路交友 (online dating) 來認識另一半。

Part 1 自我介紹
Part 2 日常雜務
Part 3 職場應對
Part 4 休閒娛樂
Part 5 出國旅遊
Part 6 愛情來了

315

01 My friend set me up on a blind date.

我朋友設局要我參加相親。 set up 設局；計畫

02 I am planning to hook up my best friend with my brother.

我打算要把我的好友介紹給我哥。 hook up with 和…有聯繫

03 Do you have any suggestions for conversation starters on a blind date?

對於相親的開場白，你有什麼好建議嗎？
conversation starters 破冰開場白

04 Don't go into a blind date with expectations that this will be "the perfect man".

不要帶著對方會是一個完美男人的期望去赴相親之約。

05 My biggest fear of a blind date is that I might say the wrong thing at the wrong time and blow the chance of scoring a second date.

對於相親，我最大的恐懼就是在不對的時機講錯話，把第二次邀約的機會搞砸。 blow 失去良機 score 取得

06 There's nothing worse than sitting in silence on a blind date.

相親最糟糕的就是面面相覷的無語場面。 in silence 靜靜地

07 It was really awkward because we ran out on things to talk about.

場面真的很尷尬，因為我們無話可聊了。 awkward 尷尬的

08 I don't like to go on a blind date because I don't know how to break the ice.

我不喜歡相親，因為我不知道冷場的時候該怎麼辦。
break the ice 打破冷場

09 Talking about the weather on the first date is so cliché!

第一次約會聊天氣真的很老梗！ cliché 陳腔濫調

⑩ What if I bring up some subjects and my date cannot come up with a response?

萬一我提到了什麼話題，而我的約會對象沒辦法回應我怎麼辦？

⑪ Practice ahead of time by going over possible topics of conversation.

最好事先練習，準備好可能會聊到的話題。 go over 檢查

⑫ All these worries will only make you more tense and serious.

這些擔憂只會讓你更緊張。

⑬ I would suggest that you try to avoid topics such as religion, politics, money or past relationship failures.

我會建議你避開如宗教、政治、錢財與過去失敗的感情經驗等話題。 failure 失敗經驗

⑭ Try to ease into more substantial topics.

試著慢慢引導對方和你聊比較實際的話題。 ease into 慢慢帶入 substantial 有價值的

⑮ Try to start with some easy and interesting topics like jobs, travel, cooking, sports, current events, movies and television.

試著聊點輕鬆有趣的話題，例如工作、旅遊、烹飪、運動、時事、電影跟電視等。

⑯ Don't be too eager if you want to arrange a second date.

如果你還希望有第二次約會，就別表現得太急切。 eager 渴望的；急切的

⑰ Come on! Just look at it as networking.

別這樣！就把它當作是社交活動。 networking 建立關係網絡

⑱ I didn't meet my boyfriend in a club. Actually, my friend introduced him to me.

我跟我男友不是在夜店認識的，其實是我朋友介紹的。

⑲ Don't let first impressions get in the way.

不要讓第一印象決定一切。 get in the way 擋路；妨礙

317

雙人實境對話

對話情境① 參加相親

A : I am going on a blind date.
B : Who arranged that for you?
A : My mom, **aka** the annoying **matchmaker**.
B : Haha. Good luck to you. Be sure to **suit up**!
A : Whatever.

A：我準備要去相親啦。
B：誰幫你安排的？
A：我媽，也是所謂「惱人的媒婆」。
B：哈哈。祝你好運，記得要打扮一下喔！
A：隨便啦。

aka (also known as) 縮 又稱為

matchmaker
[`mætʃ`mekə] 名 媒人

suit up 片 打扮；準備

對話情境② 準備話題

A : What should I talk about on a blind date?
B : Just briefly introduce yourself and be a good listener at the same time.
A : Sounds so **complicated**.
B : Not at all. Just be yourself and act natural by talking about something you are familiar with.
A : I think I might need to practice **beforehand**.

A：相親的時候我該聊些什麼？
B：只需要簡單地自我介紹，並當個好的傾聽者。
A：聽起來好複雜。
B：一點也不會，只要聊些你熟悉的話題，做自己，表現得自然點。
A：我想我需要事先練習。

complicated
[`kɑmplə.ketɪd] 形 複雜的

beforehand
[bɪ`for.hænd] 副 預先地；提前地

對話情境 ③ 快速聯誼

A : They **hooked up** on a speed date.
B : They did? I thought they met in a bar.
A : At first, both of them didn't want to attend the event.
B : Then what happened?
A : Their friends **forced** them to go. Now they should thank those friends!

A：他們在快速聯誼當中相識。
B：是喔？我以為他們是在酒吧認識的。
A：一開始，他們兩個都不想參加這個活動。
B：然後呢？
A：他們的朋友逼他們去的，現在他們可得感謝彼此的朋友了！

hook up 片 變成一對（情侶）
force [fors] 動 強迫；迫使

對話情境 ④ 說錯話不打緊

A : I think I blew the chance of asking this girl I just met on a second date.
B : What makes you think so?
A : I said a **dirty joke** and she didn't laugh.
B : Maybe she didn't find it funny, but it doesn't mean you don't **stand** a chance of asking her out.
A : It's a **relief** to hear that!

A：我想，邀那個剛認識的女生第二次約會的機會，全被我搞砸了。
B：怎麼說？
A：我講了一個黃色笑話，她沒有笑。
B：她可能只是覺得不好笑，不表示你沒有機會約她出來啊。
A：聽你這樣講，我鬆了口氣。

dirty joke 片 黃色笑話
stand [stænd] 動 經得起
relief [rɪˋlif] 名 放心；寬慰

Part 1 自我介紹
Part 2 日常雜務
Part 3 職場應對
Part 4 休閒娛樂
Part 5 出國旅遊
Part 6 愛情來了

含情脈脈
Love in your eyes

便利三句開口說

I can't stop thinking about him. He is driving me crazy.

▶ 我一直想著他，想到快瘋了。

替換句▶ I can't get him out of my mind. 我沒辦法不去想他。

☑ ➔句型提點 **Using It Properly!**

stop 後面若接動作，動詞須為 V-ing（現在分詞）形式；「can't+
stop+V-ing」意思是無法停止做後面的動作；而片語「drive+ 人名 / 代名詞 +crazy」則是指把某人逼瘋。

. . . .

He is totally flirting with you!

▶ 他絕對是在跟你調情！

替換句▶ He is making a pass at you. 他一直在跟妳眉來眼去。

☑ ➔句型提點 **Using It Properly!**

「flirt+with+ 某人」表示與某人調情、搞曖昧。例：
She is already taken, so just try not to flirt with her. 她已經名花有主了，所以別試著跟她調情。

. . . .

I'm wondering whether he will ask me out or not?

▶ 不知道他會不會約我出去？

替換句▶ I'm wondering if he's ever going to ask me out. 我在想他到底會不會約我出去。

Part 1 自我介紹

Part 2 日常雜務

Part 3 職場應對

Part 4 休閒娛樂

Part 5 出國旅遊

Part 6 愛情來了

☑ ⇨ 句型提點 〈 Using It Properly! 〉

「whether...or...」表示不論…還是…，若句子對比的名詞或片語相同，可省略 or 之後的名詞或片語。例：I am not sure whether I should bring an umbrella (or shouldn't bring an umbrella). 我不確定要不要帶傘。

有來有往的必備回應

Q I can't stop thinking about him. He is driving me crazy.

A You really like this guy, don't you?

你真的很喜歡這個男生，對吧？

Q He is totally flirting with you!

A Really? Why can't I see the signs?

有嗎？為什麼我都看不出來？

Q I'm wondering whether he will ask me out or not?

A I don't know. Let's wait and see.

我不知道，拭目以待吧。

小知識補給站   Some Fun Facts

在描述談戀愛的感覺方面，常常聽到的還有「have butterflies in one's stomach」，指極度緊張、就像有蝴蝶在肚子裡面飛拆騰，可用來描述看到暗戀對象，小鹿亂撞的心情；chemistry 原意是化學，也可用來指相互吸引、來電的曖昧情感。

321

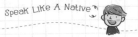
01 **Thanks to modern technology, now you can even flirt with text messages.**
由於現代科技發達，你還可以用簡訊調情。 flirt 調情

02 **The whole point of flirting is striking a balance between revealing your feelings and keeping the person you like intrigued.**
搞曖昧的重點在於，在表露感情及讓對象產生興趣之間取得平衡。 strike a balance 取得平衡 intrigue 激起好奇心

03 **Compliments get people's attention and create a receptive mood for good conversation.**
讚美可以取得對方的注意，並營造出互動良好的對話情境。 receptive 能容納的 mood 心境

04 **Eye contact is the best and easiest thing you can do to start flirting.**
眼神交流是最棒、最不費力的調情方法。 eye contact 眼神接觸

05 **I met a girl I am really interested in and want to ask her out.**
我認識一個女孩，我對她真的很有興趣，想約她出去。 ask...out 邀約

06 **I really don't know how to chat a girl up.**
我真的不知道要如何與女生搭訕。

07 **How do I pull off the flirtation?**
我要怎麼做才能調情成功？ pull off 成功完成

08 **I really like this girl and want to keep my approach casual by first saying hi.**
我真的很喜歡這個女孩，想先以輕鬆的態度上前向她說聲嗨。 approach 靠近 casual 漫不經心的

09 **You have great eyes. They're very pretty.**
你有雙好看的眼睛，它們很美。

⑩ You are an angel sent from above.
妳就像從天而降的天使。

⑪ I've noticed the cute kitty in your profile picture. Is that who you spend most of your time with?
我看到妳的檔案照片上有隻可愛的貓咪，妳大部分的時間都跟它一起過嗎？

⑫ Do you want to hang out tonight?
你今天晚上想不想一起出去？ `hang out 輕鬆相處`

⑬ I enjoy spending time with you and would like to be more than friends.
我很喜歡跟你相處的感覺，希望我們能不僅僅是朋友。

⑭ So I'll see you around tomorrow?
所以明天還會看到你嗎？

⑮ Are you talking to your crush on the phone now?
你正在跟你暗戀的對象講電話嗎？ `crush 迷戀對象`

⑯ Do you think I should call him or wait for his call?
你覺得我應該要主動打給他，還是等他打來呢？

⑰ Are you going to ask her out or what?
你到底要不要約她出去啊？

⑱ Tell me everything about your date last night and spare no details!
快告訴我你昨天的約會，不要省略細節！ `spare 省略`

⑲ Dude, she is so out of your league.
老兄，你配不上她啦。 `out of one's league 某人高攀不起`

⑳ I think he is really into you.
我覺得他真的很喜歡妳。 `into 對…極有興趣`

㉑ He focuses on your hobbies and interests so much.
他非常認真去了解你的嗜好跟興趣。 `focus on 集中於`

㉒ She swept him off his feet.
她讓他為之傾倒。 `sweep sb. off one's feet 使某人傾心`

自我介紹

日常雜務

職場應對

休閒娛樂

出國旅遊

愛情來了

323

雙人實境對話 oh!

對話情境 ① 堅持不主動

A : I can't seem to get him out of my mind!

B : Why don't you just call him?

A : Are you **nuts**? How could I **take the initiative**?

B : Is there a rule?

A : It's just that I don't want to be too **aggressive**.

A：我沒有辦法不想他！

B：你何不乾脆打電話給他？

A：你瘋囉？我怎麼可以主動？

B：有人規定不能主動嗎？

A：我不想要表現得太過激進。

nuts [nʌts] 形 (俚) 發瘋的

take the initiative 片 帶頭；採取主動

aggressive [əˋɡrɛsɪv] 形 侵略的；好鬥的

對話情境 ② 沒希望了

A : Do you think he is going to ask me out?

B : Have you heard from him since the last blind date?

A : Um, just on the same night after I got home. He sent a **brief** text message.

B : And that's it? No more **interaction**?

A : OK. So, there won't be a second date, will there?

A：你覺得他會約我出去嗎？

B：上次相親結束後，你還有跟他聯絡嗎？

A：嗯，只有當晚上我回到家後，他傳了一則簡短的訊息。

B：就這樣？沒有其他互動了？

A：好吧，沒有第二次約會了，對吧？

brief [brif] 形 簡短的；短暫的

interaction [ˌɪntəˋrækʃən] 名 互動

對話情境 ③ 有互動才有機會

A : He is totally flirting with you!

B : You think?

A : Duh. Look at those flirtatious text messages!

B : I am such an idiot! What should I do?

A : If you like this guy, flirt back!

A：他絕對是在跟你調情！

B：你覺得是嗎？

A：當然，看他傳來的曖昧訊息！

B：我真是太白癡了！那我該怎麼辦？

A：如果你對這傢伙有興趣，就給他點
曖昧的回應啊！

flirt with sb. 片
與某人調情

flirtatious [flɝ`teʃəs]
形 打情罵俏的

對話情境 ④ 兩情相悅

A : So are you planning on spending all night
online or do you have more exciting plans for
this evening?

B : I won't say it's exciting, because I am planning
on walking my dog in the park.

A : Such an attractive girl like you? Don't you
think you need company?

B : Um...I guess it does no harm to have someone
tagging along.

A : I certainly will tag along!

A：所以你是計畫掛在網路上一整晚，
還是有什麼其他有趣的活動？

B：稱不上有趣啦，我晚上要去公園遛
狗。

A：像你這麼迷人的女生，不覺得需要
有人陪著嗎？

B：嗯，多一個跟班應該也無妨。

A：我絕對跟到底！

company
[`kʌmpənɪ] 名 陪伴

tag along 片 尾隨

certainly [`sɝtənlɪ]
副 一定；必定

自我介紹

Part 1

Part 2
日常雜務

職場應對

Part 3

Part 4
休閒娛樂

出國旅遊

Part 5

Part 6
愛情來了

找到真愛好幸福
I found the one!

便利三句開口說

I am falling for you.
▶ 我被你迷倒。

替換句 You stole my heart. 你偷走了我的心。

✅ **句型提點** Using It Properly!

「fall for+ 人 / 事 / 物」，有兩種意思，此句表示迷戀、傾心，另一個意思則為受騙、上當。例：She is falling for online shopping recently. 她最近很迷線上購物。/ I shouldn't have fallen for your schemes. 我不應該中你的計。

· ·

I am so in love with you.
▶ 我如此愛你。

替換句 I love you so much that my heart aches. 我愛你愛到心都痛了。

✅ **句型提點** Using It Properly!

「be 動詞 +in+love+with+ 人 / 事 / 物」表示愛上某人 / 事 / 物。例：He is in love with antique collecting at the flea market. 他愛上了在跳蚤市場收集古物。

· ·

I adore you.
▶ 我愛慕你。

替換句 I cherish you. 我很珍惜你。

✅ **句型提點** Using It Properly!

動詞 adore 的意思是愛慕、敬重、極喜歡。例：She

adores going to the musicals. 她非常喜歡看音樂劇。/ The knights were adored for their loyalty. 騎士的忠心使他們備受敬重。

有來有往的必備回應

Q I am falling for you.

A Keep your voice down! People are watching.

小聲點啦！大家都在看。

Q I am so in love with you.

A I don't know what to say.

這讓我無言以對。

Q I adore you.

A Me, too.

我也是。

小知識補給站

Some Fun Facts

「愛」除了最基本、常見的 love 以外，還有許多不同的表達方式：crush 指暗戀、迷戀；一見鍾情可以說 love at first sight；unrequited love 為單戀；戀情除了 relationship，也可以說 romance；短暫的迷戀、一時的癡迷是 infatuation；最後，affection 除了指愛慕，也常用來表示親情。戀情的發酵過程也有特定的說法，從一開始為對方心神不寧 (hung up on someone) 到認定對方就是另一半 (better half/ perfect match)，戀情也是需要時間來經營的。

自我介紹 Part 1

日常雜務 Part 2

職場應對 Part 3

休閒娛樂 Part 4

出國旅遊 Part 5

愛情來了 Part 6

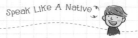
01 **I think we two are a perfect match!**
我覺得我倆是絕配！ match 相配者

02 **Honey, we are meant for each other.**
親愛的，我們是天造地設的一對。 be meant for 指定；預訂

03 **Do you want to go steady with me?**
你想要跟我穩定交往嗎？

04 **It was love at first sight!**
這是一見鍾情！ at first sight 初見

05 **Don't you see that Michael is all over you?**
妳看不出來麥可為妳痴狂嗎？ be all over sb. 為某人瘋狂

06 **I think I just found my soul mate.**
我覺得我找到心靈伴侶了。 soul mate 心靈伴侶；性情相投的人

07 **He is the love of my life.**
他是我此生的摯愛。

08 **You are my heart's desire.**
你是我心所嚮往。

09 **He made my heart skip a beat.**
他讓我心跳漏一拍。 skip 漏掉

10 **I can't live without you.**
沒有你我活不下去。

11 **Our mutual affection is something that I hold dear.**
我們之間的愛意是我最珍惜的東西。 mutual 相互的；彼此的

12 **She is the kind of girl that I've been longing for.**
她就是我朝思暮想的那種女生。 long for 渴望

13 **You manifest the meaning of true love.**
你證實了真愛的存在。 manifest 證明；證實

⓮ **I want a lifetime with you.**
我要跟你共度餘生。 lifetime 一生；終身

⓯ **My love for you is unconditional and eternal.**
我對你的愛是無條件也無止盡的。 eternal 永恆的

⓰ **You are my dream come true.**
你讓我的美夢成真。 dream come true 夢想成真

⓱ **She cast a spell on him.**
她讓他著迷。 cast a spell on 用符咒迷惑

⓲ **You are the best thing that ever happened to me.**
認識你是我生命中最棒的一件事。

⓳ **You mean the whole world to me.**
你就是我的全世界。

⓴ **I get weak-kneed whenever you walk by.**
當你經過我身邊時，我全身都感覺輕飄飄的。

㉑ **I feel moonstruck whenever you kiss me.**
每次你吻我，我都覺得如痴如醉。 moonstruck 迷亂的

㉒ **When the guy brought the girl home, they made out on the front porch.**
那男生帶女孩回家時，他們在門廊前親熱。 make out 親熱

㉓ **He and his girlfriend are so passionate about each other.**
他跟他女友兩人打得火熱。 passionate 熱情的

㉔ **He gently gave me a peck on the cheek when we parted.**
我們分開的時候，他在我的臉頰上輕吻了一下。 peck 啄

㉕ **They are madly in love, so they show no modesty in their public displays of affection.**
他們在熱戀，在公眾場合也完全不掩飾對彼此的愛意。
modesty 羞怯 display 展現；炫耀

㉖ **There's some chemistry between the two.**
這兩人有來電。 chemistry 化學作用；來電

自我介紹

日常雜務

職場應對

休閒娛樂

出國旅遊

愛情來了

329

雙人實境對話 〈oh!〉

對話情境 ① 爛漫之人

A : I am **falling for** you, and I couldn't take my eyes off you since the day I met you.

B : That's really straightforward.

A : I **can't help it**.

B : I don't know what to say.

A : Just **follow your heart**.

A：我被你迷倒了。從我遇到你的第一天，我的視線就無法從你身上移開。

B：你還真直接。

A：我忍不住呀。

B：我實在不知道該如何回應你！

A：跟隨你的心吧。

fall for 片 傾心；迷戀

help [hɛlp] 動（與 can/could 連用）避免；阻止

follow one's heart 片 追隨（某人的）內心

對話情境 ② 木頭般的伴侶

A : I am so in love with you.

B : I am **pretty** sure you said that yesterday.

A : But you ignored me last night! So, I just want to make sure you get the message.

B : Yeah, yeah, yeah. I got it alright.

A : Is that the only **response** you've got?

A：我如此愛你。

B：我很確定你昨天講過同樣的話。

A：但是你昨晚都忽略我啊！所以我只是想確定你有接收到訊息。

B：有啦，我收到啦。

A：你就只有這個回應嗎？

pretty [`prɪtɪ] 副 相當；很

response [rɪ`spɑns] 名 回應

對話情境 ③ 真愛煞風景

A : I adore you.
B : You light up my life.
A : You hold the key to my heart.
B : You are holding the key to our front door.
A : You are such a killjoy.

A：我愛慕你。
B：你照亮我的生命。
A：你握有解開我心鎖的鑰匙。
B：你則握有我們家大門的鑰匙。
A：你真的很煞風景耶。

light up 照亮；
點燃
killjoy [`kɪl.dʒɔɪ] 名
令人掃興的人／事

對話情境 ④ 真愛確實存在

A : Do you believe in true love?
B : Yes. I think it's the beautiful thing our world possesses! My parents are the perfect example.
A : I am so jealous. I have always doubted its existence.
B : Don't be such a pessimist. You'll find your prince charming someday.
A : Alright. I'll keep my fingers crossed.

A：你相信世上有真愛嗎？
B：我相信，我認為真愛是這個世界上最美麗的事物！我爸媽就是很好的例子。
A：真令人羨慕，我總是懷疑真愛的存在。
B：別那麼悲觀，你會找到心目中的白馬王子的。
A：好吧，我只能祈求好運囉。

pessimist
[`pɛsəmɪst] 名 悲觀主
義者
prince charming
白馬王子
**keep one's
fingers crossed**
祈求好運

自我介紹

日常雜務

職場應對

休閒娛樂

出國旅遊

愛情來了

小三老王閃邊去
How dare you cheat on me!

便利三句開口說

Why didn't you answer my phone call?
▶ 你為什麼不接我電話？

替換句 Why was my call sent to your voice message the other day? 為何我那天打給你是轉語音信箱？

✓ **句型提點** ﹤Using It Properly!﹥

接聽電話的動詞要用 answer，此句的「answer one's phone call」即表示接聽某人的電話。例：She got fired just because she didn't answer her boss's phone call immediately. 她只是因為沒有馬上接老闆的電話，就被解雇了。

- -

You've been acting weird lately.
▶ 你最近的行徑很怪異。

替換句 There's something weird about your behavior. 你舉止怪怪的。

✓ **句型提點** ﹤Using It Properly!﹥

當行為舉止異常，可以用 act weird 來表示。例：Why do you think that Hank has been acting weird lately? 為什麼你覺得漢克最近行為怪怪的？

- -

Where were you last night?
▶ 你昨天晚上去哪了？

替換句 Why couldn't I reach you yesterday? 為什麼我昨天找不到你？

☑ ➡句型提點 Using It Properly!

看到疑問詞「where」，就可以馬上知道對方是在詢問地點。例：Where would you like to travel on your next vacation? 你下一個休假想去哪裡旅遊呢？

💬 有來有往的必備回應

Q Why didn't you answer my phone call?

I had bad reception. *A*

我手機的收訊不好

Q You've been acting weird lately.

Have I? *A*

有嗎？

Q Where were you last night?

I was at home, sound asleep! *A*

我在家，睡得很沉啊！

小知識補給站 Some Fun Facts

劈腿、戴綠帽的英文說法是 cheat on 或是 two-time，外遇可說 have an affair，或是用 seeing someone on the side 表示背地裡偷吃；而小三或小王，可以說 the other woman/man，mistress 則特別指情婦。台灣有徵信社，國外則常雇用私家偵探 (private detective) 來掌握對方出軌的證據；在懷疑對方的忠誠時，不妨靜下心來，等握有確切證據時，再來指控對方也不遲。

Part 1 自我介紹
Part 2 日常雜務
Part 3 職場應對
Part 4 休閒娛樂
Part 5 出國旅遊
Part 6 愛情來了

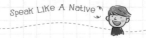
01 Why haven't you changed your Facebook relationship status?
你為什麼都不修改你臉書上面的感情狀態？
relationship status 感情狀態

02 Are you seeing someone else?
你在跟別人約會嗎？ see someone else 與其他人約會

03 Don't you lie to me.
你不要騙我喔！ lie to 對…撒謊

04 Why did you turn off your cell phone yesterday?
你手機昨天為什麼關機？ turn off 關掉

05 Why do you all of a sudden need a lot of space while talking over the phone?
為什麼你講電話的時候突然需要很多空間了？
all of a sudden 突然地

06 Don't you think you're being overly sensitive?
你不覺得你過度敏感了嗎？ sensitive 神經過敏的

07 I have a feeling that you are having an affair.
我覺得你有外遇。 affair 風流韻事；外遇

08 She suspects her boyfriend isn't being faithful.
她懷疑她男友對她不忠。 faithful 忠貞的

09 Something's fishy!
感覺有點可疑。 fishy 可疑的

10 I suspect that he's been fooling around while I am not around.
我懷疑他趁我不在的時候到處亂搞。 fool around 胡搞

11 I think you're doing some funny business behind my back.
我覺得你在我背後搞七拈三。 funny business 不道德的行為

12 Why are you making these false accusations?

你為什麼要做出這些不實的指控？ accusation 指控；指責

⑬ There must be some misunderstanding here.
一定有什麼誤會。

⑭ My friend snooped through her man's Facebook to find proof of his affairs.
我朋友偷看她男友的臉書，想要找出他外遇的證據。
snoop 窺探 proof 證據；物證

⑮ I am going to confront my boyfriend over that flirtatious text message.
我要跟我男友對質，問他那封曖昧簡訊是怎麼回事。
confront 對質 text message 簡訊

⑯ Lighten up! It was just a totally harmless text.
放輕鬆！這只是個無傷大雅的簡訊而已。 lighten 變得輕鬆

⑰ My girlfriend has been sneaking out of the house recently.
我女友最近常常偷溜出門。 sneak 偷偷地走

⑱ He confessed what he did.
他坦承他的所作所為。 confess 坦白；供認

⑲ He is cheating on his girlfriend.
他背著女友偷吃。 cheat on 對…不忠

⑳ It was just a fling. Nothing happened.
這只是玩玩的，什麼都沒發生。 fling 一時的放縱

㉑ The girl doesn't know she is a mistress and a home wrecker.
這女生不知道自己是破壞別人家庭的小三。 mistress 情婦

㉒ He is involved in a love triangle.
他陷入三角戀情。 love triangle 三角戀愛

㉓ Why can't you be honest with me?
你為什麼不能對我坦承？ be honest with 對…坦承

㉔ If you still don't trust him, don't date him.
如果你還是不信任他，就別跟他交往了。 date 與…約會

Part 1 自我介紹

Part 2 日常雜務

Part 3 職場應對

Part 4 休閒娛樂

Part 5 出國旅遊

Part 6 愛情來了

雙人實境對話

對話情境 1　傳簡訊被發現

A : You've **been obsessed with** texting lately. Who were you texting just now?

B : What? No one! I was just checking an online weather forecast.

A : Come on! Your fingers were moving **rapidly**.

B : Well, my fingers need some exercise **from time to time**.

A : Just save it. Hand me your phone right now!

A：你最近很沉迷在傳簡訊喔，你剛剛在跟誰傳訊息？

B：什麼？沒跟誰啊！我在上網查天氣預報啦。

A：少來！你的手剛剛明明就動得很快。

B：嗯，我有時候需要運動一下手指嘛。

A：省省吧你，手機馬上給我交出來！

be obsessed with
片 沉迷於

rapidly [`ræpɪdlɪ]
副 迅速地；很快地

from time to time
片 有時；偶爾

對話情境 2　舉止怪異

A : You've been acting weird lately.

B : No, I haven't.

A : You have been wearing **perfume** for the past two weeks.

B : I **used to** wear perfume all the time.

A : Yeah, like five years ago you did.

A：你最近的行為很怪異。

B：哪有？

A：你最近兩個禮拜都有擦香水。

B：我以前都會擦香水啊。

A：對啊，大概五年前吧。

perfume [pə`fjum]
名 香水

used to 片 過去經常⋯

對話情境 ③ 在家熟睡

A : Where were you last night?

B : I was at home.

A : Liar. I called your cell phone and it was off. I called your home and no one answered.

B : I was beat, so I hit the sack very early.

A : Am I supposed to believe that?

A：你昨天晚上去哪裡了？
B：我就待在家啊。
A：騙人。我打你手機沒通，打家裡電話也沒人接。
B：我很累，所以提早上床休息了。
A：我應該要相信你的說辭嗎？

beat [bit] 形 筋疲力盡的

hit the sack 片 睡覺；就寢

對話情境 ④ 荒唐藉口

A : Just be honest with me. Are you seeing someone else?

B : I am not! You are paranoid.

A : Then can you explain why you have been sneaking out of the house in the middle of the night recently?

B : I've been sleepwalking perhaps.

A : That's the most ridiculous excuse I've ever heard.

A：老實跟我說，你在跟別人約會嗎？
B：我沒有！你太神經質了。
A：那就解釋一下，你最近為何半夜都偷溜出去呢？
B：可能是夢遊吧。
A：這是我聽過最荒唐的藉口。

sneak out 片 偷偷溜出去

in the middle of 片 在…當中

sleepwalk [`slip.wɔk] 動 夢遊

ridiculous [rɪ`dɪkjələs] 形 荒謬的

自我介紹　日常雜務　職場應對　休閒娛樂　出國旅遊　愛情來了

吵架怒翻桌

Having a big fight

 便利三句開口說

I don't want to see you anymore.
▶ 我再也不想見到你。

替換句▶ Get out of my sight. 離開我的視線。

✓ **句型提點** Using It Properly!

> 想要進行某事，除了前面講過的 would like，也可以
> 用此句的「want to+ 原形動詞」，但語氣較為強硬，
> 常用來強調很想要某物 / 做某事。例：Jenny wants
> to immigrate to Canada. 珍妮想要移民到加拿大。

I want you to get out of my life!
▶ 我要你在我生命中消失！

替換句▶ Get lost! 滾開！

✓ **句型提點** Using It Properly!

> 「get out of+ 名詞」表示離開某處或某狀態，後面
> 常接 my life/face/sight，以表示「不要再出現在我
> 面前」、「我不想看到你」。例：You should get
> out of your comfort zone and try new things. 你
> 應該離開舒適圈，去嘗試新事物。

Why are you being so paranoid?
▶ 你為什麼要這麼神經兮兮的呢？

替換句▶ Don't be so suspicious. 不要這樣疑神疑鬼的。

✓ **句型提點** Using It Properly!

> 形容詞 paranoid 意指偏執的、想太多的。使用
> being 表達維持在某種狀態，口語中使用的話，也帶

有強調的口吻。例：Why are you being so mean to that little girl? 你們為什麼對那個小女孩這麼壞？

有來有往的必備回應

Q I don't want to see you anymore.

A Me, neither!
我也不想！

Q I want you to get out of my life!

A No, YOU get out of my life.
不，是你滾出我的生命裡。

Q Why are you being so paranoid?

A Why are you being such a jerk?
那你為什麼要那麼混蛋？

小知識補給站   Some Fun Facts

　　激烈爭吵還可以用片語 be at war，藉戰爭比喻爭吵的程度。常見的吵架用句還有 Wise up, please. 聰明點好嗎？ / How dare you! 你好大的膽子啊！ / Cut the crap. 廢話少說。 / Don't push me around. 不要對我頤指氣使。當然，碰到有爭執的情況，不妨就事論事 (take the matter on its merits)，盡量不要做人身攻擊或過早下判斷。根據國外的調查，有吵架的情侶因為有機會一起成長，有時候反而會走得長久；相反地，完全不吵架的話，怒氣反而會一點一滴累積，累積的憤怒可能吞噬自己的理智呢。

Part 1 自我介紹
Part 2 日常雜務
Part 3 職場應對
Part 4 休閒娛樂
Part 5 出國旅遊
Part 6 愛情來了

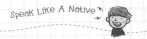
01 What is up with you?
你到底是怎麼回事？

02 Will you stop moping now?
你可以不要再悶悶不樂了嗎？ mope 鬱鬱寡歡

03 I'm giving you the silent treatment.
我決定要開始跟你冷戰！ silent treatment 沉默以待；冷戰

04 Have I done something wrong?
我做錯了什麼嗎？

05 How could you do this to me?
你怎麼可以這樣對我？

06 I am so sick and tired of you.
我真的厭倦你了。

07 I am so fed up with you always trying to pick a fight!
我真是受夠你了，老是找架吵。 be fed up with 厭煩

08 Can you stop whining?
你可以不要再抱怨了嗎？ whine 發牢騷

09 Who are you? I don't know you anymore.
你到底是誰？我已經快不認識你了。

10 Enough is enough. Give me a break!
夠了！讓我喘口氣吧！ enough is enough 適可而止

11 You have a serious issue of anger management.
你在脾氣控制上出了很嚴重的問題。 issue 問題；爭議

12 Is that all you have to say? After all we've been through?
我們一起經歷過這麼多風風雨雨，你就只有這些要說？

13 I'd take that back, if I were you!
如果我是你，我會收回那句話。 take sth. back 收回說錯的話

⑭ **You are the most selfish person I've ever met. I'm so done with you!**
你是我遇過最自私的人，我受夠你了！
be done with 與…再無關係

⑮ **You screw everything up!**
所有事情都被你搞砸了！ screw up 弄糟；搞砸

⑯ **He is such a pain in the neck.**
他真的有夠煩人的！ pain in the neck 令人厭煩的人事物

⑰ **I need you to leave this instant!**
我要你現在馬上離開！ instant 頃刻

⑱ **Just listen to yourself! You're not making sense at all!**
你自己聽聽你講的話！根本是胡謅！ make sense 有意義

⑲ **Get lost, you big fat liar!**
滾開，你這個大騙子！ get lost 滾開

⑳ **You are going to regret this. I'm warning you!**
你會後悔的，我警告你。 warn 警告

㉑ **Shut it! I don't want to listen to a word you say.**
閉嘴！我不想要聽你講任何一句話！

㉒ **You've gone too far this time.**
這次你真的太過分了。 go too far 做得過分

㉓ **I can't take it anymore. It's over.**
我再也受不了了，我們分手吧。

㉔ **Don't be such a drama queen.**
你不要這麼小題大作好嗎？ drama queen 喜歡小題大作者

㉕ **You've gone overboard.**
你真的太超過了。 go overboard 做得過頭

㉖ **Don't you dare say that again!**
你再說一次試試看！

㉗ **You're going to pay for this!**
你會為此付出代價的！

對話情境 ① 再也不想看到你

A : You're such a **player**. Get out of my sight! I don't want to see you anymore.

B : Me, neither! I'm sick and tired of your **hysterical** behavior.

A : Here are your clothes and **suitcase**.

B : What for?

A : You need to leave the house now.

A：你實在是太花心了。從我面前消失吧！我再也不想見到你了。

B：我也不想！我已經受夠你歇斯底里的行為了。

A：這裡有你的衣服跟皮箱。

B：要幹嘛用的？

A：你現在就給我搬出這裡。

player [ˋpleɚ] 名
花心的人

hysterical
[hɪsˋtɛrɪkl] 形 歇斯底里的

suitcase [ˋsut.kes]
名 手提箱；行李箱

對話情境 ② 消失明天生效

A : You've gone too far this time. I want you to **get out of** my life!

B : I **am more than happy to** get out of your life!

A : Then what are you standing here for?

B : Well, It's 2 a.m. I'll do that tomorrow.

A : You are **impossible**.

A：這次你真的太超過了。我要你從我的生命中消失！

B：要從你生命中消失，我真是高興得不得了！

A：那你現在還站在這邊幹嘛？

B：這個嘛，現在半夜兩點，我明天早上再消失。

A：你真是不可理喻。

get out of 片 離開

**be more than
happy to...** 片 非常樂意做某事

impossible
[ɪmˋpɑsəbl] 形 不可理喻的；不可能的

對話情境 ③ 不講理

A: I was just saying hi to my colleague! Why are you being so **paranoid**?

B: No. You were obviously **making eyes at her**.

A: Chill out! I was trying to be reasonable.

B: Are you **implying** that I am not reasonable?

A: I think you're just trying to **pick a fight**.

A：我只是跟同事打聲招呼而已呀！你為什麼要這麼神經兮兮的呢？
B：才不是，你很明顯就是在跟她拋媚眼。
A：冷靜點！我試著要講理。
B：你是在暗指我很不講理嗎？
A：我覺得你只是故意要找架吵。

paranoid
[`pærənɔɪd] 形
多疑的；偏執的

make eyes at sb.
片 向某人拋媚眼

imply [ɪm`plaɪ] 動
暗示

pick a fight (with sb.) 片 找碴

對話情境 ④ 冷戰中

A: Don't be mad.

B: I'm not mad.

A: Yes, you are. I'm sorry. I admit it was my fault. Will you stop moping now?

B: I'm not moping. I'm giving you the **silent treatment**.

A: I knew it! You're still **peeved** at me. What can I do to **make it up** to you?

A：別生氣了。
B：我沒有生氣。
A：有，你有。對不起啦，我承認是我的錯，你可不可以不要再悶悶不樂了？
B：我沒有悶悶不樂，我是在冷戰，不想講話。
A：我就知道你還在氣我，我該怎麼彌補我的錯呢？

silent treatment
片 冷戰

peeved [pivd] 形
惱怒的

make (it) up 片
彌補；和解

Part 1 自我介紹
Part 2 日常雜務
Part 3 職場應對
Part 4 休閒娛樂
Part 5 出國旅遊
Part 6 愛情來了

343

互相溝通

Calm down and talk issues through

便利三句開口說

It's all my fault.
▶ 都是我不好！

替換句 I am responsible for this. 我該為這件事負責。

✓ ⌐**句型提點** **Using It Properly!**

fault 是名詞，意為錯誤，向別人認錯時，常使用此句。例：It's not your fault. 這不是你的錯。It's all her fault that my project had failed. 都是因為她，我的計畫才會失敗。

Let's chill out and have a talk.
▶ 我們冷靜下來好好談一談。

替換句 We need to communicate. 我們需要溝通。

✓ ⌐**句型提點** **Using It Properly!**

片語 chill out 表示請對方冷靜，比起 calm down，更常用在與熟識朋友的對話當中。例：Chill out, pal! I didn't even touch your wallet. 冷靜點，老兄，我連動都沒動過你的錢包。

Will you ever forgive me?
▶ 你會原諒我嗎？

替換句 Will you accept my apology? 你會接受我的道歉嗎？

✓ ⌐**句型提點** **Using It Properly!**

「Will+ 人名 / 代名詞 +forgive+ 受詞？」用來詢問對方願意原諒後面所指的人嗎。例：Will you

forgive Liam for all the mistakes he had made?
你會原諒里安所犯下的所有過錯嗎？

 有來有往的必備回應

Q It's all my fault.

A I should apologize, too.
我也應該要道歉。

Q Let's chill out and have a talk.

A I don't want to chill! The fight isn't over!
我不要冷靜！架還沒吵完！

Q Will you ever forgive me?

A Over my dead body.
下輩子吧。

 **小知識補給站** Some Fun Facts

　　就算是生活在同一個文化背景，想法也難免會有差異，而且生活習慣的不同，也有可能造成摩擦；在溝通時，可以先試著不要翻舊帳 (rake over the ashes) 或拒絕溝通 (stonewalling)，也別只為了反對而反對，甚至大發脾氣 (lose one's temper)，這樣不僅無法解決問題，還有可能火上澆油 (add fuel to the flame)，把事情愈弄愈糟。有效的溝通方法，無非就是用心傾聽、控制音量及語氣、適度給予對方回應、避免讓他人感到不受尊重，並盡量讓對方了解自己的感受，若是自己有錯在先，也要有勇氣道歉、努力尋找解決的途徑。

自我介紹 日常雜務 職場應對 休閒娛樂 出國旅遊 愛情來了

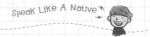
01 I made up with my boyfriend last night.
昨天晚上我跟我男友和好了。 make up with 與…和好

02 Can we make peace?
我們可不可以和好？ make peace 講和

03 What can I do to mend your broken heart?
我可以怎麼做來彌補你受到的傷害呢？ mend 修補

04 I am sorry for being too judgmental.
我為我的挑三揀四感到抱歉！ judgmental 妄加批評的

05 I love you, and I want our relationship to work.
我愛你，也希望我們的關係可以長久。 relationship 關係

06 Can we sit down and discuss what went wrong?
我們可否坐下來討論我們之間哪裡出問題了？

07 I don't want to give up on us.
我不想要放棄！ give up on 不再相信…會成功

08 Let us try to love again.
我們再試試重新來過吧！

09 I shouldn't have doubted you.
我不應該懷疑你的。 doubt 懷疑

10 I shouldn't have yelled at you.
我不應該吼你。 yell at 對…大吼

11 I'll change! I can fix this.
我會改，我會彌補錯誤。

12 Just give me one more chance.
再給我一次機會吧。

13 I can prove it to you.
我可以證明給你看。

14 We can work this out. Just have faith!

我們可以一起解決問題，抱持著信心吧！ `work out 能夠解決`

⑮ **I promise I will never let that happen ever again.**
我保證不會再犯了。

⑯ **Let's come clean and start over.**
讓我們敞開心胸，重新來過吧！ `come clean 和盤托出；招供`

⑰ **From now on, we need to spend more time communicating.**
從現在開始，我們需要花更多的時間在溝通上。
`communicate 溝通`

⑱ **I still believe in us.**
我仍然對我們有信心。

⑲ **I am so sorry for being so sensitive and insecure.**
我很抱歉表現得這麼敏感又缺乏安全感。
`insecure 侷促不安的`

⑳ **I should have told you that I am so lucky to have you.**
我應該早點告訴你，有你在我真的很幸運。

㉑ **Don't you think we both deserve a second chance?**
你不覺得我們應該再給彼此一次機會嗎？

㉒ **Please don't leave me! You mean the world to me.**
拜託不要離開我！你是我的全世界。

㉓ **I don't want to lose you!**
我不想要失去你！

㉔ **I never meant to break your heart.**
我從來都不想要傷妳的心！
`break one's heart 使某人傷心、心碎`

㉕ **I want to make things clear.**
我想要把話說清楚。

㉖ **Let's stop the silent treatment.**
我們停止冷戰吧。 `treatment 對待；處理`

Part 1 自我介紹

Part 2 日常雜務

Part 3 職場應對

Part 4 休閒娛樂

Part 5 出國旅遊

Part 6 愛情來了

對話情境① 和好吧

A : It's all my fault! I should have spent more time with you instead of being so **workaholic**.

B : I should have been more **open-minded**. After all, you've got so many **burdens** on your shoulders.

A : Can we stop fighting?

B : I was going to say the same thing.

A : Let's kiss and **make up**!

A：都是我的錯！我應該要多花點時間陪你，而不是只知道要工作。

B：我應該要心胸寬大點才對，畢竟你肩上承擔了很多的責任。

A：我們可以不要再吵了嗎？

B：我也正打算這麼說。

A：那我們就親一下，和好吧！

workaholic
[ˌwɝkə`hɔlɪk] 形 醉心於工作的

open-minded
[`opən`maɪndɪd] 形 心胸寬大的

burden [`bɝdn] 名 沉重的責任；負擔

make up 片 和好

對話情境② 怎麼做都不對

A : Let's chill out and have a talk.

B : Why should we? I am still very mad at you.

A : If that's the case, I'll **leave you alone**.

B : Argh! You are always capable of **pissing me off**!

A : What have I done? I just want to give you some **space** to **think it through**.

A：我們冷靜下來，好好談談吧！

B：為什麼要冷靜？我還是很生你的氣。

A：如果是這樣，那我先離你遠一點。

B：吼！你總是有辦法把我惹毛耶！

A：我又怎麼了？我只是想給你點空間想清楚而已啊。

leave sb. alone 片
避免打擾；不理會

piss sb. off 片 惹怒某人

space [spes] 名 空間

think through 片
徹底想清楚

對話情境 3 意外地很好打發

A : Will you ever forgive me?
B : Let me think about it.
A : Please. I'll buy you flowers and take you to **fancy** restaurants.
B : **In that case**, I forgive you.
A : Wow, that was quick. I thought I was just **asking for the moon**.

A：你就不能原諒我嗎？
B：我考慮一下。
A：拜託啦，我會買花送你，還會帶你去高檔餐廳用餐。
B：這樣喔，那我原諒你。
A：哇，還真快。我還以為我只是異想天開咧。

fancy [`fænsɪ] 形
高檔的；豪華的

in that case 片
既然那樣

ask for the moon
片 異想天開

對話情境 4 三省吾身

A : The last thing I would do is leave you. Just give me one more chance to make it up.
B : Well, I think both of us deserve a second chance.
A : I agree. Let's stop the silent treatment and **work things out**.
B : Yeah. I am going to be 100 percent honest with you **from now on**.
A : And I am going to stop being **cynical**.

A：我最不希望的事情就是離開你。再給我一次彌補的機會吧。
B：嗯，我覺得我們都該給彼此一個機會。
A：我同意，我們就別再冷戰，一起解決問題吧。
B：是啊，我往後會對你百分百的坦承。
A：我再也不會這麼憤世嫉俗了。

work (something) out 片 解決某事

from now on 片
從此以後

cynical [`sɪnɪkl] 形
憤世嫉俗的

Part 1 自我介紹
Part 2 日常雜務
Part 3 職場應對
Part 4 休閒娛樂
Part 5 出國旅遊
Part 6 愛情來了

349

便利三句開口說

I want to break up.
▶ 我要分手。

替換句▶ I am breaking up with you. 我要跟你分手。

✓ ➔ 句型提點 Using It Properly!

動詞片語 break up 表示分手，其名詞 breakup 即
為兩字的合併。例：She finally broke up with that
psycho. 她終於跟那個瘋子分手了。/ Aiden just
went through a bad breakup last week. 艾登上周
才經歷過一段糟糕的分手。

- -

**I don't think our relationship is going to
work out.**

▶ 我覺得我們沒辦法在一起。

替換句▶ We are not meant to be together. 我們不適合
彼此。

✓ ➔ 句型提點 Using It Properly!

用 I don't think... 可以表達自己的否定意見；片
語 work out 意為發展、有結果。例：I don't think
yelling at me is going to work it out in any term.
我不覺得對我大吼大叫可以解決任何事情。

- -

We are getting back together.
▶ 我們復合了。

替換句▶ Let's start over. 我們重新來過吧。

☑ **句型提點** **Using It Properly!**

get back together 為動詞片語，意指情侶復合。例：
They are not going to get back together in the
near future. 他們近來不會復合了。

有來有往的必備回應

Q I want to break up.

A What have I done wrong?

我做錯了什麼？

Q I don't think our relationship is going to work
out.

A Why? We've been together for almost a
year.

為什麼？我們在一起快一年了。

Q We are getting back together.

A Are you sure this is the right decision?

你確定這是對的決定嗎？

小知識補給站   Some Fun Facts

流行歌曲中，常常聽到歌手們以感情故事來譜出
心聲，像是泰勒斯在 We Are Never Ever Getting
Beck Together 唱出分手就要堅決一點；火星人布魯
斯的 Just The Way You Are 描寫戀愛當中，完美情
人怎麼看都很美；當然也可以聽聽西洋老歌，像是皇
后樂團 (Queen)、披頭四 (The Beetles)、木匠兄妹
(The Carpenters) 等樂團的曲子，在聽歌放鬆之餘，
還可以從歌詞裡面學習到口語上的常用說法！

351

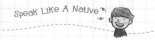
01 Are you dumping me?
你要把我甩了嗎？ dump 拋棄

02 I just feel that I'm not the right one for you.
我只是覺得我不適合你。

03 I don't think our lives were meant to be spent with each other.
我覺得我們彼此不適合生活在一起。

04 Breaking up with my first love is the hardest thing I've ever done.
跟我的初戀情人分手是我做過最困難的一件事。

05 I thought we had it all.
我曾以為我們擁有全世界。

06 He thought we were perfect for each other.
他以為我們是天造地設的一對。

07 Don't you know how much I sacrificed to be with you?
你知不知道為了跟你在一起，我做了多少犧牲？
sacrifice 犧牲

08 We are so over!
我們徹底結束了！

09 We are through!
我們分手了！ through 完結的；斷交的

10 I am still under her.
我還是忘不了她。

11 It's only a matter of time. You'll be over her!
這只是時間早晚的問題，你會忘記她的！

12 I tried so hard to make it work with her.
我很努力想維持我和她的感情。

⑬ **This relationship isn't right for us.**
我們不適合談戀愛。

⑭ **I can't believe that my boyfriend just broke up with me by text message.**
我不敢相信我男友竟然傳簡訊跟我分手。

⑮ **It's not you. It's me! I need to work on myself.**
不是你的問題，是我！我需要自我成長。
`work on 從事；致力於`

⑯ **Should I try to get my ex back?**
我應該要挽回我的前任嗎？`get...back 取回；重新得到`

⑰ **I regret breaking up with my ex, and I want him back so bad.**
我後悔跟我的前男友分手，我極度想要挽回他。

⑱ **I want to rekindle our relationship.**
我想要重燃我們之前的關係。`rekindle 再點火；再振作`

⑲ **Can we get back together?**
我們可不可以復合呢？

⑳ **She is going to win her ex back.**
她要重新贏回前男友的心。`win back 重新獲得`

㉑ **Let's start from scratch and take things slow.**
我們重新來過，並放慢腳步吧！
`start from scratch 從頭開始進行`

㉒ **You are the most perfect partner that I could ever dream of.**
你 / 妳是我夢寐以求最完美的另一半。

㉓ **Don't beg your ex-girlfriend to come back! That makes you look desperate.**
不要懇求你的前女友回來，這樣顯得你很可悲。
`desperate 絕望的；極度渴望的`

㉔ **Please don't turn your back on me!**
拜託不要背棄我！`turn one's back on 某人轉身不理`

Part 1 自我介紹
Part 2 日常雜務
Part 3 職場應對
Part 4 休閒娛樂
Part 5 出國旅遊
Part 6 愛情來了

對話情境 ① 不歡而散

Ⓐ : I want to break up.

Ⓑ : Honey, what's wrong? Did I do something wrong?

Ⓐ : No. It's not you. It's just that I need to work on myself.

Ⓑ : Cut it out. That's the worst breakup excuse I've ever heard.

Ⓐ : Whatever. Take it or leave it!

A：我要分手。
B：親愛的，怎麼了？我做什麼了嗎？
A：沒有，不是你的問題，只是我需要自我成長。
B：別說了，這是我聽過最爛的分手藉口。
A：隨便，信不信由你。

cut it out 片 停止；別說下去

take it or leave it 片 接不接受由你

對話情境 ② 提出承諾

Ⓐ : I don't think our relationship is going to work out.

Ⓑ : I don't know what you mean. We've been together for over three years.

Ⓐ : That is the point. I don't think you want to commit to this relationship.

Ⓑ : Where does this idea come from?

Ⓐ : Have you ever thought about proposing to me?

A：我不覺得我們的關係能夠長久。
B：我不懂你的意思，我們在一起三年了耶。
A：這就是問題，我不覺得你想要在這段關係中許下承諾。
B：這想法是從哪裡冒出來的？
A：那你有想過跟我求婚嗎？

work out 片 有進展；解決

commit [kə`mɪt] 動 承諾；做出保證

propose [prə`poz] 動 求婚

對話情境 ③ 胸寬似海

Ⓐ : My ex-boyfriend and I are getting back together.

Ⓑ : Are you sure this is a good idea?

Ⓐ : Sure! We are still so much in love.

Ⓑ : But he cheated on you! Don't you remember?

Ⓐ : Well, I think that's forgivable...

A：我前男友要跟我復合了。

B：你確定這是個好主意嗎？

A：當然！我們彼此仍相愛。

B：但是他劈腿耶！你忘了嗎？

A：嗯，我覺得那可以原諒啦…

cheat on (somebody) 片
對某人不忠

forgivable
[fəˋgɪvəbl] 形
可原諒的

對話情境 ④ 復合真心話

Ⓐ : Please don't leave me. Let's work out the problem together.

Ⓑ : But you've never listened.

Ⓐ : I promise I will do whatever you ask me to. I'll never find anyone like you.

Ⓑ : Oh, that's the sweetest thing you've ever said to me!

Ⓐ : Let's go back to square one and start all over again.

A：拜託不要離開我，我們一起解決問題吧。

B：但是你都聽不進去。

A：我發誓，將來你要我做什麼，我都會去做，我再也找不到像你一樣的人了。

B：喔！這是你對我說過最貼心的話了！

A：我們一起重新來過吧。

promise [ˋprɑmɪs] 動 承諾；答應

go back to square one 片 回到起點；重新開始

start over 片 重新來過

自我介紹　日常雜務　職場應對　休閒娛樂　出國旅遊　愛情來了

355

Unit 57 我們結婚吧
I think I wanna marry you.

便利三句開口說

Will you marry me?
▶ 嫁給我好嗎？

替換句 Will you spend the rest of your life with me?
你願意跟我共度餘生嗎？

✓ **句型提點** Using It Properly!

中文雖然有嫁、娶之分，但英文只要用一個動詞 marry 就可以表示嫁或娶，後面不需要加介係詞，直接加受詞即可。例：Charlotte is going to marry the guy she met at a local bar. 夏綠蒂即將要嫁給在本地酒吧認識的那個人。

. . . .

How will I propose to my girlfriend?
▶ 我要怎麼向我女友求婚呢？

替換句 How am I going to ask my girl to marry me?
我該怎麼讓我的女友嫁給我？

✓ **句型提點** Using It Properly!

動詞 propose 原意有提議、打算的意思，動詞片語「propose to+ 某人」，則表示向某人求婚。例：He intends to propose to his girlfriend on a sky writer. 他想要用天空寫字的方式來向他女友求婚。

. . . .

I am waiting for the right moment to pop the question.
▶ 我在等待求婚的好時機。

替換句 I am waiting for the perfect time to propose.
我在等待完美的求婚時機。

✓ **句型提點** **Using It Properly!**

pop 有突然提出問題的意思，而片語 pop the question 專指「求婚」，若只是提出問題，千萬別用此句引人誤會囉。例：Are you ready to pop the question? 你準備好要求婚了嗎？

有來有往的必備回應

Q Will you marry me?

A This is not the right time!

現在問這的時機不太好！

Q How will I propose to my girlfriend?

A Try to surprise her with an unpredictable approach.

試著用出乎意料的方法來給她驚喜。

Q I am waiting for the right moment to pop the question.

A I do hope you'll pull it off!

我真心希望你成功！

小知識補給站

在美國結婚，必須先申請結婚執照 (marriage license)，才能舉行婚禮，請公證人公證、向政府登記、拿到結婚證書 (marriage certificate) 後，便是已婚之身了。而美國最熱門的結婚地點，不外乎拉斯維加斯、夏威夷等地，甚至還有公司提供套裝行程，從結婚地點到婚禮規劃全都包含在內。

Part 1 自我介紹

Part 2 日常雜務

Part 3 職場應對

Part 4 休閒娛樂

Part 5 出國旅遊

Part 6 愛情來了

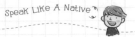
01 We have been together for over five years, and I think it's time we move on to the next level.
我們已經在一起五年了，覺得該是時候往下一階段邁進。

02 I want to ask my girlfriend to marry me.
我想要請我的女友嫁給我。 marry 嫁；娶；與⋯結婚

03 She is the love of my life, and I want to settle down with her.
她是我的摯愛，我想要跟她定下來。 settle down 安頓下來

04 My boyfriend got down on his knees and proposed last night!
我男友昨晚跪下來跟我求婚了！
get down on one's knees 某人跪下

05 Will you be my wife?
請當我的妻子吧！

06 I think it's time we took some vows.
我想該是我們許下誓言的時候了。 take vows 立下誓約

07 I want to be with you forever.
我想與你相守一輩子。

08 I think it's time we settle down.
我想該是我們定下來的時候了。

09 I want to have your baby.
我想為你生小寶貝。（較為露骨的表達方式）

10 Let's get hitched!
我們結婚吧！ get hitched 結婚

11 Are you going to accept his proposal?
妳要接受他的求婚嗎？ proposal 求婚

12 Are you ready for a life-long commitment?
你已經準備好接受一輩子的承諾了嗎？
commitment 承諾；保證

⑬ **I am not ready. I think you are going too fast.**
我還沒準備好,我覺得你太急了。

⑭ **This is the worst proposal ever.**
這是最糟糕的求婚。

⑮ **I'm sorry, but I don't want to be tied down by marriage.**
很抱歉,但我不想被婚姻綁住。 `tie down 束縛;約束`

⑯ **I've decided to make a big commitment to him.**
我決定要跟他共結連理。

⑰ **I can't believe my best friend is going to tie the knot!**
我不敢相信我最好的朋友要結婚了! `tie the knot 結婚`

⑱ **I'm so glad you're getting married.**
我好高興你要結婚了。 `get married 結婚`

⑲ **I am engaged!**
我訂婚了! `engaged 已訂婚的`

⑳ **My fiancé and I will be married in June.**
我的未婚夫跟我準備在六月結婚。 `fiancé 未婚夫`

㉑ **It's so hard to choose the perfect engagement ring for my wife-to-be.**
要幫我未來的老婆找訂婚戒指真困難。

㉒ **This engagement ring is a token of our steadfast love.**
這枚訂婚戒象徵我們堅定不移的愛。 `token 象徵;標記`
`steadfast 堅定的;不變的`

㉓ **I have an announcement to make. "Ophelia and I are engaged!"**
我要宣布一件事情:「奧菲利亞跟我訂婚了!」
`announcement 通知;宣告`

㉔ **From now on, our futures are tied together.**
從現在開始,我們的未來緊緊相繫。 `from now on 自現在起`

Part 1 自我介紹

Part 2 日常雜務

Part 3 職場應對

Part 4 休閒娛樂

Part 5 出國旅遊

Part 6 愛情來了

雙人實境對話

對話情境 ① 錯誤的求婚時機

A: Will you marry me?

B: Are you proposing to me while I am doing the dishes?

A: I know I am not asking the question properly.

B: Duh! I don't know how to respond.

A: OK. Let's do it some other time.

A：嫁給我，好嗎？

B：你現在是在我洗碗洗到一半的時候跟我求婚嗎？

A：我知道現在求婚不太恰當。

B：廢話！我都不知道要怎麼回答了。

A：好，那我們改天重新來過吧。

do the dishes 片
洗碗盤

properly [ˋprɑpɚlɪ]
副 適當地；正確地

對話情境 ② 狗頭軍師

A: How will I propose to my girlfriend?

B: It's easy. Girls like fancy restaurants and engagement rings with big diamonds.

A: Besides that, what am I going to say?

B: Just follow your heart and pop the question.

A: Yeah right. I should ask someone who is more experienced.

A：我要怎麼向我女友求婚呢？

B：很簡單，女生都喜歡高檔餐廳跟大顆鑽戒。

A：除了這些之外，我要說些什麼？

B：就隨心所欲，想求就求囉！

A：最好是。我應該去問比較有經驗的人才對。

engagement ring
片 訂婚戒指

diamond
[ˋdaɪəmənd] 名 鑽石

對話情境 ❸ 貼心男子

🅐 : I am waiting for the right moment to pop the question.

🅑 : I am so nervous for you! Have you prepared a proper speech?

🅐 : I am going to be **sincere** and **straightforward**.

🅑 : Good **strategy**. And where are you going to propose to her?

🅐 : At home! I am going to cook a perfect meal first, and then pop the question.

A：我在等適當的時機求婚。
B：我都替你緊張了！你準備好要說什麼了嗎？
A：我決定要真誠坦率。
B：很好的策略，你要在什麼地方跟她求婚？
A：在家！我要先端出完美的餐點，然後再求婚。

sincere [sɪn`sɪr] 形 真誠的

straightforward [ˌstret`fɔrwəd] 形 坦率的；直接的

strategy [`strætədʒɪ] 名 策略

對話情境 ❹ 鑽戒是女孩的好友

🅐 : Guess what? My boyfriend just asked me to marry him!

🅑 : Congratulations! When are you going to get married?

🅐 : We haven't **gone into details**. But **check out** this engagement ring!

🅑 : Wow, it must have cost your **fiancé** a fortune!

🅐 : I am so happy I could fly!

A：猜猜怎麼了？我男友剛剛向我求婚！
B：恭喜！那你們什麼時候要結婚？
A：我們還沒有討論到細節，先看看我這顆訂婚戒吧！
B：哇！你未婚夫一定花了不少錢！
A：我高興到快要飛起來了！

go into details 片 詳細敘述

check out 片 看看

fiancé [ˌfiən`se] 名 未婚夫

自我介紹 Part 1
日常雜務 Part 2
職場應對 Part 3
休閒娛樂 Part 4
出國旅遊 Part 5
愛情來了 Part 6

步入禮堂
A perfect wedding

便利三句開口說

Are we going to plan our own wedding?

▶ 我們要自己規劃婚禮嗎?

替換句 Are you going to hire someone to plan our wedding? 你要雇用專人來規劃我們的婚禮嗎?

✓ **句型提點 Using It Properly!**

規劃婚禮,用英文來說就是 plan a wedding,因為有許多細節需要籌畫,故搭配動詞 plan 來表達。例:I am going to help my best friend plan her wedding. 我會幫忙我的好友規劃她的婚禮。

· ·

We need to set the date for our wedding first.

▶ 我們得要先選好結婚的日子。

替換句 When are we going to get married? 我們什麼時候要結婚?

✓ **句型提點 Using It Properly!**

片語 set the date 表示確定日期、把日期訂下來。例:We should plan ahead and set the date for our next project. 我們應該事先規劃好下一個企劃的內容,並把日期訂下來。

· ·

My father is going to walk me down the aisle.

▶ 我父親將會牽著我走向紅毯另一端。

替換句 My father is going to give me away at the altar. 我父親到了教堂會將我交出去。

Part 1 自我介紹

✓ 一、**句型提點** **Using It Properly!**

「walk+ 人名 / 代名詞 +down+the+aisle」字面上是帶著某人走向紅毯另一端，此指結婚典禮由父親把女兒交到新郎手中，故也可直接指「結婚」。

 **有來有往的必備回應**

Q   Are we going to plan our own wedding?

 Part 2 日常雜務

> How about hiring a wedding planner? *A*
>
> 找個婚禮顧問如何？

Q   We need to set the date for our wedding first.

 Part 3 職場應對

> I agree. Then we can book a reception hall in advance. *A*
>
> 同意，這樣我們就可以先預約婚禮會場了。

Q   My father is going to walk me down the aisle.

 Part 4 休閒娛樂

> I am so moved I could cry! *A*
>
> 我感動得要落淚了！

💡 **小知識補給站**   *Some Fun Facts*

 Part 5 出國旅遊

在西洋的結婚典禮，新娘通常將四樣物品穿戴在身上：一樣舊物 (something old)，象徵代代相傳；一樣新的物品 (something new)，象徵承舊啟新；一樣借來的東西 (something borrowed)，象徵幸福美滿的祝福；還有一件藍色的物品 (something blue)，象徵純潔、忠貞。而婚禮結束後，賓客們會向新人們灑紙片或米表示祝福、新人們再坐上掛著一串空罐子的禮車開走，氣氛熱鬧非凡。

 Part 6 愛情來了

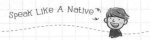
01 Are we going to hire a wedding planner?
我們要不要雇用婚禮顧問呢？ planner 計畫者

02 How many guests are we going to invite?
我們要邀請多少位賓客？ invite 邀請

03 I am on a tight budget, so I am planning a small wedding.
我的預算吃緊，所以只規劃小型的婚禮。
tight budget 吃緊的預算

04 Do I get to decide on the wedding venue, the dress and the cake?
我可以自己決定結婚地點、婚紗跟蛋糕嗎？ venue 發生地

05 I want to design my own wedding invitations.
我想要自己設計結婚邀請函。 invitation 邀請函

06 I am looking for my wedding favors. Do you have any idea?
我正在物色婚禮小物，你有沒有什麼建議？

07 The bridegroom put on his tuxedo and was surprised to find out that it was too small.
新郎穿上燕尾服後驚訝地發現衣服太小，不合身。
bridegroom 新郎 tuxedo 燕尾服

08 I'll make you my best man.
我希望你能當我的伴郎。 best man 首席男儐相

09 Have you ever been a maid of honor?
你有沒有當過伴娘？ maid of honor 首席女儐相

10 The best man made a toast at the wedding reception.
伴郎在喜宴上舉杯敬酒。 toast 祝酒；敬酒

11 The bride asked her bridesmaids to pick the dress together.
新娘要她的女儐相們一起去選禮服。 bridesmaid 女儐相

⑫ We'll throw him a bachelor party.
我們要幫他辦一個告別單身派對。 bachelor 單身漢

⑬ How many people did you invite to your bridal shower?
你邀請了多少人參加你的婚前暖身派對？ shower 送禮會

⑭ I am holding a bachelorette party for my best friend, who will soon get married.
我要幫我即將結婚的好友舉行一場告別單身派對。
bachelorette 單身女子

⑮ I'll walk you down the aisle someday.
我總有一天會牽著妳走向紅毯的另一端。

⑯ It's a shotgun wedding.
那是一場先上車後補票的婚禮。

⑰ Where is the gift registry?
送禮登記處在哪裡？（美國結婚俗是送禮物，由新人決定禮物內容、準備好禮品清冊，賓客只要直接去「認購」一件清單上面的禮物即可。）

⑱ I, Timothy, take thee Tina to be my lawful wedded wife.
我，提姆西，願娶妳蒂娜成為我的妻子。 lawful 法律認可的

⑲ The wedding rings were exchanged during the ceremony.
結婚戒指在婚禮儀式當中交換。 ceremony 儀式；典禮

⑳ After the ceremony came the wedding reception.
結婚儀式之後就是喜宴。 wedding reception 婚宴

㉑ It is very important to plan the seating for our guests at the reception.
喜宴上賓客的座位分配非常重要。 plan the seating 分配座位

㉒ A sit-down meal is the type of reception I want.
我想要的是坐著用餐型態的喜宴。（國外喜宴有站著喝雞尾酒聊天的、戶外野餐、海灘、遊艇上…等等各種不同形式的婚禮喜宴。）

自我介紹

日常雜務

職場應對

休閒娛樂

出國旅遊

愛情來了

雙人實境對話 oh!

對話情境 ① 婚禮幫手

A : Are we going to plan our own wedding?
B : I don't think we have time for that.
A : Why do you sound impatient?
B : I am just concerned how little time we may have.
A : You don't need to worry about a thing. My sister will help.

A：我們要自己規劃婚禮嗎？
B：我覺得我們沒時間搞這些。
A：你為什麼聽起來這麼不耐煩？
B：我只是擔心我們的時間不夠。
A：你什麼都不用擔心，我妹妹會來幫忙。

impatient
[ɪmˋpeʃənt] 形 沒耐心的；急切的

concerned
[kənˋsɝnd] 形 擔心的；憂慮的

對話情境 ② 取得共識

A : We need to set the date for our wedding first.
B : Exactly. Then we can decide on the location for our reception.
A : I've heard that most of the sites are booked a year ahead.
B : If that's the case, we'll marry in "off-peak season" then.
A : I am okay with that!

A：我們得先選好結婚的日子。
B：沒錯，然後我們就可以選定婚禮的地點。
A：我聽說大部分的場地在一年前就被預訂了。
B：如果是這樣的話，那我們就在「淡季」結婚好了。
A：我沒意見！

decide on 片 選定；決定

reception
[rɪˋsɛpʃən] 名 接待；婚宴

off-peak [ˋɔfˋpik]
形 淡季的

366 🎧 MP3 ▶ 174

對話情境 3 感性父女

A : My father is going to walk me down the aisle.

B : I guess your father is going to be very **emotional** when he **gives** you **away**.

A : I think so, too. I think I will be all tears.

B : Did you hire a wedding **photographer**?

A : Yes. But I don't want him to take any photos with me crying.

A：我父親將會牽著我走向紅毯另一端。

B：我猜你爸在把你交出去那一刻，一定會非常激動。

A：我也這麼覺得，我覺得我會淚流滿面。

B：你有請婚禮攝影師嗎？

A：有，但我不想要他拍我哭的樣子。

emotional
[ɪ`moʃən] 形 激動的；
情感強烈的

give away 片 此指
（在婚禮上）把新娘交
給新郎

photographer
[fə`tɑgrəfə] 名 攝影師

對話情境 4 婚宴跳舞

A : The reception is about to begin.

B : I've heard that the father and the bride are going to **lead** the dance.

A : So I've heard. Can't wait to see them dancing.

B : After their first dance, are you going to join the crowd?

A : Nah, I think I'd better **keep off** the **dance floor**.

A：婚宴即將要開始了。

B：我聽說新娘跟爸爸要跳舞開場。

A：我也聽說了，等不及看他們跳舞的模樣。

D：他們跳完之後，你要加入跳舞的人群嗎？

A：不了，我想我還是遠離舞池比較好。

lead [lid] 動 引領

keep off 片 遠離

dance floor 片 舞池

自我介紹

日常雜務

職場應對

休閒娛樂

出國旅遊

愛情來了

國家圖書館出版品預行編目資料

走跳國外一定要會的生活便利句 / 張翔 編著. --
初版. -- 新北市 : 知識工場出版 采舍國際有限
公司發行, 2017.7 面 ; 公分. -- (Excellent ; 86)
ISBN 978-986-271-769-1(平裝)

1.英語　2.會話

805.188　　　　　　　　　　　　106006649

知識工場 · Excellent 86

走跳國外一定要會的生活便利句

出版者 / 全球華文聯合出版平台 · 知識工場

作　　者 / 張翔　　　　　　印 行 者 / 知識工場
出版總監 / 王寶玲　　　　　英文編輯 / 何毓翔
總 編 輯 / 歐綾纖　　　　　美術設計 / 蔡瑪麗

郵撥帳號 / 50017206 采舍國際有限公司（郵撥購買，請另付一成郵資）
台灣出版中心 / 新北市中和區中山路2段366巷10號10樓
電　　話 / （02）2248-7896
傳　　真 / （02）2248-7758
ISBN-13 / 978-986-271-769-1
出版日期 / 2017年7月初版

全球華文市場總代理 / 采舍國際
地　　址 / 新北市中和區中山路2段366巷10號3樓
電　　話 / （02）8245-8786
傳　　真 / （02）8245-8718

港澳地區總經銷 / 和平圖書
地　　址 / 香港柴灣嘉業街12號百樂門大廈17樓
電　　話 / （852）2804-6687
傳　　真 / （852）2804-6409

全系列書系特約展示
新絲路網路書店
地　　址 / 新北市中和區中山路2段366巷10號10樓
電　　話 / （02）8245-9896　　傳　　真 / （02）8245-8819
網　　址 / www.silkbook.com